THE GHOSTLY GIANT

Detail by detail, the long-dead ship was revealed. She was lying, listing to starboard, bow down, on a gentle slope. Originally dull black, the wreck was now graced with a ghostly shroud of pale ooze almost like a woman's heavy face powder.

The stern, an angular jumble of propellers and steering planes, swelled slowly into the long, molded waist, then finally narrowed again slightly into the bow, which had a bulging overhang not unlike an overdeveloped forehead.

Overhead, leaning to one side and disappearing into the murk like a shadow, rose the conning tower. And on the tower was the final giveaway, the big rectangular windows, almost picture windows, with which so many Foxtrots were built.

But something was missing. The wreck and the surrounding bottom were all too quiet. Lifeless. There was nothing swimming or burrowing or squirming. Could it possibly be the radiation or was it just his imagination?

SEAGLOW

WILLIAM S. SCHAILL

LEISURE BOOKS NEW YORK CITY

A LEISURE BOOK®

September 1998

Published by

Dorchester Publishing Co., Inc.
276 Fifth Avenue
New York, NY 10001

Copyright © 1998 by William S. Schaill

ISBN 0-8439-4429-3

Printed in the United States of America.

Part One
October–November 1993

Moscow (Russian Federation)—The disorders (at times near chaotic) that followed the disintegration of the Soviet Union continue both in the semi-autonomous republics that comprise the Russian Federation as well as in a number of the newly independent former Soviet republics. In Moscow, large troop formations loyal to President Yeltsin are engaged in pitched battles with the president's legislative opponents. Just days earlier, Eduard Shevardnadze (president of the independent Republic of Georgia and former foreign minister of the Soviet Union) is compelled to flee a Georgian provincial capital one step ahead of advancing rebel forces. Throughout the region, reformers and reactionaries battle with both bullets and words while gangsterism, and de facto gang rule in some areas, is widespread.

Baghdad (Republic of Iraq)—President Saddam Hussein continues his genocidal assault on Shiites,

William S. Schaill

Kurds, and any other group that fails to embrace him totally. With his ambitions for home-grown nuclear, biological, and chemical warfare capabilities recently shattered by a storm in the southern desert he is now highly receptive to other suggestions concerning the humbling, or destruction, of his many, many foreign enemies.

St. Petersburg (Russian Federation)—A very senior Russian naval officer receives confirmation from Zurich of a large payment made to him by the Trans-Caspian Trading Corporation. The payment is compensation for the revelation and delivery of certain secret and extremely valuable information. Prior to this transaction the officer in question, who both detests and distrusts President Yeltsin, had been very concerned about the financial arrangements for his impending retirement.

Moscow (Russian Federation)—Ultranationalist politician Vladimir Zhirinovsky, called a Fascist by many supporters of President Yeltsin, continues to lay the groundwork for the surprisingly (some say threateningly) strong showing by his Liberal Democratic Party in the December Parliamentary elections.

Miami (United States of America)—The Trans-Caspian Trading Corporation, a private Russian commercial enterprise whose ownership and precise business are far from clear, registers with the State of Florida as a Foreign Corporation Doing Business in the State and opens a small office on the Dolphin Expressway near Miami International Airport.

Port-au-Prince (Republic of Haiti)—The United Nations reimposes its embargo and naval blocade of Haiti when General Raw Cedras refuses to return power to the elected, then deposed, president, Jean-

Bertrand Aristide. Haitians continue to flee the ongoing violence in large numbers.

San Juan (Commonwealth of Puerto Rico)—By a narrow margin the electors of Puerto Rico choose to continue as a commonwealth rather than either apply for statehood or declare the island's independence.

Chapter One

"Where the hell've you been, Cornie? My arm's about to fall off!" snapped Al Madeira over his shoulder as he heard the door to the engine room open behind him. He tried to turn, to glower, but found he couldn't. He was trapped; tangled in a mass of electrical and control cables, pipes, tubes, and manifolds. There was nothing to do but remain as he was, spread-eagled across the big yellow Caterpillar diesel.

"Sorry, Al," replied *Wave Runner*'s grimy, troll-like engineer. His tone was one of almost childlike sincerity.

"You find the small wrench?" The retired U.S. naval officer, who was holding one end of a long hose, squirmed in discomfort and irritation as he spoke. What the hell was the wrench doing outside the engine room, anyway?

"Yup! I had to look all over, even up in the pilothouse, but I finally found it forward, next to the anchor winch. . . . And I also found two guys looking for you up on deck."

"Who?" wondered Madeira aloud. And what were they trying to sell him?

"Never saw 'em before," replied Cornie, now standing

next to the big main engine in which Madeira was entangled. "They say their names are Linevich and Novikoff . . . Look like Russians to me."

What do Russians look like, Cornie? he wondered. "You ask them to wait in the cabin? I'll go up in a minute."

"They're right here, Al," said Cornie, sounding as if he was about to start giggling. "Standing beside me. They insisted. . . ."

Pushy bastards, thought Madeira, feeling uncomfortably exposed and defenseless in his current posture. He considered telling them to get lost, then didn't. "In that case, come on over here and help me secure this damn hose."

"Yessir!"

"I'll be right with you," Madeira said. His face remained jammed against the cooling water manifold while the sweet-sharp smell of oily machinery flavored every shallow breath he took. "As you can see, you've caught me in a difficult position."

"If anybody understands difficult positions, Captain Madeira, we do," said a heavily accented voice. It sounded as if the speaker was suffering from an early-fall cold. "Please take your time and finish the job to your satisfaction. Then we can talk."

Madeira considered his two unexpected, and still unseen, visitors while he held the end of the hose tight against the valve and watched Cornie apply the wayward wrench.

The names Linevich and Novikoff meant nothing to him. They did sound Russian, but that proved only that Cornie wasn't a total fool. Neither did he recognize the one voice he'd heard so far.

They didn't feel like a threat, but that didn't mean anything. Over the years he'd managed to overlook any number of threats, even the all-too-obvious ones. Most he'd totally failed to detect until it was way too damn late. In a few cases he'd watched stupidly as disaster approached and done nothing, or not enough, to prevent it.

What could these guys possibly want?

Cornie grunted softly as he gave the wrench one final, mighty twist. "Okay, that's it."

Madeira withdrew his head and shoulders from the nightmarish, three-dimensional spiderweb that surrounded the engine and turned toward the visitors. As he straightened up, a bolt of muscle pain shot across his stiffened lower back.

There appeared at first to be nothing remarkable about the two strangers standing next to the engine-room door.

One was dressed in a dark business suit and looked at Madeira with an intelligent but far-from-enthusiastic interest. He was tall, balding, and slightly stooped. Madeira placed him somewhere in his mid-sixties, assuming the deep folds on his face were really the result of passing years and not of disease, genetics, or some sort of official, character-building abuse.

The other was a shortish, well-built fellow with a full head of brown, almost curly, neatly trimmed hair and a tweed sport coat and slacks. He appeared to be a few years younger than Madeira, somewhere in his late thirties or early forties.

Madeira wiped his hands on a reasonably clean rag as he continued to study the second visitor. The silence was broken only by the distant rumble of the blower forcing damp, fresh air into the normally stifling engine room. Perhaps he'd been wrong; there was something notable about this one.

There was a tremendously alert expression on the younger man's face as his brown eyes moved quickly and confidently around the brightly lit, immaculate space. He examined the two big main engines and the much smaller generator, the pumps, the electrical panel, and the tools hanging on the bulkhead. Clearly he knew what everything was, and what it was there for.

And as he looked, he evaluated. Everything.

It was obvious to Madeira that the younger Russian was a professional sailor of considerable experience and authority. And also one very much on edge. Why else would he keep flexing, then clenching his fists slightly as he surveyed the space?

"What can I do for you, gentlemen?"

"My name is Anton Linevich, Captain Madeira," said the older man. It was the heavily accented voice he'd heard before. "I am with the Commercial Section of the Russian Consulate in New York."

Madeira shook his hand.

"And this," continued the Russian diplomat, "is Captain Novikoff of the Russian Federation Navy."

"A pleasure," Madeira said.

"The pleasure is mine, sir," replied the younger man as he grasped Madeira's hand firmly and held it, a smile on his face.

"What can I do for you?" Madeira repeated after an awkward pause during which he felt the deck shudder, then sort of hop to one side. As he spoke he continued to study the younger Russian. There was an intensity about him that was striking, even by naval standards. Submarines, he decided, totally off the top of his head. Or some other elite branch.

What interest might he, and the Russian Federation Navy, possibly have in whale-watching? Or in Al Madeira?

"Would it be possible, sir," Linevich asked, stooping still more as he spoke, "to have a brief conversation with you in confidence?"

Madeira found himself caught between an unruly impulse to break out laughing at Linevich's melodramatic air and an equally uncontrollable sense of unease. Do real people really talk this way?

Was either of them armed? he wondered. Linevich looked tame enough, although some of history's greatest butchers had looked like little more than tired old men, but Novikoff seemed a pretty high-powered guy, the sort who could be counted on to do whatever was necessary to carry out his orders.

The Cold War was over, he reassured himself. We're almost allies now, he mused, although he couldn't be sure precisely against whom, so whatever intrigues these two might have in mind must be of a private sort. Smuggling the Tzar's long-lost jewels into New York, or something like that.

Unconvinced by his own logic, Madeira scrolled frantically through his past. Had he ever, during his twenty-three years in the navy, done anything for which they might want revenge? Had he ever known anything they might want to know, even now, years after the fact? Had he ever seen anything they might want forgotten and buried?

"Let's go on up to the main cabin and get a cup of coffee," he proposed, having found no answers in his own past.

"Some hot coffee will taste very good on a day like today," replied Novikoff.

"Cornie. Would you mind finishing up number one by yourself? I'll be back in half an hour or less to help you with number two." In truth, Madeira thought, Cornie should've been doing the whole damn thing by himself.

"No problem!" Cornie's put-upon expression belied his words.

Madeira still found it difficult to accept that at least one of Cornie's ancestors had arrived on the *Mayflower* . . . or that so many high Commonwealth officials were his relatives. The only part of the grimy engineer's background he did consider even faintly possible was the often-denied rumor that the first ancestor, the one aboard the *Mayflower,* had arrived in irons.

But then, who was he to cast stones? His own grandfather, the Portuguese fisherman who'd come to America to catch the *bacalhao,* the cod, had arrived under some sort of a cloud. It was a cloud that Al's father had hinted at many times but never explained.

The thought of *bacalhao,* especially the dried, salted variety, made his stomach turn. It'd been a staple of countless generations of Madeiras. All but his own.

With Madeira leading, the party climbed the aluminum ladder out of the brightly lit engine room into the twilit main passenger cabin. The linoleum was cracked here and there but highly buffed, just as it would be on a warship. The row upon row of well-worn seats resembled the pews of a waterborne chapel, while all the way forward stood a small, altarlike table, behind which *Wave Runner*'s whale expert generally stood to deliver the sermon. Only the stained glass seemed lacking.

"I'm all ears, Mr. Linevich," Madeira said. He poured a cup of lavalike black coffee from the simmering pot for each of his visitors. Outside, a cold, wind-driven, autumn rain filled the air and pounded the gray waters of Provincetown Harbor, making it impossible to see even the two-hundred-and-fifty-foot-high Pilgrim Monument, which normally towered over the town.

The tall Russian diplomat looked intently into the steaming contents of the cup cradled in his hands. Then, straightening his back, he looked at Madeira with equal intensity. "Captain, we . . . me, Novikoff here, our whole nation . . . have a very difficult problem. We are hoping you can help us with it."

Madeira nodded for him to continue.

"You may consider our request preposterous, or even outrageous, but please hear us out before—"

"There's very little I find preposterous these days," interrupted Madeira, "and even less that merits my outrage. I just don't seem to have the energy for it."

Madeira sat on one of the benches and gestured to Linevich and Novikoff to do the same.

"If you remember your history lessons you will remember the so-called Cuban Missile Crisis, which occurred in October of 1962."

"Yes, I'm even old enough to remember the TV news about it. . . . Your merchant ships, supposedly carrying ballistic missiles to Cuba, steaming right at our blockading destroyers . . . Our president waving a handful of aerial photographs showing the missile silos and saying he's going to stop the ships . . . Your premier saying there'll be war if he so much as breathes on one . . . At the time I was certain there was going to be a war."

"During the course of that unfortunate misunderstanding," interrupted Linevich hastily, as if desperate to move the discussion on from the distasteful past and back to the present, "one of our early, experimental nuclear submarines sank with all hands aboard."

Madeira sat bolt upright, a look of suspicion on his face. Had more really happened during that historic showdown between Kennedy and Khrushchev than either side had ever admitted in public? A collision? Gunfire? Depth charges? Why would the Russians want to drag it out into the open now?

"Where did it sink?" he asked carefully.

"About fifty miles north of Puerto Rico," replied Linevich.

Madeira's expression deepened into a frown.

"No, Captain," continued Linevich, "we have every reason to believe this tragedy was due to some sort of equipment failure or human error on the part of the vessel's crew."

"We didn't sink her?" Madeira asked, still alert for some hint of hostility or calculation.

"We have never known exactly what happened, but as far as we know, the United States did not even know she was there at the time. Only recently has the CIA learned of it."

"Fifty miles north of Puerto Rico? Near the Puerto Rico Deep?" It was still damn hard to believe—not that it'd happened, but that it had never been exposed.

"Yes. Along the southern edge. In about three hundred meters of water."

A smile appeared on Madeira's face. "Why do you want her back? To put her in a museum? But at that depth she must've been crushed. She can't be anything more than junk now. A tangled mass of pipes and steel plate."

"We don't want all of her." It was the younger man, Novikoff, who spoke this time. "We want her reactor and some of her other machinery."

Understanding, as bright as the tropical sun, dawned on Madeira. "She's leaking radiation!"

"I am afraid so," Linevich said. "Our civilian research ships have been monitoring the area for several years. A few months ago we detected a sharp increase in radiation close to where we think the submarine is resting."

"We should also tell you," Novikoff said, "that the reactor is a very primitive, plutonium-fired system. . . ."

"Nasty stuff," Madeira mumbled. "Working on her's going to be a mess . . . but you have very adequate and experienced salvage resources of your own, don't you? Why come to me?"

"Surely," said Linevich, the diplomat, "you can imagine the circus that would develop if a Russian naval task force showed up fifty miles from Puerto Rico and announced it was going to recover the reactor from a nuclear submarine that had been sitting there, leaking radiation, for almost forty years. As I have indicated, your government is aware of the problem and is willing to let us handle it. President Clinton is just as eager as President Yeltsin to keep the operation as low-profile as possible."

"Captain Madeira," Novikoff said heatedly, "we're tired of being pointed at, laughed at, pitied and blamed. We admit this is our mess, a problem we created. It's our intention to clean it up as efficiently and responsibly as possible." As he spoke, his fists clenched and unclenched rapidly. "It's also our intention," he continued, "to do it as quietly as possible. Ten thousand press conferences will contribute nothing to the recovery . . . and neither will the hysterical, self-serving opinions of the countless instant experts who will suddenly appear out of nowhere on your morning news programs."

"Our pride is not the point!" snapped Linevich, his lower jaw pointing accusingly at Novikoff, "although I will admit that it *is* a factor. What we are facing here is a serious threat to the environment, to the world's oceans, and an even more serious political threat, a threat to the spirit and progress of reform in Russia. Without reform, Captain Madeira, Russia will slip back into barbarism and aggression and the world will be at risk again.''

Linevich paused to take a breath and then continued. ''I must tell you there are many at home who say President Yeltsin—our current, democratic government, that is—is incapable of protecting Russian interests, Russian honor. On the one hand it must maintain excellent relations with the United States, but on the other it must continue to prove it can take care of itself in a world filled with thugs of all colors and political beliefs.''

''You're absolutely right, Anton,'' Novikoff said hastily, almost biting his tongue.

''At that depth she may not really be a threat anyway,'' Madeira said, realizing as he spoke that they still hadn't answered his question.

''I'm afraid that's not totally correct,'' Linevich said with an almost embarrassed expression. ''The radiation already appears to be spreading beyond the wreck. Both on the ocean bottom and in the water.''

As the diplomat spoke, the totally irrelevant image of a pulsing, black and orange mushroom cloud flashed into Madeira's mind. It was the same cloud Johnson had used to defeat Goldwater. Ironically, within a few years it was Johnson himself who ended up as the warlord everybody loved to hate.

Madeira stared out the window at the rainwater raging along the decks and over the boat's side. In his mind he continued to watch with unease as the desert dust was sucked up into the blooming flower of nuclear death.

Too much television! he told himself. Mention the word *radiation* in any context and he'd been conditioned to see the glow-in-the-dark atomic fungus.

There was a slight shudder, then a long, metallic groan, as *Wave Runner* fetched up against one of her mooring lines.

''Furthermore,'' continued Linevich, dragging Madeira back to reality, ''the submarine is resting in an area where two of the moving plates that make up the earth's crust meet. A number of our experts feel that very strong earthquakes and volcanic activity are to be expected. They feel it is possible that some geologic force may yet split the reactor completely open, or even burst it into thousands of tiny fragments, and create a mass of highly radioactive water that would be carried slowly along the Antilles Barrier and then up the east coast of the United States."

The diplomat delivered the explanation with a tone of regret, almost as if he personally were responsible for the hooliganism of the earth's tectonic plates.

"Faced with this possibility, and the proximity to Puerto Rico, we don't wish to take any chances."

Madeira turned and looked out the picture windows, away from the harbor and across the big, battered, water-soaked parking lot. Fronting the lot was a row of dingy eateries and tourist shops, their gaudy facades now sad, funguslike, in the pounding downpour.

Beyond the jumble and nearly lost in the rain, P-Town's fabric of narrow streets and classic clapboard wove its way up a long slope until it faded into the murk. Only the outline of the cupola-crowned town hall was faintly visible.

During the summer, even in the heaviest rains, the lot, the streets, the eateries, and the trinket shops were all jammed with life. Now it was almost empty. The noisy, colorful vacationers had all gone home, leaving him and Cornie and these two Russians almost alone in the universe. That sense of melancholy, of isolation and alienation, which existed as an integral part of Al Madeira, flowered briefly then subsided again.

It's all built on sand, he thought. Why hasn't P-Town just slid into the Bay at some point over the past three or four hundred years?

"Three hundred meters . . . a thousand feet . . . that's only about thirty atmospheres, more or less. There're hundreds of people now with experience at that depth. . . . You've got a number yourselves. Why don't you go to them?"

"There are many fewer than you seem to think," Novikoff replied, now clearly in charge of presenting the Russians' position, "and none has a reputation quite like yours.

Of greatest importance, we're confident you have no desire to see your own picture on the front page of the newspaper.''

"Of greatest importance?'' Madeira wondered aloud.

"Yes," replied Novikoff. "Surely you can see what a threat the news media is to an operation like this. They're like starving dogs these days. If they get their teeth into this they'll never let go. They're the only force capable at the moment of bringing Yeltsin down and restarting the Cold War.''

Madeira nodded in reply as he continued to stare out at the cold rain. "A thousand feet," he said to himself. Four hundred fifty pounds per square inch. Water so hard it'll demolish steel and crush a person into pinkish jelly. Bitterly cold and dark as a tomb. And even more lonely.

Less than a year before he'd lost Tina, the one woman with whom he'd ever felt totally in sync. Now, watching summer being driven away by autumn's violence, his whole adult life seemed to boil down to two monumental deep-sea disasters: the accidental destruction of a naval undersea station he'd commanded, and the murderous fury that had ended the excavation of a Spanish treasure ship.

Fire and water. Each had proved deadly. And his many successes, for his rational side insisted that there had indeed been many, were totally irrelevant.

On both occasions he'd been in charge. On both occasions, as far as he was concerned, he'd been responsible.

The truth, he told himself, was that he never wanted to go down again. He'd lost his taste for diving. He feared the depths more than he'd ever feared anything before.

"I'm surprised my reputation didn't chase you away.''

Why the hell was he saying that? Why wasn't he just saying "No, thank you, now please get lost''?

"You were placed in impossible positions and succeeded in doing the best that could be done," Linevich said in an almost fatherly tone. "We admire that. You are our first choice for the job.''

Listening to the two Russians, Madeira felt a strange

21

flicker of enthusiasm. What they were offering was a total mess, a foul, incredibly stupid mess. At the same time, it was something he could really get his teeth into and wallow in. It might even be his salvation.

And the irony was interesting. Attractive, in fact. He'd be working for the very Russian Navy from whom he'd been defending America for over twenty years.

What would his uncle Carlos do? he wondered. Carlos was one of the very few people he knew who really demanded, and received, every penny's worth of value from life. Carlos would continue to fight the hook right up until he was gaffed, hoisted aboard, dropped into the fish box, and buried.

Carlos would undoubtedly take the job.

There was a faint thud as another gust of wind slammed into *Wave Runner*. The preliminaries are over, he thought. The big guy, the long-predicted nor'easter, is now in the ring.

Returning to the past, he could still feel the pain, and the deathly chill, that had followed the agony. But there were to be no excuses, and he knew he must feel no regrets. He'd done what he'd thought had to be done. Tina and all the others were gone forever and that was that. He wasn't quite ready yet to follow them.

Still holding his empty coffee cup, Madeira turned and looked around *Wave Runner*'s main cabin.

When he'd returned from his last misadventure, determined to hang up his swim fins and take up farming, he'd found that Carlos, the eternal cod fisherman, the only member of the family to follow in Grandpa's footsteps, had finally wised up. He'd sold his fishing boat and was in the process of purchasing *Wave Runner,* both the vessel and the business. Madeira had immediately signed on, along with a number of cousins, as a junior partner. He'd also agreed to act as relief captain. Not even Carlos, who at the age of seventy-one still insisted upon commuting from Gloucester, wanted to chase whales seven days a week.

Hell! The Cape was jammed with operators qualified to

skipper *Wave Runner.* Carlos would have no trouble finding a replacement for him for the few weeks remaining in the season! For that matter, he'd find his own replacement.

"What do you plan to do with the machinery once we have it?"

"That remains to be decided," Novikoff replied with the satisfied smile of a fisherman who knows he'd just set the hook. "Our scientists are studying that question right now."

Yet another, even harder gust belted the whale-watcher, heeling her and driving her against the groaning fenders that protected her sides from the pier.

"What sort of resources do we have?"

"You and Captain Novikoff will get whatever you need," replied Linevich. "The two of you will plan and execute the project under the auspices of the All-Russia Oceanographic Institution."

"Pay?" Madeira was surprised at his own sudden interest in money. Between his pension and his portion of *Wave Runner*'s profits he was more than comfortable. But then the world was changing, he decided, and so was he. It was just a matter of his catching up and getting with the program.

"Anything within reason," replied Linevich.

"A million dollars. No cure, no pay." You're only worth what your pay stub says you are, he thought.

"Those are traditional salvage terms."

"After taxes," Madeira concluded, as astounded at the Russians' willingness to agree as he was at his own greed.

"Since you are a foreign consultant, we will not hold you to our own pay standards." Linevich smiled at his own joke.

"Project SeaGlow," mumbled Madeira.

"SeaGlow?" Linevich asked.

"Yes, Anton," Novikoff laughed. "SeaGlow is perfect! If the press, or the environmentalists, catch us, they'll undoubtedly accuse us of making the whole ocean, and everything in it, glow."

As the Russian officer spoke, Madeira's imagination lurched into overdrive again. He could see a large blob of glowing, highly radioactive water that moved slowly northeast. Carried first by the Antilles Current, it soon oozed into the mighty Stream itself. Onward it went, pulsing slightly, from Puerto Rico to Key West and then to Nantucket, mutating or destroying all it flowed over and past. A fluid mass of death.

He laughed at his own idiocy; the damn thing wouldn't really glow!

"Are we agreed, then, Captain?" asked Novikoff, the smile still on his face.

"I'm interested," Madeira replied as he thought how nice it was to be wanted, "but you're going to have to let me think it over a day or two. I'd like to discuss it with one or two people who, I can assure you, will be very discreet."

"Of course," Linevich said.

Chapter Two

Madeira walked the two Russians out to the tiny gangway. After shaking their hands he wished them a good trip back to New York. He then remained on deck, watching the pair trot down the wind- and rain-swept dock to their car. It was a nondescript four-door of some sort that was parked almost beside his own at the harbor end of the empty lot.

"Yo! Al!"

Madeira turned and look at Cornie, who was standing in the open door, looking out at him.

"How're you doing?" he asked.

" 'Bout half done, but I could sure use some help."

Madeira struggled to control his irritation, both with the tone and with the content of Cornie's near demand.

"Good work," he finally said. "Keep at it. Do what you can for a while, then I'll be down to help you finish up."

"Fine!" the engineer replied sullenly. "Didn't I hear those guys say something about a sunken sub? It around here someplace?"

Loose lips sink ships, thought Madeira, unsure how much

Cornie had heard and hoping to minimize the damage. "Yes," he said, "it was supposedly carrying a big load of gold bars. They said the gold was stolen from Russia, but they were damn careful to not tell me much. If I decide to do anything with them they're going to have to tell me a lot more. I want to start checking on them right now, so you get back to work and I'll be down in about fifteen minutes."

"Right!" said Cornie.

One glance at his eyes told Madeira that the engineer had overheard enough to find Madeira's intentionally vague explanation confusing. In time, after he'd had a chance to think it all out, he might even become suspicious.

"And Cornie, keep this sub bit under your hat for now. We don't want a thousand treasure hounds running around here looking for it, do we? Unless, of course, they're willing to pay a super bonus to charter *Wave Runner*."

As he cracked the feeble joke Madeira chuckled the greediest, most conspiratorial chuckle he could come up with.

"Yeah, Al. We'll keep it private. Just between you and me."

After ushering Cornie to the engine-room ladder, and down it, Madeira returned to the main cabin and poured himself a fresh cup of stale coffee.

There'd been a lot of truth in the lies he'd told Cornie. The Russians really hadn't answered his questions, but that wasn't the biggest mystery of the moment. The mystery was why he was so eager to do it at all, even without knowing more.

He liked his current life. He got to drive a boat and live beside the ocean, and he could be home every night and even have a real social life. And, thanks to his retirement benefits, he could pay all his bills—just as long as he didn't get carried away—whether or not he ever raised a finger again.

Yet the trashed sub called to him like a radiation-poxed siren.

At his age he should know better, he told himself as he reached for the telephone to call Lane Williams, the now-retired admiral to whom Madeira had reported while in command at Cabot Station.

Before the disaster, Williams had been the only one who tried to help. Afterward, it was Admiral Williams who'd stood by him, saved him from ritual execution, and insisted in a very loud voice that the gravest portion of blame be placed on his own massive shoulders.

Williams was one of the few men in his position who would have even considered coming to Madeira's defense. Tough, incorruptible, outspoken, he had, over the years, served with practically everybody who was anybody in the navy. Williams was also one of the very few men who could have protected Madeira. In the course of forty years of naval service the admiral had done a lot of favors. He'd also tripped over and remembered more than a few skeletons in many, many closets.

"The number you have just dialed," said the recording a few seconds later, "has been changed. Please make a note. The new number is . . ."

Area code 305? thought Madeira as he dialed the number given him by the synthesized voice. Where's that? Florida? South Florida? They're sure as hell on the move again!

"Hello?" said a vibrantly feminine voice after the second ring.

"Hello, Kate. This is Al Madeira."

"Al! It's wonderful to hear from you. . . . It's been so long. How's the whale-watching business?"

"It's very good. Much to my surprise, I'm enjoying it."

Kate Williams laughed with a gaiety that belied her almost sixty years. "I'm very glad to hear that. You deserve something good for a change."

"And you two . . . how are you? And *where* are you?"

Again the relaxed, almost girlish laugh. "We're in the Keys, at a marina on Desconocido Key. That's one of the benefits of living on a big, old powerboat. When we tire of

27

a place we just cast off and head on. . . . Just as long as we have gas money.''

"How's the admiral?''

"Getting younger every day. . . . I know you won't believe that, but it's true! Retirement has done wonders for him. For both of us. You'll just have to come see. . . . Soon. He's even got a project to work on now. One they're paying him for and that doesn't involve his having been an admiral.

"He's on the dock cleaning some fish at the moment. I think he makes believe the fish are really certain people he served with over the years. . . . You can imagine who!''

Listening to Kate's muffled voice calling down to the stocky fisherman, Madeira looked out into the fast-falling night at the nor'easter now lashing the harbor. It was the sort of wind that carried winter on its shoulders as it tore the few remaining leaves from the cringing trees. At the other end of the phone line, he thought, were palms, white sand, and the golden sun slipping quietly into Florida Bay's delicate blue-green depths.

Thwack! . . . Thwack, thwack, thwack.

He felt as much as heard it. The machine gun–like rapping. Something had come loose in the tearing, whistling wind and was already beating itself to death.

Shit! It must be the canvas cover over one of the deck lockers.

"Al,'' rumbled Lane Williams a minute or two later. "How's whaling?''

"Couldn't be better,'' he replied, torn between the necessity of resecuring the flapping cover and the desire to discuss the Russians with Williams. "Been coming home every night with a hold full of oil and whalebone.''

"You rascal!'' Williams chuckled as he spoke. "I hope for your sake the telephone isn't tapped.''

"You know how it is, Admiral. Old habits die hard among us Portuguese. Kate tells me you finally got a real job, too.''

Williams laughed again. "Ran into a couple fellows who'd just bought a half-finished super-resort down here

28

from the FDIC. All sorts of special effects and exotic entertainments. Even virtual reality! Some of it comes *this* close to making call girls obsolete.

"The engineering was a disaster. I convinced them I could straighten the mess out for half of what anybody else would charge, and by God I am! Be done in about a month. There was a little trouble at first because I don't have a Florida Civil Engineering License, but we worked that out."

Williams paused, the chuckle vanishing from his voice. "What's up?"

"I'm not entirely sure. . . ." He could now hear the cover's heavy brass grommet flogging the locker, undoubtedly destroying the latter's paint job. For that matter, the whole damn thing might tear off. "About an hour ago two Russians showed up in my engine room and asked me to help them salvage an old Soviet nukie which they say sank during the Cuban Missile Crisis. And they want it done quietly."

"There weren't any casualties during that. I was there. No action at all, in fact . . . It was just a lot of huffing and puffing."

"They say it was an accident. The problem is the sub had an experimental, plutonium-fired reactor which has started leaking radiation."

"Where is it?"

"A few miles north of Puerto Rico, near the Deep."

"Ha! Do we know about it? Officially?"

"They say we do. They say both Yeltsin and Clinton want them to do it."

"Perceptions are everything. Have been throughout history, actually. You want to do it?"

"It looks interesting."

"I thought you'd given up diving."

"So did I. . . ."

"*Can* you do it?"

"It'll be a challenge, but yes! Assuming I can get a basic minimum of gear."

"Then why'd you call me?"

29

"I'm not really sure why they want me, and . . ."

The wind gusted again, slamming the boat into the dock and driving the flapping cover into a fury.

"They want you because you've proven you're very good at picking up scrap from the bottom of the ocean. Besides, outside experts, especially retired U.S. naval officers, make excellent scapegoats."

"Yes, I hadn't thought of that."

"You've survived before. If you want to do it, I think you should. I can't see any ethical problems, although, frankly, you'll be swimming with bigger and meaner sharks than you've ever faced in the past."

"The Russians, you mean?"

"Among others. The Kremlin, the Agency, the Libyans, and everybody in between. Even the Russian Mob. They've become a major player these days, and it's sometimes hard to tell them from what passes for a legitimate government over there. Since the Cold War ended, the whole world's turned into a seething mass of power-hungry factions. Even here in the U.S. Christ! The President, not that he doesn't deserve it, is being massacred by his own party and Congress has splintered into six hundred would-be Caesars. Fortunately, TV's our preferred weapon. The Russians and most of the rest of the world, except the Brits, seem more interested in real blood than opinion polls."

"Ummmmmm."

"I hope I'm not discouraging you. . . ."

"No. Not at all. I do read the newspaper from time to time."

"Good! It does sound like your kind of job; just the sort of royal screwup the rest of us would run like hell to avoid. And who knows? If you succeed, you'll probably be doing your country a favor. How's the pay?"

"Very good."

"No doubt you'll earn it. I still have a few contacts left in Washington. It'd probably be a good idea for me to check with them on this, just to make sure . . . Just because they say the President says he approves doesn't mean a damn thing. I'd hate to see you lose your pension.''

"I'd appreciate that."

"I'll have them get in touch with you. Remember, these people aren't necessarily my friends. They're contacts. Most of them are also the sort of sharks I was warning you about. They're all especially dangerous now because they're confused; they're not sure where their next meal's going to come from."

"Understood."

"Just make sure they don't make a snack of you!"

Madeira hung up and raced, cursing, out into the storm to save what was left of the lacerated canvas cover.

As he hunted for some light line to secure the cover he remembered he had a dinner date with Sally Carton, the new manager of his local bank branch. Sally of the ear-to-ear smile. Sally who knew a million good jokes and talked a mile a minute through her own laughter. And when she stopped talking for a moment, it was Sally who looked at you as if you were the only person in the world.

A good dinner in a nice restaurant, now largely free of the horde of summer visitors. Some dancing, maybe . . .

He looked at his watch. He might have time!

No. He didn't have a chance in hell. Not if he stayed to finish up with Cornie, and that seemed unavoidable. He had no choice but to cancel. He'd plead the demands of business; maybe a banker would accept that.

Fat chance! He certainly wasn't the only male in town who'd noticed her arrival.

He could already imagine the conversation: "Hi, Sally, this is Al. . . ."

"Hi, Al. What's up?"

"I'm really sorry to call so late, but I've got to stand you up on this date I've spent over two months trying to talk you into."

"I hope nothing bad has happened."

"No, it's just that I've got to romance a ten-ton hunk of iron into performing like it's supposed to do."

"Oh, I'm so sorry, Al. Maybe some other time."

Some other century, most likely.

The whole prospect reminded him of life in the navy, although there you often weren't even supposed to explain why.

He found a length of line and secured the cover as quickly as he could, desperate to get back to the phone and save what he could with Sally. And he wondered just how successful the Russians would be in maintaining security around an operation that was to take place so far beyond their own tightly controlled borders.

"Shit!" he growled as he hunched forward and stared out intently into the black hole of a night. It should be here! Or maybe just ahead.

Could he have already passed it?

He should've spent the night aboard *Wave Runner*. At least Sally had taken it well. She'd even agreed to reschedule.

The monster nor'easter's wind and rain pounded with the force of steel on the station wagon's roof and flowed down the windshield in sheets. The roar of the wind and water, combined with that of the window defroster, made it difficult to talk, even to himself.

The headlights revealed little—a dozen feet of Route 6A, normally a narrow parking lot jammed with cars but now a shallow, empty river, and the faintest glints of drowning shrub pines along the highway's side. Then, having failed miserably in their duty, they simply disappeared into eternity.

He continued creeping down the highway, uncertain which side of the yellow line he was on and no longer caring, trying to penetrate the night as he went. Suddenly his windshield burst into life, filling with a thousand glittering white diamonds that made it impossible to see anything else.

Somebody was coming right at him, he realized. Somebody who must've just rounded the curve. Whoever he was, he was coming fast. Very fast. Too fast! The guy must be drunk, he thought, to be going that fast under these conditions. And neither of them, he felt certain, had the slightest idea which side of the road he was on.

Almost without thought Madeira slowed further and pulled off onto the narrow, sandy shoulder, skidding on the mixture of sand and wet pine needles and almost hitting a twisted little pine in the process.

Even before he'd oozed to a halt the other car blew by, hidden behind a solid sheet of glittering water thrown up by its front tires.

Shaking his head and grinding his teeth, Madeira crept back onto the pavement. A gust of storm-maddened wind slammed into the wagon, forcing it to skip sideways across the slick surface.

Further infuriated by the wind's slap, Madeira grasped the steering wheel even harder. Christ Almighty! he thought. It wasn't as if he'd never been there before; it was his own goddamn driveway he couldn't find.

Goddamnit! He *had* passed it. There, just ahead, was that crummy little vegetable stand, now boarded up for the winter. He glanced into the mirror and saw absolutely nothing at all. Interpreting the nothing-at-all as an all clear, he made a sharp U-turn and headed back down the all-but-invisible highway, keeping carefully to the wrong side as he went. If some other jerk was out blundering around in the storm, it was just too goddamn bad. For both of them.

Five endless minutes later he spotted the small sign and swung the wheel almost viciously to the left. The driveway was long and narrow, little more really than two shallow ruts in the Cape's sandy soil. On either side, and overhead, barely-seen walls pressed in, forming a tunnel even darker than the storm-lashed highway had been.

A hundred yards in the tunnel expanded into an open lawn and the driveway forked; the right branch led to the main house, the left to the caretaker's house, which he rented.

Madeira stopped at the fork, his attention suddenly drawn to the main house. The wind and rain continued unabated, so he could hear nothing . . . but he was certain he'd seen a light.

It'd been the wagon's headlights, he told himself, reflecting off the windows. But when he saw the faint glimmer again he knew it wasn't his headlights, because they were now pointed away from the house.

The headlights of a car passing on the highway? No. They wouldn't be visible in this weather.

Damnit! This was the second break-in in the month since the Boltons, the owners, had returned to New York.

He remained seated until the light flickered yet again through the intense dark. The prudent thing to do, he reminded himself, would be to drive on to his own house, call the cops, and let them handle the situation. Except there were probably only about two and a half of them at this time of year and the nor'easter was undoubtedly keeping them more than busy.

He watched the light and listened to the storm. It has to be a kid, he told himself. Or kids. No serious felon would waste his time breaking into summer houses. It was up to him to investigate. To earn the discount he was getting on the rent.

He killed the wagon's lights, then backed blindly along the driveway to where it entered the scrub. After parking across the drive he struggled into the slicker that had been lying on the seat beside him. He then grabbed the flashlight in the glove compartment.

The storm, solid water and a furious wind that reeked of salt, seaweed, and power beyond imagining, roared into the wagon the instant Madeira even began to open the door. He slipped out quickly, pulling up his hood as he did, and slammed the door behind him. Unlighted flashlight in hand, he marched down the watery driveway, then across the squishy lawn toward the main house.

He climbed the steps and crossed the front porch, then paused at the open front door. Did he really want to catch the intruder or just scare him, or them, away? Should he reach in and turn on the lights or slip in and sneak up on him?

The howling furies of the night swirled past him and into the living room.

Serious felon or not, he thought, the son of a bitch might still be armed. And Madeira wasn't.

Deciding his advantage lay in darkness since he undoubtedly knew the house better than the intruder did, Madeira stepped into the living room and paused, dripping a mixture of water and grimy oil, he learned much later, on Mrs. Bolton's prized Virgin White couch.

The light flashed again, reflected off one wall. He, they, were back in the kitchen.

It was definitely *they,* he decided after listening a minute or two. Despite the storm's ungodly roar he could hear them talking as they banged around, slamming doors and drawers and rattling pots and pans. They were obviously in a hurry and seemed to think they were still alone.

Walking as gently as he could and trying to stay on the rugs, he edged past the couch and around toward the short hall leading to the dining room.

The beam of a large flashlight exploded in his face, stunning and blinding him. Then there was a shout from the kitchen and the light went out.

Madeira charged forward several steps, then stiffened.

There was something! A click. A glint. A hoarse whisper. A clink. Something almost imperceptible to his consciousness yet capable of shouting "Down!" at the top of its lungs. Down! Down! Down!

Driven by hint, instinct, and luck, he threw himself onto the floor and to the side.

A mass of orange-black flame erupted from the muzzle of a sawed-off shotgun. The heavy pellets screamed over him and slammed into the wall.

What the hell was he doing!

Panting now as much from fear as exertion, he lay where he was, in as near absolute silence as possible, and listened.

There was the sound of hoarse whispering, then of feet running heavily. Then something slammed.

A cold blast of air hit him in the face as he crept into the chaotic kitchen and turned on the light. The sweetish smell of burnt black powder was strong despite the wide-open back door.

Still panting, and shaking, he flipped on the back floods and looked out, taking care to stand to one side of the door. The small, rain-soaked back lawn and dense, glistening scrub beyond were visible, but there was no sign of motion except for that caused by the wind and rain.

"This is Al Madeira," he said into the phone after the police dispatcher had answered. "I live out in the care-taker's house at the Bolton place. . . ."

"Yes, Mr. Madeira?"

"About an hour ago I returned home from Provincetown and found intruders in the main house."

"Are they still there?"

"No. They ran off into the woods."

"Has anyone been injured?"

"No . . . but they fired a shotgun at me."

"You're sure you're not injured?"

"Yes."

"Didn't we have a similar report from you a couple weeks ago?"

"Yes, somebody broke in then. Nobody shot at me."

"What's been taken?"

"I'm not sure yet. They also broke into my house. They must have done that before I arrived."

"You say they ran off into the woods. . . . What about their vehicle?"

"I haven't been able to find one. They must have parked along the highway."

"Do you feel you're personally in danger? They may be back, you know."

"No. I'm fine. I'm sure I surprised them and they panicked. They were just trying to make time to get away."

"As long as you're not in imminent danger, the earliest we can get somebody out there to take your report will be sometime tomorrow morning. We've got half a dozen serious accidents to deal with. In the meantime, if you feel in any danger, leave immediately."

"Thanks. I'll be waiting."

Goddamn kids! thought Madeira as he broke the connection and looked around his own ransacked living room. He then dialed Carlos to tell him he might not make it in to *Wave Runner* the next morning.

When did the little bastards start carrying guns around here? he wondered. For that matter, was it kids this time?

Whoever it was was obviously after more than some leftover booze or costume jewelry. They hadn't even bothered with his antique sextant, which, he was certain, could be easily sold to any one of a thousand antique shops.

He looked down at the puddle growing around him on the rug as his soggy clothes drained and groaned. It'd take him at least a day, maybe two, to straighten out the messes in both houses. And that was before he called in the cleaning service and then had to keep an eye on them.

Chapter Three

Race Point Light was now almost directly to starboard.

Madeira glanced briefly at the tall, black and white banded tower and thought how lonesome it looked rising over the barren, sandy point. But that's the essential nature of lighthouses, he decided. Forever on watch, standing alone at stiff attention, while life races and frolics around them. The light, he decided, was more forthright, even noble, than the thin, square, Italianate tower of the Pilgrim Monument, which was still also visible on this most crystalline of days.

Ahead great, blue North Atlantic swells rolled and tumbled under the bright sun and clear skies of an autumn high. The sapphire seas, white-crowned by the brisking easterly breeze, seemed to gallop at him as they pivoted around Cape Cod's low, almost insubstantial tip. Surging then into Cape Cod Bay, the waves flushed out the moldy, brown-green water of summer.

Balanced on the balls of his feet, his motions automatic, Madeira leaned slightly forward, then aft again as *Wave Runner*, steered by her automatic pilot, rose to and topped one of the cresting, blue and white hills.

All in all, he thought as he glanced down at the compass, a dynamite day! A Sally Carton sort of day, he concluded, thinking of last night's rescheduled dinner date and the sensation he had that some of Sally's perpetual, but far from tiresome, cheerfulness had rubbed off on him. The sort of day that made you wonder why anybody would want to leave it all and go down *there,* possibly never to return. To suffer the cold, dark silence. To suffer the oppression of a thousand feet of thick water mindlessly determined to crush you.

What the hell was he going to do about the Russians?

He heard no reply to his question. The pilothouse was silent, a silence underlined by the low mumble of the almost two thousand horses that drove *Wave Runner,* the quiet moaning of the wind, an occasional creak and the radio's hisses and burps.

Madeira glanced at the little painted plaster Virgin Mary that Carlos insisted be kept in the pilothouse and then allowed his eyes to wander around the horizon. A mile or so to port, *Evie G,* another whale-watcher, also raced northeast toward Stellwagen Bank. *Evie* was Frank Urban's boat. Madeira kind of liked Frank, although he'd found that Frank could be a little slippery at times.

Like *Wave Runner, Evie* was charging into the rolling, slightly choppy seas with her bow held high. Up she went, riding up and over every approaching swell, then down she pitched, thundering down the back side of the last and up into the next. All the while her stern remained almost buried in the boiling, exhaust-fouled wake that trailed out behind her.

It's always been a race, he thought. The objective used to be to catch and kill the whale; to carve it up and cook it before somebody else did. Or before the whales swam away.

Madeira had no hold to fill, but he did have passengers to satisfy. The men, women, and children who filled the cabin below weren't suffering the tortures of seasickness for just any boat ride. They were there to see whales.

ASAP!

And the only way the boat could support her crew and make a decent return on the large investment she represented, not to mention paying the mortgage, was to keep the passengers satisfied and get in two trips a day during the season.

"Does anybody know how the right whale got its name?" The amplified but muffled voice of Sandy Alvarez, *Wave Runner*'s whale expert and Madeira's unbelievably distant cousin, wafted into the pilothouse from the cabin below. So distant, in fact, was the relationship that Madeira wasn't sure he could even explain it if asked to do so. He did know it was on his mother's side.

He'd heard the spiel a hundred times before and was sick of it. Especially the preachy part. Unfortunately, he knew if it was even the slightest bit audible a part of his mind would anticipate, and grab hungrily for, every tedious word. His only defense was to get away from the door to the cabin, to step out of the pilothouse onto the boat's tiny bridge. He glanced again at Race Point, then at the compass. With a sigh of great relief he stepped out into the breezy port wing where he could watch *Evie G* drive through the growing chop and slowly pull ahead. Frank was clearly feeling competitive today . . . and willing to squander a little extra fuel in the process.

It was going to be just the two of them, decided Madeira. *Evie* and *Runner*. It was late in the season, and most of the other boats were operating on abbreviated schedules . . . or not at all. The majority of his passengers were school groups, along with a few older couples who were enjoying the fall, crowd-free weather. Many of the whales were leaving, or had already left. Heading south, to calve in the warmer waters between Bermuda and the Antilles. Heading right for an old Russian submarine that was leaking radiation.

"Bertie, this is Hank," the radio spat suddenly. "You gitt'n any over where you're at?"

"None to speak of," came the laconic reply.

"That's acouse Bertie don't know howta get nuttin," suggested a third, unidentified voice. "Not even afta all these years. . . ."

Madeira smiled at the fishermen's exchange, then wondered if *Runner* was making any money today. School groups never ended up paying full fare, especially when Carlos booked them. Even though he was old enough to know better, Carlos continued to believe children possessed some special virtue, almost nobility. Nothing was ever too good for them, as far as Carlos was concerned.

With luck, Madeira consoled himself, half the kids will have forgotten their lunch, or sat on it, and have to buy some overpriced junk food from Sandy at the snack bar.

He wondered if *Evie* was doing any better.

Another forty-five minutes, he thought, looking at his watch.

Why hadn't Lane Williams's contacts gotten back to him about the Russians? Unless Novikoff and Linevich had lied to him, what sort of complications could there be?

Maybe they *had* lied. Maybe the government knew nothing about the operation. Maybe the United States wanted to handle the matter itself . . . or didn't want it handled at all. No, that wasn't it. The Russians wouldn't have lied to him, not about things he could so easily check.

Could the problem be in Moscow?

The possibility had bothered him the last few days, ever since he'd seen the TV footage of Yeltsin's troops hammering the Parliamentary office building and realized he hadn't the slightest idea who were the good guys and who the bad. The news anchor had assured him that the black-garbed special troops driving the tanks and firing the artillery, the ones that reminded him of Hitler's SS troops, were loyal to Yeltsin and therefore on the side of the angels. But none of it computed. Not for him, anyway.

Did he really want to be involved in all of it? Especially when he didn't even understand what was going on?

But why would that seemingly one-sided clash, the Battle of the White House, disrupt the operation? They said that

Yeltsin had won. And the recovery of the sub was Yeltsin's operation, wasn't it?

The problem, he decided, would prove to be American-made. The Cold War might be over, the Age of Aquarius might even be near at hand, but the United States government hadn't changed one bit. Mumble something about the risks, just for the record, then wink and wait and watch as some other fool leads the charge.

If things worked out, nobody'd remember the timidity of your mumblings and there'd be more than enough photo ops to go around.

If, on the other hand, disaster resulted? Outrage, condemnation, and investigation were always very satisfying.

Nobody'd ever sign off on anything, except with disappearing ink.

He stepped back into the pilothouse and checked the Global Positioning System. They were getting close!

It looked, in the distance, like some sort of strange nun buoy. Vaguely conical in shape and more or less pointed at the top, it was an uneven, splotched hue of gray. If he hadn't known better, Madeira would've assumed it was something the navy'd designed and built absentmindedly, then ordered a madman to paint. Only upon closer examination were the throat folds visible. Then the great, somber eye at the cone's base, almost lost in the chop.

Stellwagen Bank. They'd arrived. Although there was no land in sight, nothing but a heaving expanse of blue and white in all directions, there could be no mistaking their destination. The depth sounder, the Global Positioning System, and the whale all vouched for its identity.

Madeira leaned on the rail and studied that great eye as it studied him, the whale spinning ever so slowly to follow *Wave Runner* as she ghosted to a stop.

"Oh, look!" boomed Sandy's voice over the external PA system, "That's a right whale off the port bow. . . . In fact, that's a whale we know very well. She's a female who we call 'Granny.'"

Seaglow

Madeira was aware of his unimaginably distant cousin's voice and of the rush of passengers toward the foredeck. He was equally aware of wind and wave slowly forcing *Wave Runner*'s bow to starboard. But his concentration was centered on Granny's eye.

How much intelligence, how much understanding really did lie behind that eye? It was a question he'd been asking himself for almost twenty years now.

His first close contact with whales had been with the detachment of porpoises attached to the undersea station he'd commanded until it was destroyed. Agile, animated, resourceful, seemingly playful and human in size, it'd been easy to attribute great intelligence to them. Unfortunately, it was proving much more difficult for him to relate to the Great Whales. They were simply *too* great, and aloof.

"Granny," continued Sandy, "is a very important member of this pod, or herd, of whales. . . . We believe that up to eight of the other members are all her children."

As Madeira pondered what he suspected was unknowable, Granny allowed herself to sink demurely back into the ocean's obscurity, only to be replaced by another, this time off to starboard. A minke whale, he guessed, based on its size.

There was a rush from one side of *Wave Runner* to the other.

It could, of course, be a young right whale, he admitted to himself. He wasn't always good at telling them apart and minkes were fairly rare, but this did look like one.

For that matter, he hadn't always been sure about the porpoises, either. They'd always seemed so smart, but how much did they really understand?

Did whales know they were each going to die? He didn't know. Sandy wouldn't know either. Although she had an advanced degree in something-or-other, there was much she didn't know.

Even Susan Constantine, the marine biologist who had worked with the porpoises at the undersea station, didn't know. She'd tried to find out, run a hundred experiments to

43

plumb the depths of the porpoises' understanding, but all had failed.

By now the minke had also disappeared and *Wave Runner* was starting to roll heavily, her white-painted steel rails swooping all too close to the churning foam. He was going to have to get her bow back around into the wind. Otherwise, some of the passengers might end up joining the whales.

Madeira walked all around the wheelhouse, carefully examining the surrounding water. He felt certain that no whale, at least none of the Stellwagen regulars, would be stupid enough to get caught by his maneuvering, but . . .

As satisfied as he was ever going to be, he returned to the wheelhouse and started to twist. Rudder hard left. Port shaft back. Starboard shaft ahead.

The engines growled. The chop slapped at the hull. The boat shivered and shuddered, and all the while, Sandy's near-continuous commentary gushed on in the background. She'd make a damn good auctioneer, he thought.

Almost as soon as *Wave Runner*'s bow was back into the wind, a large right whale surged alongside, swimming on the surface, blowing and studying the boat as it passed.

Madeira noticed one of his passengers, a small school kid, jumping and shouting in delight and found himself smiling. The smile quickly turned to uncontrollable laughter as the full darkness of his own vision hit him. The kid, and many of the other passengers, those who were jumping or bending, could easily pass for twitching, shrimplike krill, the whales' favorite food.

The Gentle Giants of the Deep, he concluded, weren't there to communicate. They were really just checking out the jumbo shrimp dinner.

So hard was Madeira laughing that it was several minutes before he realized the phone was buzzing.

"Yes?"

"Al? This is Cornie. There's a guy here says he has to talk to you. I told him passengers ain't allowed in the wheelhouse. . . . He says to tell you he's an old friend of Lane Williams?"

Madeira felt the laughter ebb out of him. The contact was already lying to him. "It's okay. Let him up."

"Al, it's good to meet you!" said the individual who stepped into the wheelhouse a moment later. "I'm Charlie Nash.

Shortish. Wearing slacks, a turtleneck, and boating shoes. Clearly very fit. Thinning hair, cut close. A square, tensed jaw. Compressed lips. A faint, demanding smile. The sort of face that said "If it's important to me it damn well better be important to you, too."

Madeira looked over the new arrival and both disliked and distrusted him immediately.

"Good to see you, Charlie," he replied in kind. "I wondered when you were going to show up."

"You know how it is, Al. Ten assignments all at once. Things to be checked into. People to clear with. Heavy-duty meetings and paperwork. Exhausting! No different from the navy."

Madeira nodded, checking *Wave Runner*'s heading as he did. He'd have to twist again soon.

"So what've we got here, Al? What do you know about all this?"

Madeira started to tell him all he knew, which was limited to his conversation with Linevich and Novikoff.

"Yeah. Okay. We know them," Nash mumbled at one point.

About halfway through his account Madeira excused himself for a few minutes to concentrate on turning *Wave Runner*'s bow back into the seas. Then he led Nash out into the fresh air, where he concluded by mentioning his call to Lane Williams, carefully skipping over the admiral's references to fish with big teeth.

"Okay, Al. That's how we read it too," Nash said after Madeira'd finished. "We want that reactor rendered harmless and we want to see *them* do it. It's important to their government that they do it themselves. Yeltsin's under a lot of pressure, now more than ever, to prove he can handle things. It's also very important to Clinton. He wants to prove he can work better with Yeltsin, with the Russians, than the Republicans ever could. That's why we want you to do what you can to help them.''

"Why doesn't he loan them some navy salvors?''

"I told you, it has to be their show. They said they wanted a civilian, you in particular. A number of people seem to have a very high opinion of you.'' Nash's tone hinted that he might not share that same high opinion.

"That trouble they had in Moscow a few days ago . . .''

"You mean the showdown with the reactionaries in Parliament? Don't worry about it. Our guy won. You concentrate on what you know.''

As Nash spoke, it occurred to Madeira that the whales would be among the first to suffer from the wreck's leaking radiation. It'd probably start as stillbirths—or grotesque birth defects of some sort—and they'd never know what'd hit them.

He scanned the surrounding waters, then the foredeck, watching the passengers shoot roll after roll of film. One passenger in particular caught his eye: a short, fat guy with what looked like a 700-millimeter telephoto lens. He was shooting everything! Whales. Other passengers. The sea-gulls diving astern. For a moment, Madeira almost felt as if that immense lens, glinting in the afternoon sun, were aimed directly at him.

"You see that little guy with the huge telephoto?'' asked Madeira, turning back to Nash. "I could swear he's taking our picture.''

"Where?'' Nash asked, stepping to the rail to get a better look.

"There,'' Madeira replied, turning and pointing.

But the photographer was nowhere to be seen.

"Shit! He's gone.''

Nash laughed. "Don't get carried away with the 'secret agent' bit. We know who you are and so do they. Who'd want to take your picture when we'll give them a dozen?''

The phone buzzed.

"Al?"

"Yes, Sandy?"

"Could we move about two miles to the east, to where Festus and his pod tend to hang out?"

"Sure thing. Do the passengers seem to be enjoying the show? And how are food sales?"

"They're loving it, Al, and they're eating their heads off. Especially coffee and hot chocolate."

Super-high-margin stuff, Madeira thought as he hung up the phone. And Sandy's a good kid.

After looking carefully around to make sure no whales were trying to make out with *Wave Runner*, Madeira advanced the throttles slowly and turned east.

"Is that all you want me to do? Help them recover the reactor?"

"For the most part, yes. That's the primary objective. But we also want you to keep your eyes and ears open. There's a lot going on in Russia these days . . . it's much more open now than in the past, of course, but we can still use every resource we can get."

"What exactly do you want me to find out?"

"Everything! There are some days when even we're not sure exactly what's going on there. Just keep your ears and eyes open. We'll get what we need when we debrief you."

"There's been a lot in the news lately about the Russian Mob. Are they going to be a problem, do you think?"

"You mean the plutonium? It's possible, although this stuff is far from fresh. It's been degrading for almost forty years, so it's not worth as much as the new stuff, but there's still a lot of it here. What I'm saying is that anything's possible. So keep alert."

"How do I communicate with you?"

"Don't worry about that. I'll contact you from time to time if we feel it's necessary. We don't really expect you to run across anything hot or super time-sensitive. It's background, mood, context that we expect you to pick up along with the wreckage."

Madeira must have looked a little skeptical, because after a pause, Nash continued: "They're not going to shoot you, you know. Or take you to Lubyanka. They're turning that into a museum, anyway. Like I said before, they know you're a United States naval officer and they know where your loyalties lie. They've hired you as a technical expert, and we're the employment agency that's providing your references."

"It all seems simple enough," Madeira said as he allowed *Wave Runner* to coast to a stop in what he suspected was Festus's turf. "Except for the recovery itself. That may prove to be a ballbuster."

"It *is* simple. And you'll be pocketing a hefty chunk of change in the process. You just make sure the recovery doesn't turn into an environmental horror show of some sort. If you blow that, there *will* be real trouble."

Madeira nodded, more irritated than ever at Nash's manner.

Whooosh! A whale popped up alongside and cheers rose from the deck below him. Madeira couldn't tell if the new arrival was Festus or not.

"I'll be seeing you, Al," Nash said as he headed for the door to the ladder back down to the main cabin.

"Roger," Madeira replied, noting that the wind's heading seemed to be holding steady but its force was increasing. The return, the downwind run to P-Town, was going to be rough on the passengers. He considered cutting the expedition short a few minutes. He also considered Nash and the Russians. He didn't feel very comfortable with either.

He listened to Sandy's patter. He liked the whales as much as anybody, he decided. In fact, he suspected he understood them better than many of the experts did, almost empathized with them, although there was so much he didn't understand.

Despite Nash, despite the prospect of a sloppy, rolling trip back, it really was a beautiful day. But for Madeira the beauty couldn't last.

A deep sense of gloom, and of foreboding, settled over

him. While he thought he'd managed for the most part to reconcile himself with the sins and stupidities of his past, he'd never really recovered from losing a woman with whom he was almost insanely in love. The experience had left him lost and incomplete, staring intently into the pit of despair.

He knew he was still perched on the edge of that pit, and the jumbo shrimp bit was the tip-off. He had to go down again into the cold and dark. He had to feel the nearness of death and overcome it. If he was to ever live again, he had to accept the challenge.

"I'll do it for the whales," he told himself.

Once back in the main cabin, Nash rejoined the girl with whom he'd boarded. Had he seen her, Madeira would've considered her very pretty. Hard but pretty.

"How'd it go?" she demanded as Nash sat down next to her.

"Fine," Nash replied. "It's all go, and no matter what happens, we're golden. He's not Navy anymore, he's not ours. He's mercenary now. We can't lose."

"You think he can do it?"

"Get the sub up? Yes. His record says yes, as long as Primakov doesn't want to stop him for some reason." As he spoke, Nash noticed that Madeira had turned the boat so that the waves were now coming from behind. They were now jamming *Wave Runner* forward, into the back of the next wave ahead, and making her yaw and roll most uncomfortably.

"You think Primakov's the boss?"

"That's Company policy at the moment, isn't it?"

"Why would he want to kill this operation?"

"I don't know, but anything's possible."

"You don't believe he's loyal." It was a statement, not a question.

"Primakov? To whom?"

"The State."

"Which one?"

"To Yeltsin, then."

"He was Gorbachev's man while Boris was still doing vodka ads."

"Then you don't think he's loyal to Yeltsin?"

"I'm sure he's as loyal as any KGB chief ever has been."

"It's not the KGB anymore."

"It's not the Cheka either, but nobody I know can see any real difference. For all I know, it's the Mob now. Even Madeira was bright enough to realize that *they* might turn out to be a factor in this whole affair."

"I'll be back in a minute, Nash. . . ."

"Your stomach still bothering you? It must be those greasy french fries you insisted on having."

Chapter Four

"Mike!" said Viktoria Galin, her electric blue eyes snapping at Madeira even though her words were directed at Novikoff. "You're giving Captain Madeira the wrong impression."

Novikoff, sitting across the conference table from the *Academik Asimov*'s tall, blond chief scientist, smiled and shrugged almost timidly. The gesture, Madeira thought, seemed to belie the flash of anger clearly present in the Russian's eyes. And the rapid clenching and unclenching of his fists. "You may be right, Viktoria . . ."

"It's important that he fully understand the situation," she continued. Although she never looked away from Madeira she was certainly aware of her superior's anger. "We, the ship's scientists, are fully in agreement with the basic objective of this voyage—somebody has to clean up after the ideologically pure—but we will be more than just a cover. We will continue to perform real research to the maximum extent possible."

"Yes, Viktoria, of course. I never meant for him to understand anything else," Novikoff replied, his smile still pasted on.

"No," Madeira said quickly, feeling it was up to him to defuse the situation, "I'm afraid I'm the one who caused the confusion. A certain amount of research shouldn't cause any significant problems. I'm sure there'll be some critical points in the operation where you'll have to hold off for a while, but most of the time . . ."

While struggling to choose his words carefully, he realized the two Russians both seemed to be waiting intently for him to finish. It was almost as if he was some sort of mediator, or buffer, instead of just a hired technical expert.

"What bothered me was the suggestion that you might try to man the habitat with scientists while we're working on the wreck. That's just asking for trouble! We simply don't have enough resources to support both activities at once. We'd be totally unable to aid them if they get into difficulty."

Where, he wondered, had the geophysicist's outburst come from? Why did she appear to feel such fury over what seemed to him a very minor misunderstanding? And at whom was her venom really directed? Was it a matter of turf? Was it politics? Or did she just hate Novikoff's guts?

"That's not what I suggested," she replied, some of the anger gone. "I was talking about during the early stages."

"I understand that now. I apologize." A note of mild irritation crept into Madeira's voice. "To tell the truth, I really don't want to see the habitat used at all. As we all know, it's totally obsolete. That's why I don't plan to use it for the recovery; the time and resources required to support it would far exceed any savings it might offer."

"We feel it's an important part of the cover," Novikoff said in a tone that hinted he was tiring of the discussion and preparing to assert the final authority that undoubtedly was his to exercise.

"Okay," Madeira said. His legs hurt from all the sitting—driving to Logan Airport, sitting on the shuttle, and then the cab drive in from La Guardia—and he was beginning to develop gas. "We'll take it along, but while we're working on the wreck, the empty habitat will simply be parked on the bottom."

"Okay."

Viktoria and Novikoff leaned back in their chairs, each seeming to take a deep breath. Even though they were seated almost directly opposite each other, they somehow managed to avoid exchanging so much as a glance.

"Thank you," Viktoria said. "You've clarified a great deal."

Madeira chewed over the exchange. Looking back on it, he realized he didn't have the slightest idea what it was really about. As he attempted to decrypt Viktoria's last comment, his eyes wandered aimlessly around the silent conference room. It was small and sparely furnished with blond, contemporary furniture. A blue rug covered the floor. One door. No windows. Nothing on the walls but off-white paint. The door looked a little thick, and it was hard to be sure if it was really wood. Located in the Russian Consulate's midtown commercial annex, it could have been anybody's conference room. Except for the big brass samovar, intricately decorated and very antique-looking, that stood on the sideboard along one wall.

He then noticed, without surprise, that there was something set back in the ventilation duct, behind the grating. An acoustic baffle, maybe. There was probably also some sort of electromagnetic shielding present.

The room was designed to be secure from eavesdropping. Totally understandable, he decided, in a world where even fast-food franchisers encrypted all but their most routine communications.

What the hell could he possibly have clarified for them? For her? Maybe nothing. Maybe Viktoria's last remark had been nothing more than a face-saving means of ending the exchange.

"Very good, Al," Novikoff said suddenly. "May I assume, then, that you're satisfied with our selection of *Asimov* for this operation?"

"Yes," Madeira replied, thinking of the video they'd shown him of the big Russian research catamaran. The ship's twin gray hulls, open, clear decks, and great beam all promised a roominess and stability he'd never enjoyed before. Her lift capabilities seemed more than adequate and, except for the habitat, her diving inventory was both extensive and composed of up-to-date gear. "She looks almost perfect to me."

"Excellent!" beamed the Russian, all hint of his past anger gone. "And I'm pleased to report that my superiors have approved your suggestion to use a modified TexFac robotic pipe-welding system as the vehicle for the laser cutters. They already have one on order, along with spare parts."

Madeira couldn't help but smile in both satisfaction and anticipation. The Russians were proving to be an absolute dream to work with. Whatever he asked for he got. They were totally professional and truly enthusiastic. Indeed, the only false note had been Viktoria's outburst. And that, he assured himself, was probably easily explained.

He reminded himself there'd be problems, there always were, but he was confident he and Mike Novikoff could overcome them all.

His glance returned to Viktoria, who was reading a sheet of paper. She was tall—taller than Novikoff but slightly shorter than Madeira—and slender but not skinny. Her nose was a little too large, but who was he to talk? Hers, at least, looked as if it belonged where it was.

Elegant was the word, he decided, in her white blouse and blue skirt.

And very demanding. It was the eyes! They matched the skirt.

Which still didn't explain why she was at the meeting.

Where was *Asimov*'s captain?

What the hell! Novikoff was the operational commander. There was no reason the ship's master had to be there too.

"I'm still not sure I understand my exact role in this operation," Madeira said, breaking the second long silence. "The term 'salvage master' has never been very precise. It can mean anything from a figurehead adviser who's there to be seen but not heard to God's chosen agent. How exactly do I fit in?''

Novikoff laughed deeply. ''You'll be the chosen agent— God's chosen agent, as you put it. When we're on the wreck, everybody will work for you: the divers, the ROV unit, Captain Bukinin of *Asimov*. And you will work for me. But I'm only interested in results, not in details of execution. The project's success is totally dependent upon your experience, your skills, and your leadership. Let me assure you, you'll earn your fee and the victory will be yours.''

Madeira nodded in acceptance, although still far from convinced that his position would really be as clear-cut as advertised. ''Has the final decision been made yet on exactly what we are going to do with it after we get it up?''

''Yes, and Viktoria is best qualified to explain, since she helped make it.''

Madeira turned and found himself skewered again by the two blue eyes. At least the minor mystery of her presence was now solved.

''We considered resinking it in deeper waters, we gave that very serious consideration, but there's simply too much tectonism. People, especially American tourists, tend to forget that the Carribbean islands, the Antilles, are volcanic in origin and that many are still active or potentially active. All the deeper areas near the site are along boundaries where various tectonic plates, the moving plates which make up the earth's crust, meet. That means earthquakes, volcanism, the real possibility of creating the very disaster we're trying to prevent.''

''What about the Atlantic deeps? The stable ones?''

''Scientifically they'd probably be fine. But think of the publicity!''

Madeira smiled slightly at what the headlines might say. At the same time, he was struck again by the Russians' paranoia about the press.

''You're going to bury it? Take it home, cut it up, and bury it?''

"That's the plan."

"Where?"

"We have places. . . ."

"We're going to need pontoons. We can't possibly drag it all the way back to Russia hanging under *Asimov*!"

"Can we drag it a hundred miles?" Novikoff asked, a look of concern on his face. "Our people have told me it can be done."

"If we're careful, I suppose. And if the weather cooperates. If we're careful and if the weather cooperates we could drag it ten thousand miles, but the weather never cooperates for ten thousand miles."

"But you do think one hundred is possible?"

"A hundred miles . . . Three knots max . . . Thirty, thirty-five hours, depending on the current. If the weather's bad, more. Yes, it's possible. What then?"

"We load it aboard a seagoing dry dock."

"In the middle of the ocean?"

"No. We've arranged to use several possible locations, depending on the weather. The Bahia de Samana in the Dominican Republic and another location on the north edge of the Silver Banks, near a small island. All well out of public view, we hope."

"It's doable, I guess," Madeira replied with less than total enthusiasm. "We'll still need pontoons to get it from under *Asimov* into the dry dock."

"They'll be aboard the dry dock. We'll install them when we meet the dock."

"Now," Novikoff said before Madeira could do anything more than nod again, "would you mind going over, for Viktoria, how you imagine your part of the operation is going to proceed? Highlight whatever problems you can see coming and that sort of thing."

Madeira leaned back in his chair, reviewing in advance what he was going to say. "The most difficult part's going to be cutting and rigging. That's assuming, of course, that you can get us back to the wreck. As for the lift itself, the weather's the biggest factor. We'll have to be very careful, but I doubt it will be anything compared with trying to cut with the small crew you want to use.''

"It's unavoidable. The smaller the crew, the better. Security's going to be enough of a problem anyway.''

"What do you think the main threat is? Terrorists of some sort?''

"Yes. They seem to be the principal threat. We are taking precautions.''

"Just out of curiosity, who's in charge of security? This is plutonium we'll be dealing with, isn't it? The stuff they make bombs out of?''

"Yes,'' Viktoria said, "it's the stuff they make bombs out of.''

"Security's being taken care of,'' Novikoff said. "It's not your concern. If you have any problem, come to me and I'll make sure the proper person takes action.''

"Okay.''

"What about the radiation?'' Viktoria asked. "Not only is the wreck itself radioactive, but it's undoubtedly filled with very hot silt.''

"That's one of the main reasons for using the pipe cutter. So we can spend as little time as possible near the wreck . . . and even less in it. Between our diving dress and the seawater itself we should be okay, although I assume we're willing to accept some exposure.''

"Of course!'' Viktoria replied. "*We* have no choice. What are you willing to accept?''

It was a question that Madeira had asked himself before. It was, for him, a matter of balancing the challenge, and the million dollars, against what they said happens to you when you're overexposed.

"I don't know exactly,'' he replied finally, "but probably more than I would have twenty years ago.''

"Some more details, please,'' Novikoff continued with a big, encouraging smile.

Madeira reached out and pulled the submarine's lines across the table. As he did, Viktoria and Novikoff moved their chairs so they were sitting on either side of him.

William S. Schaill

How easy it all looked, he thought as he leafed through the big book of plans. How neat and clean and precise! Everything in its place. Everything labeled—in Russian, of course, but Novikoff had arranged for many English translations to be entered for Madeira's benefit. It was all just a matter of cutting through the fairwater and outer hull here, into the ballast tank. Then through the inner side of the tanks, into the inner hull, into this storeroom. All on *this* side of *this* bulkhead. Well away from the machinery spaces, where the radiation was assumed to be.

And then the stern will pop off, just like the tail of a shrimp when it's headed.

The thought of shrimp brought briefly to mind the thought of whales.

It was obvious. Except that the plans were now little more than a fantasy. The sub was a wreck. The Russians' photographs showed her on her side, tilted forward down a steep slope and partially buried in silt and ooze. Her guts, her machinery, cables, stores, and piping were undoubtedly all tangled. Nothing would turn out to be where they expected it to be. Nothing would look like they expected it to look. Nothing would be labeled. Up would be down and down up. Or nowhere.

"Mike," Madeira said as he looked up from the plans, "as I understand it, this is essentially a specially modified version of what we've always called a Foxtrot-class sub. About three hundred feet long and twenty-five hundred tons displacement . . ."

"Yes, it is basically what you in the West have always called a Foxtrot."

"Weren't Foxtrots diesel-powered? Wouldn't it have made more sense to use a bigger hull, one designed for nuclear propulsion?"

"The Soviet navy was no more logical than anybody else's," Viktoria remarked dryly.

Novikoff looked at her a moment, then smiled and turned back to Madeira. "It was a matter of resources, Al. Consideration was given to using what you call a November hull;

they were nuclear-powered antisubmarine submarines of about four thousand tons and one hundred ten meters—about three hundred and sixty of your feet. We were building a number of them at the time, but they cost almost four times as much as a Foxtrot and, to tell the truth, we were desperate to get as many Novembers to sea as we could to protect against your new submarines. So the decision was made to modify a half-built Foxtrot. By that time we were building them primarily for export anyway. They were our principal export model, so, as you can imagine, we had many available."

"As you will learn, Captain," Viktoria interjected, "resources are and have always been a problem for us. Much more than for you. This is a reality which your President Reagan seemed to grasp long before many other, better-informed individuals did, which explains why we were able to bluff you successfully for so many years."

She does have a sense of humor! Madeira thought. Of some sort.

"How up-to-date were these lines when the sub was lost?" he asked, returning to business.

"Those are the builder's plans. I think we have to assume that alterations may have been made after she was launched, and I'm afraid those things weren't always well documented."

Shit! thought Madeira. How many hundreds of undocumented alterations had he tripped over, and hit his head on, over the years?

"What more can you tell me about the reactor?" Madeira said. "I see it here in the lines, but what's inside it and how well is it stuck together?"

"It's an experimental, hybrid design," Novikoff replied carefully. "It was designed both to produce steam and to create more fuel at the same time. Our engineers were hoping to reduce the need to refuel."

"Were any more of them built?"

"Just one . . . and it proved to be difficult to control."

"What the hell does that mean?"

"It means it didn't do everything they hoped it would do, so no more were built!"

"What happened to it?"

"It suffered a partial meltdown."

"And it's fueled with plutonium?"

"There's also uranium in there, it's the raw material for the breeder part of the operation. But none of this makes any difference to our recovery operation!"

"Look! You've laid out a very tricky salvage operation here: recovering almost half the sub, towing it a hundred miles, and loading it aboard a dry dock in the middle of the Atlantic. It would probably be a hell of a lot easier to cut a big hole in the wreck and pull out the reactor piece by piece—"

"No!" Novikoff shouted, all humor now gone. "You were hired to do a job that we have already defined! No shortcuts! This has to be done right. *All* the machinery is probably radioactive now. And the hull. And the silt! We can't afford to have some big-mouth writer shouting that we did a sloppy, shortcut job!"

"Okay," Madeira said. "You're the boss."

As he paused, Madeira could hear, or maybe feel, the tidal murmur of Viktoria's breathing. Was it his imagination, or was the icy geophysicist composed of more than just case-hardened steel? Pondering the question, he almost forgot about Novikoff's existence.

Keep this on a professional level! he reminded himself. Remember what happened last time. With that warning he forced himself to proceed down the technical path.

"We're going to have to use the laser on the pipe cutter to do all the heavy cutting." As he spoke, Madeira's right index finger moved up and down on the sub's plans, across the big storeroom located just forward of the reactor room.

"Al!" snapped Novikoff, his eyes on Madeira's finger. "I thought we just agreed to cut through the berthing space forward of that storeroom."

The sudden and intense fury, almost hatred, in the Russian's expression stunned Madeira momentarily. It also seemed to catch Viktoria off guard as her eyes narrowed and her slow, rhythmic breathing missed several beats.

Madeira looked dumbly down at his own finger. "Yes, we did," he agreed, "but that extra volume, and weight, will make it just that much harder to lift the wreckage."

"I must insist," Novikoff said, his expression making all too clear the totality of his determination. "We want that storeroom as a buffer between the reactor room and the outside."

Madeira still wasn't convinced the extra buffer was necessary, unless the bulkhead had failed, but it was obvious that further argument would lead nowhere. Except, he realized with renewed shock, possibly to violence.

He could handle another twenty feet, another fifty or sixty tons at most.

And if the bulkhead had failed? he asked himself. Then something else would also have failed. In that case, they'd have to wrap the whole damn thing in a giant plastic bag.

"Of course. We cut through the berthing compartment."

"Excellent!"

For the next two hours Madeira continued almost without interruption, explaining how, using a bare minimum of human divers, he would carve the stern off and then levitate almost two thousand tons of radioactive rubbish, intact, to the surface.

"How much effort do you want to put into trying to determine the cause of the sinking?" Madeira asked.

"I wondered when you'd ask that," Novikoff said. "The question seems to bother you more than it does us."

There was a knock on the door. Novikoff walked over and opened it a crack, listened, then turned to Madeira. "Will you excuse me for a minute? I'll be right back."

"Of course," continued Novikoff about five minutes later as he resumed his seat, "we'd like to know what happened to the submarine, but under the circumstances it's not our highest priority." Calm and matter-of-fact though the Russian's words were, Madeira sensed that Novikoff's fury remained just under the surface. It was a cold, satanic fury that pulsed and burned.

"Is there a problem?" he asked. "Something to do with the operation?"

"No," Novikoff replied, clearly struggling to get his emotions under control. "Not really a problem, just one of those thousands of administrative details that keep popping up and must be taken care of promptly and vigorously before they have a chance to develop into something truly irritating."

By the time Novikoff closed the meeting, the chill, late-autumn gloom had turned into bitter, bone-chilling night.

"Good night, Captain," Viktoria said as she shook his hand. "I'm looking forward to going on this expedition with you."

"Al," said Novikoff as he walked Madeira to the annex's entrance, "I think we got a great deal done today. I'd hoped to dine with you tonight, but I must return to St. Petersburg very early in the morning. There is much to do aboard *Asimov*, and I want to see that it's done right."

"That's half the battle," agreed Madeira, his empty stomach now growling in response to the mention of dining.

"Yes," Novikoff replied. "See you in two weeks, and bring your suntan lotion." The Russian laughed at his own joke. "I'll meet you at the airport myself. I want to be with you when you first see my homeland."

"I'm looking forward to it."

After carefully buttoning his trench coat and shaking hands with Novikoff, Madeira stepped out into the wet, dark Manhattan night. He was greeted by near-solid sheets of rain hissing past dim streetlights and raging, rubbish-filled cataracts racing down the street toward the storm drains. Hunching forward and clutching his briefcase, he wondered if the sun would ever shine again.

Somewhere out there, probably within twenty or thirty feet of him, was a taxicab, but all he could see clearly were the head- and taillights of the slowly passing traffic and the dark, inert shapes of the cars parked along the street.

There it is! he realized at last as his eyes began to adapt to the dark.

He stepped hurriedly across the sidewalk, between the parked cars, and out into the street where he dove into the waiting cab. His feet were soaked from the icy rapids roaring along the curb.

"The Hilton, please," he said. He started to settle back in the seat, only to be forced stiffly upright again by the stream of painfully frigid water that continued to cascade down the back of his neck and spine. He thought of Lane Williams lounging on the fantail of his yacht, listening to the palms rustle in the night breeze. The admiral, he decided, was going to get a visitor. Just as soon as the job was done. If they hadn't moved again.

Novikoff had been right, he thought as the water dribbling down his back started to warm up. They had gotten a lot done today.

Yet, despite the technical progress achieved, the meeting had also rekindled a sense of unease within him. He should, by now, feel comfortable around the Russians. They were, after all, only people. Naval people, in fact. Naval people just like him.

Unfortunately, he didn't. No matter what you were talking about or doing with them there was always something else, something dark and fearful, swimming just beneath the surface.

Was there really something there, he wondered, or was his dread just the residue of Cold War conditioning?

He sighed slightly, then realized that a sea of blinking taillights lay ahead. The cab was just sitting, caught in a traffic jam and smelling dank and wet. When the cabbie leaned on the horn Madeira was tempted to tell him to knock it the hell off, but he decided that would be just as ineffectual as the honking itself.

He still had to find somebody to replace him aboard *Wave Runner*. He'd assumed it would be no problem, but it was. Lots of candidates had shown up, but none had been qualified. All the best prospects seemed to have headed south for the winter.

Damnit! He couldn't leave Carlos in the lurch, even if it was for only a few weeks.

And he had to perfect his own cover story, that he was going down to the islands for a little sport diving in shallow, sunny seas. It wouldn't have been such a problem if Cornie weren't going from one end of the Cape to the other telling everybody that Al Madeira had been hired to salvage another wreck filled with gold, this time a Russian submarine. Fortunately, he'd also swallowed the hint that the sub was somewhere close by.

He also had to do something about Christmas shopping.

Then he wondered if Handy Harry the Fixitman had finished repairing the shotgunned wall in the Boltons' house. And if the new alarm system he'd had installed would make any difference.

Even if it did work, who'd have time to respond?

Finally he thought of Viktoria Galin. Of her tall, slender form. Of the hollow of her throat and the gentle rise and fall of the fullness within her blouse as she breathed through slightly parted lips. Of her golden hair. And of her eyes, her disconcertingly blue eyes. He didn't feel much more comfortable around her than he did around the other Russians, but the reasons for his discomfort were somewhat different.

The night was dark, and Madeira's thoughts were many and far away. There was no reason for him to have noticed the unoccupied yellow sedan parked fifty yards from the annex entrance. Neither could he have seen the photograph of himself, standing with Charlie Nash on *Wave Runner*'s bridge, which was partially wedged down into the crack below the passenger seat back.

Chapter Five

A glowing pinpoint.

It started as an infinitely tiny point of burning white light, lost in an eternity of darkness. Then it flashed, and in less than an instant its brilliance was everywhere.

Was it a beginning? Or an end? Was it the Creation of the Universe? Or was it a locomotive running her down?

Viktoria Galin awoke on the telephone's first ring. Though she was immediately alert and clearheaded, the dream remained as sharp and focused as when she'd witnessed it.

On the third ring she rolled over and reached for the receiver, running her hand through her tousled blond hair as she did.

"Yes?"

"Commander Galin, this is Mishkoff," said the voice of the consulate's chief of security.

"Yes, Pavel?" she replied carefully. The Soviet system was dead, or so they said, and it was the era of reform and renewal, but only a total fool would let her guard down completely.

"A body has been found in a car parked down the street from the annex."

"Is it one of ours?"

"No. Some sort of Hispanic, I believe, but it's very hard to tell."

"Why do you think it has anything to do with us? You're as bad as the Americans. You suspect us of everything."

"He was badly abused before he died. Tortured. I recognize some of the techniques."

Damnit! she thought. Mishkoff never let anybody, and especially her, forget he was traditional, old-line KGB. The man had over thirty years in the devil's service and undoubtedly looked back on each and every one of them fondly. "It still probably doesn't involve us. Drugs, maybe. Just about everything these days seems to be connected to drugs somehow."

"I have a hunch that it does involve us, Commander, perhaps even your operation, but if you have no interest that is your business. I have informed you. I have done my duty."

Cursing again to herself, Viktoria sat up and switched on the bedside lamp.

"Have you notified Novikoff?"

"No. He's already left. He's over the Atlantic now."

"Where are you?"

"On the first floor. At the front desk."

"I'll be there in ten minutes."

"Dress warmly. It's sleeting."

Fully reconciled now to the reality of the night, Viktoria hung up and crossed the bedroom of the annex's small guest apartment. She glanced briefly at the window, which faced out on an alley. A crummy view, she thought as she slipped quickly into jeans, boots, and a short fur jacket, but at least the window didn't have bars on it.

Damn Leo and his insane enthusiasm for the grand gesture! In the end all he'd managed to do was get himself killed. And, as a final legacy from him, she undoubtedly *would* end up in a room with a barred window. Twenty years, if not more, for treason. Or insurrection. Or some damn thing. Just as soon as Mishkoff's associates back in Moscow learned more about her and Leo. As far as they were concerned, there was no difference between love and conspiracy.

"Here," Mishkoff said, shining a flashlight into the car as Viktoria halted beside him. "Look for yourself."

Viktoria looked in and was revolted. The face was barely recognizable as such; it'd been pounded so severely that its eyes, nose, and cheekbones were lost from sight in a hash of reddened goo.

"Why do you think he's Hispanic?" she asked, trying not to gag as she spoke.

"The skin, or what's left of it . . . The way he's dressed . . . He's wearing a cross on a chain around his neck. After you've seen enough of them, you can just tell."

"What's that!" Viktoria demanded suddenly. "Something's stuck down behind the passenger seat."

Mishkoff aimed the flashlight at the seat.

"It's a photograph, I think," Viktoria said.

"Yes, I think so also," Mishkoff replied with what seemed to Viktoria to be a note of irritation.

"Is . . . was this person armed?"

"I see no weapon, although it may be in the glove compartment or under the seat."

"Or in the trunk?"

"Or in the trunk. The only way we can be sure is to open up the car and get in, and that is something I don't wish to do."

"Is there any more to see?"

"No. I don't think so."

Damn him! she thought as she looked up and down the wet, almost lifeless street. He had to let me in this far to protect his own back, because it might be related to my mission. But he's not going to let me in far enough to learn anything. "You're going to report it to the New York police?"

"And the FBI, of course. They do still keep us under surveillance. In fact, they're probably wondering right now why we're standing around out here in this shit and making jokes about dim-witted Russkies."

"It wasn't done in the car," Viktoria observed. "Not enough blood."

"Of course not! It takes time and room to do work like this."

The voice of experience, thought Viktoria with a mixture of irritation and disgust.

"Can they hear what we're saying?"

"I hope not. These conditions aren't good."

"How much can they see?"

"We're probably little more than solid shadows to them, even with computer enhancement. Given time, of course, they'll undoubtedly identify each of us."

"Where are the cameras mounted?"

"You want to get the photograph out!"

"Of course! And his identification. And I want to know if he was armed. You did imply that he may be related to my operation. If you're right, I want to know everything about him. Don't you?"

"It may be too late. The Americans will almost certainly assume we're somehow involved."

"But they won't know for sure. It could be anything from drugs to a jealous husband."

"Commander, neither your assignment nor your rank gives you the authority to order me to do this, but I do think you make a certain sense."

"Thank you, Pavel."

"I suppose," Mishkoff continued with a contrived sigh, "that it is my duty, as a citizen of Planet Earth, to determine if this poor fellow might not still be alive. Surely they would not blame me for trying to help him!"

"You're a model citizen of the new world order," replied Viktoria, relieved that she wouldn't have to get into the car herself.

Mishkoff opened the passenger-side door and dove into

the yellow coffin. In less than two minutes he was out. "There's a knife in the car, under the seat, but no gun. And no identification on the body," he said as he emerged and closed the door.

"Do you recognize this fellow?" the chief of security continued as he turned and handed Viktoria the photograph, then shined his flashlight on it. "Isn't that Novikoff's pet American?"

"Yes," Viktoria replied. "This man must have been following him."

Mishkoff limited his response to a nod.

"It's good we recovered this photograph before you turned the case over to the Americans. We can't afford to have them become nervous about our handling of SeaGlow, can we? What will Moscow say if Washington decides to step in and take over the operation on the grounds that we can't maintain security?"

Mishkoff grunted.

"Pavel?" she asked, wondering if she really wanted to know the answer.

"Yes?"

"You're sure you don't know who did this?"

Pavel's cold stare said no, he didn't know. Or maybe his expression was saying that he might know, or definitely did know, but wasn't going to tell her.

Viktoria straightened up and looked around into the rain-thickened darkness. Even the supercharged sodium lamps were able to provide little more than faint yellow halos in the surrounding gloom. She had no choice but to assume Mishkoff knew more than he was telling her. For the time being, anyway. Neither did she have any other choice but to push a little harder to learn more for herself, since Mishkoff's objectives, those of the former KGB, might not be the same as those she had been sent to achieve.

She tossed her soggy fur jacket on a chair and sat on the edge of the bed, leaning over to pull off her boots.

A pack of wide-eyed Siberian or Chechen nationalists.

A boatload of Greenpeace fanatics.

Or even Ukrainians.

She'd expected some sort of interference, but this, she suspected with a sinking heart, was direct from Moscow. Either President Yeltsin was much more serious—deadly serious, in fact—than she'd realized about maintaining the operation's security or somebody else, somebody big, was up to something. And very possibly that something they were up to was calculated to topple Yeltsin.

But which was it? Or was it something entirely different?

Why had the man been following Madeira? As far as she could tell, he hadn't been armed to kill so all he could have been was a tail. But there was no mystery for any of the major players to be chasing after. They all already knew about SeaGlow and about Madeira's part in it.

And why had the man in the car been killed? Both Moscow and Washington were in on the operation, so there was nothing to hide. Nothing she could see, anyway.

Unless he was a reporter. But even the KGB, or the SVG as it was now called, understood just how stupid that would be. Killing a reporter would just drive the rest of them into a feeding frenzy.

Why had the body's identification been removed? Even without a wallet the New York police would eventually succeed in identifying him.

Why was he so horribly mutilated?

That, at least, could probably be explained. It was a warning. But to whom was it addressed and what was being warned against? What good was a warning if the addressee didn't understand it?

Something was missing!

Of course! She was the one who didn't understand the message. For all she knew, the addressee understood it perfectly.

And, for that matter, the affair didn't have to be political at all. They'd assumed all along that the plutonium might prove irresistible to one or more criminal elements. They'd blossomed in Russia and were now spreading across the

Atlantic and beyond in search of ever-higher returns on their thuggery.

Was the Mob following Madeira? If so, then who was warning them off? Another gang, or the KGB?

If it was the KGB, then they'd certainly become careless in their old age. Or Mishkoff had, anyway. The photograph should never have been overlooked.

On the other hand, it was possible that the failure to remove the photograph meant that Mishkoff, and the KGB, weren't involved at all.

Angered at her own ignorance, she rolled on her side and reached for the telephone.

"Pavel," she asked after dialing an internal number, "are they ready?"

She listened, frowning, then said, "I understand . . . but I still want to look at them myself."

An hour later she was again seated on the edge of the bed. Mishkoff had been all too correct. The consulate's own enhanced videotapes of icy dark street showed no more than, she hoped, would those made by the FBI.

The car was visible, but well off to the edge of the camera's field. A number of people passed it during the afternoon and one or two may have paused next to it, or looked in, but she couldn't be sure.

Then, in the deceptive gloom of the sodden dusk, a dark blob had appeared. The blob, a group of three or four individuals, all very indistinct, moved slowly down the street and past the car. There was a stutter, a pause in the blob's flow, and then it resumed.

That was it! In that instant she knew she'd seen something happen—but she couldn't say what. Then, several hours later with the dark now total, the same group, or one much like it, may have again passed, and paused, and moved on.

The first time past, she realized after thinking a few moments, the man had been yanked out of the car. And on the return trip his body had been stuffed back in.

It had been done with incredible speed, which might explain why the photograph was overlooked.

William S. Schaill

Or it might explain nothing at all.

Damn Pavel! she thought. He claimed no further enhancements were possible. Was he afraid to dig any further, or had he been ordered to not let her dig any further? Or did he already know all the answers himself? There was nothing more she could do. As long as she was in New York, he was the boss.

Viktoria lay in bed, unable to sleep and equally unable to find any sure answers. Many possibilities, no answers.

Her thoughts turned to the photograph. Who was the man standing with Madeira? His banker? His brother-in-law? An unhappy passenger?

Of course not! The man with Madeira was Charlie Nash, one half of the control team Langley had assigned to supervise the retired naval officer. She knew it and so did Pavel, yet the consulate's security chief refused to admit he knew. He'd done as much as he was going to for her.

Then she smiled slightly. Madeira, standing on the bridge of his whale-watching boat and wearing an old sweater and khaki pants, looked so much happier and more at home in the photograph than he had in the pin-striped business suit he'd been wearing the day before.

She wondered how happy he'd be looking at the end of this operation.

She hoped he'd still be happy. He seemed to deserve to be happy. But then, almost everybody deserved to be happy and yet so many never managed to get what they deserved.

Leo certainly hadn't.

Chapter Six

The hot, dry summer of the eastern Mediterranean had just about run its course as the afternoon flight from Amman, Jordan, passed over Cape Sunion and turned on its final approach to Athens International Airport. A minute or two ahead, standing on its sacred hill far above the surrounding city, lay the Acropolis, its ancient ruins glowing almost golden in the slanting sunlight. Although the cool, damp air masses of Europe and the Atlantic had yet to fully settle in, there was a very noticeable brown tinge to be seen in the bluish sky around the high temples, a corona due largely to the modern city's infamous horde of cars, trucks, vans, motorbikes, and smokestacks.

Among the passengers aboard the Air Jordan flight, most of whom were merchants or other business travelers, was an almost painfully thin young man with a face both smooth and harsh, depending on his mood and purpose, and thick, wavy, jet-black hair. His features and coloration spoke faintly of the East—the dark hair, the intense brown eyes, the thin but prominent nose—yet they spoke with no precision, refusing to say exactly from where he came.

According to his passport, the young man's name was Niko Avalaridze and he was a citizen of the Russian Federation. As he'd told the Boeing aircraft salesman sitting next to him on the flight, he was shopping for oranges and other fruit to import into produce-starved Russia.

In fact, Niko did import citrus. And, in the best tradition of the merchants who have worked the eastern Mediterranean over the millennia, he and his associates, primarily relatives, were also prepared to deal in anything else from which a satisfactory margin could be squeezed.

In terms of international trade, both legitimate and otherwise, Niko was not a big player . . . but he was now certain that was about to change.

Having only carry-on luggage and nothing to declare, Avalaridze was able to move quickly through Customs and Immigration. He then grabbed a taxi, which took him into the center of Athens to a small commercial hotel located partway between Syntagma and Omonia Squares, a few blocks from the National University.

By the time he'd finished showering and dressing in a clean polo shirt and slacks the warm Mediterranean day was cooling into night. He passed quickly through the lobby and out into the still-crowded street, where he turned right. After walking a block or two, alert every step of the way for the caress of a pickpocket or the glint of a knife in the hand of a mugger, he stopped in front of a dimly lit open-air taverna located right at the edge of Omonia.

"Niko!" said a voice to his right. "Over here."

Avalaridze turned slightly and squinted, then walked over to a table almost completely hidden in the shadow.

"You trying to hide, Ari?" he asked the pudgy, middle-aged man in jeans and cowboy boots who was sitting at the table and drinking a glass of milky ouzo.

"Of course not," Ari said as he picked his nose. "Who do we have to hide from? Do you want a drink?"

"A beer," Avalaridze said.

"Local or American?"

"I'll try local. You're the expert on Greece. You order for me."

"Okay," Ari said, waving the waiter over as he spoke.

"How did it go?" Ari asked quietly but intensely after the waiter had brought the beer and left.

"It went very well, but I'm glad I'm out of Baghdad. Our new customer's a psychopath. Have you ever looked at his eyes?"

"I've never met him."

"In the newspaper pictures, you've seen him there. He reminds me a lot of Stalin. One minute he loves you, and the next he's spitting and roasting you. Just for the hell of it."

"Then he's going to buy from us?"

"Yes. He wants it very badly."

"How much?"

"Five hundred million dollars."

"Can he raise that much money? From where? The Americans still won't let him sell any oil."

"He only has to pay two hundred and fifty when we deliver it to his agents. He will pay the rest over the next year."

"Installments? The cheap bastard!"

"Also a means of making sure we keep our mouths shut. He wants his new toy to be a surprise."

As he spoke, Niko looked out onto the street and the square. It was a brightly lit, noisy mass of people, cars, trucks, tavernas, shops, and deep shadows.

He smiled slightly when he noticed a mob of American sailors wandering around, still wearing their whites and looking for action. Like everybody else, he told himself, they have their needs. Unlike so many, however, they also have the cash to pay for them.

"What do we care where he gets it?" Niko continued. "I'm confident he can. He'll squeeze it out of the Iraqi masses. Maybe somebody will give him some foreign aid. As I said, President Saddam wants our product very badly. He understood immediately when I explained how it's the

75

perfect Doomsday Weapon, one for which nobody—not Moscow, not Washington, and nobody else—has a defense."

"Congratulations!"

"And the Americans won't be able to take it away from him, because they won't know he has it until he decides to use it."

"Congratulations again."

"Not until we've delivered and received payment. Now tell me, what's this about Novikoff in New York?"

"It worked out okay, Niko," Ari replied, alarmed by Niko's tone of voice. "It seems that somebody, I think it must have been those damn Chechens, hired a guy to follow the American. They must have heard the rumors that he's going to salvage a Russian submarine filled with gold and decided to sniff around a little. When he learned about it, Novikoff flew into a rage and told the KGB officer at the consulate that the Chechens, or whoever they are, were endangering an operation of extreme importance to Moscow."

"They believed him?"

"Yes. Citizen Primakov does seem to feel the recovery of the submarine is important. I guess he's trying to kiss up to Yeltsin until he gets the chance to do something else to him. The KGB did the job for us, thinking they were doing it for themselves," concluded Ari, laughing.

"Then you did nothing yourself?"

"I didn't lift a finger. I was in Brooklyn when they did it."

Niko sat a moment, rolling the still-untasted bottle of beer between his hands. "I've never known the KGB to do a favor for anybody, not even accidentally."

"Things are changing, Niko, and you should know that better than anybody. Everybody knows they're getting sloppy."

"We were lucky this time, but we may not be if Novikoff loses control again," Avalaridze said, his eyes now glinting in the light of the street.

"I thought you would approve."

"At least you weren't involved, but I'm worried about Novikoff's judgment. There are better ways of warning off the Chechens without drawing all this attention to the American."

"What can we do about it?" Ari asked, irritated.

"Nothing. We can't very well replace him, so all we can do is hope."

Ari noticed that Avalaridze's eyes were now following a girl walking past. "You want a girl? A reward for yourself?"

"No. Not tonight. I have an early flight tomorrow and the past week has been very tiring."

"Food, then?"

"Yes, in a moment. . . . I'll be flying to Miami tomorrow. I want you to stay here until I call for you, and I want you to keep out of trouble in the meantime. Stay sober. Stay out of jail. Stay away from the police and keep your mouth shut."

You're the one who's always acted like Stalin, Ari thought as his younger cousin's suddenly sharp tone slashed him again. "Of course I'll stay out of trouble!"

"Make sure you do! And don't try to do any little drug deals in your spare time. Everything is going very well, and I won't allow you to screw it up."

"You can count on me. But some of our bigger customers got very nervous when I told them not to expect another delivery for eight to ten weeks."

"We gave them enough to make it."

"They're worried that we're getting ready to cut them off, or that somebody else is cutting us off."

"Didn't you tell them we're changing suppliers to get a lower price?"

"I told them, but I don't think they all believed me. Some are probably talking to the Chechens right now."

"No, they're not. The Chechens won't talk to them until they're sure they're desperate. We'll have time to get another shipment in after we finish our business with Saddam. Remember, we'll make more on this than we have on cocaine during the past fifteen years! Five hundred in, less than ten going out. It's amazing how little it takes to buy a few Russians these days.''

"Okay, Niko. Do you have a new supplier who will give us the stuff at a lower price?''

"I've changed my mind, Ari, I do want a girl. A young one. You know what I want.''

"What about your food?'' Ari asked, glancing at Niko's still-full beer bottle and afraid to force the issue about the price of cocaine.

"I'll order that for myself. You find me a girl. Quickly!''

"Okay,'' Ari said as he stood and headed for a pay phone. He knew better than anybody that his little cousin Niko was just as capable of spitting and roasting somebody as Saddam or Stalin was.

Part Two
January 1994

Moscow (Russian Federation)—Following the somewhat confusing results of the December 12 elections
(in which a majority of Russians voted in favor of
President Yeltsin's Draft Constitution but, at the
same time, Yeltsin's Russia's Choice Party received
only about 15% of the votes cast while the ultranationalist Liberal Democratic Party of Vladimir Zhirinovsky received 23%), Yeltsin scales back his
reform efforts. Two key pro-reform government
ministers, Yegor Gaidar and Boris Fyodorov, con-
demn Yeltsin's actions and resign from the government. Confused civil wars and insurrections,
warlordism, and ethnic warfare continue in several
of the newly independent republics as well as in a
number of republics and autonomous political units
which remain parts of the Russian Federation.

Washington, D.C. (United States of America)—President Clinton reiterates his very strong support for

President Yeltsin as Russia's (and the world's) best hope.

Baghdad (Republic of Iraq)—The United Nations and its local inspectors and agents continue to tighten the screws on, and infuriate, Saddam Hussein as they locate, identify and dismantle, one by one, each of the dictator's numerous nuclear, biological, and chemical weapons facilities.

San Juan (Commonwealth of Puerto Rico)—A fully loaded petroleum barge runs aground and ruptures in the vicinity of San Juan, threatening many of the island's most important tourist beaches.

Chapter Seven

The five-thirty Aeroflot flight from London to St. Petersburg galloped loudly down the runway, lifted smoothly into the clear night sky, and turned northeast almost immediately.

Madeira, who'd barely made it aboard the plane in time, settled back into his seat and closed his grit-filled eyes. His body was stiff and sore from the long, trans-Atlantic flight and his mind felt as rumpled as his white shirt and blue business suit.

"The cabin attendant tells me you're an American."

Startled, Madeira opened his tired eyes and turned to look at the previously unnoticed young man sitting next to him.

"Yes, I am."

"And you're a naval officer?" continued his slim, intense neighbor.

Fully alert now, Madeira sat up. "Retired, yes."

"I'm sorry," replied the neighbor quickly, with a smile. "I also learned that from the attendant. We live in a time of great change, and of great opportunities, and knowledge is the key to grabbing those opportunities.

"My name is Niko Avalaridze," the neighbor continued as he handed Madeira a business card. "Don't try to pronounce it, I was born in one of the southern republics. Georgia, to be precise. At the east end of the Black Sea, just north of Turkey. Just call me Niko."

Madeira, his mind still fogged, studied the card a moment. "Niko Avalaridze," he read. "Trans-Caspian Trading Corporation . . . Miami—Moscow—Tbilisi—Baku."

Miami and Moscow? Okay.

Tbilisi?

Tbilisi, he decided, was the capital of Georgia. It'd been in the news a lot recently. The Georgians had been busy shooting each other.

But Baku?

"Where's Baku?" he asked.

Avalaridze laughed easily. "Azerbaijan. It's the capital of the Republic of Azerbaijan. It's also a port on the Caspian Sea."

"Aren't they at war with somebody?"

"Azerbaijan? Yes, they're disagreeing with Armenia. Without the KGB and the Soviet Army to maintain order, everybody seems to be fighting with everybody else these days. Most of the feuds go back hundreds of years, if not thousands. I just try to keep my head down and stick to business."

"Georgia . . . Tbilisi . . . They're not on the Caspian Sea."

"No, but Baku is, and Trans-Caspian sounds more poetic than Trans-Black."

Madeira must have looked confused, because Avalaridze hastened to continue: "There are three little countries stuck between the Caucasus Mountains and the northern border of Turkey: Georgia's on the west, up against the Black Sea; Azerbaijan's on the east, up against the Caspian Sea; and Armenia's sort of in the middle and below the other two, between them and Turkey. They all used to be part of the Soviet Union, but now they're independent."

Madeira nodded, beginning to visualize the layout.

"And then there's Chechnya," Avalaridze continued, a hint of disapproval creeping into his voice. "Chechnya's just north of Azerbaijan. You've undoubtedly heard of them—the Chechens are always in the news for something."

Madeira nodded again. "Are they now independent too?"

"No, although the Chechens seem to think so. Chechnya's still just one of the republics in the Russian Federation. You Americans might think of them as states."

Madeira wiped his hand across his face, now realizing that his brain had been functioning at half speed. "Al Madeira," he finally said, shaking Niko's offered hand. "Sorry if I seemed a little dopey."

"Don't worry about it. Airplanes seem to have that effect on everybody."

"So you live in Tbilisi?"

"No. I was born there, but I am now a resident of Moscow, and a Russian citizen."

"Your English is very good."

"Thank you. I'm in the import-export business, so I get a lot of practice."

Madeira smiled. "What do you deal in?"

"Many things. At the moment we're working especially hard on bringing oranges and other fruit into Russia. You wouldn't believe the demand! Up north, that is. Moscow. St. Petersburg. Some of the southern republics, like Georgia, grow and export some citrus, but there's always a shortage up north and now people have some money to spend."

"It sounds promising."

"More than just promising! It's booming! So much so that we've been seriously thinking about buying a motor yacht for our Miami office. Something we can entertain the big citrus growers on. Not an ocean liner, of course, but something big and fast enough to get around the Caribbean in, something that would impress the growers, convince them that we're solid. As a retired naval officer you must have some very good ideas of what exactly I should be looking for."

83

"I'm really no expert on yachts, especially the big, fast Maxis, but . . ."

"Welcome to Russia, Al," Niko said three hours later as he and Madeira stepped out of the crowded, overheated cabin and into the bitterly cold St. Petersburg night.

"Thanks," Madeira replied as he pulled up the collar of his overcoat and started carefully down the boarding stairs and into the bus waiting on the snow-and-ice-covered tarmac. All around the void was filled with thick, blowing snow that whirled madly in all directions, dimming the otherwise harsh floodlights.

"Frankly," Niko said, "I hate this weather. It's much nicer where I come from, but the action's here and in Moscow, so we all just suffer with it."

One or two other passengers, who had overheard the comment, smiled grimly in agreement. Then the bus, even more jammed than the airplane had been, rumbled to life and crept off through the storm toward the terminal.

Hell! thought Madeira as he stepped out of the bus and another icy blast slammed into him. Feeling the growing pressure of the other passengers behind him, he headed for the door to the terminal with Niko still at his side. Just one of the cattle, he thought as he went with the flow.

"You see, Al?" Niko said as they worked their way through the door. "Isn't it just like I said it was? Russia is absolutely filled with people, and the more the people the more the needs. And needs are what business opportunities are made of." The Georgian's big brown eyes positively glowed as he spoke.

"Al!"

Madeira stopped and turned. Novikoff, dressed in a blue pin-striped suit and overcoat, was standing alone and rocklike some distance away in the center of the Arrivals area. Smiling and waving, the Russian naval officer seemed larger, more imposing somehow, on his own turf than he had in New York. He also appeared totally unaware of the rising tide of passengers who surged carefully around and past him toward Passport Control. He seemed equally un-aware that few, if any, of the passersby dared so much as a glance in his direction as they hurried past, intent upon their own affairs.

"Mike!" Madeira replied, returning the wave and feeling a touch of the relief we all feel upon greeting an old friend in surroundings foreign to us. For a moment he wondered what Novikoff was doing on this wrong side of Customs and Immigration. But then, whatever Novikoff might look like at the moment, he was a Russian naval officer acting on government business. Nobody would expect him to cool his heels in the waiting area.

"Is that your party?" Niko asked after shooting a glance at Novikoff. "I've enjoyed traveling with you," he contin-ued quickly, offering his hand. "And thanks for the advice about boats and ships. Best of luck with whatever it is you're here to do."

Madeira shook Niko's hand, wished him the best, and watched him join the flow toward Passport Control. He then angled off toward Novikoff.

"Good to see you again," beamed Novikoff as he grasped Madeira's arm and guided him away from Passport Control, toward a small door in the side of the room. "Sorry about the bus. I should've warned you. . . . But soon we'll have an all-new, totally modern terminal here, complete with jetways. Just like New York or Atlanta."

Madeira forced a short-lived smile on his face. "I'm not that delicate. It's all part of the adventure." As he spoke he could have sworn he saw Niko Avalaridze breeze through Passport Control and Customs without even stopping.

"Good man!" As he said it, Novikoff clapped Madeira on the shoulder.

"Don't worry about the formalities," he continued after noticing Madeira's uncertain expression. "You're here on government business. You're our guest. We're going out this way."

"What about my luggage?" Madeira asked as he eyed the door's prominent lock and remembered the cold dark that lay beyond. He was being foolish, he told himself. He should feel flattered. Novikoff was just giving him some sort of VIP treatment.

"Two of my men are taking care of it. How was your flight? More comfortable than mine, I hope. Aeroflot's improving, but it's not there yet."

"Can't agree with you on that," Madeira replied, making every effort to be a good guest, not to mention an agreeable employee. "My flight was great. Looks to me like Aeroflot's going to be a tough competitor from now on."

"Thanks, Al. When you compliment Aeroflot you are complimenting all Russians. I'll arrange to forward your remarks to the proper authorities."

As he stepped through the door, Madeira felt the weight of the hundred furtive glances that followed him. Each of them asked where he was being taken. Some wondered who he was. Even now, although the Soviet Union had been relegated to history, few Russians would dare to even speculate on why a man might be led off, out a locked side door, into the horrific night.

"I've already told the cabin crew."

"Excellent! That's very good for their morale."

While Novikoff laughed, Madeira allowed himself to be squired back out to the slush-covered apron. I'm just tired, he thought. It'd been a long trip. He'd slept fitfully, and his shoulders were cramped. His mouth tasted like a trash can, and he'd awakened to this dark and shitty night. Of course he was a little on edge!

This must be what it feels like after you turn fifty, he thought. But he'd feel better in a couple of minutes, just as soon as he settled into the warm, dry limousine that was undoubtedly waiting just ahead in the thickening brew of wind, snow, and bitter Baltic night. An hour or less from the airport to the hotel, where he'd catch up on his sleep. And then a day or two of sight-seeing, with Novikoff as guide. He'd read up on the city, and there was much he wanted to see.

He'd traveled so much over the years and seen so little,

he thought. Now was his chance, so he'd better lighten up and take advantage of it.

"Have you had a chance to work up our itinerary for the next few days, Mike?" he asked cheerfully.

"This way," Novikoff, said, leading him out of the snow-shrouded floodlights and around a corner of the terminal.

Madeira froze.

It'd been there all along, he realized later. A heavy, pulsing pounding. A deep melody played to the storm's harmony. He'd felt, and dismissed, it when he'd first stepped out of the bus.

Now, in the lee of the terminal building, the sound overpowered the wind's raspy howl. He found it impossible to dismiss the shadowy helicopter parked about fifty yards ahead, its slowly turning rotors creating a muffled, but very solid, *caa thunk, caa thunk, caa thunk.*

They sure as hell weren't using a big military chopper to take him to his downtown hotel!

Chapter Eight

In P-Town and New York it'd been easy enough for Madeira to believe the Cold War was long past. The massed armies, the captive nations, the hammer and sickle, the torture cells were all supposed to be gone. Boris Yeltsin was now leading Russia along the path, twisting though it might be, to a future filled with hope and light, freedom and justice.

But he wasn't in P-Town or New York. He was in St. Petersburg, once the capital of some of history's greatest despots. The nearest ACLU office was over three thousand miles farther away than the Arctic Circle, he didn't speak a word of Russian, and he was all alone.

He looked around again at the thick, swirling snow and thought of how the other passengers had hurried past Novikoff, their eyes averted.

Russia was still the largest nation on earth. Countless millions of square miles of emptiness. How easy it must still be to make somebody disappear in all that emptiness!

What could they possibly want from him? he asked himself. For most of his career he'd been little more than a seagoing garbage collector!

Maybe that was a little harsh, he decided. He'd been in the repair business and he'd made house calls. With a little towing on the side.

"Don't worry, Al" shouted Novikoff quickly when he realized Madeira had stopped dead in his tracks.

"It's nothing to worry about," continued the Russian, clutching Madeira's elbow. "We've had to advance *Asimov*'s sailing date. The Neva has frozen a little earlier than usual, and so has much of the harbor. The ship's anchored in open water off Kronshtadt. Just as soon as we board her she'll get under way."

Madeira was now able to make out the dim light shining from the helo's big side door. It looked to him like the door to Hell.

Still, he thought, Mike's explanation did sound reasonable. He was letting his imagination and years of Cold War conditioning fly out of control. How many thousands of schedule changes had he suffered over the years? How many thousands had he, himself, ordered?

He took a deep breath, tasting the mixture of wet snow and engine exhaust that swirled around him. So much for the sight-seeing, he thought with a pang of disappointment. Maybe he'd be able to return after the job was completed. When he had one million, after taxes, in the bank.

Realistically speaking, he didn't have a choice at the moment anyway.

"What about the gear?" he asked.

"The special stuff?" Novikoff replied in a relieved tone. "All aboard. I know you wanted to look it over before we loaded, but there simply wasn't time. You know as well as I do that the weather, the ice, is a terrible and unpredictable master."

Madeira pondered terrible and unpredictable masters as he stepped up into the shuddering helo, instinctively bowing his head as he did to avoid losing it to the long, sharp rotors whipping the white air above him.

William S. Schaill

One look around, at the dings and dents, the chipped paint and dirt, convinced him the copter was not normally used for transporting VIPs.

A figure in a black flight suit and crash helmet saluted him. Then he felt Novikoff's hand on his arm again, guiding him to one of the very temporary-looking seats set up along the sides of the dim cabin.

"Is that all of it?" Novikoff shouted in his ear a moment later. Madeira looked up from the foreign seat-belt assembly he was trying to secure and watched as two new figures appeared out of the darkness. Dressed in long parkas and carrying his luggage, the two seemed to fly in the door like huge bats with the dark wind at their backs.

A suitcase and two duffels.

"That's it," he shouted back. "I try to travel light."

Novikoff laughed, and signaled to the helmeted figure in black.

"This is Grivski and Mendalov," he shouted, nodding toward the new arrivals, who were now seated and adjusting their own seat belts.

"They're two of the divers you'll be working with."

Madeira nodded and smiled, not really liking what he saw, especially the chillingly lifeless stare the biggest diver bestowed on him. That must be Grivski, he thought. And the other's Mendalov. He, at least, seemed able to smile, although it was a far-from-comforting one.

The figure in black slammed the door shut.

"Hang on!" shouted Novikoff as the rotors' muted song rose in pitch. The shaking, roaring helo then lifted off the snow-covered apron and almost immediately skidded sickeningly to one side, only to be slammed violently in the opposite direction as it rose above and out of the terminal's lee.

"Afghanistan!" Novikoff shouted in Madeira's ear. "These fellows each did a tour or two in Afghanistan. They're tough and steady. Our best! They'll get us through."

Get us through what? Madeira wondered as his stomach

suddenly dropped. I'm the salty dog who's supposed to get us through the salvage operation.

He didn't like the helo, either. He didn't like any of them, of course. They all sounded as if something very important had come loose and was banging around. This one sounded even worse; it sounded as if the co-pilot were pouring a steady stream of nuts and bolts into the gearbox. Or maybe it was the pilot who was pouring the nuts and bolts and they had a chimp doing the driving.

And why did those rivet heads seem to be dancing across that bulkhead? Weren't they supposed to be tight against the aluminum? Holding the sheets together?

Even before they'd totally cleared the terminal's roof, the helo tilted and spun violently to the right. The pilot rammed the joystick forward, the tail rose, and they shot westward, directly into the raging storm.

Madeira nodded to Novikoff and hung on. Having nothing intelligent to say about service in Afghanistan, he concentrated on blanking out the worrisome grinding sound. Furthermore, he already felt a roughness in his throat from trying to bellow over the engine's roar and hoped to hell he could avoid aggravating it further.

"Mike!" he shouted suddenly, forgetting about his throat. "Yes?"

"Did you see that fellow I was talking to when I walked into the terminal?"

"I noticed you were talking to somebody. Who was he?"

"A Russian businessman, a Georgian he said, named Niko Avalaridze, or something like that. Said he was in the import-export business. Citrus. Oranges."

"What did you talk about? Oranges?"

"Yachts, mainly. He said business is very good and he's thinking of buying himself a yacht. . . . Don't worry. Nothing was said about what I'm here for."

"I wasn't worried about that. You understand the need for security as well as anybody. You know nothing more about him?"

"No."

"Did he hint in any way he might already know why you're here?"

"No," Madeira said.

"So what's the problem? You sat next to a chatty fruit merchant. One who says he's making big money. Lots of people say they're making big money these days. Lots of people *are* making big money these days."

"It looked to me as if he passed through Passport Control and Customs without stopping, and without being stopped."

"That's possible. He said he was in imports and exports?"

"Yes."

"He may have been lying to you. He may be government. Imports and exports provide a lot of freedom to travel."

"Why would he be so interested in me? Don't your intelligence people know what we're doing?"

"Of course! Those who need to know, do know. He may have just been curious. Or it's also possible that President Yeltsin decided to check up on you and me." As he spoke, Novikoff winked.

"And," the Russian continued, his smile already gone, "there's another possibility. I won't lie to you; he could be a rich and powerful businessman who's reasonably honest and also has a lot of political influence, or he could be a gangster. During the past ten years certain criminal elements—gangs, to be honest—have become very powerful. You've heard of the Chechen gangs, of course, but they're not the only ones. Many others also come from the southern republics and even from those in Asia. I'm very embarrassed to say, there are also a growing number of gangs run by Russians. Some of them act as if they were as powerful as the government itself."

"The plutonium?"

"Yes. We still consider that a very real possibility. We're taking precautions, of course. Unfortunately, they've infiltrated not only the civil government but also some army and naval units, and we're never sure exactly which, so we can't be too careful."

Forty kilos, thought Madeira. Five or six bombs. Maybe more.

There're a dozen countries, mostly small and unstable, who'd pay their entire annual gross domestic products for forty kilos of refined plutonium, even if it was a little more than slightly used. That must explain Grivski and Mendalov, the two Russian Rambos.

"What did you say his name was?" Novikoff shouted. "I think I will check a little more into him."

"I'm not sure I can pronounce it. Here's the card he gave me."

Madeira fished the card out of his pocket and handed it to Novikoff, who studied it a moment and then consigned it to his own pocket.

"I'll check into this in the morning."

Fighting its way into the Baltic gale, the rattling helo passed first over an industrial park or facility of some sort, its precise layout revealed by the rectilinear pattern of fuzzy lights faintly visible in the white darkness below. The chopper continued on over the great open fields and marshes to the south of the city, already nothing more than dark, almost invisible expanses of snow and ice, and along the coast. Then the pilot turned north, out over the wind-maddened waters of the Gulf of Finland. All the while, the machine soared, shuddered, and swooped—slammed from side to side like a soccer ball in active play.

I guess that's it for my sight-seeing in Russia, thought Madeira as he turned away from the viewless window.

The cabin was bitterly cold, and there was nothing to look at except the dancing rivets and shuddering bulkheads. The noise, the pounding, thumping racket, was overpowering, making further conversation not worth the effort.

Madeira tried to withdraw into himself and doze off. That proved just as impossible as had conversation.

"There she is, Al!" Novikoff shouted, grabbing Madeira's arm as the copter banked sharply to port.

Madeira stared stupidly at the Russian a second, then

looked out the miserable little window and spotted a faint white glow far below.

The helo continued its fast, swooping approach toward the research ship's lighted landing pad, shuddering worse than ever as it descended.

With a jerk, the swoop changed to a hover. For a moment, the world was level and unmoving. The roar of the engine dropped . . . and so did the helo, thudding down sickeningly onto the pad.

It bounced. And slid to one side. And bounced again. And continued to skitter to the side. For a few seconds Madeira was convinced they were going to bounce right off the pad and overboard into the enraged Baltic.

The instant the wheels touched steel the second time the shadowy figure in black threw the door open and Novikoff jumped out. Madeira, the two divers, and the luggage all followed immediately, tumbling onto the pitching deck. Even before they were clear of the rotors, the door slammed shut and the roaring shriek of the helo's engines increased again until it filled the darkness. Then it was gone, its blinking red light disappearing immediately into the wind-tortured murk.

Madeira looked all around and saw nothing but flying snow glistening in the feeble floodlights. Even with the helo gone it was still blowing like hell. Hard-driving, lightly salted snow. Icy little granules blasting his exposed face and burrowing down the neck of his knee-length parka. And in the distance there was nothing. No lights. No shadows. Nothing but a white darkness that shaded into blackness.

Instinctively, he noted the ship's motion: the pitching, the shudder as she jerked her anchor chain taut, the vibration of her engines. She's under tremendous strain, he thought.

Christ! he realized with a start. We're in the middle of the Gulf of Finland. And they're steaming to an anchor, using the engines to keep from dragging. No seaman in his right mind would arrange a rendezvous like this unless he had some very compelling reason.

The ice! he reminded himself. The Neva's frozen over.

But there didn't seem to be ice in the Gulf.

"Where's Kronstadt?" he shouted at Novikoff the minute it was possible to hear anything beyond his own thoughts.

"About ten miles to the east," Novikoff replied.

"Is there ice there? In the harbor? At the naval base?"

"No. Not yet."

"Why aren't we in there? Why are we out here?"

"Time is absolutely critical in the operation, Al. We had to be certain to get out ahead of the ice. We have to get that wreck cleaned up before too much of its radiation gets out and kills people. We wanted to be ready to go the instant you arrived."

"Oh!" Madeira said, the stress of the past day catching up with him again. He felt tired, very tired, he had a headache, and the exceptionally sharp, fresh air was doing nothing to make him feel any better.

Only then did he realize that several dark figures had joined them, materializing out of the driving snow into the feeble yet still harsh aura of the helo platform's working lights.

"Al," Novikoff shouted, determined, as usual, to keep things moving right along, "this is Captain Bukinin, *Asimov*'s master." As he spoke, Novikoff pointed at what Madeira could now recognize as a tall, heavyset man with close-cut gray hair and a less-than-welcoming expression on his round, puffy face. "Captain, this is Captain Madeira, our new salvage master."

Before Madeira could get his half-frozen hand out, Bukinin had saluted him coldly, then turned to talk to the figure standing next to him.

Madeira, not sure how to respond, just nodded.

"Chernov," Novikoff said, gesturing toward the individual talking to Captain Bukinin. "Vasily Chernov, *Asimov*'s chief mate."

Chernov, still listening to Bukinin, nodded and smiled briefly.

"And Viktoria, of course . . ."

Madeira turned to the chief scientist. Like the others, she was dressed in a full-length padded coat and fur hat, which contained most of her blond hair. But nothing, not even the darkness of the night, could contain the blue fire of her eyes. For the first time that night—hell! for the first time in over a year—he felt warmed to the core. Warmed and challenged and excited.

"We're all very glad you could make it," she said, offering him her hand and a broad smile as she nailed him with the manic intensity of her eyes.

God! he thought. These people really do know how to suffer with gusto!

"We get under way immediately," interrupted Bukinin, his inexplicable hostility still obvious. "Chernov is attending to the anchor right now. Unless, of course, Comrade Galin objects—"

A flash of irritation shot through Viktoria's eyes as she turned to him and snapped something in Russian.

"Yes," Bukinin replied in English, smirking as he spoke. "I know you don't want to be addressed as Comrade, but weren't you once a loyal member of the Party? And please remember Captain Novikoff's order that we speak only English when Captain Madeira is present."

"I was young and didn't fully understand," she replied almost defensively. "I've corrected my mistake."

"You made no mistake," Bukinin snapped. "It's an honor to belong to the Party. I remain a member and always will. There are many who now feel the worst mistakes have been made since the Party was so brutally suppressed by the so-called reformers."

Before Viktoria could reply, Bukinin, still smirking, turned away. "I'm needed on the bridge."

"Bukinin can be a very difficult person," Novikoff said. "He has always been a very loyal Communist and now seems to feel abandoned by history. He remains, of course, a loyal Russian and an excellent seaman. Are you ready for your tour of *Asimov*?"

96

"I probably shouldn't admit this, but the only thing I'm ready for is sleep."

"I can understand that. I'll show you to your quarters."

"Thank you."

He paused a moment, looking at Viktoria. She was still smiling, telling him that despite the appearances everything really was under control. Telling him they really did want him to be there.

Should the fact that she'd been a member of the Party make any difference to him?

He hadn't the slightest idea.

"I'm looking forward to working with you, Dr. Galin," he finally said as he allowed Novikoff to lead him off to his stateroom.

Something had happened!

Despite his bone-deep exhaustion, Madeira found himself suddenly wide awake. Because of that same exhaustion, his thoughts were heavy and fuzzy.

What was it that'd happened?

He'd felt something. A bump? A shudder maybe. A difference in the ship's motion?

He didn't know what his sleeping mind had detected, but the sea sense developed over a lifetime screamed that something wasn't right.

He lay in his bunk. Fighting his way to the surface. Trying to clear his head. Listening. Struggling to identify what it was that his subconscious had heard or felt.

The ship was so damn big, her motions so muted by bulk. He wasn't used to big ships, the salvage force tending toward smallish, overgrown tugboats. He wasn't accustomed to big-ship motions, especially those of giant catamarans, yet he knew something was wrong.

Was that a bell ringing? Everything else now seemed normal. No general alarms shrieking. Nobody shouting over the PA system. Now he didn't even hear the bell. Maybe he never had.

His head still ached, as did his arms and legs. His eyes

still felt gritty and his skin felt tender in the stale, overheated air. The better part of a day spent in a jetliner, followed by the thumping inflicted by the helo, had done nothing good for his middle-aged body.

He dragged himself out of the rack and shuffled stiffly over to the very large porthole with which his accommodations were graced. His view was aft, over the dimly lit main working deck, then on over the stern into the darkness. The wind was still blasting and the icy snow still attacking and glazing everything in its path, but, essentially, all appeared quiet.

Through his bare feet he felt the steady vibration of *Asimov*'s main engines. His knees flexed slightly in response to the ship's labored pitching and pounding as she entered the Baltic from the Gulf of Finland. He didn't envy the exposed lookouts who he assumed were posted in weather like this.

He opened the stateroom door just as a sailor ran by, wide-eyed, then disappeared down a ladder at the end of the passageway. He looked more closely at the hatch into which the sailor had disappeared. A faint, bluish haze seemed to be rising up from it.

Alarmed and confused, Madeira turned to the chair and grabbed the suit trousers he'd arrived in. After slipping into them and securing the belt, he sat down on the edge of his bunk and hunted for his loafers. If it had been his ship he'd have called the bridge and interrogated the officer of the deck. But it wasn't his ship.

He pulled on the stiff, rancid socks he found in the loafers. He then stood and slid his feet into the loafers themselves.

Still half asleep, he charged out the door into the chill, dimly lit passageway, which looked, at best, only vaguely familiar. It could, he thought, have been almost any ship. Or cheap hotel. Or prison.

The sailor was nowhere in sight, but Madeira could hear him as he scuttled down ladders far below.

Madeira sprinted down the passageway, which he decided

in passing could use a fresh coat of paint, and stopped at the hatch. The haze was real and it had an acrid tang to it. Electrical fire! he thought. He dropped down the first ladder, following the sailor, who sounded as if he were several decks below him.

Down he went in pursuit, sliding down the handrails of one ladder, then spinning around and sliding down those of the next. Down into the ship's guts. And the deeper he went the more his head cleared and the more at home he felt. Big or small, Russian or American, they're all the same, he thought. Steel, oil, paint, and bilgewater. And the constant, pulsing vibration of machinery running.

At the foot of the sixth ladder he realized he was now near or below the ship's waterline, and the acrid haze was stronger than ever. Once again he could hear the sound of the sailor running. Running aft now, it would seem. Along the passageway behind him. He followed, ducking through two watertight doors, then came to a sudden halt at the next door when he realized men were shouting and snarling on the other side.

After catching his breath and briefly debating the wisdom of doing so, Madeira stepped through the door. About twenty feet aft of him three sailors were cowering. Between them and him another lay on the deck, bent and retching, attempting futilely to both hold his groin and, at the same time, stop the blood from pouring out his nose and mouth. To his left, Grivski was mechanically slamming yet another sailor's face into the blood-spattered steel bulkhead. As he worked, Novikoff's favorite Afghanistan vet showed no emotion at all. Neither pleasure nor excitement nor doubt. Not even boredom.

Behind Grivski, presiding over it all, stood the chief mate, Vasily Chernov, with the runner next to him.

"What the fuck's going on!" Madeira snarled, nauseated by the whole scene.

Twisting his victim's arm up behind him, Grivski slammed the broken face into the bulkhead again, then spun the man around and kneed him. "This is ship's business,

Captain. Russian business. You leave. Go back to your quarters."

"Yes, Captain," Chernov said, the grin of deep pleasure on his face giving way to irritation. "This has nothing to do with you or your duties. You are no more than a passenger here. You have no authority. Return to your quarters!"

"Is Captain Novikoff here?" As he asked, Madeira studied the faces of the three so-far-unharmed sailors. He saw fear and resignation. And not the faintest spark of rebellion.

"Yes," Chernov replied, nodding toward the opposite end of the passageway. "He's with the chief engineer."

When Madeira started to move in the direction indicated, Grivski dropped the sailor and moved into Madeira's path.

"Return to your quarters, Captain," repeated Chernov. "Captain Novikoff is busy now. I will ask him to call you when he has the time."

Madeira looked around him, his emotions a crippling mixture of fury, frustration, and fear. St. Petersburg was only one of many places where it was all too easy to make somebody disappear. Russia might be big and empty, but the Atlantic was even bigger and emptier.

"This man will escort you," Chernov continued, nodding toward the messenger, "and I will ask Captain Novikoff to talk with you just as soon as possible."

Faced with his own powerlessness, it was all Madeira could do to keep from imagining himself as the poor bastard whose face Grivski was smashing. He shuddered inwardly at the thought, stiffening as he did in an effort to conceal the weakness from Chernov and Grivski.

Within a few minutes of his return to his stateroom, Madeira's phone buzzed. "Al, I'm sorry I missed you. We had an explosion in one of the main generators. . . . Some son of a bitch sabotaged us!"

"What the hell were Chernov and Grivski doing?"

"Chernov and Grivski? Yes, that was reported to me. That was a mistake, a very serious mistake on their part, and I have already disciplined them. It's time they learned we don't do things that way anymore."

All right, thought Madeira. Everybody's always said they're a rough bunch. I suppose it takes time to turn things around. And, he forced himself to admit, he'd seen a few fists and knees used in the United States Navy over the years. He'd always come down hard on the offenders, and so had everybody else he knew, but he also knew that there were still a few who tolerated and even encouraged it. Brutality seemed to be just as eternal, and universal, as love.

"What's the plan now?"

"We'll repair it, of course. We're returning to Kronshtadt. They say they can repair it in twenty-four hours or less."

"Roger," Madeira responded, hoping that Novikoff really did have the situation, and Grivski, under control now.

Three or four hours later, Madeira was jolted into full alertness by a muffled but protracted rumble that resonated both through the air and also through the ship herself. It was the sound of anchor chain pounding down and out the hawse.

He bounded over to the port and looked out. There was nothing to see but the dirty gray light of a snowy dawn.

He listened to his knees and feet. The main engines were still running, but they were no longer under the same load as when the ship was under way. And the ship's motion was totally different. The sensations of slipping and swooping were missing, replaced by a violent pitching that was cut short on each rebound by the telltale shudder of an anchor chain snapping taut.

They were anchored, all right. But not in any harbor he could imagine.

What the hell was that hanging from the overhead? he wondered as he stepped out into the gloomy passageway.

A sensor of some sort. A smoke detector?

Hell no! It was a TV camera. The damn passageway was under surveillance, and he hadn't even noticed it the night before.

Madeira was unable to read the signs posted on the bulkheads, and it took him a while to reach the bridge. When he finally got there he found Novikoff, red-faced, shaking his fist and shouting in Russian at Captain Bukinin. Viktoria was also there, standing off to one side and eyeing the two of them with a strange expression, one that hinted at both suspicion and resentment.

Novikoff spotted Madeira and immediately spun in his direction.

"Good morning, Al," said the Russian, his rage seeming to disappear almost magically.

Madeira continued to concentrate on the ship's motion. It still didn't feel to him like they were in port.

"When do we move alongside the pier?"

"We won't be. We're going to make the repairs out here, where we are."

"Anchored out in the middle of the Gulf?"

"Yes. The parts we need, and the technicians, are on their way right now by helicopter."

"Why?"

"Al," a note of apology appeared in Novikoff's voice, "we've been having some labor problems recently. We Russians are only beginning to learn how to deal with the new freedoms. And you know how dockyard workers are."

"Traitors!" Bukinin mumbled.

These people really are fucked up! Madeira thought, scarcely able to believe they were afraid to use their own shipyard.

"Do you know who did it? And why?"

"Not yet," Novikoff said, suddenly enraged again, "but we'll find him and hang him by his balls. I won't permit anybody to disrupt this operation. It's too important."

"Goddamn Balts," Bukinin growled. "It was one of them . . . or maybe a Ukrainian. Look what *they've* done to the Black Sea Fleet! They stole all the electronics and other valuable supplies for use in their own fleet. They even stole some of the ships! They're all traitors. And thieves! They'd like nothing better than to make fools of us. I've repeatedly demanded an all-Russian crew, but they keep sending me these . . . others. What do you say, Comrade?"

"I say you're the fool, Captain," Viktoria replied. "Both the Baits and the Ukrainians much prefer Yeltsin to the alternatives. And I've warned you before: Don't call me Comrade!"

Bukinin nodded, a faint look of amusement on his face.

"And my mother was Ukrainian," Viktoria added.

"I had no intention of insulting your mother," replied Bukinin as Viktoria turned and headed for the ladder.

"I'll find him and kill him," Novikoff mumbled, clenching his fists as he stared out into the all-obscuring snow.

"Viktoria," he snapped suddenly. "I want to talk to you. Come to my quarters!"

Chapter Nine

Just when Madeira was close to giving up hope, the northern sun finally showed itself. Wrapped in one of the Russians' big parkas, his tortured sinuses about to explode, he stood on *Asimov*'s windward bridge and watched as the liquid silver circle winked briefly through the skudding overcast, then dove for cover again.

Bubbleheads, naval divers, aren't supposed to have sinus problems. No asthma, no pollen-related allergies, no sinuses. It was right there in the book. He'd told them at the very start that he'd always had sinus problems. They hadn't cared, because they were always desperate for otherwise-fit bodies. So for the next twenty-plus years he'd popped antihistamines, just like everybody else, so he could get on with the work at hand. Now his sinuses were worse than ever.

The sun was much too feeble to do anything for his sinuses, but it was a start. And it would return, he reassured himself. It always did. Especially when you were headed south.

He still couldn't get over the size of the ship, as he looked down at least eighty feet to watch the milk-gray seas pound against the ship's towering starboard hull. Seven hundred feet long. Almost one hundred and fifty feet of beam and a displacement of over thirty thousand tons. It was like being on an aircraft carrier.

He turned and walked across the long bridge, which extended from outboard of one hull to outboard of its mirror-image partner on the other side, and stopped at the door to the pilothouse. After opening the door, tightly closed against the weather, he stepped in and found only two people, the captain and a helmsman, on watch.

The helmsman, whom he'd seen around but didn't know, glanced at him briefly with a faint, furtive smile.

"Good morning, Captain Bukinin," he said, as cheerfully as he could, to the towering, beefy officer.

Bukinin turned and glanced at him, his distaste all too obvious. Then, without saying a word, he turned back to looking out the window.

Fuck him, thought Madeira as he returned to the door and stepped back out onto the bridge.

To the west and slightly astern ran a long, dark smudge. Jutland. Denmark.

To the east, and now totally invisible, lay Sweden. Also to the east and clearly visible, two giant, slab-sided containerships, along with several even larger and equally graceless tankers, plowed crisscrossing tracks through the Kattegat's choppy gray waters.

He'd expected to see more traffic. The last time he'd been here it'd been a madhouse. It must be the time of year, he decided. No matter how hardy the local salts were, there had to be some sort of slowdown with the coming of the ice.

They really were ugly, he decided, returning to the ships themselves. Especially the containerships. They looked more like the truck-trailer containers they carried than they did ships.

He watched out of the side of his eye as Captain Bukinin lowered his binoculars and walked over to the radar. After studying the screen a moment the captain spat out a rapid order to the helmsman. The sailor grunted in reply and turned the wheel one revolution to port. After studying the compass a moment, he returned the wheel to its original position and grunted again. Bukinin briefly studied the navigational plot, then, with one final grunt, returned to the window and raised his binoculars again.

Madeira had to admit to himself that Bukinin knew his business. In fact, the son of a bitch was damn good.

Once his sea legs accepted the big catamaran's unusual motion, Madeira had concentrated on learning his way around the ship and familiarizing himself with the Russian gear—everything from the little SeaFairy ROVs to the clunky underwater habitat, even though he really hoped he wouldn't end up having to use the latter.

Thanks to Novikoff's guidance, along with that of Boris Timon, one of the divers, he did now have a good feel for the ship and the gear. He was just about ready to give up on his second objective, however, that of trying to fit in.

The officers, the divers and technicians, the few scientists who were actually aboard, could all speak English but did so only when it suited their convenience. As for the sailors, the only English most of them seemed to know was "Can you give me a cigarette?" and "How many rubles will you take for that?".

What the hell did he expect? He was the hired hand. He should've learned some Russian. Maybe, he thought for one mad moment, his linguistic ignorance was precisely what qualified him for the job.

Madeira continued to look through the window into the pilothouse and found himself looking at half a dozen TV monitors, all blank, mounted on the aft bulkhead. They're just as secretive and surveillance-happy as everybody always said, he thought. The whole damn ship was covered by little TV cameras. Yet he'd never seen anybody actually looking at the monitors.

He felt the ship start her long turn to port and glanced

back at Bukinin. He did seem to have everything under control.

The respite from the weather was over, he thought as he started down the ladder and toward the passageway leading to the aft boat deck. Once they rounded the northern tip of Denmark they'd pass from the relatively protected waters of the Kattegat to the Skagerrak. There they'd be fully exposed to the furious westerlies tearing across the North Sea.

As he entered the passageway he encountered Boris Timon, the diver who'd been assigned to familiarize him with the ship and her gear.

"Hang on, Captain," Timon said. As he spoke a big smile crossed his broad, almost playful face and revealed the hole left by two missing teeth he claimed to have lost in a diving accident.

"It'll just make our dry run this afternoon that much more exciting."

"You still wish to do it? Even in this weather?"

"We won't be launching. I just want to play with the controls."

"Yes, you're undoubtedly right. It's very important that you feel at home in our little Beluga."

By the time he reached the boat deck they'd already entered the Skagerrak. He leaned on the rail and looked aft over the main deck. He could feel the seas growing sharper and harder and the ship responding, her twin prows rising high on one wave only to slam down and bury themselves in the next gray-green wall.

He looked aloft, at the smoke emerging from the funnel only to be torn away by the wind, at the Russian ensign held straight out and almost motionless by that same fierce breeze.

Then he sneezed.

"God bless you!"

Madeira turned and looked at Viktoria. Like him she was wearing a parka along with a slight grin. And the wind had liberated a few wisps of her golden hair. He wondered if she'd been standing on the boat deck when he arrived.

"Thank you."

"We don't have that problem, you know."

He stared at her a moment. "What?"

"Russians, real Russians, that is, don't get colds. Just ask Captain Bukinin. That's why we never wasted our socialist resources developing the hundred different cold pills you Americans have."

She was still smiling as she joined him at the rail.

"What about Ukrainians? Do they get colds?"

"Half-Ukrainian geophysicists do. That's why I have my own supply of American cold pills. Just don't tell the political officer."

"Is there one aboard?"

"There's not supposed to be. Not anymore. . . ."

"Then I'd like to take a look at your collection sometime. Mine doesn't seem to be doing the job."

They both laughed.

"I hear you're satisfied with the equipment Mike's gotten for you."

"Yes. It's all fine. . . . Great, in fact! Some got banged up a little, but we're repairing it now."

"And the divers?"

"Very professional."

Madeira glanced aft and noticed a small group of sailors dressed in a variety of outfits, none of which looked very clean, milling around on the main deck. Hands in their pockets, they didn't seem to be doing anything except talking and pacing back and forth, as if waiting for something, and they didn't seem to be sure what, to happen.

Why the hell doesn't somebody give them something to do? he wondered. He knew that idle sailors inevitably stumbled into trouble. He hadn't spent half a lifetime in the navy for nothing.

"Then you think we'll succeed?"

"Yes, I think we'll get that hot piece of junk up and packed into the dry dock. I'm not sure where I'd hide if I screw it up. I've got a reputation to keep up, you know."

"And what will you do with all your new money?" she

asked, smiling at first, then frowning as she looked past him at the growing crowd of sailors.

"Does it ever stop snowing in Russia?"

"Yes. Of course. In the summer."

"Good, because I think I'd like to visit, as a tourist. I think there's a lot I'd like to see, to learn."

As he spoke, Madeira noticed it'd begun to snow again. He glanced at Viktoria, then at the patrol boat pounding along to port. Low and gray, about a hundred feet long, the Danish naval vessel was nearly lost among the wind-driven mass of snow, spray, and solid water.

"Where'd *she* come from?" he asked, glancing up at one of *Asimov*'s twin funnels as he did. Although it'd been painted over, and although Russia's traditional red, white, and blue stripes were flying aft, the Soviet hammer and sickle welded to the side of the stack was still visible. Its complete removal, Novikoff had explained, was just a matter of adequate funding.

"They've been there for some time," replied Viktoria. "They always are. The Danes still don't trust us, although the Norwegians are much worse. They were following us almost the entire length of the Baltic. This boat will follow for an hour or two and then leave."

If they don't drown in the meantime, Madeira thought.

"There'll be so much for you to see," Viktoria said, returning to a topic she clearly preferred. "Russia's a very big country. It spans both Europe and Asia. Many hundreds of millions of people have been doing things, making things, dreaming things for so many centuries. Much was suppressed, but now it is possible to see it all again."

As she paused, Vasily Chernov, anger showing clearly on his face, hurried past them, headed aft.

"What's going on back there?" Madeira asked.

"I don't know," Viktoria replied, still frowning. "You do understand that we have many labor problems these days. Captain Novikoff was right when he said now that our people have tasted a little bit of freedom they want so much more . . . and they really don't know what to do with it."

Madeira started to remark that management's tendency to beat the crap out of the troops might have something to do with the labor problem but then slammed his mouth shut. Viktoria was a geophysicist. She wasn't really part of management.

The crowd, which seemed to number at least fifty, immediately formed itself into a loose circle around Chernov, who was shouting and waving his arms wildly in the wet, driving wind.

The crowd replied in kind and the circle began to close around the chief mate.

Before Madeira could ask Viktoria what Chernov was saying, the mate fumbled with his holster, drew a pistol, and fired repeatedly into the air. Despite the wind's shrieks and moans, the sharp cracks were clearly audible to Madeira.

"Shit!" Madeira mumbled under his breath as he looked down at the drama. A hard, salty mist, spray thrown up by *Asimov*'s windward bow and carried all the way aft by the howling wind, peppered them with its icy birdshot.

At first the mob didn't move. Then it backed off slowly, separating itself from Chernov and forming a tight knot about twenty feet aft of him. The mate holstered the pistol and began shouting at the sailors again. They swayed back and forth as they listened, a few slipping and skidding, as the slick deck beneath them pitched, rose, and fell in response to the hostile seas.

Beyond them the ship's wake—slick, straight, and dirty white—pointed back in the direction they'd come from.

Just as Madeira noticed that Viktoria had developed what seemed a death grip on the rail, the watertight door in the bulkhead immediately below them crashed open and Captain Bukinin stormed out, bellowing as he came.

The sailors surged forward, forcing Chernov and Bukinin back against the bulkhead. With the ruckus now almost directly beneath them, Madeira could hear the shouting clearly. The words were, to him, totally incomprehensible, but the spirit, the unquenchable rage on both sides, was all too clear.

"What're they saying?" he demanded. "What's the problem?"

Viktoria was already leaning far over the rail, listening intently.

"They say they want to be paid," she said finally with a look of disgust. "They say they won't work anymore until they're paid. They want to turn around and go back to St. Petersburg."

"Is it true?"

"That they haven't been paid? Yes. None of us has been in two or three months. There's some administrative problem."

Bukinin's voice now shrieked up at them.

"What's he saying?"

"That they'll get paid when we arrive in San Juan. That they don't need any money while we're at sea anyway."

The sailors were all shouting and moving toward the two officers, their rage heating the chill air.

"They say they're not going to wait. And they say they don't believe him. One just called the captain a lying . . . turd. They want the ship turned around now."

They're getting awfully close to the line, thought Madeira. Not even I'd be willing to take too much more than this. Of course, he added to himself, I'd have done something about the pay problem months ago.

"Bukinin's now calling them all traitors and telling them he'll turn them all over to the KGB."

As she spoke over her shoulder, Viktoria seemed to Madeira to be examining the crowd carefully. Face by face.

Of course! he thought. There has to be. . . . "Is there a KGB officer aboard?"

"The KGB doesn't exist anymore, but there's probably at least one SVG officer aboard. That's what most of them are called now. The Foreign Intelligence Service. I don't know for sure . . . but probably. Now more than ever the authorities feel order must be maintained. Crime is out of control. Without any order, reforms are impossible."

There was a sudden, sharp motion in the crowd. One of

111

the sailors had thrown something at the officers. Something hard-looking.

Whatever it was, Madeira could see it tumbling in the air, black against the gray sky. It seemed to hang a moment, as if held aloft by the wind, then started to fall toward Bukinin.

Hell no! It was way too high to hit the captain.

"Watch out!" he hissed as he grabbed Viktoria's arm and yanked her to the side.

A three-foot Stillson wrench whistled by and slammed onto the steel deck about five feet directly behind where the chief scientist had been standing.

Everybody on the main deck looked up at them. The two officers drew their pistols again. This time it was Bukinin who fired twice into the air. He then lowered the muzzle so it pointed directly into the mob.

Chernov followed suit.

One sailor, a very big, bearded man, stepped forward. He was shouting something. Waving. He paused, then pointed his finger at the captain, snarling again as he did. Then he launched into a hissing, spitting diatribe.

There were two sharp reports and pale smoke curled out of Chernov's pistol.

The bearded man lurched backward, skidding on the slush, an expression of shock, or anguish, on his face. Then he crumpled to the deck and was still.

"Goddamnit to hell," Madeira snarled as he stared down at the body, a growing, dark red stain already spreading along one side of its chest and running down the icy, snow-covered deck. Chernov had just shot and killed one of his own fucking sailors! And the man wasn't even armed.

People just don't do this sort of thing, he found himself thinking over and over, stunned by the act's suddenness and fury. Especially not over a few crummy rubles.

Nobody went to help the fallen man. For a moment, nobody even moved. The only motion was the rolling of the ship, the only sound the howling of the wind. Then the mob went mad, scattering in all directions.

Of course they do, Madeira reminded himself. You just

watched a man shot down over a few rubles of back pay. And in New York people are killed for a five-dollar necklace or a pair of used sneakers.

Maybe there was more to it than he realized. What were they all *really* saying when they were shouting at each other? Who was the dead man? What was his history?

Why in God's name had he allowed himself to be sucked into this sewer? He didn't know the players. He didn't know the rules. He was totally out of it.

It was the money, he reminded himself. The million dollars and the challenge of a super-nasty project. And the need to prove something to himself, something he should have settled to his own satisfaction decades ago.

But the money should have alerted him. He should have known something was wrong when they agreed, with no argument whatsoever, to pay him almost as much as a second-string football player gets. You really are worth what your pay stub says you are. That's what you're worth to your employer, anyway.

When he returned his full attention to the deck the crowd had completely melted away, its members having dived into various doors and hatches.

Madeira turned and looked again at the wrench, black and greasy and harder than any cranium made by God, as it lay in state on the slushy deck. At whom had it really been aimed? Bukinin? Chernov? Himself? Why would any of them want to throw a wrench at him? Why had it been thrown so high?

"Now what?" he asked Viktoria, noticing as he did the expression of revulsion that filled her face.

"The man will be buried at sea and Captain Bukinin will write a report explaining that Chief Officer Chernov had to shoot him during a mutiny," she replied without looking at him.

"Will there be an inquiry?"

"Perhaps . . . after we complete the operation . . . but I doubt it."

"What about Chernov?"

"What about him?"

"He overreacted."

"I'm sure Captain Bukinin's report will establish beyond doubt that his action was justified under the circumstances."

It must be fucking awful, he thought, to be Russian on a full-time basis.

She turned and looked at him. "That's not how you would have dealt with the situation, is it? You're a good man, a good officer. I bet your men, most of them, were happy to see you every morning. Most of the men aboard this ship are good men, too, but this is still Russia. Life is still very hard for us.

"You know," she continued, turning away, "I'm certain the pay problem really will be corrected when we reach Puerto Rico."

"What will happen to those other sailors?" he asked, thinking of the application of Russian discipline he'd seen the night the generator was sabotaged.

"Notations will be made on their records. Other than that, probably nothing."

How can she say that? he wondered. Whether or not she's a scientist, she's no fool. . . . She knows all too well what goes on down below and in the dark of night.

As she spoke Viktoria must have sensed his skepticism, because she continued, "There are too many of them involved to do much of anything. If they can identify the ringleaders, something will happen to them. But otherwise . . ."

"After the ringleaders are identified, do they have to be tried and convicted?"

"Al, I'm not the President of Russia!"

"If it really was just about money, then it should never have gone as far as it did."

"Yes. Chernov's a fool, an animal. He made trouble where there should have been none. He tries too hard to show he's a tough guy, to please Bukinin."

"You see what I mean, Comrade?"

Madeira turned away from Viktoria and discovered Bukinin standing at the top of the ladder, pistol still in hand.

"It's those fucking Balts and . . ." continued the captain. "They're all undisciplined troublemakers. They lack any sense of loyalty."

"Don't call me Comrade!" Viktoria snapped to Bukinin's retreating back as the captain stormed forward, holstering his weapon as he went.

Chapter Ten

"You say this's been meggered?" Madeira asked, hunching his shoulders as he spoke in an effort to maximize the parka's warming power.

"Meggered?"

"Tested for electrical grounds."

"Yes, Captain," Timon replied, his broad face raw from the harsh wind blowing fiercely down the boxlike tunnel formed by *Asimov*'s two towering, rust-streaked hulls. It was a wind heavily flavored with the scents of ships and the sea—paint, rust, petroleum, salt, and the indefinable aroma of decay that afflicts all ships almost as soon as they are launched. "When we onloaded it we let part of it hang in the water and tested as we wound it aboard."

"No bad spots?" He had to shout to be heard above the roaring, rushing rumble that filled the air around them.

"None, sir."

"Are you sure?"

"Yes, sir."

Madeira stood back and looked at the huge steel reel, over

twenty feet in diameter, and the three thousand feet of black, four-inch waterproof power cable wrapped around it. Boris better be right, he thought. They'd be pumping thousands of amps through it. One break in the plastic cover, one tiny crack in the insulation, and the damn thing'd explode.

Both Madeira and Timon instinctively grabbed at rails as the deck beneath them rose, tilted, and shuddered slightly. A solid, slapping thump reverberated deeply around them, then blended into the surrounding concert of nature's winds and percussion.

Madeira half-consciously noted the change in motion and walked to the edge of the reel well, a partially enclosed platform hung below the ship's main deck between her twin hulls. A freak cross-sea of some sort, he decided. He glanced forward into the tunnel. About a hundred feet ahead, and maybe forty clear of the water, the Beluga worksub rested in its cradle. Forward of that he could see an end of the cylindrical habitat, also resting in a special cradle. Below it all a churning, gray-white millrace tore past, snapping and heaving as it flowed.

When, he wondered, had *Asimov* last been dry-docked? There were thick masses of greenery and mollusks trailing through the gray water along both sides of the tunnel.

A scarcity of resources, no doubt.

"Have all the ROV umbilicals been meggered also?" he shouted as he returned to the limited protection of the well's partial enclosure.

"Yes, sir, although sometimes they fail even after we have just tested them. We have prepared everything we can."

Madeira nodded in understanding. The same sort of thing had happened to him hundreds of times. Murphy, the Murphy of Murphy's Law and its infinite corollaries, had been a sailor.

He stepped over to the rail and looked down into the millrace. The plans had been made and discussed, the gear tested. Bukinin continued to make clear that he had no taste for Madeira, but Madeira was now confident that the Russian captain could be counted on to perform his duties both faithfully and very well. Similarly, Madeira continued to loathe and even fear Grivski and Mendalov, but he was equally sure they would do their jobs. Try as he might to find something, there was very little left for him to do until they reached the wreck.

Except worry.

No matter what Viktoria had said, he'd been certain there had to be repercussions from the mutiny. The Russian concept of discipline seemed to demand some active response. Something more than the simple horror of Rustoff's exemplary death.

He hadn't had to wait long. The next morning there were at least three broken arms, half a dozen badly bruised faces, and God only knew how many concealed wounds. And the ship's boatswain, whom Bukinin might well hold responsible for not warning him of trouble, seemed even more surly and hangdog than usual.

And nobody, not even Olga, the ship's doctor, seemed to find the injuries worth mentioning.

Other than that, Captain Bukinin himself continued to rage openly, cursing Estonians, Ukrainians, Georgians, and a dozen other groups that Madeira suspected weren't even represented in the ship's crew. Novikoff, for his part, continued to burn silently, trying hard not to show it.

And Chernov?

Chernov seemed to have already forgotten the whole matter.

Once the price of revolt had been levied and collected from the crew, Rustoff's death, just as Viktoria had predicted, seemed destined to be reduced to an exercise in paperwork.

Which made him even more uneasy.

Then Novikoff had mentioned that metal shavings were found in the gearboxes of half a dozen deck winches—undoubtedly put there to disable the very winches he would need to raise the wreck.

There were no suspects. At least not yet.

"That was a very good drill we had in the Beluga," observed Madeira, turning back toward Timon and trying to shift his thoughts to the positive side of the ledger.

"Yes it was. You're now right at home in it."

"Do you see any reason we can't use her in place of the habitat for saturation diving?"

"No. None at all. That was one of her designers' intentions."

Timon smiled a strange little smile as he said it.

"Is there something you wanted to add?"

"Speaking for myself, I am very happy you don't intend to use the habitat. It's a coffin!"

Madeira glanced around again to reassure himself there really were no TV cameras in sight. Hell, he thought. It's impossible to cover every single space in a ship this size. Even for the Russians.

Which didn't mean there wasn't a listening device of some sort.

"Boris," he asked, "is it really money the sailors are so unhappy about?"

"That is what I understand," Timon replied carefully.

"You say that as if you're from another planet; as if you're not aboard the same ship as they are."

"We're navy, sir. They're not. We understand our duty. Their objectives and motivations are confused. We don't mingle much with them, either."

Madeira already knew the divers were naval personnel while most of *Asimov*'s crew were not. He'd assumed some sort of gulf would exist, but Boris's tone gave him pause.

"What about Mr. Chernov?"

"He's a merchant officer. Just like Captain Bukinin. They both also have reserve naval commissions."

"Are all your merchant officers like them?"

"They are all employed by the state. . . ."

"Are they all like Chernov?"

Now it was Timon's turn to look around. "No. Most are not like him. Many are forceful men, but few go as far as he does . . . as often."

"Will they do their jobs?" Madeira asked, not wishing to force Timon to say any more about his superiors. "While we're underwater, will the sailors attend to business? On the wreck?"

"Yes. I think so."

"Are you all combat swimmers?"

Boris considered his answer. "No, sir. I am what you would call a salvage diver. Like you. Grivski and Mendalov are 'special.' They're not as experienced at salvage and deep diving as I am, but Captain Novikoff feels they'll prove their worth. As you know, this is a very sensitive operation. I understand he is especially worried about the reactor's fuel, the plutonium."

Madeira'd wondered about Grivski and Mendalov ever since he'd gotten his first close look at them at the airport. He now began to wonder about Boris as well. His English was very good—too good, he asked himself, for a run-of-the-mill Russian Bubblehead?

"Did you serve in Afghanistan?"

"No. My services were not needed. Despite our most heroic efforts, the Soviet navy failed to sink any of its own ships there."

Thanks to Timon's deadpan tone and expression it took Madeira a second or two to register the joke. Then he burst into laughter along with the Russian diver.

Still laughing, Madeira looked around the reel well. Although the ship's sides were rusting and her bottom badly fouled, her diving gear was all clean and polished. Most was also totally up to date and ready for immediate use. The Russians knew as much as he did about caring for the equipment. They also seemed to know perfectly damn well how to use it.

So why was he worth one million dollars to them? The question had continued to nag him for weeks now and he was no closer to a reasonable answer.

Well, he wouldn't push it. It wouldn't be the first time he'd had to conduct an operation about which others knew more than he.

"I'd really hoped to spend a few days in St. Petersburg," he remarked to Boris. "Captain Novikoff was going to give me a tour."

"Yes," replied the big, blond diver with renewed enthusiasm, the hole left by his two missing teeth now clearly visible. "I'm from St. Petersburg, too. Just like Captain Novikoff. It's a very interesting and beautiful city. The museums, the parks and palaces, the Neva. You would have learned much about us . . . but it may be just as well for you to wait for summer. Even I find the city cold and dreary at this time of year."

There was another rumbling thump, then *Asimov* lurched again. This time it felt to Madeira as if the whole ship were skidding sideways down the face of a huge wave.

The phone buzzed.

We're turning around again! thought Madeira as he watched Boris pick up the receiver. Why the hell are we turning around in the middle of the Strait of Dover?

"Captain Novikoff would like you on the bridge, sir."

There was almost a sense of relief in Boris's voice, thought Madeira. As if the Russian were happy to be rid of him, or to end the conversation, at any rate.

"Very well. Tell him I'm on my way."

"Can you believe it, Al?" Novikoff shouted as Madeira stepped onto *Asimov*'s huge, windswept bridge. "They're trying to cancel the operation!"

"They're not trying, Captain," Bukinin said with a look of satisfaction at Novikoff's discomfort, "they *have* canceled it. We've been ordered to return to Kronshtadt."

Novikoff looked at Bukinin, a snarl on his lips. "We have *not* been ordered to return! Not yet. We've been advised to be prepared to return if so directed after the President and his advisers finish their reevaluation of the recent elections."

"The Russian people have spoken," Bukinin replied dryly, "and if Yeltsin had any honor he would resign immediately and move to America. And take his fat-assed advisers with him. Let real Russians run Russia."

"I tell you again, Captain Bukinin, we have *not* been ordered to return. You are anticipating what will not happen. As overall commander of this operation, I order you to turn west again!"

At first, neither of them moved. Then both turned, almost simultaneously, and looked at Viktoria as if the final decision was hers to make.

"I found the message very imprecise," she finally said, her voice softened by the collar of her parka, into which she was speaking. "However, I tend to agree with Captain Novikoff. We have not, yet, been ordered to return. I've also found that prudence does wonders for one's longevity. I think it would be prudent for us to turn back and request immediate clarification."

"Why would they recall us?" Madeira wondered aloud. "Have they changed their minds about the whole thing, or is it that sailor Chernov killed?"

Bukinin laughed contemptously. "No, Captain, nobody cares about that criminal being shot. He was of no significance. A flea. A tick. It is a matter of state. Many of our most clear-eyed leaders disagree with Yeltsin. They see absolutely no reason to bow and scrape before your government."

"You're a fool, Bukinin," Novikoff said. "A fool and a fascist."

Madeira looked off to port at the huge, foaming seas and the distant, dirty-white cliffs. The sky was clearing rapidly and the wind was screeching to beat hell. In another hour they would've been through the Strait, out into the Channel, and headed more or less southwest on their final leg to the New World.

Would they *really* cancel the operation? Anything's possible with this gang, he decided.

If they did, he reasoned, he'd be off the hook! A surge of anguished relief swept through him. Freed from this nightmare ship. Freed from the obligation to go down again.

Then a shudder, all sense of relief fleeing before it as he caught himself, embarrassed by his own thoughts. He didn't like either the ship or the project anymore, but he'd set a task for himself and he'd carry it out, damnit!

Looking outside, he spotted the plume of spray as it erupted far off the port quarter, midway between *Asimov* and the cliffs. At first he assumed it was a rock. Then he realized it was a patrol vessel turning in the brutal seas, mimicking *Asimov*'s maneuvers. She had to be British, he realized after spotting the white ensign snapping at her truck.

It was all very simple, he told himself. If he failed to recover the reactor the world would end. The whales' world and his own.

He glanced up at the TV camera. The camera stared back with an indifference as icy as any Bukinin had shown. It cared no more about his world than it did about that of the whales.

"Latrines, Sergei, latrines!" said Oleg Markovich, almost shouting in his bitterness. "In some units even *senior* lieutenants, like you, are cleaning latrines!"

"The world has changed, Major, and so must we."

"Clearly it has, Sergei, and, as you can see, it confuses even me at times . . . but we must remember, despite the current humiliations we suffer, that so long as we wear these uniforms our duty remains unchanged. To do what is best for Russia . . . Russia must always come first!"

As he spoke, the major looked aft through the open stern of the floating dry dock. Out of sight, just over the horizon, lay the Canary Islands. And beyond them, Africa. "I've served so many years. . . . But you are right, life is like war. We can't afford to be sentimental, to continue to follow obsolete tactics. We must act when it's time to act, and we must adapt! All the same, and remember this well, our objective does not change!"

"I understand and totally agree, Major."

"Good. Then also remember that if we are confused at times the men are even more confused. Our principal duty these days as officers is to keep the men on course."

Sergei nodded his continued agreement. "Have you decided yet about Kardon?"

"Yes. I'm convinced he's gone bad; he's in deep with one of the St. Petersburg gangs and he's tried to recruit at least two others to join him."

"Do you plan to court-martial him?"

"No. The normal procedures can't be trusted these days. I'll do something about him."

The two naval commando officers stood in silence a few moments, looking out over the choppy gray Atlantic, as the great, boxlike dry dock was dragged slowly, reluctantly, westward by an equally boxlike black tug.

"We have a long trip ahead of us," Markovich said suddenly, turning toward his subordinate. "Remember, keep your men occupied. Otherwise, they'll become bored and careless and get us all into trouble."

"Yes, Major."

"And keep them away from vodka. The tug's crew is bound to have cases of it.

"Yes, Major."

"Very well. Now reassemble your boat crew and return to the tug."

Chapter Eleven

Viktoria watched the image standing in the lee of lifeboat number three, waving its hands and shifting its great weight from foot to foot as it appeared to harangue four sailors. Its back was turned most of the time and her view was often obscured by the wind-driven snow. Still, there was no doubt that she was looking at Karl Rustoff, his huge beard swaying like an elephant's trunk. Although his body was long gone, he remained alive and well in her file of digitalized videos.

As Madeira had noticed, nobody usually monitored the many TV cameras positioned all over the ship, but that didn't mean they weren't on duty. Each and every one of them was operating, twenty-four hours a day, and each was feeding all it saw into the ship's extensive computer system.

Viktoria could only guess at precisely what Rustoff was saying, but she felt certain it was inflammatory. His gestures gave it away. And his animation. And his record. He'd been a minor troublemaker for years. A bigmouth. Why, she wondered, had he been selected for this operation? Was it a beauracratic screwup or was it his almost pure Russian genes that had gotten him aboard?

Take this footage out of context, as would almost certainly be done, mix in a few reasonable assumptions along with the sorry details of Rustoff's record, and Chernov was off the hook, she decided. In fact, if Zhirinovsky and his gang of radical nationalists really had gained as much as they seemed to have in the election, then Yeltsin might well be history in a few weeks. With Zhirinovsky running things, Chernov might even turn out to be a national hero!

She dumped the image, then the whole program, and turned to stare out the pitch-black port.

Nothing!

It was past four in the morning, and although they were now in the Bay of Biscay, rather than the North Sea, the wind and sea were still pounding hard on the ship . . . and her nerves.

She'd spent the past ten hours looking at videos and still knew absolutely nothing she hadn't known before.

Ten hours of sailors. Sailors talking. Sailors working. Sailors sleeping and eating and picking their noses. Laughing sailors. Angry sailors. Bored sailors. Individual sailors and sailors in groups. None bothered to even glance at the cameras except Al Madeira, who kept shaking his head in disgust every time he looked into one.

And out of all that footage no suspicious gatherings, not one hint of who the mutiny's ringleaders were or who'd committed the sabotage. She should have known it would lead to nothing. The videos were good only for confirming what was already suspected or in the rare case that some moron committed an offense directly in front of a camera.

She'd known it would lead to nothing, but she'd had to try it anyway because nothing else was leading anywhere either.

It should have been easy. One of her informants should have been able to identify the ringleaders . . . or the individual perpetrators, at the very least.

But they couldn't. Or wouldn't.

Nobody had seen anything. Nobody knew anything. There didn't appear to be any leadership. It was as if the seeds had been sown by the wind and then left to germinate, sprout, and bloom on their own.

Damnit! she thought as she fiddled with a small black tektite, one of the few personal souvenirs she carried with her.

But none of *Asimov*'s troubles had been random or spur-of-the-moment. Somebody had thought it out. The saboteurs had disabled only machinery that wasn't covered by a TV camera. It had all been planned. Except Rustoff's death. That may not have been anticipated.

There were over one hundred officers, sailors, and scientists aboard *Asimov*. Every one was competent and every one had more than enough opportunity, especially if several were working together.

She'd carefully reviewed their KGB records, which she kept buried in the ship's computer mixed in with her geophysical data. Most had been carefully chosen for the project, and yet every one now seemed to have *something* in his or her past, or present.

Greed. Ambition. A relative who'd disappeared late one night. Friends who'd shown a little too much appreciation for Western values. Even Olga. But then, she was a physician.

She thought of her own parents, of her father who was sentenced to twenty years at one of the labor camps in Asian Russia and proved to be one of the few who ever returned.

He returned, all right. Reformed and rehabilitated after only five years because his skills were needed for the advancement of the State. And he was never the same again.

But it was her mother whom they'd destroyed. The fear, the uncertainty, the indignities and contempt heaped upon her by the authorities, the bitter struggle to keep herself and her young daughter, Viktoria, from having to live in the gutter.

Goddamn them! she thought in a rising fury.

Them? Who was them? she asked herself for the millionth time. She was always tempted to blame the Russians but knew it was far bigger than them. It was the system. The brutality had always been there, from time immemorial, but it was that great Georgian—not Russian—statesman, Joseph Vissarionovich Djugashvili, known to history as Joseph Stalin, who'd extended and institutionalized the franchise.

She found herself clutching the edges of the desk, the blood in her head pounding.

She had to get control of herself! If the past was to be prevented from returning, then she, and others like her, had to keep chaos at bay until freedom and justice and decency could be reestablished.

She took several very deep breaths and forced her hands to relax. Then she forced her mind back from the grand scheme of things to the more immediate problems of mutiny and sabotage.

No one could be considered totally above suspicion when the future, like a loose American football, bounced wildly all over the field, eluding everybody's firm grasp. Everything was wide open. Everything was up for grabs. A new order was coming and the possibilities were limitless.

She wished those facing her at the moment weren't quite so limitless.

If today were yesterday, she thought with bitter irony, and I were somebody else, I'd round up another two dozen suspects and have the answers beaten out of them.

It was an approach tried and true and still much in use . . . but not by her. It was simply not part of the new Russia she hoped she'd live to see.

Unfortunately, she wasn't the boss on *Asimov* any more than she had been in New York. When told to do so, Grivski was, as always, more than pleased to handle the details. The only thing he'd managed to learn, however, was that Rustoff and his golden tongue had single-handedly engineered the revolt . . . and that much of the crew liked neither Yeltsin nor Zhirinovsky, nor Chernov for that matter.

And that was all he'd been able to get out of them without resorting to more sophisticated methods. Methods that Novikoff had prohibited. For the time being.

She stood a moment to let the blood flow back into her

legs and felt the ship roll slightly, then slip slowly sideways down the faces of the beam seas. Was it organized political dissidents she was dealing with? Out to make a fool of Yeltsin?

Or was it a hundred angry sailors demanding a minimum of fair play and eager to avenge seventy—make that seven hundred—years of abuse?

Whatever the cause, she decided, the ship was a bomb, primed and waiting to detonate. So was the whole operation, for that matter. Thrown together in confused haste, its risks equal to, if not greater than, its rewards.

She wondered if Novikoff possessed enough self-control to pull it all off. Then, wondering precisely what she was going to do if he didn't, Viktoria walked over to the neighboring desk, picked up the phone, and dialed a three-digit number.

"Captain, this is Galin. I haven't been able to find anything of use to us. Not in the files, not on the videos . . ."

She listened a moment, then sighed. "At this time, everybody aboard the ship is a suspect. Except you and me, of course, and Al Madeira."

Again she listened. "No," she finally said, "I simply don't see how it would be possible for him to be involved."

As she spoke she felt like laughing. Madeira was probably the only sane person aboard the whole ship. And one of the two or three honest ones.

"Tell me, Captain," Timon asked as Madeira carefully examined one of the SeaFairy ROVs, "are all retired American naval persons able to find good jobs like yours?"

"You mean this one?" Madeira said, looking up from the three-foot-long ROV, which resembled a small torpedo with a proportionately small lobster pot mounted on the front.

"No." Timon laughed. "Even a stupid Russian sailor like me knows the pay you're getting for this is unusual, even for an American. . . . I mean your job back home . . ."

"I have that job because I own part of the boat, along with several of my relatives. I understand there're many

129

fishermen in Russia who own boats with their families. . . ."

"Do you like it?"

Madeira looked down again at the ROV. Two months earlier he'd felt whale watching was growing a little tedious. A week earlier, slogging across the Bay of Biscay with an awful head cold and feeling almost totally isolated and alone, it'd looked pretty good. But now, with *Asimov* transiting the Sargasso Sea and Puerto Rico only a day or so away, he found his enthusiasm returning.

"Yes, I do. It gets a little boring at times, but there are no midwatches and the pay's good. It's a good thing to be able to go back to. Why do you ask?"

"I worry. Many of us worry. Our army and navy are being cut back even more than yours, I think, and there are no jobs. None at all. I have a wife and two daughters. . . . My wife works in a cannery and makes almost nothing. Without my pay all four of us will starve, just like in the days of the Tzar."

Madeira glanced up at the TV camera and wondered uneasily if Timon was angling for a career in espionage.

"I say nothing they don't already know," Timon said, waving his hand to brush aside Madeira's concern. "All of Russia agrees what the problem is. It's agreeing on the best solution that causes trouble."

"Everything seems to be changing the last few years," replied Madeira, very uncomfortable with the lameness of the non-answer he was about to offer. "Everywhere! I've been lucky, so far. I picked my relatives well. Let's just hope all this change does really bring new opportunities. If it does, I think you're just the sort of guy to find yours."

"I hope so, Captain."

"You will. And your daughters will have wonderful lives. Now, about these SeaFairies . . . They're very small."

"Yes, they are."

"What sort of videos do they provide? Aren't they too small to hold steady?"

"They're a little shaky sometimes, but they're very useful. They can get in where bigger units can't. I think we will end up using them a great deal the next few weeks."

"Just let me tell you, Mr. Avalaridze," the big, blond yacht broker mispronounced the name with total confidence in a deep, rich southern drawl, "that if you go with *Velociraptor* here you're making one hell of a good choice. Frankly, she's going to impress the shit out of them back-country citrus growers. . . ."

Standing on the foredeck of the ninety-seven-foot Maxi yacht, Niko smiled back at the man, then continued to view the midmorning scenery. As they glided out Government Cut, the entrance to the main channel into the Port of Miami, the southern tip of Miami Beach was to port. To starboard lay tony and exclusive Fisher Island. Ahead, open all the way to Europe, or Africa, depending on your objective, lay the Atlantic, resting now under the gentlest of breezes.

The broker waved to the pilothouse's tinted windows, jet black from this angle as were all the huge, rectangular windows along the Maxi's sides. "Hang on, sir," he shouted.

Niko grabbed the lifeline just in time as the Maxi's four huge turbocharged engines, generating a total of almost four thousand horsepower, burst to life and the yacht turned sharply to starboard.

"As you can see," the broker shouted, "you've got plenty of power and speed. Over sixty knots in four- to six-foot seas. Good seakeeping, too. Roomy quarters below for entertaining, and lots of style! *Velociraptor* was built to an Italian design. The Continental look—long, sleek, fast, and elegant—is very much in fashion these days."

The Georgian citrus merchant nodded his understanding. What he couldn't get over were the colors. The greens and blues and whites. So totally different from the world into which he was born.

It was all so totally different!

He thought back to his childhood, spent on the outskirts of Tbilisi. Unpaved roads, stinking mud in the summer, icy mud in the winter, and a dismal shack that had housed six families, none of which ever seemed to have enough food.

The Soviets had given him so little and yet, he now realized, had provided more than enough. They had taught him to read. And, through their corruption, incompetence, and utterly misguided determination to prohibit everything, they had taught him and everybody else to need.

Driven by his own needs, guided by a sharper-than-average perception, he had quickly learned the value of others' needs. Biological needs. Material needs. Emotional needs. Needs so great as to seem limitless. And every need represented an opportunity. Wealth and power were to be obtained simply by satisfying the needs of others; those needs that they were too stupid, too lazy, or too timid to satisfy for themselves.

As for *Velociraptor*, he'd already determined that she would suit his purposes perfectly. The cargo weighed only about a ton and a half. He could distribute it among the fancy cabins for the short trip to the rendezvous with Saddam's people.

"What's the story about this yacht's owner?" he asked the broker.

"It's a sad one," replied the broker as sweat began to form on his big, blond mustache and sunburned forehead. "In a way, the boat turned on him and ate him. He ran into a little business difficulty, something with the Customs Service, and his expenses, mainly lawyers, soon grew to be more than his income, which was dropping fast at that point. In the end, as it turns out, it was the cost of maintaining *Velociraptor* that pushed him over the edge. His lawyers beat the Customs people, but he ended up in bankruptcy court. The court has hired me to dispose of her."

"I'm sorry to hear that. I guess he just wasn't the big player he thought he was."

"I guess not."

"Then the court is willing for her to be chartered to me?"

"The court's objective was to sell her, and I have a customer for her if I can charter her for a year or two for him."

"Well, then. I wish to charter her for eighteen months.

132

. . . Did you say ninety-five thousand a month?''

"Yes, that's the number. Will you require a captain? The current owner's captain," and as he spoke, the broker nodded at the pilothouse, "is available. So's the engineer."

"No, thank you. We will provide our own personnel if that is satisfactory with the new owner. Our captain is fully licensed. . . ."

"I'm sure it's no problem," exhaled the broker, already calculating the double commission, one on the charter and one on the sale, "since this is a bare-boat charter. When do you wish to take possession?"

"Just as soon as possible. We have a great deal of entertaining to do."

"This is certainly the boat to do it on!"

"How far is it from here to Key West?" Niko asked.

"Key West? About a hundred and fifty miles."

"Then we could be there in three hours?"

"Yes. Very close."

"I've never been there. Why don't we take a run down there and seal our deal over lunch. Is that possible?"

The broker looked a little skeptical, although he refused to drop his smile. "Let me talk to the captain a moment. . . ."

"I'm more than willing to pay for all the operating expenses, the fuel, the captain's pay, whatever is called for."

"That's very generous of you, sir. I'm sure we can work something out."

Twenty minutes later, *Velociraptor* was abeam of Fowey Rocks and thundering south. Ahead lay Hawk Channel, the passage that runs between the Keys to the west and their shallow but still-submerged outer reefs to the east.

Niko continued to stand in the bow, looking southeast, in the direction of Puerto Rico. It's all coming together so nicely, he thought.

He smiled. He was growing to like America, already beginning to think of it as home. Who knows? Someday he might even find his own name on the Forbes list of richest Americans.

He decided to look into becoming an American citizen.

133

Chapter Twelve

The small black dot flashed occasionally in the crisp morning light as it skipped silently toward them over the gently rolling blue waters. Madeira stood on the boat deck and watched it approach, squinting as he did and wishing he had a pair of binoculars.

Puerto Rico was barely in sight, no more than a gray bump in the horizon, its mountains still more cloud than stone and soil. The pilot boat was undoubtedly still moored securely to its dock, the pilot enjoying a cup of *tinto,* or perhaps Coca-Cola. And yet *they,* and it had to be *they,* were not only well on their way but almost there.

Curious how the Russians would handle their first exposure to the news media they so obviously hated and feared, he walked forward to the first of the several ladders he would have to climb to reach the bridge.

"*Asimov, Asimov,* this is helicopter November Echo Seven Eight Three Four Six," intoned the radio on the research ship's bridge. "Stand by to receive me."

Novikoff turned to Madeira, who'd just stepped into the

pilothouse. "What does he mean 'stand by'? We haven't given him permission to land! He hasn't even asked for permission. Is he official? Coast Guard? Customs? Police?"

"No, he's not official. If he were he'd identify himself more fully."

"Then who the hell is he?"

As Novikoff spoke, Madeira watched Captain Bukinin pick up a telephone and start shouting Russian into it.

"Reporters, Mike. The press."

"How do you know?"

"Anybody else would have identified himself and asked permission to land. They're trying to catch us off guard, to get aboard before we have time to hide anything."

Novikoff snarled something in Russian, then picked up the radio mike: "This is the Russian Federated Republic research ship *Asimov* calling the helicopter approaching us. . . . Stay away! You do not have permission to land."

There was a whooshing fan-roar as the helo came in fast and dipped down low over the ship, only to rise again and glide off a short distance to the east, leaving a trail of ruffled water behind it.

"*Asimov,* this is November Echo Seven Eight Three Four Six. Request you clear those personnel off the pad so I can land!" The speaker, probably the pilot, thought Madeira, sounded as if he had a southern accent and a mouthful of bubble gum. He also sounded as if he were still in Vietnam, barking orders at gooks.

Madeira glanced aft and almost laughed at the flock of Russian sailors milling around on the pad. Hands in pockets and dressed in their parka-less tropical outfits, which were composed of whatever they had lying around, they were making it totally impossible for the helo to land. Some of them were smiling and even laughing. It had become a game to them. Much as Madeira hated to admit it, Bukinin had come up with a good solution to the press problem.

"Mike," said Madeira, "may I talk to them? I may be able to get rid of them."

"They should be arrested and shot," Bukinin shouted. "I

will shoot them down if they come back again!"

Unfortunately, thought Madeira, the son of a bitch wouldn't hesitate to do it.

"Captain, I agree we don't want them aboard the ship, but we can't go overboard. If we start shooting at them they're really going to be suspicious."

"You're absolutely right," Novikoff replied, a look of crafty concern replacing the angry discomfort that had dominated his face. "They're as much of a threat to the operation if they're too suspicious as they are if they actually get aboard. Please see what you can do."

Madeira stepped out onto the wing of the bridge and looked up. Good! Quebec, the solid yellow flag indicating the ship was under quarantine, was already flying. He stepped back into the pilothouse and picked up the mike.

"November Echo Seven Eight Three Four Six, this is *Asimov*. Be advised that this vessel is still under quarantine and that it is illegal for you to land until we have received pratique. Be further advised that we will be holding a news conference at seven P.M."

He was certain they already knew about the news conference, since it'd been scheduled for weeks, but he wanted to appear as friendly and reasonable as possible. For the sake of the operation.

In fact, he would just as soon see them all in hell. Al Madeira both disliked and distrusted the media. They, a number of them anyway, had gone out of their way to crucify him on those occasions when he'd come to their attention.

Don't flatter yourself, he thought. There was nothing personal about it. They were unaware of you as a person. You were no more than a blob of raw material to be shaped to their purposes, which often seemed to have little to do with objective truth.

At first the helo didn't respond. It just hovered about a hundred feet off the water, vibrating. Then it banked and slid around behind *Asimov*. It continued forward until it assumed station abeam and to leeward, still about a hundred feet off the water and matching the ship's forward speed of seventeen knots.

That stupid bastard! thought Madeira as he watched the copter tilt suddenly forward and dart toward *Asimov*'s broad fo'c'sle platform. He glanced quickly at Bukinin, ready to restrain the captain from opening fire, but the helo's move had been too quick. Before Bukinin could grab a weapon or shout an order over the PA system, the helo was hovering a few feet above the platform and three figures, one with flaming red hair, had jumped down and were stumbling across the platform out from under the rotor's furious downdraft.

Jesus! It was right out of *Apocalypse Now*. How the hell had the pilot avoided all the antennas and stanchions? Madeira continued to wonder as the helo tilted forward and shot off to windward. Then he noticed that Bukinin was shouting into the phone again.

"These people are criminals!" Bukinin shouted as he hung up the phone. "They will wish they never did this!"

As Bukinin raged, Madeira noticed the faintest hint of a smile skip across the helmsman's face. Then, looking forward, he could already see Chief Officer Chernov leading an armed party toward the uninvited guests.

"Please, Captain! We've got to jolly these jerks along. We can't overreact! If you rough them up they'll stick with us every second of every day until they find out why you did it."

"Silence!" Bukinin snarled. "I never wanted you aboard my ship, and I have no interest in your opinions!"

"Bukinin!" The voice cracked like a whip. So icy was it that it took Madeira a moment to realize it was Novikoff's. He stepped back and watched as the Russian naval officer, hands clasped behind his back, walked slowly toward the civilian captain.

Bukinin turned and glowered at him. "Yes, Captain Novikoff?"

"Do I have to remind you, again, of the supreme importance of this operation," Novikoff asked in a voice so calm as to be beyond fury, "and the importance of Captain Madeira to it?"

Bukinin started to reply but was cut off by one look into Novikoff's eyes.

"You would be well advised to remember that I can have you relieved at any time. I will not hesitate to send you home for insubordination."

Bukinin continued a glower for a moment, his face growing redder with every passing second. Then he turned away, seeming to stare forward, at the press, who was now surrounded by Chernov's party, and at the green-black smudge growing rapidly along the horizon. "What is it that you want done?"

"I'm going to ask Al to explain what he thinks should be done. If it seems reasonable to me we'll do it."

Bukinin continued to face forward, staring fixedly out over the bows and saying nothing.

"What did you have in mind, Al?" Novikoff asked, turning away from Bukinin's back.

"To make the best of a bad situation . . . A warm welcome and a guided tour," Madeira replied as he and Novikoff joined Bukinin in looking out over the bow. "We'll show them the labs. We'll let them crawl into the habitat and even try on a diving dress if they want. We'll show them everything and explain every detail. I'll describe the research program. . . . Even better, Viktoria can do that. They'll love her!

"We'll be in and anchored long before we finish, and they'll be desperate to get ashore with their scoop."

"Um . . ." Novikoff said. "Are you sure you can control the tour?"

"Yes. And even if one of them does wander off there's nothing aboard this ship, except maybe the pipe cutter, which even hints at our mission!"

"What *about* the pipe cutter?"

"Only an expert would know what it is, and even he wouldn't know how we're going to use it."

"If they *do* see it?"

"I'll tell them it's a . . ."

"A laser-based precision seismograph."

Novikoff and Madeira turned, startled slightly to find Viktoria standing behind them.

"I was going to say a geological sample cutter," remarked Madeira, "but I like Viktoria's idea better."

"Yes," Novikoff said, a small smile of relief crossing his face. "I would believe either story. I think."

"Hell!" Madeira snapped as he glanced forward again. "You'd better call off Chernov before he does something really stupid!"

Novikoff followed his glance and saw Chernov fiddling with his holster as his party approached the interlopers, who had stopped with their backs to the ship's huge anchor winch. Eyes wide, the Russian officer jumped to the bulkhead and grabbed the PA system mike. A thunder of rapid Russian boomed out in all directions.

"What did you say?" Madeira asked.

"He told Mr. Chernov to welcome our guests and escort them to the main salon for tea and a brief overview of our project," explained Viktoria, "to be followed by a tour of the ship."

"The sailors!" Madeira said, a look of alarm passing across his face. "I forgot about them. They'll want to talk to the crew!"

"I thought you're going to keep them in the habitat."

"Al's right," Viktoria said. "Several common sailors—dependable people, of course—must be available to them. They won't be satisfied by just hardware."

"Just don't make them too available," Madeira remarked with a smile. "I'm sure they'll want to root out the facts for themselves."

As he heard his own words, he wondered if maybe he'd been around the Russians for too long already.

"Al," Meg Jefferson said sharply as he started to explain the Beluga worksub's capabilities, "I've seen these before, been down in one, in fact. One just like it, anyway. You've got all sorts of neat toys here and Viktoria's dynamite, but we're not here for technology. I want to know what's really going on in Russia and what the crew of this ship thinks about it. Is there going to be a coup? A civil war? I want meat!''

Madeira straightened up and looked at her. Flaming red hair. Hands on cocked hips. She should be strutting around in Congress, he thought. Or on TV.

Then he laughed to himself. From what she said, she was on TV at least once a week! As a commentator of some sort.

''All right. Let's go find some sailors to talk to. Do any of you speak Russian?''

''Yes,'' Meg said, a small look of triumph on her face. ''Hal speaks some.'' As she spoke, she nodded toward the other reporter.

''Good. Many of them speak English, but sometimes they're a little hard to follow.''

''We'll pick them. I especially want to talk to that dickhead who started to pull a pistol on me.''

''Okay. You find them, but I've still got to be with you.''

''What the hell are you, the warden? Or just some sort of window dressing?''

''I'm the deep operations director . . . and I also seem to have some liaison responsibilities.''

''Who do you really work for? Not that you'd ever tell me the truth!''

''I'm retired, you know. At the moment I'm working for the Russian Federation, the All-Russia Oceanographic Institution.''

''They want you to keep an eye on us!''

''They don't need me to do that,'' Madeira replied, pointing at the TV camera mounted over their heads. ''They're just as up-to-date as we are.''

Madeira paused and checked his watch. He'd give himself ten more minutes. Then he'd get back to help Viktoria.

Meg and her two pals, escorted by Viktoria, were busy

interrogating a half-dozen sailors about their political preferences. The harbor pilot had come aboard. The ship would soon be passing between Cabra Island and Morro Castle and on into her anchorage in San Juan Bay. And Novikoff needed Madeira's passport for Immigration.

He took a deep breath and sprinted the length of one passageway, then down a ladder, and finally along the passageway on which his stateroom was located.

Puffing slightly, he stopped at his door and reached in his pocket for the key. As he did he heard something. A whisper-faint shuffling sound. And it seemed to be coming through the door.

Shit! he thought at first. There's a goddamn rat in my room. Then he heard a loud *thunk* and knew it was no rat.

Furious, he grabbed the door handle and twisted it, shoving the door inward as he did, thinking he was about to catch some petty thief in the act.

The door flew open, and there was Vasily Chernov sitting at his desk, sorting through his papers.

"What the hell are you doing there, Mr. Chernov?" he snarled as he lunged through the door.

Chernov turned slowly, trying to hide his surprise behind a weak smile. "I need the specifications for the lifting wire assemblies, Captain. My men will soon be putting them together, and you were very busy showing the journalists around."

"How'd you get in?"

Chernov's expression turned to one of smug amusement. "Captain, I am the chief officer of this vessel. I have master keys for almost all of the spaces aboard her."

"Get out!" Madeira snapped. "I'll get the liftwire plans to you in plenty of time."

"Of course, Captain."

"And from now on, if you want something, ask for it!"

"Of course, Captain," Chernov replied cheerfully as he rose and walked out the door.

Madeira slammed the door shut, then returned to his desk. At least the bastard hadn't made a mess of it. All he'd done, in fact, was pull out the sub's plans. It almost looked as if he'd been studying them.

It was more obvious, however, that he hadn't been studying the liftwire plans, which were still in their file folder.

Then he remembered the passport and looked at his watch. He had to get back to Viktoria!

He unlocked the desk's one locking drawer and removed the passport. Then he locked the drawer and, after taking one more look at the papers on the desk, turned and stepped out the door, which he carefully locked after him. Just out of habit.

The noon sun was beating down hard on San Juan Bay's mirrorlike surface when Meg stormed back out on deck, Madeira and her two associates trailing behind. *Asimov* was moored, her anchor chain as limp as the yellow quarantine flag hanging from the yard, the pilot long gone, and Madeira already missed the wind that had been tormenting them for almost two weeks.

"Okay," she said, not bothering to turn to Madeira as she spoke to him. "We didn't hit any home runs, but we got a few singles and a double or two. Like I said, Viktoria's world class and Mike's not bad either."

"I'm glad if you're glad."

"It's a start."

There was something about Al Madeira that Meg Jefferson did not like. Unfortunately, Madeira could not for the life of him figure out exactly what it was, unless she suspected that he didn't like her, either.

Pondering the question, he looked north at Old San Juan wrapped across the mouth of the bay, and watched as the Customs launch headed toward them. It couldn't arrive too soon, he thought, tiring rapidly of his new career in flackery.

He noticed a small speedboat slicing toward them from the south, from the direction of the Bacardi Rum factory. It was coming fast, trailing a tall rooster tail and a broad, creamy wake, and he couldn't see any sign of a girl in a bikini or of water skis.

"Will you be at the press conference tonight?"

"Wouldn't miss it for the world," she replied.

Suddenly Uribe, the press photographer, dashed for the rail and threw a yellow bundle over the side. Within seconds, the speedboat turned sharply across *Asimov*'s bow and shot down her side. As the boat screamed past, one of her crew leaned far over and snatched the bundle with a large fishnet.

"Yes!" Meg shouted, doing a little dance and punching at the hot sun with her clenched fist.

"That was very dramatic," remarked Madeira after she'd calmed down. "Do you always end your interviews that way?"

"We do what we have to do. We can't always count on our subjects' cooperation.

"And there're others who just don't get it either," she added in an ominous tone.

"Then you really do think you got something worth getting today?"

"Like I said, it's a start . . . and before I'm finished I'll find out why you're really here."

While Madeira struggled to breathe normally, the Customs launch pulled alongside the ship's lowered gangway. Two men in uniform jumped across to the stage and started the long climb up the gangway.

When the two officials reached the deck they were greeted by Bukinin, who somehow managed a faint smile, and a jovial Novikoff. The Public Health officer went off with the two captains while his companion, a small man whose mustache was as crisp and trim as the crease on his trousers, walked aft to Madeira.

"*Bienvenido a Puerto Rico*, Captain Madeira," said the dapper little Customs officer, nodding his head ever so slightly.

"*Muchas gracias, señor,*" Madeira replied, stumbling slightly in his accent and wondering why he rated such a special welcome.

"I have read of your past adventures. It is an honor to

meet you." He spoke English with a noticeable Castilian lisp.

"And you, Ms. Jefferson! What a surprise to find you already here. This is the third, and last, time you do this to me and Dr. Ribera."

"What, Mr. Perez? What do you think you can do? Arrest us for breaking quarantine? That's been tried."

"Shortly before we came alongside we observed one of your party throwing a parcel overboard. Since this vessel has not yet cleared into San Juan, I am forced to assume that the parcel was some sort of contraband . . . very possibly narcotics."

Meg Jefferson burst into laughter. "You're going to arrest *us* for drug smuggling?"

"*Suspicion* of drug smuggling, *señora*. Until the matter is clarified. Until I am satisfied concerning the contents of that parcel, yes." He pronounced it "jess."

"Cut the crap, Perez! You know perfectly goddamn well we're not drug smugglers!"

"All I know, Ms. Jefferson, is that certain journalists do not believe the laws apply to them. You are not to leave this ship, you and these other two, except with me. In my launch!"

Perez then nodded to Madeira, turned, and sauntered forward.

"Sorry," Madeira said as he watched a single-engine plane drone into the airport.

"Fuck him!" Meg responded. "Where's the radio? I've got to call my editor."

After guiding Meg and her party to the bridge, Madeira stepped out onto the wing and idly stuck his right hand into his pants pocket.

There was something in there that hadn't been before! He withdrew his hand and found a folded piece of paper. It was a note from Charlie Nash. A suggestion that they meet while he was in San Juan.

How, he wondered, had Perez done it? The man was an absolute magician! A master at sleight of hand.

Chapter Thirteen

"I might add," Viktoria said to her audience of journalists, "that these volcanic microvents we hope to study are quite transitory. As the tectonic plates continue to shift, existing vents are closed off and new ones open. Thus—"

"Is it true," interrupted a nasal voice from the back of the room, "that a mutiny occurred during your trip from St. Petersburg? Was it politically motivated? Would you care to comment on it?"

While Viktoria paused, changing gears, Madeira scanned the four rows of folding chairs but was unable to match a face with the voice.

"Yes," replied the geophysicist, "I'm very sorry to say we did have a labor dispute concerning pay. Perhaps it would be best if Captain Novikoff—"

"What about the man who was killed?" demanded the voice.

"One of our sailors, a member of the ship's engineering department, assaulted Captain Bukinin," Novikoff said with surprising smoothness as he stood and Viktoria sat down.

"In the struggle he was shot . . . and later died."

How'd they find out about that so quickly? Madeira wondered as he turned his attention back to the Russian. Somebody on the ship must've somehow told Meg Jefferson without his hearing it, unless it came from Moscow or St. Petersburg. But why would the Russian Navy announce the miserable affair at all, let alone without warning the ship they were going to do it? God! Were they that screwed up?

And where was Meg? He looked out over the small crowd and saw no sign of her fiery hair. She said she was going to attend.

"Why did he attack the captain?"

"We're still not completely sure. As Dr. Galin mentioned, there was a dispute about pay. My own feeling is that the unfortunate fellow was unbalanced. According to his records he's had trouble before and shown definite signs of instability. Unfortunately for him we seem to have underestimated the problem in the past. If we'd been more alert we might have been able to help him sooner."

"Will you be releasing his records so they can be reviewed by experts?"

"The release of personal records to the public is prohibited."

Madeira squirmed in his chair. He continued to feel Chernov had overreacted, yet he suspected that many courts, even American ones, might well view the matter the way Novikoff was describing it. Somebody, and Madeira'd come to believe it was Rustoff, *had* thrown a wrench that could easily have been fatal if it'd hit its target.

Despite having spent two weeks aboard *Asimov,* Madeira felt he knew little more about the incident, or the man, than the reporters seemed to know. Was Rustoff a flaming radical of some sort or just a tormented madman? Was he victim or instigator?

And who'd been the real target of the wrench?

He wished the press conference would end quickly. He wanted to get on with the job and get it over with. He found himself thinking fondly of the whales, the Pilgrim Monument, *Wave Runner,* and his unimaginably distant cousin Sandy's continuous eco-prattle.

Even the room was depressing: worn red-and-gold carpet, brown walls, and a pair of dim chandeliers that were totally out of place. One of many tired banquet facilities in one of the more overworked of Condado Beach's many resort hotels. It reeked, he thought. The room, the carpet, the very air reeked of people and of coffee. How many thousands of steaming urns had been dispensed and consumed in this dreary place? How many sales conferences, get-rich-quick schemes, and weddings had been solemnized and celebrated here? Why the hell had the Russians selected this place?

Probably because it was cheap. Limited resources.

"Is an investigation being conducted?"

"Yes. Very definitely!" Novikoff said. "We fully understand your interest in this tragic event and we will do our best to keep you informed. And now—"

"Can you tell us more about the man and his motivations? Why he assaulted the captain," demanded another voice. Madeira was able to identify the questioner this time, a tall, skinny guy in the first row. Sitting next to him was a strikingly pretty girl.

Very pretty, he thought, but with an expression hard as nails. She's got to be even tougher than Meg.

"At the moment, no," Novikoff said, showing not the slightest irritation or impatience at the question. "He was originally from Moscow and he was unmarried. As I have already said, according to our records he had been in trouble many times before. That is probably why, at the age of almost forty, he was still what you would call a fireman, the lowest position in the engine room. The matter is being investigated and you will be kept posted."

He's really quite an actor, thought Madeira, so long as he doesn't lose his cool. Maybe that's an act, too. The uncontrollable anger. Maybe that was all for effect.

"Do you have any evidence that drugs were involved? Smuggling, maybe . . . Was he a member of one of the Moscow Mafias?"

147

"No. Not that we know of."

"You seem in a great hurry to leave. Shouldn't you remain here until the authorities have learned more?"

"The authorities are investigating—"

"The FBI?"

"Our authorities. Russian authorities."

"So what's the hurry?"

"*Asimov* is a very expensive ship to operate. The project, like all scientific projects, has a definite budget. We can't afford to spend any unnecessary time in port."

"Captain Madeira, what can *you* tell us about this?"

The question caught Madeira by surprise. "I'm afraid I know little more than you do. I don't speak Russian."

"Why are you really aboard that ship?"

"To help with the ultradeep operations. I'm just a diver, a technical consultant." Where the hell was Meg Jefferson? he wondered with an unease he didn't understand.

"Will visitors be allowed to visit you?" shouted another voice.

Madeira drew a blank.

"We have every hope of arranging for one or two visits by the news media," Novikoff replied, getting Madeira off the hook.

"When?"

"We'll have to get back to you about that."

"What makes you so sure there wasn't more to it than just an argument over pay?"

"We have found no evidence of anything else."

The questioner rolled his eyes, as if to say that it would take more than that for the Russians to convince him that they weren't still beating their wives.

Madeira leaned back and inhaled deeply, savoring the damp tropical night. The floodlit royal palms were motionless, and the flags lining the hotel's driveway were limp, yet the heavy air couldn't have been more full of life. It's all there, he thought: sea, palmetto, soil mold, cooking oil, automobile exhaust. And floating above it all, majestically aloof, an exquisite cloud of cigar smoke.

The night air was far from perfect, but it was infinitely better than that in the conference room. And, he decided, he'd reached a point in his life where he could no longer hold out for perfection. Better, he now believed, was the best he could ever hope for.

Question after question. The same ones over and over again. Nobody was interested in the cover story. All they wanted to know about was Rustoff, Yeltsin, and Zhirinovsky. And none of them believed a word they heard.

He laughed. Novikoff should have saved himself a lot of strain and just told them the truth. They wouldn't have believed that, either.

The cigar, he decided, was a very good one. He turned, seeking the source of the rich aroma, and found himself staring, almost face-to-face, at an elderly, but very spry, Puerto Rican gentleman, dressed in pale blue slacks and a magnificent white guayabera.

"*Señor?*" asked the small man, smiling slightly at Madeira.

"I beg your pardon. I was enjoying the aroma of your cigar."

"*Muy sabroso, no?*"

Before Madeira could answer, the man pulled another out of his shirt pocket and offered it to him.

"That's very kind of you," Madeira said, smiling, searching for a graceful way of declining. "I'm afraid that would be wasted on me."

The man smiled more broadly now as he returned the cigar to his pocket. "I'm sorry you've never had the opportunity to develop your tastes for the finer things in life, young man. Don't delay too long in doing so. The day will come when you discover it's too late."

After nodding a friendly good-bye, the man sauntered off to a blue Mercedes that was idling in the glistening, dew-dampened driveway.

"Al!"

"Over here, Mike," he replied as he watched the Russian head toward him from under the porte cochere.

"How did we do?" Novikoff asked quietly as he reached Madeira's side.

"All right, I think. They're going to want more on Rustoff's death—how the hell did they know about it?—but I didn't hear or see anything that made me think any of them suspect what we're really here for."

"Yes, that's what I think," said Novikoff as Madeira wondered what had happened to Meg Jefferson. "It's good they're so interested in other things that have nothing to do with our mission, although we're going to have to come up with something more on Rustoff."

"And how do you plan to get out of your invitation to come visit at some point?" Madeira asked.

"I've been thinking about that," replied Novikoff with a little smile. "What I think we'll do is pay another call on San Juan. We'll invite them all aboard and let Viktoria show them the work she's done."

"Will she have anything to show them?"

"I think so. Don't fool yourself. Viktoria's very capable. She'll manage to get in a lot of science while we're working on the wreck."

"I've never had the slightest doubt about her abilities," said Madeira.

"No," Novikoff said. "You shouldn't."

Hell, Madeira thought. They've made a terrible error. Instead of hiring a million-dollar salvage expert they should have hired a million-dollar flack. In today's virtual world all they had to do was create the desired perception, put the right spin on the story. They'd never even have to actually touch the wreck itself.

"Viktoria wants to return to the ship now," Novikoff continued, "but there're several things I'd like to take care of while we're here and Chernov seems to need more time to complete the ship's business, so the boat'll be making two trips instead of one. You are free to return now or stay, of course. We'll meet at the dock at one A.M."

Madeira couldn't help a slight, grim smile. He pitied whatever girl Chernov had selected to do business with but welcomed the opportunity to stay ashore a little longer. To stretch his legs. To escape the stench of vinegar and cabbage and humans all cooped up in a big steel box too long. To meet with Charlie Nash. To see if Nash could explain why any sane man would continue to suffer the nightmare Madeira was living.

Then he noticed Viktoria standing behind Novikoff. She traveled well; she looked just as good standing next to a palm tree as she did in the middle of a blizzard.

He thought of the dapper cigar smoker. The man was right. Only a fool would let the finer things in life pass him by.

To hell with Nash. And to hell with professionalism.

Throughout the transit of the Atlantic he'd been almost constantly aware of her presence, or absence. Her smile and intelligence had taken the edge off so many mealtime confrontations. Her eyes had beckoned, very possibly without her conscious intent.

At least he'd thought he'd seen something in them.

And when he'd realized she was spending most of her time working with Riki, the ship's Armenian head biologist, he'd felt a wave of undoubtedly misplaced jealousy.

Faced by the attraction he felt, he'd retreated, hidden behind professionalism and dedication to the mission and memories of the past. For him, the ship was filled with danger, disorder, and horror. And she was part of the ship.

But the past was past, and tomorrow he might be dead from a heart attack. Novikoff was obviously busy with other matters and wouldn't have any objection anyway. And Nash couldn't explain anything to him. Nash would want him to do the explaining.

He'd be a fool if he didn't ask Viktoria to have a drink with him. As for the note, it was a request, not a subpoena!

Then he remembered Rustoff. Rustoff heaving the huge wrench. Rustoff waving his fists. Rustoff crumpling onto the slushy deck.

He hadn't *seen* Rustoff throw the wrench. He hadn't the slightest idea who'd thrown it. Or why. Or at whom. And then there was the memory of Grivski, the Grand Inquisitor, pounding a man's face into mush.

A sudden, almost overpowering impulse toward caution shouted at him to avoid the woman; that he knew too little about her, and about everything else, to stick his neck out. Then he looked at her again. She looked much better under that palm tree than she ever did in a blizzard! It had to be the tan.

"Viktoria," he said, walking over to her. "Can I buy you a drink?"

Novikoff, who was still standing near the geophysicist, turned and watched a moment with a slight grin, then wandered off.

"I'm sorry, Al, but I've got so much to do."

"One, then you can get back to your computers. We'll have it right here, at the hotel bar, on the lanai. It's the only liberty we're going to have for a while. . . ."

"Liberty?"

"Shore leave, time we can be off the ship."

"Okay, sailor," she said finally, a smile spreading across her face. "One drink, then I get back to work."

"I'm glad that's over," sighed Viktoria after they'd settled at a table in a corner of the lanai off the hotel bar and ordered some rum concoctions that the waitress assured them were excellent for stress relief. "I can never get over how good your reporters are at interrogation. They keep asking the same question over and over, always in a different way, and keep asking it until they get the answer they want."

Madeira leaned back in his chair and looked out into the night, at the faintly visible beach and the shadowy palms rustling dryly in the trade winds. "I've never been interrogated, really interrogated, by the police or anybody else," he finally remarked as much to himself as to her. "I got a speeding ticket once . . . and a lecture from the trooper, and then a few weeks ago I walked in on a burglary at the place where I live. The police did finally come by to ask me for some details, but they spent most of their time commiserating with me.''

The drinks arrived. Viktoria picked up hers and took a sip. Then she looked all around, making sure that there were no recognizable journalists, or Russians, close by.

''You're a very lucky guy, Al. Your country is filled with lucky people, whether they appreciate it or not,'' she said, then took another big sip of her drink.

Madeira turned and looked at her. ''I would have thought that somebody in your position, with your skills, would be immune from that sort of thing. Especially now.''

''Now maybe, but not then, not when I was a child.''

Madeira waited, feeling a surge of anger at the thought that she'd ever been abused.

''When I was very young my father was an important engineer, he designed petroleum refineries, and my mother taught French. We lived in a big, airy apartment of our own and really lived very well. Then, when I was five, my father made the mistake of criticizing, loudly and publicly, a new design that was to be used to build half a dozen new plants. He said it was junk; that it would never work well and that it might very well kill the people who would work at it.

''Everything he said turned out to be true, but that was after he had been sent to Siberia. You see, the man who made the design was very important politically. Even though Father's criticisms were all technical, the designer felt he had been mortally insulted.''

The waitress approached, and Madeira waved her off while Viktoria paused and then continued: ''Father was charged with expressing technical opinions which were politically unacceptable. I know that sounds ridiculous to you, but at the time it was perfectly accepted. He was sentenced to the camps for twenty years. Even though he always was a loyal Communist.''

Madeira looked into her eyes, which were themselves focused intently on the past, and tried to imagine the Siberian prison camps. He found he couldn't; the gentle winds, the sound of waves on the beach, and the shadows of waving palms made it impossible.

Then he thought of Grivski and his vision was clarified.

"Mother lost her job," Viktoria continued after sipping her drink, "and was assigned to scrub the floor of a cafeteria. We lost our nice apartment and had to live in a horrible little corner of a filthy basement. To be honest, I didn't totally understand what was happening, but I do know it was terribly hard on my mother.

"And then, after five years, Father was suddenly back. And with a better job than before. Things had a way of changing sometimes in the old Soviet Union, and he also had a lot of friends. It was, I suspect, one of those relatively rare occasions where somebody really was sent to the camps for rehabilitation rather then termination. To teach him a lesson he would never forget.

"Mother got her old job back and we got a nice, new apartment and I was assigned to one of the special schools run for the promising children of important professionals."

Madeira squirmed, then took a large belt of his own drink.

"But Father was never the same. He never spoke of the camps, never smiled and never expressed an opinion again. Not even to me. Just numbers. Dimensions. Velocities. Weights. He did his job the best he could and never let science stand in the way of politics, of survival. And then he died a few years later.

"Whatever his pain, it had been even worse for my mother. The shame, the drudgery, the fear. She outlived Father, but it might have been better for her if she hadn't.

"By the time he died the authorities had already decided I had enough of an aptitude for mathematics to be an engineer or even a physicist, so I remained on the privileged track right into university. I wanted to be an astrophysicist— I think I thought it might be a way of looking for God without having to publicly renounce atheism—but they decided they needed geophysicists and that seemed close enough for me."

Madeira, who had been slumping slowly into his chair as he listened, sat up and took a deep breath.

"It's a miserable story, Al," Viktoria said as her eyes returned from the past to him. "I'm sorry I inflicted it on you."

"I'm surprised they expended so many resources on you if you were the child of somebody whose loyalty was suspect," replied Madeira, still dumbfounded, even though he knew he shouldn't be, by her story.

"Father's loyalty was never suspect, not really. I told you, he was always a good Communist. And what you also don't seem to understand is that it wasn't ideology. It was simple politics. Many of the important people spent time, at some point in their careers, in exile. They weren't sent there because they were disloyal to communism but because their bosses thought they might be disloyal to them personally."

Madeira sat in silence, feeling totally incapable of responding in any reasonable way.

"You think I should hate my country for what it did, don't you?" Viktoria continued after she'd finished her drink. "Yes! It's a nation of drunks and bullies and sadists, but I don't hate it, because it's no different from the whole human race and I don't hate that. The West seems so much more civilized these days, and I devoutly hope Russia will develop in that direction, but civilization is no more than a dream, a fantasy that must be believed in to exist. Abandon the dream, stop believing for just a second, and the fabric tears. Then all the old, ugly realities break out again."

"And the future?" Madeira asked, hoping to see her smile again.

"Yes, the future," she said, turning to him and smiling. "The future may bring a return to the horrible realities of the past or it may bring the beauty of a great dream."

"Let's get some dinner. I'm famished."

"I'm sorry, Al, but I really do have to get back to the ship," Viktoria said as she stood. "Thanks for the drink and for listening to me."

"I'm . . ." I'm what? thought Madeira. Glad you told me

about yourself? Sorry you went through all that? Nauseated by every word you uttered? Totally in love with you?

"Some other time?" he concluded lamely.

"I think we can count on that," she said with a devious smile. "At least for the next month or so."

Then she was gone, the swish of her dress still echoing in his mind.

Madeira looked around the almost empty lanai and considered ordering another drink, then decided not to. After two long weeks of being a part-time Russian, the thought of talking to a card-carrying American for an hour or two sounded very attractive.

Even if the American was Charlie Nash.

"I'm glad you could make it, Al," Nash said as he opened the door to the rented condo. "We expected you'd have to go right back to the ship, especially after that scene at the press conference."

"I didn't see you there."

"I wasn't. I don't think you've met Jen. . . ."

Madeira turned and found he was only slightly surprised to see the girl from the first row, pretty but hard as nails, standing in the living room.

"Al," Jen said with an absolutely minimal smile as she accepted his offered hand.

"Jen has credentials for everything," said Nash. "Want a beer, Al? From what Jen tells me, you probably need it."

"Thanks," Madeira said, "I could use one. How the hell did they know about the shooting?"

"No way of knowing," Nash said over his shoulder as he entered the small kitchen and disappeared into the refrigerator. "Hell! *We* didn't know about it. Nobody mentioned it to those reporters who attacked from the skies, did they?"

"Not that I saw. They were only allowed to talk to 'dependable' personnel."

"Obviously at least one of them wasn't so dependable," replied Nash as he handed Madeira a Heineken, "but then, that's just what I'd expect. Factions within factions within factions. We're having one hell of a time figuring for sure who's on whose side . . . and for how long.''

''Tell us about it, Al'' Jen said as she settled into what struck Madeira as an extremely ugly and uncomfortable-looking couch. The whole place, he decided, looked as if it'd been furnished at a clearance sale.

''The shooting?'' asked Madeira, still standing.

''Start there, if you want. What was its real cause?''

''I really don't know.'' He then described what he'd seen and what Viktoria'd told him.

''Galin,'' Nash remarked, ''she's something of an unknown. We know Novikoff was handpicked by the President and we know this Captain Bukinin is clearly sympathetic to the radical nationalists, he was included to provide political balance, but we know very little about Dr. Galin except that she's written some articles our people say are pretty good. What's your opinion?''

Madeira's personal opinion was that she had a difficult past, a quick wit and a nice laugh, tanned well, possessed the most amazing eyes, and was worth dying for. ''She's very bright and can be quite forceful when she feels strongly about something. My own feeling is that she's a top-notch scientist. As for her politics, she seemed upset about the shooting but also seemed to accept it as almost . . . inevitable. She used to belong to the Party but now says it was a terrible mistake. She's quite sensitive about it. She's also quite sensitive about being half Ukrainian.''

''We already knew that much,'' snapped Jen. ''Now tell us why the ship didn't sail from St. Petersburg on schedule.''

Madeira told them about the explosion in the generator, resenting Jen's accusatory tone with every word he uttered.

''Pretty much as we suspected,'' Nash mumbled. ''Do they think it was sabotage?''

''Yes.''

''Do they know who's behind it?''

"No, but they beat up most of their crew trying to find out."

"What can you tell us about the mini-coup in Moscow, Al?" Jen demanded.

"Can't tell you shit about it, Jen," Madeira replied, sick to death of both of them. "Didn't even know it'd happened."

"Yes, you did," Jen said, her expression now severe to the point of anger. "That's why the ship pulled a three-sixty right in the middle of the English Channel."

"We received an order to prepare to turn back. There was some doubt about whether to actually go ahead and turn back or wait for a more precise order. Novikoff, Bukinin, and Galin all finally seemed to agree it would be prudent to go ahead and turn. Then, a few hours later, another message came in telling us to continue with the operation."

"How did they explain it?"

"They said it was some sort of policy disagreement in Moscow; that Yeltsin was reassessing the results of the election. I got the feeling such things have happened before."

"What was your reaction?"

"Me? It pissed me off. I wanted to get on with it."

"The truth is," Jen said, "we think a number of Yeltsin's key supporters threatened to jump ship. Several, including Yegor Gaidar, the vice premier, did. Then some sort of a deal was struck, and now we're not at all sure who really has the power. It's even possible that Yeltsin's just a dummy now, a front man; that he's doing what somebody else's telling him to do. On the other hand, we're not even sure if there really was a coup. It may have all been smoke and mirrors."

That's just what I should be giving serious consideration to, thought Madeira. Jumping ship! Ditch the Russians and ditch you two while I'm at it.

"I should think that since the operation is still 'go' and Novikoff's still in charge then Yeltsin's still in charge. Didn't you say Novikoff's his man?"

"Yes," Nash said, standing and starting to pace the

length of the living room as he spoke, "we think so. That's how it looks, but that may not mean anything." The CIA agent then stopped in his tracks and spun suddenly.

"So listen up very carefully, buddy boy," he snarled, pointing at Madeira with the index finger of the same hand that was holding his sweating bottle of beer. "The balloon's up on this operation! The President's people aren't happy. They've got a lot of capital invested in this guy and they don't want him to take a tumble . . . or change course. If they smell even the slightest whiff of fuckup, or see any more shit like what's going out on the wires from here right now, he'll pull the plug and hang you and some others out to dry."

Madeira stared fixedly at him, thinking fondly of right whales and rabid environmentalists.

"Before I forget, keep an eye on that first mate . . . Chernov? Our people say he's closely connected to one of the Chechen gangs and he may be up to something that's not in our interest—or Yeltsin's, either."

Madeira nodded his understanding, hoping as he did that the tirade was over. It wasn't.

"And let me tell you something else," continued Nash, his face now totally flushed. "There're rumors around of real big trouble at our firm. The old high-level-mole shit, although this time it almost sounds for real. They say it's some guy with a South American wife. A Colombian."

"Shut up, Nash!" Jen snapped.

Nash stared at her a moment, then turned back to Madeira. "Jen and I can finesse the shooting for you, but that's it! The Russian political situation is unstable. The Russians themselves are unstable. It's up to you to make sure this whole operation doesn't blow up in our faces, because we can't afford any more bombs at the moment.

"If it does," concluded Nash, his face still twisted, "don't bother trying to go home. And don't think you're ever going to collect that million dollars. Or any more of your pension."

Chapter Fourteen

The trades, which had been strengthening all day, tugged at Boris Timon's thinning blond hair and raised armies of small waves that slapped at *Asimov*'s high sides as the ship swung gently to her anchor.

Standing far forward, in the ship's starboard bow, the Russian diver leaned on the lifeline and looked out into the night, exhaling a pale cloud of cigarette smoke. After watching the blinking lights of Isla Grande Airport a few moments, his attention shifted to the north, to El Morro, the great, looming fort that guarded the entrance to the bay. Tier upon tier of massive, age-darkened stone walls rose high out of the almost invisible sea. Chains of lights strung along the ramparts. Sinister shadow otherwise.

It was a sight he could understand and feel at home with. All but the palm trees. How, he wondered, did the Puerto Ricans look upon the four-hundred-year-old fortress? As a symbol of protection or as one of oppression? Then his thoughts returned to his wife and kids.

"Boris?"

He turned, straightening up as he did. "Yes, Dr. Galin," he replied in Russian, "I'm here. How'd the press conference go?"

"The principal objective was achieved, I think, but there was one very bad surprise," replied the tall scientist as her dress and long blond hair both moved gently in the breeze.

"Yes?"

"Several of the reporters already knew about Rustoff. They asked a number of very difficult questions."

"How much did they know?"

"Almost as much as I do. When those reporters were aboard, did you see them talk to *anybody* other than the people Captain Novikoff and I approved?" As she asked, her fingers skipped lightly along the lifeline.

"No, but I wasn't with them every second. One, as I remember, had to go to the bathroom . . . and we did let them wander a little on their own. Was it one of them who asked about Rustoff?"

"No. Neither of them was there, which also worries me."

"Could the leak have come from Moscow or St. Petersburg?"

"It's certainly possible, but until we learn so for sure we must act as if it came from this ship."

"Captain Madeira?"

"That's what I was going to ask you. You've spent more time with him than anybody else."

"He had many chances to do it, but I don't think he did. He's not a very good liar. Do you think the Americans are getting cold feet?"

"They've been known to change their minds, or the CIA may have been planning this all along, planning to discredit us. Who else had a chance to speak to the reporters?"

"Mr. Chernov? Those who were with him when the reporters first arrived?"

"Yes, I'd forgotten about that. One of them might have blurted something out. I know Chernov won't tell you anything, so I'll talk to him. You talk to the others."

"I'll see what I can learn, but I haven't learned much by

161

listening the past week or two." And neither have Novikoff and Grivski, he added to himself.

"Do what you can, Boris, and keep alert about the sabotage, too. We don't want that starting up again while we're working on the wreck."

"I understand."

"Good night, then."

"Good night, Dr. Galin."

He watched as his superior disappeared into the superstructure.

A very attractive woman, he thought, not that it could possibly make any difference, considering their relative positions. He wondered if she was really the right person for the job. Her background involved mainly analysis, they said. Processing scientific data in search of little treasures. Very little field experience. None, probably, in the really dark and dirty stuff.

What the hell! as Madeira would say. What business was it of his? Whoever selected her for her job must have known what he was doing.

He paused a moment. From what he'd heard, it was Captain Novikoff himself who'd picked her.

The cabbie accepted Madeira's fare and tip with a cheerful *"Gracias, señor."* As soon as Madeira had dragged himself out of the cab and closed the door, the cab immediately squealed off into the night in search of another fare or two.

"¡Cerrado!" snapped a voice from the shadows. "The first ferry isn't until eight in the morning!"

Madeira looked around the floodlit front of the darkened ferry terminal, finally locating the security guard. "I'm from the Russian research ship anchored out in the bay. A boat's supposed to be here in a few minutes to pick us up."

As he explained he continued to look around, watching the tourists straggle back to the cruise ship parked on the far side of the pier to the east. A few tourists, he thought, and three or four dockside idlers, but no sign of Novikoff or Chernov.

"I know nothing about that," replied the guard with a mixture of boredom and irritation. "I was told there would be only one boat, and that left hours ago."

Madeira looked at his watch. He was about fifteen minutes early. "There's supposed to be another at one."

"You wait here," the guard said. "I will check."

Madeira nodded as the guard disappeared into the terminal. The pavement was wet, there having been a rain squall while Nash and Jen were reading him the riot act, and the trades were spotty in the lee of Old San Juan, although there was a chap out in the bay.

After waiting several minutes he ambled out of the light a few yards, along the seawall toward the cruise ship pier. Not wanting to go so far that the guard couldn't find him, he stopped next to a parked truck, then turned to look back across the dark, choppy water at the ferries moored alongside the terminal.

Nash's an ass, he thought, grinding his teeth. An utter ass. And so's his henchperson, or boss, or whatever she is.

Why the hell was he taking so much shit from so many different people? It certainly wasn't the money. He'd already come to think of that as sort of a joke.

He glanced out toward the center of the bay and tried to pick out *Asimov*'s anchor lights from the constellation of shore lights beyond.

By this time tomorrow they'd already be over the wreck and he'd be on his way down. Or already there. He felt his body tense, and a band of steel seemed to tighten around his chest. He forced himself to take a deep breath.

There was a scuffing sound somewhere behind him. He looked around in the dimness and saw nothing. Wharf rats, he thought. On their way to check out the cruise ship's garbage.

He could handle the job. By itself. He could handle the Russians and Nash and Jen. By themselves. But mix them all together and then throw in all that he didn't understand and hadn't been told and you had a stew he just might not be able to handle.

Niko Avalaridze, for example. He'd never liked mysteries or surprises, especially when he already felt threatened. And seeing the Georgian businessman in San Juan qualified as just such an unwanted surprise.

Coincidental?

Perhaps. He'd said he was in imports and exports. Citrus, he said. Did Puerto Rico export oranges and grapefruits?

Avalaridze's card had said he maintained an office in Miami, but it wasn't the sort of coincidence Madeira was comfortable with.

Motor yachts, my ass!

Madeira hadn't really expected the cabdriver to stop at the red light, but he had. While waiting for red to become green, Madeira'd looked out the window to his left, watching as another cab turned the corner. Then the other cab stopped suddenly.

Two figures, standing on the sidewalk directly under a streetlamp, had waved the cab down. One was a big, thuggish-looking guy dressed in jeans. The other was smaller, slimmer. . . .

The second figure rang a bell in Madeira's memory. He sat there in the darkened cab and studied the figure, who was only a dozen feet away. He looked a lot like Niko.

He *was* Niko!

"Hey, man . . . you!" The challenge was delivered in a high, singsong voice. "You got something for us? Like money?"

Oh shit! thought Madeira, his attention returning to the waterfront where he was and wondering if it was already too late. Two-legged wharf rats! At least six of them. While he'd been daydreaming they'd surrounded him.

He looked around quickly. At the distant cruise ship all lighted up to resemble a great, white wedding cake. At the ferry terminal. At the road. At the inky shadows in his immediate vicinity. There wasn't another soul in sight, not close enough to understand what was going on, except for the six predators themselves. And the few cars passing by on La Marina all seemed to have their radios turned up to full volume.

He opened his mouth to shout, but shouts didn't come naturally to him and it probably made more sense to just hand them his wallet and write the loss off to his own stupidity.

He sensed as much as he saw the motion, and the decision was made for him. They weren't waiting for him to surrender gracefully, and they were interested in more than just money and credit cards. They were after the thrill of the kill. He was surrounded, and one of the muggers was already swinging something dull and dark at him.

It was a baseball bat.

Chapter Fifteen

Great black and gold battlements, an ascending jumble of billowing turrets, massive towers and rolling parapets all pulsed across the horizon. Here and there yellow-white flashes appeared like battery after battery of siege guns discharging. Then a bloodred glow flickered across the whole, appearing first at the base, then slowly ascending, silhouetting and dwarfing El Morro's rock-solid, pale shadows.

Forgetting for the moment his tender gut and very real fear, Madeira stood, transfixed, as he witnessed the awesome glory of the dawn. It was, he'd always felt, God's reaffirmation that all past follies could somehow be corrected; that yesterday's sins could be atoned for; that today's dreams might yet be realized.

Red sky in the morning, he thought. Sailor take warning.

The ancient warning rang loudly in his mind while a chill coursed up and down his spine.

As far as the weather went, he decided, this particular dawn would prove to be one of the many exceptions to the rule. The storm drums were silent, the dark curtains of rain

166

absent. And the flashes were merely the sun's rays burning their way up and over the horizon. In time, he suspected, the ramparts would be revealed as nothing more threatening than the fair-weather cumulus clouds that so often act as the trade winds' puffy handmaidens. A little overdeveloped, perhaps, but nothing to worry about.

But what about everything else? Him? The goddamn Russians? This damned job?

His gut hurt, although Olga, the ship's usually sour doctor, didn't think the damage was too severe, and he was scared.

He'd been scared before, many times, but this time it was different. It wasn't just a matter of icy black depths and decompression; of gas pressures and electronics and the ever-present risk of mechanical failures. It wasn't the coldly dispassionate sort of threat he'd learned over the years to face. It was intentional, willful, calculated violence. Directed at *him*. Personally. By somebody. And he couldn't seem to escape it. It followed him everywhere. Aboard *Asimov* and ashore.

He'd reached the point where he had no idea whom he could trust. Certainly not Novikoff. Or Nash. Not even Timon or Viktoria, much as he'd like to. Not one of them was being totally honest. Not even him.

Lane Williams was right: The sharks, and everybody else, were all exhibiting their most vicious insecurities. They all had more than one agenda. They were all wheeling and dealing, and everything seemed up for redefinition.

He thought he could understand the Russians' erratic behavior. The Soviet Union, the Russian Federated Republic, the CIS, whatever it was calling itself this week, was either self-destructing or being born anew. Either was bound to be messy. And everybody'd always said the Russians are totally paranoid anyway.

But what about the Americans? What was Charlie's and Jen's excuse? The struggle's over. We won. Nothing but peace and prosperity and a kinder, gentler world ahead.

He watched as El Morro slipped past to starboard and felt

William S. Schaill

Asimov's twin prows cut into the long, smooth Atlantic swells.

A thousand feet of water. A reeking mass of radiation nobody in his right mind would want to mess with. Ever deeper, nastier, and more complex. A golden opportunity for soul-shattering failure. And all around, sharks, some big, some little, slashing and tearing at each other, and at him, in their frenzy.

The night before, even before his mind had fully identified the baseball bat, Madeira had thrown himself at the batter. Thus, when it did connect it was the handle, rather than the end, that slammed into his gut. His stomach went numb, then exploded in pain as he jammed his forearm into the batter's throat and shoved him aside.

Despite the mind-numbing deluge of pain and shock, he charged through his attacker, knocking him down. He then spun, almost losing his footing on the slick pavement, and headed for the rail along the seawall, twisting to break free from the hands grabbing at his shirt from behind.

Gasping for breath as he went, he placed his foot on the lower crosspiece, where it slipped, causing his chest to slam into and then down the rail as he fell.

Now as furious as he was frightened, Madeira stepped up onto the crosspiece again. Then, with a grunt, he vaulted to the top of the rail and continued on, thrusting forward and out into the night in a long, arcing dive. Below, the black waters of San Juan Bay glinted and danced darkly.

But how much was there of it? How deep was the goddamn water? And how many rotten but still-solid old pilings were hidden by it?

He should have thought of that before, he taunted himself as he plunged into the bay, executing the shallowest dive he could manage. Once in he continued on as far as he could underwater, praying, certain that half a dozen sharks, of the finned variety, must be swimming beside him in the inky darkness. Escorting him to hell.

Unable to see or feel anything until it was too late, he

continued to breaststroke hard, guided only by his anguished imagination.

By the time he'd managed to make it back to the surface the rat pack had gathered along the rail. Two of them were already up on it, ready to jump or dive in. "Motherfucker!" shouted a familiar, singsong voice.

Hell! he thought. I've spent most of my life in the water. If there're only two of them, I stand a chance. He sculled in place for a moment, catching his breath and developing his strategy. Should he move out to give himself time to evaluate the animals once they were in the water? Force them to come to him, to wear themselves out a little? Or should he move in? Position himself to attack the instant they splashed, before they were fully ready to defend themselves?

Something slammed into the water about ten feet away from him. Then something else. Closer. Both sounded heavy and hard. What were they? Bottles? Rocks? Chunks of pavement? Whatever they were, he was sure they'd hurt.

He was the rat now, and his assailants just a gang of boys throwing things at a swimming rodent.

There was laughter as he sculled away from the seawall. Somebody banged the rail furiously with the baseball bat. Then there was an argument in machine-gun Spanish.

The two on the rail stepped down and rejoined the mob.

"Have a nice swim, *maricón*!" they all shouted. And then they were gone, reabsorbed into the night.

Madeira took a deep, shuddering breath and inhaled half the bay. It tasted like so many other harbors he'd tasted over the years—of ships and sea life and a living city now almost five hundred years old.

He expelled the oil-dark bay water in one convulsive heave and suspected that at least one rib was broken. Foul wavelets lapped gently against his mouth and nose as he sculled, waiting to make sure they'd gone and struggling to keep his head high. His energy, his strength, his very will oozed out of him into the surrounding water, leaving him limp and exhausted.

To the left was the ferry terminal. He knew it was only a couple of minutes' walk away, but it seemed way too far to swim now. He breaststroked feebly into the stone seawall and pulled himself along its face, looking for something, anything.

Finally he came across a tiny dock. A landing, really, but enough to do the job. He dragged himself out of the water and rested. Then, after peeking long and hard over the seawall, he dragged himself back up onto the rain-damp pavement.

He was sitting, bent, dripping and breathing very, very carefully when the black Mazda screeched to a stop in front of the terminal.

Only slightly interested at first, Madeira looked up and noticed a dark flash of red inside the car. Then Mike Novikoff emerged, laughing, from the passenger's side. After closing his door the Russian walked unsteadily around to the driver's door. He leaned in the window a moment, then stepped back as the car leapt away, turned, and roared off down La Marina.

"Mike!" Madeira grunted.

"The boat here yet?" shouted Novikoff as he turned in the direction of Madeira's voice.

"Not yet," Madeira replied weakly.

"What's wrong?" Novikoff demanded as he walked toward him, weaving slightly as he came. "Are you sick?"

Then the Russian laughed with a conspiratorial air. "Ah! You had too much rum with Viktoria. I think I may be having the same problem. Where is she?"

"She went back to the ship hours ago, and I was mugged! I let a pack of animals sneak up on me."

Novikoff's laugh slowly died out as he digested Madeira's words and got a better look at him. "Did they hurt you?"

"They got me once with a baseball bat, then I managed to get into the bay."

"Where'd they get you?"

"In the side. It wasn't a good shot." Although his chest

also hurt from the fall against the rail, it somehow didn't seem worth mentioning.

"We have to get you to a hospital!"

Madeira took a deep, shuddering breath. "I feel like shit, but I think I'll survive. Maybe a cracked rib or two."

As he spoke he realized that the strong, sweet smell he'd noticed was issuing from Novikoff's mouth. The Russian certainly had guzzled a tidy tot, but not so much, apparently, as to incapacitate him.

"There may be internal damage!"

"It doesn't feel like it."

"That means nothing!"

"Help me up. We'll have Olga check me out."

Novikoff looked doubtfully at him.

"Wasn't that Meg Jefferson, the reporter, driving that car?" Madeira asked as he struggled, unaided, to his feet.

"Yes," mumbled Novikoff in a slightly surprised tone, taking Madeira's arm. "Now she has her own domesticated Russian naval officer. Her own personal window on the Kremlin. I think it's good business to keep all our lines of communication open. Don't you?"

"Yes," replied Madeira, listening to the sound of a boat's engine rumbling faintly in the distance. Was the Russian trying to work on the expedition's image or his own? he wondered. Or was he just doing what sailors have always done when in port?

"Another thing . . . You remember that guy who came off the airplane with me? Niko Avalaridze?"

"Yes. What about him?"

"He's in San Juan. I saw him get into a cab about an hour ago."

"That's very interesting, Al." As he spoke, the hand Novikoff had on Madeira's arm snapped shut like a trap. "We did check into him right after you arrived. Everything seemed on the up-and-up. I will ask them to take another look, though." Suddenly, the Russian seemed totally sober.

"It's almost as if he's following me," Madeira continued.

"Did you know a man was also following you in New York? When we met at the annex?"

"No."

"He was found, dead, after you left. A photograph of you was lying on the seat of his car."

"Why?"

"We don't know."

"Why wasn't I told?"

"We wanted to have some answers before we alarmed you."

"Well?"

"Well?"

"Do you have any answers?"

"No, not yet. According to the police, he was a private investigator. We still have no precise idea who he was working for, although I suspect it was one of the Chechen criminal gangs. They're everywhere, you know. I suspect they heard some of those stories your engineer has been telling about a Russian submarine filled with gold and decided to check into it, but that's just my personal guess."

"And who killed him?"

"We still have no idea who killed him or why. But, I must remind you, there are disloyal elements even aboard the ship. You must be very careful at all times!"

Shit! Madeira thought. "Who? Who should I watch out for?"

"It's difficult to say, exactly, but I'd definitely be careful with Bukinin and Chernov. Don't you agree?"

"Because they're hard-asses?" At the last minute he decided not to mention that Nash had already told him Chernov was Mob. Novikoff might want to know who Nash was and then take offense when he learned.

"Hard-asses?"

"Tough guys."

"Because they're known to sympathize with reactionary elements: unreformed Communists, radical nationalists, people who wish to destroy President Yeltsin and bring back the Cold War."

"Who the hell can I trust, then?" Madeira demanded as they walked slowly toward the terminal.

"Besides me, I'm not sure myself. Al, let me tell you: Things are very bad for us. It's all one damn big mess!"

"What about Viktoria? She seems decent enough."

"Did you two have a pleasant evening?"

"We had one drink at the hotel bar, then she returned to the ship."

"Ah! Do you know she's Naval Intelligence?"

"You mean KGB?"

"No, although the SVG does supervise her bosses. Her specialty is hydrographics and physical oceanography. Let me assure you that we are just as interested in those subjects as your navy is."

"Then she really is a geophysicist?"

"Yes, a very competent one. But she's also a member of a part of the navy that the rest of us, those who go to sea, are sometimes uncomfortable with."

Oh, bullshit! thought Madeira, snapping out of the half-trance he'd fallen into listening to Novikoff. The damn Russian tended to get carried away by the sound of his own words. He had no way of knowing where the lies began and the truth ended, but knew he was being fed a very small ration of one and quite a bit more of the other.

He turned and looked out into the dark bay, at *Asimov*'s lights and the lights of Catano behind her on the other side of the bay. His attention then settled on the gray launch that had surged out of the darkness into the terminal's floodlights and was turning and sidling up alongside the landing. Did he really want to return to the ship? Or did he want to grab the first cab he could find and head for the international airport? Miami couldn't be more than an hour away. Maybe he'd end up sitting next to Niko.

The thought made him smile briefly. Whatever else he was, the Georgian was a good conversationalist.

"Captain Novikoff!"

Madeira and Novikoff both turned and watched as Vasily Chernov approached.

"What happened to *you*?" asked the chief mate, staring at Madeira. "Did you go for a night swim?"

"Captain Madeira had some trouble," Novikoff answered. "Some thugs tried to rob him."

Chernov burst out laughing, bending over and slapping his knees. "That's very funny! Madeira attacked here, in one of his own country's colonies. I thought *we* were the hated enemy."

Novikoff scowled while Chernov, his normally brutal sneer temporarily replaced by a nasty smile, continued to chuckle at his own joke.

"Let me help you down to the boat," Novikoff offered as they walked along the terminal's dock toward the launch.

"I can make it. Thanks," replied Madeira, walking slowly and carefully as he did.

"Will there be any more boats tonight?" shouted the security guard from somewhere in the shadows.

"Mike?" Madeira asked.

"No," Novikoff shouted to the unseen guard. "No more boats tonight."

Chapter Sixteen

At eleven-twenty the swells remained slight and the wind was blowing a moderate ten to fifteen from the northeast. The sun was bright and hot, the sky almost cloudless, and not a speck of land was in sight from *Asimov*'s pilothouse.

Captain Bukinin looked down at the Global Positioning System plot and then shouted an order to the helmsman. The ship turned slightly to starboard, almost directly into the wind, and continued on at slow speed. Five minutes later, Bukinin again consulted the navplot and shouted another order. The engines where brought to stop. "We are there," he said, stepping back from the navigational console.

"What's the bearing to the sonar beacon?" asked Novikoff.

"It's almost directly beneath us."

"Then I too would say we're there," Novikoff announced with a hearty smile. "Now the fun begins, right, Al?"

Madeira nodded, wondering if Novikoff's definition of fun bore any resemblance at all to his own.

"Vasily," Bukinin said to his chief officer, "engage the

175

dynamic positioning system. Maintain our present position and heading."

"Yes, Captain," replied Chernov, turning to a large electronic console. "We will make it just as easy as we can for Captain Madeira. He's been having a difficult time lately."

Everybody laughed, Madeira through clenched teeth. The bastard's lucky to be alive, he thought.

Just that morning, shortly after they'd cleared Punta del Morro, he'd watched as Chernov clambered up out of a large foredeck hatch. Suddenly, from behind the five-hundred-pound watertight door, a hand whipped out and yanked away the brace holding the door up.

If the timing had been just a fraction of a second better, the son of a bitch's neck would have been broken by the door's knife edge. As it was, his leg was badly bruised and his disposition rendered even worse than usual.

Not having seen the hand themselves, neither Bukinin nor Chernov seemed really sure whether the incident was the result of carelessness or malice. Timon claimed to be convinced it was, indeed, an effort to kill the chief mate, but he had no way of being sure. Only Madeira had seen the hand, and he hadn't mentioned it to anybody. Not even Novikoff.

He felt the beat of the ship's main engines rise slightly, then diminish again as the dynamic positioning system, a technology originally developed to permit the drilling of deepwater oil wells, took control. Until further notice a computer would employ gentle nudges from the main engines coupled with steady pressure from several pairs of thrusters, small propellers mounted in little cavities in the sides of the ship below the waterline, to maintain *Asimov*'s position with surprising accuracy.

"Prepare to launch ROV," Bukinin said, in Russian into the intercom.

"I thought we'd agreed to speak English, Captain!" snapped Novikoff.

"Of course, Captain," Bukinin replied. "It's fortunate we

had the foresight to learn Captain Madeira's language before we hired him.''

Far below, on one of the platforms built between the hulls, Boris Timon and two helpers hoisted the ten-foot-long Sturgeon Remotely Operated Vehicle clear of its cradle.

"You take control now, Alexi," Bukinin boomed in heavily accented English into the intercom.

"Thank you, Captain," replied the senior ROV technician, who was located one deck below the bridge in the ship's Underwater Operations Center. "Timon, launch the ROV," he continued, having shoved the wad of bubble gum in his mouth into the pouch of his left cheek.

Timon nodded to one of his mates, who punched the Down button on the lift. He then watched as the ROV dropped quickly through the quiet, gently heaving surface. It's so nice and cool here, he thought as he watched the ROV hang just below the surface, waiting to be released. Thanks to the water's ability to bend and distort light, the Sturgeon seemed to flex gently, almost as if it were alive, swimming through the wonderfully clear fluid flowing slowly past.

"Da," he muttered under his breath as he tripped the lifting hook. The tetherless probe, now controlled by Alexi at his console in the Operations Center, disappeared almost immediately into the limitless dark below.

And soon we will follow it down, he thought.

"Everything still under control, Alexi?" Novikoff asked as he, Bukinin, and Madeira entered the operations center.

"Yes, Captain," replied Alexi between furious chews on his gum. "It's about halfway there now. In a few minutes we should be able to see something."

Madeira noticed a sneer on Bukinin's face when the captain spotted the Chicago Cubs baseball cap Alexi was wearing backward. Only a Russian would be a Cubs fan, he thought. He knew full well the cap was a gift from some relative in Chicago and that Alexi knew absolutely nothing about baseball.

177

Trying not to laugh, he glanced at Alexi's color video monitor.

Nothing. What did he expect? Mermaids? There's never anything to see at five hundred feet, especially when the bottom's another five hundred farther down.

His glance wandered over the electronics-jammed room. Viktoria, he noticed, was standing by herself in front of another monitor.

"You hoping to spot a microvent or two?" he asked, moving over beside her.

"Yes," she replied, her eyes still fixed on the featureless video screen.

Then she turned and looked at him. And laughed. "Ah! You don't believe I'm really looking for them, do you? You think they're just part of the cover for the operation and that maybe I'm beginning to believe my own lies!"

"I'm not sure at the moment. I don't think I even knew they existed before you started talking about them."

"Neither did any of those reporters. No matter what I said, all they wanted to talk about was politics, Rustoff, and drugs. Except for that one fellow who seemed so sure we're conducting some sort of antisubmarine acoustics work!"

"Are we?" As he asked, Madeira found it hard to breathe. Even in dungarees, a crisp white blouse, and small earings, she was much too glamorous for this trashy scow and its schizoid crew.

"Not with all the noise you and Mike will be making."

Lies inside lies inside lies, thought Madeira. Everybody was lying, and everybody else knew it but acted as if he didn't. Does she know that I know she's an intelligence officer?

"Then there really are microvents?"

"Yes, but they're very difficult to spot and they're not very sexy. Many only discharge a few gallons a minute, so their plumes are very small. They look like the little springs you sometimes see on the bottoms of lakes. In fact, some turn out to be just that. Little artesian springs. The only way we can be sure one's a volcanic microvent, and not just a shallow little spring, is by collecting a water sample and analyzing it.''

''How do you expect to find them if they're so difficult to spot?''

''It's not that hard. They often occur along the boundaries between the plates, especially near bigger vents, although those aren't really the ones that interest me. They're usually just offshoots from the big ones. I'm interested in the isolated ones.''

''Why?''

''I want to determine if they're precursors of big vents which are to come or leftovers from old vents which have closed off. If they are precursors, then they may be helpful for predicting earthquakes and volcanism.''

''So you just keep looking in geologically active areas, hoping to find one or two?''

''There are other things I'd also like to be doing, but I won't be able to until you and Mike finish.''

''There it is!'' said Madeira, his eyes having returned to the monitor.

''What?''

''The bottom. The probe's reached the bottom.''

Still smiling, Viktoria turned back to the screen.

Naval Intelligence or not, thought Madeira, she's mad as a hatter. Just like the rest of them, only different. Or she's a damn skilled actress.

''Alexi's very good,'' Viktoria said. ''Look, he's already found the wreck.''

Reluctantly, Madeira turned his thoughts from Viktoria and studied the screen. There, at the edge of the ROV's limited light field, was the dark suggestion of unnatural mass, of man-made edges and angles, of calculated geometric forms only now made irregular by nature.

He wanted to remain where he was, standing next to Viktoria, watching the wreck assume more concrete shape, but knew he was expected to return to Mike and Bukinin. ''Excuse me,'' he said. ''Duty calls.''

''We'll make a good Russian out of you yet,'' she replied,

her electric blue eyes smiling. A hint of doubt then flashed through them. "I heard what happened to you last night," she said very quietly. "Novikoff told me. I'm sorry. But you know it had nothing to do with us."

"Of course not. It was a pack of local punks." And that, he thought as he said it, was probably the first time in weeks that he'd heard the truth.

"Were you surprised when Mike told you I'm a naval officer like him . . . and you?"

"A little. But I shouldn't have been. I understand the importance of disinformation in this project."

She turned back to the monitor before Madeira could see her reaction to his sharp, almost bitter response.

Goddamnit! he thought, I'm getting all tangled up over this girl when I should be concentrating totally on the job.

"Al, look at this!" Novikoff said as Madeira stopped beside him. "We found it right off! A good omen, don't you think?"

"I'm impressed as hell. I've never been able to find anything this quickly, even with a sonar transponder in place."

Even Bukinin allowed a brief smile of satisfaction to cross his normally rocklike face as one of the wreck's bow dive planes appeared clearly in the center of the screen, sticking out at them almost like a whale's fin.

As he watched the display, Madeira realized just how big the sub really was. Even though the ROV's lights were simply not strong enough to illuminate the entire vessel, it was obvious that she was much bigger than he'd appreciated in New York. It was also becoming clear that she was not as twisted and distorted as he'd assumed.

"Those photos you showed me in New York were very deceptive. The wreck's in much better shape than I'd expected."

"It may even be possible," replied Novikoff thoughtfully, "for us to learn why she sank."

"I don't see why not," Madeira said, almost immediately regretting his hasty response. What if they found evidence of a depth-charge attack? Or the deep, brutal gash left by a destroyer's bow where it had been driven through the sub's flank?

After all these years would the sub's crew demand vengeance? Would their ghosts emerge to upset whatever good might come out of the operation?

"I think," Bukinin said, "we would all be interested in learning more about that."

"Captain Novikoff," interjected Alexi as he studied one of the windows that appeared only on his screen, "the probe indicates a much higher level of radiation than was recorded the last time the wreck was monitored."

"How much higher?" Novikoff demanded.

"A factor of one hundred, sir. In close to the wreck."

"Damn!" Madeira said. The appearance of solidity was clearly an illusion, he thought with a sigh. And what did he expect after almost four decades? "It sounds to me like the reactor itself, its housing and shield anyway, are going faster than we expected."

"What about the hull?" asked Novikoff.

"That must be going too," Madeira observed. "Otherwise there wouldn't be so much circulation."

Novikoff turned and looked at him. "The ball's in your court now. You're the expert."

A little under three thousand tons of hot rust, he thought. Or, at best, a badly cracked and leaking three-thousand-ton eggshell. He was expected to split the egg and then bring half of it to the surface without losing the yolk.

The soup they'd be working in was a hell of a lot hotter than he'd expected. Maybe it was best to leave it where it was.

No. It was too shallow and too close to the civilized world. And, whether or not he really cared about civilization, there were always the shrimp-loving whales to worry about.

"The first thing I've got to do is go down myself, in the Beluga, to see just how fragile it really is." As he spoke, Madeira felt a tightness stretch across his chest.

"Who do you want for your pilot?"

William S. Schaill

"Timon, I guess. Boris Timon."

"Very good."

Had Novikoff already known about the elevated radiation? wondered Madeira as he headed down into *Asimov*'s cool bowels. Despite his words, the Russian hadn't really seemed surprised when Alexi announced it. And what else wasn't he being told?

Viktoria continued to study the monitor while out of the corner of her eye she watched Madeira's form disappear down the ladder.

How he reminded her of Leo! Dear, dead Leo. Blunt. Linear. Always hoping darkly for the best but not really expecting it. Skilled in so many things, yet incapable of lying convincingly. Unable, it would seem, to truly hate. Not really qualified to be a Russian. Or anybody, for that matter.

How'd he done it? How had Leo managed to get caught between a couple hundred stubborn, possibly deluded madmen who'd turned the Parliament building into a fortress and two battalions of crack Interior Ministry troops?

Despite his many enthusiasms she knew Leo had no taste for martyrdom. He'd become one only by accident.

Once the killing was done and the fires extinguished, his body was discovered. She'd never been able to learn, without attracting too much attention to herself, exactly how he'd died. Gunshot? Explosion? Fire? She shuddered at what he must have felt.

He was, of course, immediately identified as one of the rebels, as one of those who wished to turn the clock back. But she knew damn well he wasn't. He was in there trying to make some sort of a deal. Put together some sort of a compromise. God only knew what. And he'd been caught in the middle. Just like Madeira was now. Caught between even more factions than she was sure she could identify.

Fortunately, her affair with Leo hadn't come to official attention. At least not yet. When and if it did, she was sure they'd let her know.

One way or another.

182

Chapter Seventeen

"Make yourself comfortable, Captain," Timon said, without a hint of irony in his voice. Madeira limited his response to a grunt as he wiggled his widening, and increasingly less flexible, middle-aged body into the Beluga's copilot's seat.

A white steel bulkhead pressed against him from behind. The control console was jammed up under his chin. Behind him a crummy little fan rattled as it tried bravely to give him a haircut. Electronics everywhere else. And throughout it all, the ever-present, faint stench. Of plastic cable covering. Of human bodies. Of discomfort, stress, and fear.

In a word, skintight. Just like the whole damn project.

Timon spat a torrent of unintelligible Russian into the microphone, then glanced at Madeira. "I'm sorry. I forgot."

Madeira nodded, then looked back and up while Grivski, who was standing on the sub's deck, slammed the hatch closed and locked it. With another quiet grunt Madeira turned his head forward again and looked out through the small viewing port, in the only direction that promised relief from the familiar sense of compression. He could see a por-

183

tion of *Asimov*'s luxuriant, gray-green fur swaying and rippling gracefully in the brilliant, blue swells as the worksub hung suspended between the research ship's twin hulls. As he watched he listened to Alexi and Timon go over the final prelaunch checklist.

"We're ready now," Timon said, glancing to his right at Madeira as he spoke. "They'll launch on your command."

"Okay. Let's do it," Madeira said, assuming that Grivski was clear and would get himself back aboard *Asimov*.

"*Da!*" Timon replied enthusiastically. "Launch!" he shouted into the mike.

The Beluga lurched, then shuddered, as the lifting hook was tripped. Timon immediately shoved the joystick forward and revved up the motors, eager to get well below the research ship's massive hulls before something unfortunate happened.

Madeira took a deep breath. It was always this way, he thought. Not fear, but unease. An experienced wariness coupled with a certain anticipation.

How long ago was it? he asked himself. Almost two years now that he'd sworn he'd never do a deep job again. Only fun jobs in shallow, sunlit seas. But things hadn't worked out, and here he was again. Headed down. Doing whatever it is that Al Madeira does because there's nothing else for him to do except chase whales and go deep.

He tried to stretch and found it impossible. Every cubic centimeter was jammed with hard, sharp somethings.

"Damnit!" he growled.

Timon smiled in sympathy.

Madeira stared out the viewing port a few minutes, watching as the surrounding blue darkened inexorably into a black that swallowed the floodlights' most valiant efforts. In the cabin, the only illumination came from the red, green, and yellow idiot lights on the surrounding black boxes and gauges.

"Three hundred feet, *Asimov*. All okay?" Timon asked.

"Very well," replied Alexi.

"So far," said Timon, turning toward Madeira, "all goes well."

Madeira looked down at the depth gauge. Three hundred twenty-five feet.

"So far, so good."

As they continued their spiral descent into the heavy waters, Madeira practiced aiming the two external TV cameras, even though there was absolutely nothing in sight—living, dead, or imaginary—to aim them at.

"You Americans are doing very well at the Olympics. In the downhill skiing."

"Yes, that's what I hear," replied Madeira, who hated skiing. "Do you ski?"

"No. When I was a boy that was only for very select people. And there are no mountains near St. Petersburg."

"So what did you do all winter?"

"Work. Ice-skate. And many people just drink."

"Beluga!" Alexi's voice interrupted the discussion. "How does your ammeter read?"

Timon glanced at the gauges on his console. "All readings normal, *Asimov*."

"Very well."

"What's all that about?" Madeira asked.

"The engineers were worried about two of the batteries, but they appear to be working fine."

Five minutes later, the wreck's stern was in sight.

"What now?" asked Timon.

"Let's go completely around it once. Slowly."

Timon turned the Beluga sharply to port and started along the wreck's starboard side. As they went, Madeira alternately studied the two video monitors and strained to see out the viewing port.

Detail by detail, the long-dead ship was revealed. She was lying, listing to starboard, bow down, on a gentle slope. Originally dull black, the wreck was now graced with a ghostly shroud of pale ooze almost like a woman's heavy face powder.

The stern, an angular jumble of propellers and steering

planes, swelled slowly into the long, molded waist, then finally narrowed again slightly into the bow, which had a bulging overhang not unlike an overdeveloped forehead.

Overhead, leaning to one side and disappearing into the murk like a shadow, rose the conning tower. And on the tower was the final giveaway, the big rectangular windows, almost picture windows, with which so many Foxtrots were built.

There was no doubt about it. At least they hadn't lied about the sub's pedigree. The wreck had started life as a Foxtrot-class submarine, a design of essentially World War II origins. And because, as Novikoff had put it, the Foxtrot had been their most popular export model, the American intelligence pubs had been full of pictures of them for decades. Cuba, India, Libya, Poland . . . you name it. If it had any waterfront at all, and if it'd ever had a feud with the United States, it had a Foxtrot or two.

But something was missing. It, the wreck and the surrounding bottom, were all too quiet. Lifeless. There was nothing swimming or burrowing or squirming. Could it possibly be the radiation, or was it just his imagination?

"It seems awfully quiet here," he remarked.

"Captain?" Boris replied with a puzzled look.

"I don't see any life. Nothing's moving but us."

"It's always quiet down deep."

He's right, thought Madeira. It's an absolute wasteland. A place only the French Foreign Legion would feel at home.

"There!" said Boris, pointing at the monitor.

Madeira followed his finger and saw a sea star of some sort, twitching slowly on the bottom.

"Okay," he replied, accepting that the impression of lifelessness was just in his imagination.

He leaned forward to study the bottom more carefully and caught himself looking for evidence of microvents. You moron! he thought. He still wasn't even sure they existed anywhere but in Viktoria's own obviously fertile imagination.

"Boris," he finally remarked after returning his attention

to the wreck, "I can't see anything obvious to explain what happened."

"Neither can I," answered the pilot. "I noticed one or two bent plates . . . but those may have happened when it hit the bottom."

"It also looks damn solid, though God only knows what's going on inside."

"Perhaps the skeletons are dancing . . ."

Madeira glanced at him.

". . . with joy, sir, that we have finally come back to get them. It was a joke, sir. I intended no insult or disrespect."

"I never thought you did." He tried to lean back, to take a deep breath, and found the chair and the console wouldn't let him.

"If I may say so, sir, you are in a very difficult position aboard *Asimov* and most of us understand that. These times are as confusing for us as they are for you. Those who understand the situation fully appreciate your experience and leadership."

"Thank you. That was quite a pep talk."

"A pep talk?"

"A speech designed to make me feel better."

"I say only what I, myself, feel."

They continued in silence for several minutes. Madeira studied the videos while attempting to identify a faint grinding he thought he heard, or felt, while Timon concentrated on piloting the Beluga around the wreck's bow and back along its port side.

"You hear a grinding sound?" he finally asked. "Sounds as if a bearing is failing."

Timon was silent a moment. "Yes. I think I do, but all oil-pressure and temperature gauges are in order."

Madeira knew there was nothing more to be done except abort the dive due to bumps heard in the night, until something more dramatic happened. He'd already learned that much of the Russian gear seemed to grind and moan and still keep running.

"Let's circle a few minutes," Madeira said when they

187

had returned to the wreck's stern and still found nothing obvious to explain the sub's loss.

As he spoke he studied the keypad in front of him. Not only were the labels in Russian, but the alphabet was Cyrillic. He'd spent hours trying, with Timon's help, to memorize both key portions of the Slavic script and a number of command sequences. The commands he now needed totally eluded him.

"How the hell do I shift to Virtual Mode?" he finally asked, both irritated and embarrassed.

"Here, let me show you," answered Timon, reaching across toward the keypad. "What exactly did you want?"

"The three-dimensional image of the wreck as she lies, with observed radiation levels superimposed."

"You'll have it, sir, and please don't be embarrassed. This system, like all Russian high-tech systems, was designed to be totally impenetrable by Americans."

The sound of Alexi's manic laughter reminded Madeira that everything they said could be heard aboard *Asimov*, where it was also undoubtedly being recorded.

Timon rapidly tapped a long sequence, paused, tapped in several more letters, then withdrew his arm and glanced up at his own two monitors.

All four monitors immediately blinked out, making the cabin even darker than it had been.

Timon erupted into a long, sharp string of what Madeira thought he recognized as Russian obscenities.

"What are you doing down there, Boris?"

"I'm proving the superiority of Russian technology, Alexi. Now, shut up!"

"As you can see," continued Boris to Madeira, "our designers are very, very good. This particular system has shut itself down simply because it knows you are here."

"Do you think you can fool it into believing I've left?" Madeira asked, laughing.

"All Russians can be fooled. Even electronic ones. I'll try if you will steer."

Ten minutes later, after three tries and a great deal of

explosive mumbling in Russian, Timon had the system up and running again. Before their eyes glowed a 3-D doppelgänger of the wreck; an image so detailed that even the two bent plates that Timon had noticed were clearly visible.

It was entirely possible, thought Madeira, that all Russians really were fools. But they certainly weren't necessarily stupid, even though much of the system might be based on American technology.

Constructed electronically from the sub's plans and updated by data from the Beluga's high-resolution side-scanning sonar, the neon-colored clone rested on her starboard side, bow down. The entire image was bathed in reds and pinks; the darker the tone, the greater the level of detected radiation.

At first glance the display provided no major surprises, although the intensity of the radiation was much greater than Madeira had hoped for. Other than that it showed what he'd expected to see: The red was considerably darker aft of the conning tower, where the reactor and turbine rooms were located, and the pink halo around the wreck bulged noticeably to the north, along with the Antilles Current's set.

On closer examination, however . . .

"Take a look at this," said Madeira, pointing at the virtual sub, about fifty feet aft of the conning tower. "Is that really a blob of extra-dark red, or is it my imagination?"

Timon squinted at the video a moment, then leaned across and tinkered with the video controls. "I think you're right. That spot is very certainly darker than the rest. The pressure hull must be damaged there."

"Let's go see."

Timon nodded in agreement as he turned the Beluga and headed along the wreck's aft deck.

"We should be there now," Timon said. "Can you see anything?"

"Not so far," mumbled Madeira as he tried to concentrate all the worksub's floodlights on one section of the deck. "The deck grating's the problem. It looks twisted, but it's hard to see through. Can you get any closer?"

Madeira's gut jumped a few inches as Timon suddenly dropped the trembling worksub to within a foot of the sub's canted deck.

"I am sorry about that. There are eddies around the wreck. Does that help?"

"Yes, very much," replied Madeira, his concentration centered on the video display. "I can see a shadow below the grating. I think it's a hole in the pressure hull."

"How big is it?" Timon asked as he struggled to avoid ramming the wreck.

"Hard to say. About a meter across, maybe less." Just about the size a destroyer's five-inch-high explosive projectile might make, he thought. Especially if it didn't explode until after penetrating an unarmored deck.

"Big enough to sink the submarine?"

"And to explain the hot spot . . . What the hell's that!"

"What?"

"Something just oozed out of the hole. A big eel or something. It's hiding under the grating."

"I can't see anything. Is it still there?"

"Yes. Come to think of it, it wasn't moving very fast before. Can you bang on the grating?"

Timon extended one of the Beluga's work arms and tapped. The creature moved slightly.

"I see it now," said the Russian. "Perhaps it's one of the crew member's soul. It doesn't look healthy to me."

"What sins could they possibly have committed to be reincarnated in such a hideous form, Boris?"

"Do you really believe in reincarnation? In life after death?"

"I don't think so. Do you?"

"No, but my wife does. She's a Christian and is very happy now to be able to go to church without fear that they're going to arrest her and the children."

"I'm glad for her, that she now has the choice. Do you think there's enough room for us to reach under the grating and grab that sorry-looking soul? Riki might like it for his collection."

"Not with this arm. This one will cut it in half. I'll try the other one."

"You drive the sub. I'll handle the arm."

Timon smiled and started to say something, then didn't.

While Timon folded one arm away, Madeira extended the other and spent another minute or two making sure that he had the feel of it.

"Okay. Can you move a few feet to the right?" asked Madeira finally. "I think I can get in near the hole, where the grating's bent."

"I'll try. You understand that if the arm gets caught under there and the Beluga moves suddenly the arm will break off just like a human one would?"

"Yes, I understand."

Chewing gently on his lower lip, Timon edged the Beluga to the right and down. As he did, the water streams emerging from the thrusters caused little globs of silt and gunk along the wreck's deck to burst into frantic motion and skitter away, almost as if they were alive.

Then with equal if not greater concentration, Madeira inserted the articulated arm through the grating and managed to grab the eel on the first try.

"Well done, Captain!" Timon shouted.

"It was nothing. Catching fish, any kind of fish, is second nature to us Portuguese. It's in our blood."

As he spoke Madeira pulled the barely struggling creature out into the open.

Evil-looking son of a bitch, he thought, placing it in a specimen basket. It looked as if it was covered with sores and somehow deformed. Cockeyed. Twisted. Bent. Something!

You could never be sure, though. Some of the deeper-dwelling species naturally look like they've just arrived from another planet.

Chapter Eighteen

"I understand you want to get this done as quickly as possible," said Madeira as he used a piece of black bread to mop up the remains of the meat stew, "but we have to plug that hole before we stir up all the crap inside!"

He was all too aware that his mother would be very disappointed with his table manners. His mother, however, was a long life at sea away and he was very tired and hungry, the Beluga not having completed its survey and been hoisted back aboard until almost midnight.

"I'm not suggesting we make the wreck watertight; all I want to do is keep the shit from splashing out while we're lifting and transporting. For that matter, I don't want it oozing out on us while we're working there, either."

Novikoff ground the butt of one of his rare cigarettes into an ashtray already overflowing. "We're running out of time. The situation in Moscow isn't getting any better. The radicals' influence seems to be increasing every day. Even if they don't actually seize power, they may be able to force President Yeltsin to order us home."

Madeira sipped his beer and glanced around the main salon, looking for support. Bukinin and Chernov were sitting at the other end of the table, drinking vodka and smoking. No allies there. And why did they waste their longevity on that tasteless garbage?

"Viktoria," he finally said, "please give Mike a good reason or two to agree with me."

The geophysicist put down the mug from which she'd been sipping tea as she listened to Madeira and Novikoff. "I can't improve on the ones you've already given," she said, "but if you'll all be patient a few minutes, Riki probably can."

Madeira finished the beer and went to get another. A cigar would taste good too, he thought, remembering the dapper old Puerto Rican gentleman, but if he was stupid enough to start again he'd never be able to stop.

"How much longer will he be?" demanded Novikoff, looking at Viktoria.

Viktoria picked up the telephone and mumbled into it. "He's on his way," she said, hanging up.

A very few tense moments later, Riki Akadian, the ship's senior biologist, walked in, carrying a plastic bag. "Al was totally correct about this eel," he said, looking first at Novikoff and then at Madeira. "Not only did it have several kinds of cancer but it was also a mutant, possibly a second- or third-generation mutant. I think it's the result of several generations living in the reactor."

"Or near it, assuming the shield's deteriorating?" Madeira asked.

"Yes, I suspect anywhere in the reactor or turbine compartments. We have to assume everything in those two compartments is very seriously contaminated."

"Based on the radiation readings we now have," said Madeira, leaning back and fidgeting with the new radiation dosimeter Olga had just issued him, "I'm afraid the whole wreck's more contaminated than we've been assuming."

"I have no choice but to agree with you."

"Captain Novikoff, have you had a chance to look closely at this thing?" Riki asked suddenly.

Madeira was surprised at the sharpness of Riki's tone and the violence with which the normally retiring biologist shoved the grotesque exhibit at Novikoff.

"Yes, I have," Novikoff snapped as his head jerked back, making very clear his lack of interest in looking closely again.

"Imagine the press we'll get if somebody decides we're causing more of those," said Madeira, deciding to play to Novikoff's obsession with the news media. "Or if they think we're letting them loose. A simple strongback patch will probably do the trick."

A look of almost horror swept across Novikoff's face and then was replaced by an element of calculation. "Very well!" he said finally, his face beginning to relax into a smile. "A strongback. You don't plan to spend time welding it, do you?"

"No. That won't be necessary."

"How long will it take you?"

"Two of us should be able to do it in a few hours of bottom time. Figure we're adding a day to the operation."

"It will take you at least a day to rig the power line for the hand lasers."

"I don't plan to use lasers for this. We'll use gas . . . even though it'll take a lot of it at that depth."

"Okay, I hate to lose even one day, but it's important that we do this job right. I want Grivski to videotape the damage along with the corrective action we're taking, just for the record."

"Okay," said Madeira, still amused at what he was beginning to see as Novikoff's love-hate relationship with the media. First Meg Jefferson and now he was producing his own home videos. Given a little time, he thought, Novikoff's going to develop into a regular spinmaster. Get himself a job in Washington.

"Very well," Novikoff said finally. "Get some sleep and

then get down there! I can't stress enough the need for haste!''

"Zero eight hundred?"

"Eight's fine. I understand you all need a little rest."

Madeira stood and started for the door.

"Not so fast!" Viktoria said.

"Yes?"

"Don't forget that dosimeter. Olga and I want those back the instant you return. From all of you."

Madeira smiled briefly, then returned to the table and picked up the dosimeter.

Sitting as usual in the copilot's chair, Madeira watched as Grivski guided the Beluga worksub forward between *Asimov*'s vegetation-covered bottoms and then almost immediately down into the dark, heavy waters.

The Russian, he decided, was almost always lost in some dark, cold world of his own. The blankness of his expression wasn't the result of stupidity but rather of an almost cosmic . . . disinterest? The fates of those around him seemed of no concern. Neither did his own. He was totally self-contained and showed no evidence of ever feeling pleasure, pain, or fear.

What, Madeira asked himself, could have happened to Grivski to make his eyes so stony, so dead? Had it been Afghanistan? And what was he doing there, anyway?

No, he decided. It hadn't been Afghanistan. Whatever it was had happened long before that—and probably was used there by his superiors.

The most frightening thing about Grivski, he decided, was that he, Madeira, was certain at times that he felt exactly what Grivski felt. Or didn't feel. He couldn't explain the sensation's precise origins, but he was familiar with the result. The great emptiness that he suspected dominated the Russian also existed, although on a profoundly smaller scale, within him.

"Three hundred feet. All okay," Grivski reported.

Nine atmospheres, thought Madeira. The pressure's building fast.

"Very well, Beluga," Alexi replied.

Madeira leaned forward and spoke into the intercom: "You two okay back there?" he asked.

"Everything okay," replied Timon from the small compartment directly behind Madeira.

"You wish to bottom along the port side?" Grivski asked as the wreck slowly emerged from the surrounding shadows.

Madeira turned forward and looked up at the real-time monitor and then at the one displaying the computer-generated image with overlays. "Yes," he replied. "Just aft of the conning tower."

Despite the Beluga's heavy load, Grivski settled it down onto the ooze with extraordinary delicacy, raising only the smallest cloud of silt. The man's hand-eye coordination was fabulous.

"Boris," Madeira said, "let's dress."

"Yes, Captain," replied Madeira's dive buddy as he led the way down the ladder to the Beluga's lower deck.

"Grivski," Madeira said as his head disappeared through the hatch, "that was a super landing!"

"Thank you." The tone of Grivski's reply made Madeira think of a voice-mail recording.

"As soon as Timon and I lock out," added Madeira, "you have Mendalov help you dress, then lock you out. We'll head on over to the wreck."

"Yes."

As Madeira helped Timon into his semi-armored dress he could hear Grivski and Mendalov speaking in Russian.

"Grivski!" Timon shouted suddenly. "Show some respect to the captain. Speak English!"

After a moment of strained silence, Grivski's face appeared at the head of the ladder. "We apologize, Captain. We were just talking about home. No disrespect was intended."

"They were talking about politics," Timon said in a quiet

196

voice after Grivski's face had disappeared. "They were talking about whether the President would survive or not."

"Yeltsin? Survive? You mean stay in office?"

"Survive."

"Oh," said Madeira.

What had Lane Williams said? "Fortunately, TV's our preferred weapon." And practically everybody else seemed to find real blood more satisfying?

They sealed each other's diving dress and helmet. Then, breathing from the auxiliary oxygen bottles, they entered the tubelike lock that led out from the inside of the Beluga, and secured the inner hatch.

"Flood the lock," Timon directed after they had completed one final gear check.

"Flooding the lock," replied Mendalov in a harsh, electronic voice. A voice, thought Madeira, totally devoid of humanity.

Within an instant the cold, dark waters poured in, swirling and snapping, and bringing with them a pounding tension. Madeira watched as the deep ocean rose, foaming, to his knees, and then to his waist.

He was way too old for this shit, he told himself as he listened to his own forced breathing. The cold. The fatigue. The pressure. The terrible risk of embolism, of being squeezed, of the bends or of simply drowning. The risks had been great when he was young and technically overweight. Now that he was old and really overweight—he was well over forty—the risks were completely off the chart. The navy would never have permitted him to make this dive at his age.

And on top of all that, his gut still hurt from where he'd been slugged in San Juan. Could Olga have been wrong? Was it just bruises and sore muscles, or had something serious been damaged? His kidneys? His liver, maybe? He wondered precisely which symptoms he should be looking for.

"The pressure has equalized and the outer hatch is open."

He heard Timon's report and looked down past the small

stage on which they were standing. He saw no pretty girls in skimpy bathing suits swimming by. Neither did he see any happy dive instructors feeding the local pet moray eel. All he saw was an icy blackness. And it was waiting for him.

"Follow me, Boris," he said as he stepped into the hole.

A chill flowed through Madeira as he floated down to the ooze. He checked the dress's heat control. It wasn't that, he decided.

Then Timon landed beside him.

"All okay, Boris?" he asked.

"All okay," replied Timon.

They attached their tethers, the stalklike bundle composed of their communications cables and their breathing gas hoses, tested them, and secured the auxiliary oxygen bottles.

Madeira looked at the wreck, or at that small portion of it illuminated by the Beluga's lights. They always turned out to be so damn big, he thought. As modern subs go she wasn't very big, but when you're right there, standing under them, even relatively small wrecks look very big. Over forty feet from the keel, where he stood, to the deck. Almost seven men standing on each other's shoulders. A great, looming mass, largely invisible but all too palpable, it seemed to radiate a blackness far denser than that generated by the great ocean depths.

How many hundreds of other Cold War souvenirs were lying around on the bottom? he wondered. Reminders of the decades of war-level stress and fatigue and the resulting accidents, errors, stupidities, miscalculations, and misunderstandings.

He took a step toward the wreck and stopped suddenly as a solid shadow erupted from the ooze and slithered off into the surrounding night. You ass! he thought. It was only a fish. Then he heard what sounded like a chuckle coming from Timon.

He looked up again at the wreck's great round bottom and side. Although the submarine was lying with a considerable tilt to starboard, and the upper portion of the hull was sloping away from them, there was no way they could climb up the underbody. Not even with neutral buoyancy. And he sure as hell wasn't going to screw around with positive buoyancy! Not on Timon's first dive in the semi-armored dress. That was a real easy way to kill the Russian. And himself, too.

Dragging their tethers and the gas hoses for their cutting torches, the two divers trudged aft toward the sub's stern. With each step they raised small clouds of silt along with an occasional slithery shadow. When they reached the stern they increased their buoyancy to neutral and bounded up to the port propeller guard. They glided on to the propeller itself, then forward to the shaft and finally onto the fair-water, the nonwatertight external covering that protected the two inner hulls from dings and dents and gave the sub a more hydrodynamic shape. Then, grabbing whatever hand-holds they could find on the fairwater, they crawled forward, following the slight tumblehome.

"Almost there!" Madeira said at last.

"Good!" grunted Timon.

With Timon right beside him, Madeira pulled himself up onto the canted deck and looked around. "All right," he said, shining a light through the deck grating. "I think we've got to go forward another fifteen or so feet."

"Okay," Timon replied as he stepped forward.

The Russian's weighted boot landed on the slime-slick deck and continued forward as if on business of its own. Timon slipped, then split, then tumbled backward in slow motion and slid across the deck.

"Hang on!" Madeira shouted as he grabbed Timon's tether.

"To what?" replied Timon, grabbing fruitlessly at the deck as he slipped.

Totally out of control, the Russian skied backward down the sloping deck. Then, at the very last minute, just before he toppled over the side, he was jerked to a halt by the tether.

"Okay," he shouted as he grabbed the grating and started

to drag himself back up to the high side. "I'm saved!"

"Here, look," Madeira said a few minutes later. "The deck's distorted here and I can see the hole below it. I think I'm looking right into the sub."

As he spoke he could sense water flowing up out of the hole and past him. He wondered why it didn't look red like on the computer display.

"Yes," agreed Timon, looking into the gap. "That must be the reactor room itself."

"Please describe the hole!" The voice was Novikoff's, retransmitted by the Beluga. "Can you see what might have caused it?"

Madeira peered intently through the grating, shining his light around. "I won't know for sure until we've cleared away the deck, but it looks to me as if the hull was pushed out here, as if an explosion or something forced it out, and then it rusted away. The edges look very thin and pitted."

"You are sure the force was applied from the inside out? There is no chance that the hole was made from the outside in?"

"No. No chance," replied Madeira with a sense of relief, realizing that Novikoff had told something less than the truth when he said they weren't really interested in the cause of the sub's sinking. "As far as I can see, the damage is from the inside out."

"What do you think, Timon?"

Boris bent over and looked through the grating again. "I have to agree with Captain Madeira, sir," he said finally. "The edges are most definitely bent out."

What is there in a nuclear submarine to explode? thought Madeira as he waited for Novikoff to respond. The reactor itself? There'd be nothing left! High-pressure lubricating fluids? That'd been known to happen. But it was probably steam, he decided. The superheated steam generated by the reactor, then piped to the turbines, where it drove the sub's propeller. The U.S. Navy had enough trouble with steam over the years. The Russians had always been rumored to have even more.

"Very well," Novikoff said finally, "but don't cut anything until Grivski gets a chance to tape just what you now see."

"Roger," replied Madeira as he watched Grivski climb up the wreck's side. What, he wondered, would have happened if the edges *had* been bent in? Or if they'd found a wedge-shaped gash in the sub's side?

"Okay, Boris," said Madeira after Grivski had finished documenting the hole on videotape, "let's clear away this deck. Just to make sure we have room to maneuver, we're going to cut it back a meter or so beyond the hole."

"I understand," Boris replied as he lit off his gas torch with an audible pop and watched for a moment as a cascade of smoky, blue-orange bubbles pulsed then tumbled toward the surface, a thousand feet above.

It's a long way up, thought Madeira as he also watched the bubbles rise.

Chapter Nineteen

The Long Range Survey Vehicle zigzagged slowly as it ghosted through the heavy darkness. Above its stout, cigar-shaped body lay several thousand feet of thick water. Twenty feet below, and only dimly illuminated by the ROV's floodlights, rested the silty, almost featureless slope of the Puerto Rico Deep. Driven largely by the current, the vehicle's small propeller and motor were used primarily to change course as it surveyed an area about five miles north of *Asimov*.

Sitting in the operations center, tired of studying the LRSV's video transmissions and thermal sensors and not seeing what she wanted to see, Viktoria turned that drudgery over to the computer and directed her own attention to a second monitor. This screen displayed a seismographic map of the Deep with the LRSV's track overlaid in hot pink. Running down the center of the track was a dark blue line, the path of a major geological fault.

The pink track, she decided, looked like a seamstress's stitch, like something her favorite grandmother would have shown her with great pride. It was almost as if she were using the ROV to stitch together the two sides of the fault. To prevent them from shifting and causing the earth to tremble.

The conceit amused her at first, the idea that she, Viktoria Galin, might be binding the world together. Her amusement faded the more she fiddled with the idea. In this one case, she decided, the comparison might be uncomfortably accurate.

Fifty miles from Puerto Rico. Fifty miles from the United States. A massive radiation leak poisoning the ocean. A leak that could be easily traced back to Russia.

If their mission were to fail, or even if they were just caught in the act, the press would go crazy. There would be a crisis. The whole world would point at Moscow.

"Criminals!" they would all shout. Or even worse, "Incompetents!"

The earth would shake, and Yeltsin would stumble and fall.

Who would succeed him?

She wasn't sure, but the possibilities were far from encouraging.

"Spotted anything interesting yet, Dr. Galin?"

Viktoria looked over at Alexi. "Not yet, Alexi. How's your show doing?"

"I think the good guys are winning. They've finished cutting away the deck and are about to start on the hole itself."

Viktoria stood and walked over behind Alexi. "Which is which?"

"Captain Madeira's the one with the torch in his hand, and Timon's holding that piece of steel. Grivski has the video camera."

How innocent the scene looked, she thought. How workaday. And yet how fraught with danger.

She listened a moment as the divers discussed what they were going to do next, then she looked down at Alexi. Baseball cap on backward, always upbeat, he was totally immersed in the virtual world. He's completely immune, she thought. For the Alexis of this world the real terrors the rest of us fear simply don't exist. His universe is that screen and the semiconductors behind it. As long as he's able to hook into a net there's no such thing as death.

"You want to exchange jobs for a while?" Alexi asked.

"No, thank you," she replied, returning to her own seat. "If they need help, you're much better qualified to give it than I am."

"Okay."

Ten minutes later a messenger from the radio room handed her a message, still encrypted. "Captain Novikoff would like you to call him as soon as you've decrypted this."

"Very well," she replied. And then to Alexi, "I need somebody to take over here for a while, Alexi."

"Roger!"

"That's right," said Viktoria as she stood on the boat deck and looked into the stiff breeze, out where the dark blue of the Atlantic met the almost equally dark blue of the heavens. "The private investigator was hired by somebody Moscow has identified as a known member of one of the Chechen gangs."

"Do they have this gangster under arrest?"

"No. He was identified from a photograph. Nobody seems to know where he is."

"Could he be here? What does he look like?"

"Here is what they've faxed . . ." As she spoke, Viktoria handed him a slightly blurred photograph.

Novikoff studied the photo a minute. "I've never seen this person," he remarked finally, "have you?"

"No. I'm certain he's not aboard the ship."

"Very well!" snapped Novikoff, his tone and expression showing both acceptance and determination. "This greatly complicates matters, although I suspect that we all expected something like this. We have the radicals trying to sabotage us and now the Mafia trying to . . . get the plutonium, I suppose.''

''I don't see what else would interest them, unless they really have swallowed that gold nonsense Al's engineer has been babbling about.''

''No, it must be the plutonium. We must be even more alert now than ever, and we must pick up the pace. The longer we spend on this project, the more we're exposed.''

''I'm still not convinced the sabotage is as coordinated as you seem to feel it is.''

''You feel it's random?''

''I think it may be local dissatisfaction rather than some sort of organized political dissent.''

''You yourself admit that it's all been done where you don't have TV cameras.''

''The cameras are obvious and the sailors aren't fools.''

''Of course it's the radicals! Who will benefit more if this operation turns to shit?''

''Perhaps . . .''

''The Americans, their right-wingers, are the only other possibility.''

''I don't think that's very likely.''

''Neither do I, really. For now we'd better concentrate on the known threats: ultranationalist radicals and the Mafia. I think you and I should keep a close eye on Bukinin and Chernov. They're the loudest radicals aboard, and they're also in a very good position to make a great deal of trouble.''

''Yes.''

''I'm sure you'll find I'm right.''

Viktoria watched as Novikoff walked forward, her now-chronic sense of unease growing with every step he took.

There'd been something wrong with that conversation. The identification of the dead detective's employer was important, but it still left unanswered the equally important question of who killed the detective. And why.

And why was it done the way it was? Was it a work of careful calculation or was it one of rage, of fury? Or both?

William S. Schaill

It was a question that should have been of intense interest to Novikoff, but he'd made no reference whatsoever to it.

Three time zones to the east of *Asimov* a cold, midwinter gale pounded the Atlantic's night-darkened waters and shaped them into great, heaving thirty-foot seas. Through it all, like a massive, floating rock, the dry dock crept west, wallowing slightly but otherwise almost unaffected by the chaos around it.

"How goes it?" asked the sergeant as he approached the sentry on the narrow deck running along the dock's high, rain-swept wall.

"This is stupid!" replied Corporal Kardon, who had been leaning over the lifeline watching as the seas broke at the base of the great steel cliff. "Why does the major insist upon posting sentries way out here? And in full battle dress!"

"Mind your tongue!" the sergeant snapped. Then, his tone softening, he continued: "The major is taking reasonable precautions. The Mafia, and other enemies, are everywhere."

Kardon squinted sullenly at him a moment, then turned and looked out into the dark night. "Who are you kidding, Sergeant? Out here? On a night like this?"

"Attack comes when one least expects it, Corporal."

"Where's my relief? Somebody should be relieving me soon."

"Yes, Kardon. Very soon. A few minutes."

"What I wouldn't give for a cigarette and a dry place to smoke it!"

"I understand how you feel," replied the sergeant as he stepped closer, hanging on tightly to the lifeline with one hand, a razor-sharp knife ready in the other.

The sergeant took another step toward Kardon, who continued to stare out into the storm, then abandoned his grip on the lifeline, grabbed the corporal's helmet, and yanked back. In that same instant, the knife curved through the damp air around Kardon's head, then down and back across

206

his throat. All in one smooth, rapid motion. All before the victim could respond in any way.

Moving quickly, the sergeant pressed Kardon's body against the lifelines to keep it from bleeding on the deck. At the same time he lashed the dead commando's assault rifle to what remained of his neck and then shoved the limp mass of meat and munitions over the side. He watched the dark lump splash into the surf and disappear into the heaving black waters.

"Laptev! Are you sleeping on duty?"

Alexi jerked upright in his chair upon hearing his last name and spun around. "No sir, Mr. Chernov. I was not asleep, sir."

What's this bastard doing in my operations center? thought the technician as he looked up with a mixture of fear and irritation at the ship's chief mate. How did he get in without my hearing or seeing him?

Chernov continued to look down at him with a slight smile. He reached out and plucked the Cubs cap off Alexi's head. "This is shit, Laptev!" he said as he dropped the cap on the deck and stepped on it. "How can you wear shit like that?"

Alexi kept his mouth shut.

"I'll overlook your inattention to duty this time, but make sure it doesn't happen again!"

"Yes, sir," Alexi replied, hoping that would end it.

"I want to see the plan of the wreck. Can you get that on your computer?"

"Yes, sir," Alexi said, his fingers already dancing over the keyboard. "There, sir," he said after a moment or two, pointing at one of his several monitors.

Chernov leaned forward and studied the 3-D depiction of the wreck as she now existed. He placed his finger on the reactor, then moved it forward through the storeroom and then the berthing space.

"What's this blue line here?" he demanded, tapping the screen.

"That is where Captain Madeira plans to cut the wreck apart, sir."

"Why there? Why not in the storeroom?"

"Captain Madeira says it's to provide a safety zone around the reactor room, sir."

"Is there no other reason?"

"Not that I know, sir. Perhaps you should take it up with Captain Madeira." Alexi was beginning to feel alarm at the officer's attitude and expression.

"Don't be impudent, Laptev!"

"No, sir. I'm sorry, sir. I meant no disrespect."

"Take care, Laptev. Your little black boxes can't protect you against everything."

Before Alexi could decide whether the required reply was "No, sir" or "Yes, sir," Chernov had disappeared through the door.

With gall rising in his throat, the unhappy technician leaned over to pick up his hat.

The filthy animal had left a big, greasy footprint on it.

"Major, may I speak with you?" asked the sergeant after knocking on the door to his commander's quarters and being told to enter.

"Of course, Sergeant," Markovich replied, glancing as he spoke at the dry dock's master, with whom he was drinking vodka and smoking away the evening.

"Kardon's missing."

"What do you mean, missing?" demanded Markovich, his eyes darkening and hardening.

"Corporal Donskoi went to relieve him about half an hour ago and there was no sign of him. We've searched the entire dock and haven't been able to find him."

"When was he last seen?"

"An hour ago. He was at his post on the starboard wall when I made my last tour of inspection."

"Had he been drinking, Sergeant? Did you let him go on watch after drinking?"

"It's possible, Major," the sergeant replied, stiffening at

attention. "He may have been drinking, but I'm certain he wasn't drunk."

"Damnit! How many times have I told you to be more careful about that?

"Very well! If he's fallen overboard, then it's too late. There's nothing we can do. But he may still be aboard, in some corner, sleeping it off. I want you to conduct a thorough search. Everywhere!"

"Yes, sir."

Markovich watched the sergeant as he hurried off to organize the search. The noncom seemed to have handled the problem quite efficiently. Indeed, the dry dock master, from the expression on his face, appeared to suspect nothing, although it might have been better if the sergeant had changed his jacket before reporting.

"The sea is a very dangerous place, isn't it, Captain?" said Markovich after the sergeant was gone.

"That is beyond dispute," the dry dock master replied as he poured himself another glass of clear liquid.

Markovich doubted the dockmaster had noticed the small, dark bloodstains on the jacket, since the sergeant's entire uniform was totally water-soaked. And even if he had, Markovich doubted that he would care. The follies of soldiers would be of no interest to a civilian dry dock master.

Chapter Twenty

His eyes hurt. They felt swollen and he suspected they must be bloodshot. And the Beluga's air didn't taste very good. He couldn't say it was foul—the scrubbing and recycling system seemed to be okay—but it wasn't great either.

Madeira closed his eyes and leaned back, shutting out the monitor's flickering glow. With no visual inputs to confuse the issue, the speaker-magnified sound of Grivski and Mendalov's breathing as they worked on the wreck seemed even louder than usual. Almost booming, in fact.

"Are you okay, Captain?" Timon asked.

"I'm fine," replied Madeira without opening his eyes.

The muted *thunk* of the steel stud being slammed into the sub's fairwater punctuated the two divers' rasping breaths. Madeira opened his eyes and rubbed them. He focused on the monitor as Grivski, who was standing on an already-installed portion of the framework, handed Mendalov the studgun. The big Russian then leaned over and examined the stud along with the portion of frame it was securing to the wreck.

"This is going very well," Timon remarked.

"Yes," replied Madeira. "It's a tribute to our abilities to work together." Christ! he thought. I'm starting to talk like them now!

Still, Timon was right. The work was going very well. It'd taken the two of them, with Grivski documenting every move, a little over three hours to cut away the wreckage around the hole created by the explosion, the hole that had presumably sunk the sub.

Once all the sharp, flower petal–like edges had been cut away, along with the damaged decking, they were free to get down to the hole itself. First they positioned a steel beam, the strongback, inside the inner hull across the hole. Then, with the strongback temporarily lashed in place, they laid a large steel plate over the outside of the hole, using pieces of old bed mattresses as caulking. Finally, they tightened the nut on the long bolt that ran from the center of the strongback out through the center of the plate.

After replacing the cork in the evil genie's bottle they'd made a quick trip back to *Asimov* to pick up the frame over which the automated cutter would run. And now Grivski and Mendalov were assembling and positioning the jury-rigged system much faster than Madeira had ever dreamed possible.

The two of them, he decided, were frighteningly good at carrying out orders.

A flood of Russian roared out of the speaker. Then loud laughter.

"What're they saying?" demanded Madeira, wondering at what point his heightened suspicions might cross over the boundary into paranoia.

At first Timon didn't answer. "Mendalov was telling a joke," he finally said. "About the President of Russia and the President of Ukraine having sex together . . . They're both men, you know?"

"Yes," Madeira answered, waiting for Novikoff to cut in on the circuit and cut his two divers down a little.

"How are we doing?" It was Grivski.

Madeira paused a moment before answering, surprised that Grivski had asked for his opinion and still expecting to hear Novikoff restore discipline. "You're doing first-class work," he finally replied after deciding nothing was going to come from topside. Was Novikoff absent from the Operations Center? Or was he choosing to overlook the infraction?

With a grunt of what Madeira could only assume was satisfaction, Grivski pulled himself up to the high end of the still-wobbly framework. Mendalov, who was following, reached up and handed him the studgun.

Thunk!

They could just as easily be in outer space, thought Madeira as he watched the heavily suited pair labor in slow motion on the monitor.

Thunk!

It doesn't make the slightest difference whether or not I like either of them. The important thing is that they can do the work well and quickly.

Thunk!

"Where's that thermos of coffee, Boris? I seem to be drifting off."

The framework, which resembled a row of ski-lift pylons all hooked together by a web of flexible pipes, now reached all the way up the wreck's port side. From the mudline to the deck.

"Mendalov!" Grivski said. "Hang the gun there and go down and rig that last section."

"Okay."

Madeira watched as Mendalov shoved off from the framework and floated down to the ooze, towing a light line behind him. Before the cloud of silt generated by his landing had even begun to dissipate he had the line secured to an L-shaped length of framework, the only one remaining on the ocean floor.

"Grivski, pull!" he said. "I will guide it up to you."

"Okay."

Madeira continued to watch as the section of framing,

guided by Mendalov, rose in jerks and starts up the wreck's side.

Thunk! went the studgun again when the two divers had the frame in place. *Thunk! Thunk! Thunk! Thunk! Thunk!*

"Okay," said Madeira, turning to Timon. "It's time for us to move."

"Yes, sir."

"Grivski . . . Mendalov . . . We are going to move the Beluga to the starboard side now. Shift to your auxiliary life-support systems."

"Yes. As you wish," replied Grivski as he opened the valve to his self-contained breathing gas supply system and disconnected his umbilical.

"Roger," Mendalov said, also disconnecting.

As soon as the umbilicals had been wound back onto their reels aboard the worksub, the Beluga slowly rose from the bottom.

Just another ooze-dweller, thought Madeira. An oversized one.

In fact, the more he thought about it, they were still just about the *only* large ooze-dweller he'd seen in the vicinity of the wreck.

Once clear of the bottom, the worksub turned, then churned forward as Timon guided it around the wreck's stern.

"Al." It was Novikoff. "You're doing very well down there! We are all very pleased."

"Roger, *Asimov*," replied Madeira. "Thank you."

"Very well, Grivski," Madeira said after Timon had resettled the Beluga in the ooze, "we're on station again."

"Okay," Grivski said as Mendalov launched himself over the wreck's side.

After reconnecting their umbilicals, Mendalov and Grivski unloaded sections of the plastic and aluminum framework from the Beluga, carried them the fifty or so feet to the wreck, and lifted them up to the wreck's steeply canted deck.

Thunk! Thunk! Thunk! Thunk!

Robots! thought Madeira as they finished laying the frame across the deck and started down the starboard side. Those guys are robots! He'd set a fast pace, one he wasn't sure he could maintain himself, and they were already far ahead of him. And still just warming up!

Thunk . . . Thunk . . . Thunk . . . Thunk . . . Thunk . . .

This is going to be a trophy wreck, Madeira thought as he watched the two Russian divers finish installing the frame. I'm going to have somebody take a picture of me with the wreckage in the background, just the way sport fishermen do with their record marlins.

And then I'm getting the hell home.

"*Asimov,* send down the cutter."

Thirty minutes later the boxlike laser pipe cutter appeared, sliding down the descending line and trailing its power and control cable.

"You see the cutter there, Grivski?" Madeira asked.

"Yes. We'll have it in a minute."

Between them, the two divers had no difficulty unshackling the cutter and mounting it on the frame.

"All done," reported Grivski.

"Roger," Madeira said. "Stand back while we test the system."

"Okay."

"*Asimov,* commence motion tests."

"Commencing motion tests," replied Alexi in the ship's Operation Center.

The cutter, a box about two feet square with a short nozzlelike element sticking out the side closest to the wreck, started to creep along the framework. Then it stopped and started to creep in the opposite direction, moved by little gearlike wheels that engaged a toothed edge along one side of the frame.

Beautiful! thought Madeira. "Okay . . . Try the lateral motion, then in and out."

As Madeira and Timon watched on the Beluga's displays, Alexi moved the cutter about three feet to the left of its original track, then back. He then moved it in until the nozzle was a fraction of an inch from the wreck's skin. Then back out again.

"All appears in order," he reported.

"Very well," Madeira replied, his elation growing. "Stand by to test the laser . . . but wait until I recover divers."

"Standing by."

"Grivski . . . Mendalov . . . Return to the Beluga."

"Okay."

"Alexi," Madeira said once the two divers were safely into the Beluga's hyperbaric suite, "test the cutter whenever you're ready."

"Roger, Captain!"

Alexi pressed a button on his console and thousands of amps of hot, hard power surged into the cable. An instant later half a dozen circuit breakers snapped open and the ship shuddered slightly.

"What the hell was that!" shouted Novikoff in Russian.

"A massive short circuit, sir," Alexi replied, frantically scanning his board for a more precise answer. "Something's shorted out."

"The cable's exploded!" boomed the speaker above Alexi's head as the two men in the reel well reported in. "There's been an underwater explosion about ten feet deep. The cable's been completely cut."

Beneath them, in the space between the ship's two hulls, the water surged and boiled.

"Beluga, this is *Asimov*," Alexi shouted into the microphone. "The power cable has exploded and been cut completely apart about ten feet below the surface."

"Timon," shouted Madeira, all the cobwebs suddenly blown out of his head, "lift off and head south, into the current! Full power!"

It took Alexi a moment to comprehend the reason for the almost frantic tone of Madeira's order. Then he thought of fifteen hundred feet of four-inch-diameter cable plummeting toward the Beluga, writhing and tangling as it came. If the worksub got caught in it it'd never see the surface again.

Novikoff looked at the mangled end of the cable as it dangled, still dripping, before his eyes. The sight infuriated him.

"I'm no forensics expert, sir," said *Asimov*'s chief electrician in Russian, "but it looks to me as if the waterproof cover was cut. Look here . . . this edge is straight while the remainder is jagged."

"Very well!" Novikoff snapped, his voice tight with fury. "Can we splice it?"

"No, sir. I can only agree with Captain Madeira that no splice we're able to do here would last under these conditions. One way or another, it'd short out long before we're done.

"There's still enough cable left on the reel so we can reconnect to the cutter, but it'll be very tight. Captain Bukinin will have to maintain station with great accuracy."

Novikoff stared intently at the electrician a moment, both hands hanging at his sides, clenching and unclenching rapidly. Then he turned, grabbed the telephone, and punched in the number for the operations center.

"Alexi! Instruct the Beluga to return immediately with the cutter. They're to leave the cable there."

"Yes, sir," replied Alexi, who immediately relayed the message.

"That will be all," Novikoff said to the electrician. "You may go."

Once the technician had left, Novikoff turned to Viktoria, who'd just walked through the hatch and was standing quietly next to the reel. "Do you see this! What do you suggest we do about it, Commander? It's your job to keep this sort of thing from happening!"

She stood there, searching for an acceptable response to the bitter rebuke. In the near silence she could hear faint echos: distant voices, the hum of machinery, the slap of water against steel, the groans of the steel itself as it flexed in response to the ship's motion. The swell was increasing, she'd noticed. There was a storm somewhere between them and Africa.

"I think we should request an experienced criminal investigator be sent. I'm simply not qualified to deal with this situation."

"Then you have failed to learn anything about this?"

Novikoff's fists were in violent motion again.

"The cut was made just about at the midpoint, which means it was done either during loading or when it was being paid out. When it was being paid out there were three people here: two sailors and Mr. Chernov."

"Chernov again! Doesn't that make you think?"

"Yes, but he didn't cut the cable. One of the sailors with him was mine. Anyway, why would he want to sabotage us?"

"He does have very strong, anti-Yeltsin political opinions, Commander, and your man may have been looking the other way. He might remember something if I have Grivski talk with him."

"That would be counterproductive," Viktoria replied, thinking that the only way Grivski would interrogate Timon, or any of her other people, would be over her dead body. "As you are aware, Captain, it is my opinion that much of our trouble is the result of the sailors' resentment of the way they are often treated."

However, she added to herself, I would have no objection whatsoever if you ordered Grivski to have a little chat with Chernov.

"Then it must have been done when the cable was loaded?" continued Novikoff, brushing aside her last remark. "Is that what you've concluded?"

"I think it's very likely."

"Who was in the well when it was loaded?"

"Bukinin remembers one sailor and a shipyard worker."

"Which sailor?"

"He's no longer aboard. He became ill and left at Kronshtadt."

"Where is he now?"

"As soon as we finish here I'll ask St. Petersburg to find out."

"That's a very good idea. I think we would like to speak with that man."

"There are several others, you know."

"Who?"

"Shipyard workers. The one in the well and the five or six who were ashore, tending the reel from which the cable was being transferred."

"Shipyard workers!" snorted Novikoff.

Silence again descended as the Russian naval captain leaned over to look at the cable ends as they swayed, still dripping, in the rasping wind. His nostrils flared slightly as he took a series of deep breaths, leading Viktoria to suspect he was struggling to calm himself.

"Commander . . . Viktoria," he said, turning suddenly back to her as he forced the hostility from his face, "I . . . we have a mission of incredible importance and sensitivity. As the Americans would say, it has very little upside but great downside. It is essential that we recover this wreck just as quickly and cleanly as possible. If something goes seriously wrong the results could be disastrous for Russia."

"I couldn't agree with you more, Captain."

"Good. Then you will also agree that we are reaching the point where additional sabotage might very well trigger that disaster?"

"Yes . . ."

"So we must prevent anything else from happening! Nobody is above suspicion, not even Al Madeira."

"Al? How could he have cut the cable?"

"I agree that it is highly unlikely. But it is possible that he's involved."

"Why would he?"

"Orders. A reliable source has reported that some very important Americans, both military and Agency, would be more than happy to see us screw the job up."

"And they told Al to make sure? Was he identified by name?"

"All the source has reported is that there are those who wish to see us fail. I mention this merely to show that we can be certain of nobody."

"Just how good is this source?" Viktoria asked, her curiosity getting the better of her.

"Very, very good!" Novikoff said with a smile. "It's one of the high-level moles the Americans have told themselves all these years don't exist!"

"Oh? Where is he?"

"He's right where you or I would expect him to be."

She couldn't help but be impressed by the depth of Novikoff's knowledge. He was obviously well connected with the very top levels of power. He also seemed to blab more than he should at times.

"In sum, Commander, I want you to concentrate on stopping the sabotage. The Mafia, the plutonium, yes, they're important. But our main problem is political . . . and I want it solved!"

Chapter Twenty-one

Outside, the deep, blue Atlantic continued to rise and fall in large, smooth swells that spoke of far distant storms. The sky continued largely cloudless, marred only by an occasional evening squall, and the wind blew a steady fifteen to twenty from the northeast. Inside, *Asimov*'s operations center was filled with a flickering darkness, a very faint hissing, and the hot plastic smell of electronics in action.

Sitting in one of the operators' chairs, Madeira watched as Alexi moved the cutter slowly along the track. One monitor displayed a pair of crosshairs that marked the cutter's position on the wreck's surface. In the screen's upper right field a red number, not unlike the channel indicator of a television set, indicated the distance in centimeters between the target and the cutter's tip. On a second monitor Madeira could see the tip itself in profile, a nozzlelike protuberance with a bell-shaped enclosure at the end. Trapped within the bell and bulging out the open end was a small ball of superheated, slightly glowing steam. A sharp, diamond-hard beam of energy was also visible as it surged through the

220

ball and slashed a smooth dark line in the wreck's side fair-water and deck.

"I must congratulate you, Captain," Alexi said. "You have put together a very good system here."

"Thank you," replied Madeira. He'd already reached the conclusion that Alexi was a techno-junkie who'd never met a gadget he didn't like, but he still found the Russian's enthusiastic approval of his makeshift system satisfying. He'd spent a great deal of time talking with salesmen and computer specialists, educating himself and assembling the package.

Damnit, he thought, the cutter *was* working well. In the three hours since they'd lit the laser off they'd cut almost twenty feet, and the speed was increasing as Alexi improved his technique. If there weren't any interruptions they'd be finished cutting in a day or so.

"I'm going to get some fresh air," he said. "See if I can find a cup of coffee. If anything comes up, page me."

"Okay," replied the technician, his eyes still glued to the monitor and his baseball cap protecting the nape of his neck. "You already know what our coffee's like."

Madeira stepped out onto the boat deck and looked around. The weather had been remarkably cooperative since they'd arrived, he thought, although he wasn't sure he liked the look of the swell.

The high located to the north must still be holding. Maybe even creeping down on them. It might yet develop into a blow, especially if the low to the east tried to move in. If the fronts went at each other with a will, if it developed into something really nasty, *Asimov* might find it difficult to hold her position above the wreck.

But it wasn't the weather that nagged at him. His biggest worries concerned *Asimov* herself. And her crew.

The operation now seemed to be whistling right along, but below the surface the churning, deep waves remained. Whatever the appearance of order, the whole damn ship was still about to explode. Everybody was on edge. Waiting for something. And he couldn't help feeling that they were all waiting for something different.

He looked around the horizon again, then headed forward to the salon to see if there was any coffee on.

"Madeira!" bellowed Captain Bukinin as Madeira entered the salon.

"Yes, Captain?" Madeira responded, realizing that he, Bukinin, and Riki were the only people present.

"Get yourself some coffee and come sit with me." As he spoke, Bukinin looked up from the small photographs he had been examining and squinted at Madeira through a thick cloud of cigarette smoke.

"Of course," Madeira replied. "Thank you."

He filled a cup with coffee, nodded to Riki, who was just leaving, and joined *Asimov*'s master.

"I'm impressed with your work so far," boomed the Russian between puffs on his cigarette. "I'm sure our people could get the job done, but I think you are doing very well. . . ."

Taken aback by Bukinin's sudden geniality, Madeira found himself at a loss for words. "I'm afraid this is the easy part," he finally got out. "Cutting the bottom and the keel, the areas resting in the ooze, are going to be the real test."

"I would imagine you will have to use divers for that."

"Yes. More than we are right now." Madeira noticed the two photographs in Bukinin's hands were of young girls. The Russian spotted his glance and turned the pictures so he could see them more clearly. Two preteens with very big smiles. Cute kids, he thought, wondering for the millionth time if he'd missed anything by not having any of his own.

"These are my granddaughters," he said proudly. "One of them already shows great talent as a swimmer."

"Maybe she'll be a world champion someday," Madeira said, trying to keep the conversation going. "Represent Russia in the Olympics."

"No," said Bukinin, "my daughter will not permit it. For her to become a world champion she would have to enter one of the special programs, and Anna swears she will never give either of them up.''

A mixture of what looked to Madeira like embarrassment and pain crossed Bukinin's beefy, bearded face. ''You have never married, have you?'' he continued, swallowing half a glass of vodka as he did.

''No,'' Madeira replied, ''and I even tried once or twice.''

''It's probably just as well. I've been married for thirty-five years now and have spent almost all of that time at sea. That's why Anna refuses to even consider special programs for her children. She says they are hers and she will never permit them to become the property of the state. She forgets that it is the nation which makes us great.''

Not knowing what to say, Madeira said nothing.

''When she talks like that she sounds almost like one of you, like an American.'' Bukinin smiled briefly as he said it.

''All this blather about Russia and America becoming partners,'' he continued, a scowl returning to his face. ''Why would we want to be your partners? Russia is a great nation, and has been since long before America existed. Why would she want a partner? Anyway, as everybody knows, to be partners with America means to do things the way Americans want them done.''

He's rambling, thought Madeira. It must be the vodka. He sipped at his coffee while Bukinin inhaled half the cigarette.

''I don't know what's to happen to them,'' continued the Russian, looking again at the photographs. ''I never used to worry about the future. I knew where we were all going. . . . Life has always been hard, but it was getting better. . . . And it had a purpose, a direction.

''Now? Crime everywhere! Everyone out for himself. Grabbing. Hoarding. No patriotism. No discipline. And no jobs!

''And the disease is spreading! Even Chernov!''

Madeira started slightly, fully alert now and very interested in what Bukinin had to say about his own chief mate.

"He's a hard man, no?" Bukinin continued, raising his eyebrows. "Many seem to feel he's even harder than I am. You and I both know that an officer's duty often requires toughness, but I begin to doubt Vasily's dedication to duty. For some time now I've suspected that he has become too close to the antisocials, the criminal elements, who are everywhere in Russia now that the authorities have stripped the police of their powers to maintain order. I can prove nothing, but I am on my guard and I suggest you also be on yours."

"Have you mentioned this to Captain Novikoff?"

"Of course! He said he needed more evidence than just my suspicions."

"I suppose," Madeira mumbled, unsure now what to think about anything.

"Did you know I fought in the Great Patriotic War?" asked Bukinin suddenly. "Yes!" he continued before Madeira could respond. "I was nine years old at the great battle for Stalingrad where hundreds of thousands died. It was bitterly cold and I was always hungry and tired and afraid, but it was the best months of my life. I was a part of a glorious purpose, a struggle worth suffering for!"

The memory of the misery seemed to cheer up Bukinin, to permit him to escape for a few minutes from the excruciating uncertainties of the present.

"And ever since I have served Russia to the very best of my abilities. But none of this is new to you. You also have served your country."

"I did my best for twenty-five years," answered Madeira reluctantly. "Not as many as you, but enough to understand how you feel."

Don't do this to me, you bastard, he thought as he spoke. I don't want to swap war stories with you and I don't want to drink to honor and duty and old friends long gone.

"Yeltsin's an eel. He'll say whatever sounds good to him at the moment. He can't possibly rebuild Russia!

"You will see," Bukinin concluded. "Once we get a strong leader, one who can restore discipline and direction to society, there will be no more talk of 'partnership.' "

"I don't understand Russian politics," Madeira said. "I'm not sure I understand American politics, but I think it's a mistake to lose sleep every time a politician says something stupid."

As he spoke, Madeira noticed that Viktoria was standing at the door, looking in.

Bukinin snorted what might have been a laugh, swallowed the remains of the vodka, and followed Madeira's glance. "Viktoria! Please join us."

"Thank you, Captain, but there are a number of things I must attend to. Riki and I must grab every opportunity Al gives us to fit a little research in." Then she was gone.

"A sad case," observed Bukinin. "She is sad and lonely, I fear, with so few scientists aboard this trip and so little real work for her to do. Any of my officers would be more than pleased to console her, but she will not permit it. She's a very stubborn woman! But then, that's how many of these scientists are."

More bullshit! thought Madeira. The spell broken, his mellowness quickly degenerated into irritation. Bukinin knows as well as I do that she's naval intelligence.

The two were sitting in silence, each considering the difficulty of Viktoria's present situation, when the phone buzzed. Bukinin answered, listened a minute, then handed the instrument to Madeira.

"Captain," Alexi said, "I'm having a small problem here."

"What is it?" asked Madeira, sitting up in his chair.

"It is nothing serious, sir. I'm just having trouble maneuvering the laser to cut out the supports connecting the deck and fairwater to the hull."

"I'll be right there," Madeira replied, hoping he could solve the problem for Alexi right there, in the operations center. Otherwise, they'd have to go down into that cold, drab world and do the job with handheld cutters.

* * *

Niko Avalaridze looked out the window of the small office building on the Dolphin Expressway, adjacent to Miami International Airport, and smiled in satisfaction at the sight of the carefully groomed expanses of grass and palmetto, the deep-blue, man-made ponds, and the traffic barreling along the expressway. He already felt completely at home, a million miles away from Tbilisi.

"Niko," Ari said just as a big jet thundered across the window, its roar largely absorbed by the building's insulation, "Giorgi says the Chechens have started to move in on our salesmen."

"Who?"

"Ilia, in Batumi, and several others."

The smile of satisfaction disappeared from Niko's face to be replaced by a snarl. "It won't be long now. Tell them they'll get fresh goods in two weeks. And tell Giorgi to kill the first one who tries to work with the Chechens. Make an example of him!"

"Niko . . ." Ari paused a moment, uncertain how Niko was going to react. ". . . don't you think we should concentrate a little more on our usual business? If we're not careful it's going to turn to shit."

"Don't tell me what I can or can't do!" Niko snapped, his usually placid brown eyes now blazing and almost black.

The rage was contagious. Ari had had enough of the little bastard, for that's what he really was. He reached for the knife he kept in his boot, then paused, looking up into Niko's eyes. And at the small pistol pointed at his head. "Stay cool, Cousin, otherwise I can very well do without you."

"Okay, Niko . . ." he mumbled, once again deflated.

"Novikoff says they're about ready to move the wreck, so call Arnold and tell him to get *Velociraptor* ready. We leave in a few days."

Chapter Twenty-two

Madeira tried to lean back in the Beluga's copilot chair and failed, as he should have known he would because he'd tried before. A dozen times, in fact. Every time he forgot the chairs were fixed rigidly in place. Designed, he decided, for rigid Russian backs.

Feeling slightly put out, he continued to watch one of the video monitors mounted over the steering console. This unit, which was receiving video signals transmitted from *Asimov*, showed Vasily Chernov and his crew, a thousand feet above, rigging Fixed Volume Deep Buoyancy Units along the lifting straps that Madeira intended to run under the wreck.

Satisfied with what he was seeing, Madeira shifted his attention to the second monitor, which was hooked to a camera mounted outside the Beluga. Now more than ever the wreck looked like some great whale being flensed, having its thick layer of blubber stripped off.

Using the remote-controlled laser, they'd already managed to cut and tear away an eight-foot-wide strip of deck, fairwater, and outer hull. The new wound gaped with near-

William S. Schaill

surgical precision from the mudline on one side to the mudline on the other. The pressure hull, the final, tough inner membrane, now lay exposed, ready for the Portuguese whaleman's magic knife.

His attention snapped back to the first monitor, attracted by a sudden flurry of activity. Chernov was waving and shouting furiously at a seaman who was kneeling on deck bolting one of the Buoyancy Units to the strap. Then, without warning, the chief mate kicked the man in the face. And then again in the gut, causing the victim to double over and roll onto his side.

"That son of a bitch!" snarled Madeira, startled by the violence even though he knew he shouldn't be. "What sort of a fucking navy do you people run?"

Not really expecting an answer, he turned to Timon anyway and was startled again to see the look of intense hatred on the Russian diver's face as he stared at the monitor. It really was possible, he thought, that Timon had been the one who slammed the hatch on Chernov.

"He's a merchant officer," Timon said.

"Grivski's navy, isn't he?" replied Madeira, not even caring if Grivski, who was supposed to be asleep, heard him.

Timon started to reply, paused, then went ahead.

"Our discipline has always been strict," he finally said. "I understand the policy is being reconsidered at the very highest level right now."

"Beluga, this is *Asimov*," squawked Alexi's voice in their ears. "Stand by! We're ready to send down another assembly."

"Roger, Alexi," Timon replied after glancing at Madeira and receiving a nod.

"I heard a rumor he's tied in with the Mob," Madeira prompted as they waited.

"The Mob? Criminal elements!" replied Timon, his brow furrowed. "You mean like smuggling? And stealing state property? And loaning poor sailors money, then beating them up if they don't pay him back twice as much as he

228

gave them? I've also heard such rumors, but I know nothing myself about it."

Within a few minutes the two-hundred-foot lifting strap, actually an assembly of huge wire cables and Buoyancy Units, appeared. It was dangling between them and the wreck. Descending, almost magically, from the darkness above.

"Okay, Boris," Madeira said, exhausted from his silent fuming about Chernov, "this one should be number nine. Let's grab it and stretch it out."

"Roger," said Timon as he guided the Beluga to one end of the strap, which weighed only a few hundred pounds underwater thanks to the Buoyancy Units. He hooked the eye on the strap's short towline and started to drag it in a big circle across the bottom until it was stretched out straight in the ooze, perpendicular to the wreck.

"You're doing just great down there, Al. Just great," cheered Novikoff.

"No, goddamnit! I don't think it's just caught on the keel," Madeira said as he stood in ankle-deep ooze about fifteen feet from the wreck. "I think it's wedged between the keel and something else. . . . There must be bedrock there. Or something."

Why the hell hadn't the automatic controls stopped the cutting head, or turned it, before it got wedged? wondered Madeira. Were the sensors screwed up or was it the computer? Whatever the cause, he knew, and so did Grivski, that one of them had to crawl down the tube, under the wreck, and unjam the damn thing.

"I would be more than pleased to take care of this for you," said Grivski, who was standing about ten feet away. "If you don't feel up to doing it yourself."

I'm sure you would, Madeira thought. Anything for a chuckle.

The remote tunneling system had worked like a dream for the first eleven tunnels. The big cutting head, like the head of a worm, had burrowed into the ooze and disappeared, dragging the four-foot flexible tube behind it. Hour after hour a steady stream of pudding-thick, muddy water had flowed out of the tube as the head chewed through the ooze and slipped under the keel. All the while, additional sections of tube disappeared until, finally, the head reappeared on the other side of the wreck.

And then, on number twelve, it had all come to a shuddering halt. Cursing, they'd retracted it and tried again, a few feet farther forward. Again it stopped. Someplace near the wreck's keel. Only this time it wouldn't retract. It was stuck all the way down under the wreck.

Madeira was soaked with sweat, exhausted and sick to death of Grivski's increasingly unveiled taunts . . . especially those occasions when he and Mendalov defiantly shouted at each other in Russian while glancing at Madeira out of the sides of their eyes and daring him to say something, then burst out into uncontrollable laughter.

"I'll take this one, Grivski. You can have the next."

"As you wish, sir."

Madeira stepped back and looked up at the dark, rounded mass of the wreck. It looked to him like the corpse of a great, dead whale beached on a mudflat.

And that was exactly as it should be, he thought, a faint sense of humor beginning to return. His Portuguese ancestors had been up to their chins in this business of butchering whales. Why shouldn't he be too? The only difference was that the leviathans he hacked up had even tougher skin than the great blue whale did. And, in this particular case, it was more than slightly toxic.

He took a deep breath, striving to bring his pounding heart and tensing muscles under control. You have to remember how to laugh, he told himself. If not at them, at least at yourself. He couldn't let Grivski and Novikoff and all the other bears get to him. And never forget that this is *your* wreck.

"Captain?" The note of demand and challenge was all too evident in the Russian's voice. The fucker was waiting for him to chicken out.

Get off my back, thought Madeira, his foul mood returning.

"Mind your tongue, Grivski!"

"Yes, sir."

"Boris."

"Yes, sir?" replied Boris, who was at the Beluga's control station.

"I'm about to crawl down this damn tube and clear the cutter."

"Roger."

"Make sure the power's secured. I don't want to electrocute myself. Or get my arm chopped off."

"The power is off," Timon replied. "I've locked the switch off."

"Good! I also want you to maintain a low-volume flow of water through the tube. I don't want to get trapped in a silt buildup."

"I understand, sir."

"Okay. Grivski, you ready to tend my lines?"

"Of course."

Madeira shuffled back to the end of the tube, about forty feet of which was lying fully exposed on the ooze, rolling and flexing gently with the movements of the surrounding water.

It's a huge snake, he thought as it twitched slightly. A gray-white anaconda. And it's about to swallow me.

He dropped to his hands and knees and a bolt of pain shot across his lower back. At my age, he thought, I should be sitting around at some overpriced dive resort, drinking beer and telling lies.

Grunting and cursing, he raised his hands over his head and dove into the tube.

His semi-armored dress and tether; the cutter's power cable; the water hose that provided the flow into which he was struggling. It all made for a horribly tight fit.

Madeira grabbed the water hose and pulled himself forward along the tube's slick, corrugated inner surface. After advancing about eighteen inches, he came to a stop as his elbows expanded into the sides of the tube. Already cramped beyond discomfort, he reached forward and pulled again. His helmet light burned brightly, but he could see little except pale gray, his face being pressed against the side of the tube. Once or twice he bent his head back to look ahead. Then he could see absolutely nothing at all.

Closing his now-useless eyes, he concentrated on pulling himself forward. He was inside a diving dress inside a narrow tube under a thousand feet of water. If he let himself do so he could feel each and every layer wrapped tightly around him. Pressing against him.

The trick, of course, the mental legerdemain mastered by all those salvors who manage to retain their sanity, was to not let himself feel the pressure. Focus on the objective. Be aware of the dangers, but never *feel* them. Never allow himself to start imagining what it's going to feel like when the worst does finally happen.

Neither did it do any good to think about the growing distance between him and the opening, which now lay far behind. As long as he was still above the ooze, of course, Grivski could always cut him out of the snake's belly. If the Russian felt like it.

He shuddered at the thought that his life was totally in Grivski's hands. And once he went underground it would be even more so.

He continued to worm his way forward and the tube rolled and twisted across the bottom just as if it really were an anaconda attempting to digest a freshly swallowed pig.

A million years later he realized his head was now lower than his feet. He'd finally started down the hole. He was now under the ooze. Soon he'd be under the wreck. Maybe he already was.

"What's your status, Captain?"

"I'm just starting under the wreck now," he managed to grunt out.

"Are you okay?"

"I'll make it."

"Roger."

Despite the deep ocean's deathly chill, Madeira felt as if he were in an oven. And totally, absolutely alone. Except, of course, for Uncle Carlos. At times like this, Carlos was always right there. Laughing and reassuring him that it's just this sort of sport that makes life worth living.

Madeira asked Carlos if he was about to join the sub's crew. Would he fit in? Would the ghosts accept him?

Carlos said nothing, which meant, he decided, that today might not be his day to die. Or that it was and Carlos was too polite, or embarrassed, to tell him ahead of time.

Reach and pull. Reach and pull. He found himself losing all sense of time as well as any interest in it. His life was becoming simpler by the minute. Everything boiled down to reach and pull, reach and pull. All around him, above, below, to all sides, lay a million miles of ooze. A characteristically slick material with a gritty element mixed in. All around, just an inch or two away. A marvelous substance that might do wonders for his bowels but would do nothing good for his lungs.

When was the last time he'd had to do shit like this? He found it hard to remember.

Oh yes! That mess, about ten years ago. A fully laden fuel barge had run aground and then worked itself free and sunk. He'd managed to pump out what was left of the cargo without spilling more than a drop or two and to seal the holes. Then the environmentalists, the concerned politicians, and the media had all arrived and the Navy flacks, the PR specialists, had failed to provide him with any running space at all.

After a day or two of accusations, insults, and unwanted advice, Madeira had fled to the depths.

Looking back at it, that was one of his better decisions. The greasy harbor muck, loathsome as it was, had proved infinitely more agreeable than the oozy pols.

Well, he thought, I must have survived that one. Otherwise, I wouldn't be here. Suffering through this one.

Every now and then Timon called to check on him and he replied mechanically. He failed to notice when the tube stopped plunging and returned to the horizontal. He was only vaguely aware of the artificial current's slowly increasing force and of the not-so-slow buildup of muck around him as the current sucked in ooze through the stopped cutter. Only when his hand settled on and grabbed the hose's nozzle assembly did he grasp that he'd reached the end.

"I'm there," he reported. "At the head."

"Well done!" replied Timon. Grivski continued to maintain a total silence.

"Have you found the problem?"

"Not yet," Madeira said, bending back to look forward.

Despite the powerful light mounted on his helmet, he could see nothing useful. He'd have to use his hands. Feel his way through.

He reached forward, through, and around the cutter and almost immediately found where it was jammed against the sub's bottom. He could feel the steel plates. Then he continued to feel around and under the cutter to locate whatever else was holding it, forcing it up against the wreck.

Goddamnit! There was nothing there but sand and mud. No rocks. No chunks of steel. Nothing that could be accused of having forced the cutter up against the sub's bottom.

He dug all around the cutter with his gloved hand. Then, with a snarl, he twisted it and yanked.

The damn thing came loose!

"Grivski was right," he reported in near fury. "The cutter was jammed against the wreck's bottom. There's nothing else under it."

"What do you want to do?" Timon asked.

"We have no choice," replied Madeira in disgust. "We're going to have to recover the cutter and find out what's wrong with its guidance system."

"Al, this is Novikoff."

"Yes, Mike," Madeira said, irritated at the interruption.

"Does that mean you have to recover the tube also?"

"Yes. I'm afraid so."

"How long will that take?"

"An hour to two, after I get back out."

"Then how long will it take you to decompress?"

"What the hell does that matter? If we can't fix the cutter aboard the Beluga, we'll just send it up."

"I want you back aboard the ship."

"What! Why?"

"Meg Jefferson is coming out."

"The reporter?"

"Yes."

"When?"

"The day after tomorrow."

"Christ Almighty! We're saturated at this point! Why the hell did you tell her to come now?"

"I didn't. She's been after me for several days. Today she said she's coming out with or without permission. She hinted she knows we're hiding something from her."

As the Russian spoke, Madeira thought he detected a note of desperation in his voice.

"I warned you about that, but you said you could handle her."

"I said nothing to her about this, and none of that matters at this point," snapped Novikoff, now totally back in command. "All that matters is that we convince her we really are doing scientific research."

"How do you plan to do that?"

"Viktoria and Riki are each preparing some very impressive presentations and, as soon as you get out, the Beluga's going to go over to the trench so we can show her what it looks like."

"I may still be in the pot when she arrives. You don't need me, anyway. Viktoria and Riki are more than convincing."

"But we do need you. Not only are you an essential part of the operation; you're also an essential part of the cover. You're very important to our credibility."

"All right. It's going to be close."

"You just get your ass in gear. I want you here!"

These mood swings of his are getting worse and worse, thought Madeira.

"And while you're decompressing I want the Beluga to pick up some interesting specimens, something Riki can show her."

"Roger," Madeira replied with a sigh, knowing full well that Riki had already managed, despite the complications, to acquire a number of scientifically valuable specimens.

"Grivski!"

"Yes, Captain?"

"The only way I'm going to get out of here this century is if you drag me out. I'm going to loop the tether around my foot, I hope, and then you're going to pull."

"I'll do my best."

I'm sure you will, Madeira thought glumly. "And if I tell you to stop pulling you're going to stop."

"Naturally, Captain."

The son of a bitch sounds entirely too cheerful about pulling me out, thought Madeira. And I've got to get my paranoia about him under control soon or I'll end up like Novikoff.

Chapter Twenty-three

God! thought Madeira as he reached the top of the shiny steel ladder panting. It's true! Once you pass forty, certain things, almost everything physical, seem to become harder.

He reached around and grabbed the rail to the next ladder. After taking several deep breaths he launched himself up it, two steps at a time. Only when he reached the door to Riki's bio lab did he pause to catch his long-lost breath.

"These are all absolutely fascinating, Riki," Meg Jefferson was saying as Madeira staggered discreetly through the door and into the lab. "Four previously undescribed species, you say?"

Despite the distraction of his pounding heart and laboring lungs, Madeira couldn't miss the manufactured smile on Meg's face as she stood next to a worktable and eyed the biologist's collection of exotic, formalin-marinated seafood. He also noticed that none of the specimens on display were mutants. Riki must have stashed all the really good stuff away in some corner. Then he noticed, and nodded to, Chester Uribe, Meg's photographer, who was standing silently off to one side.

"Yes," the biologist replied with a note of what Madeira interpreted as pride. "I'm very pleased with what we've accomplished so far."

And his pleasure is very well deserved, thought Madeira. Despite the complications, especially Novikoff's ranting about time being of the essence, Riki had kept at it. Badgering Madeira and Timon to set and recover traps. Purloining ROVs when Alexi wasn't looking. Much to Madeira's surprise, the Armenian biologist had managed to do some real science. So, for that matter, had Viktoria, although it was difficult for Madeira to understand the full significance of the flood of numbers gushing out of her computer.

"Al!" Novikoff said, "we're all so glad you could join us."

Madeira smiled and said hello to Meg, who still didn't seem particularly pleased to see him. He suspected her lack of warmth may have been related to Perez, the Customs officer. Or perhaps it was merely the result of Madeira's failure to prove useful to her.

"Meg," continued Novikoff smoothly, playing the part of the ringmaster. "Why don't you come over to this video monitor so you can watch our Beluga, our worksub, recover some specimen traps from deep within the Puerto Rico Trench."

Madeira followed the red-haired journalist across the lab, then stood behind her while she oohed and aahed as the Beluga churned slowly along the steeply sloping bottom, occasionally providing glimpses of the seemingly limitless depths of the Trench itself.

"This footage is just marvelous!" she said. "Really great! Do you think I can have a minute or two of it? I'm sure I can arrange to run it locally, and it just might make the network."

Despite her words, Madeira had the distinct feeling she really found it all about as exciting as the tenth rerun of a Jason Project video.

"All these years," she continued, "we've tended to think of you Russians as . . . I don't know . . ."

"Unsophisticated?" Viktoria offered.

"Yes. But it's certainly clear to me that your technology's as good as anybody's.

"And tell me, Viktoria," continued Meg, her smile back in place, "what've you been up to?"

"Come, let me show you."

With Madeira taking up the rear, behind Chet Uribe, they marched out of the biology lab and along a passageway to the earth science facilities. Every step of the way, Viktoria pitched the principles of plate tectonics, preparing Meg for the presentation she'd spent the past two days assembling.

"But don't expect to see any glittering gems or drill cores lying around," she concluded. "Most of what we're doing this trip involves deep structure one way or another. The product is numbers, the right numbers, coming out of the computer . . . and we've been getting most of those numbers by using shock waves and magnetometers of various sorts. Our equipment is very similar to what the oil companies use.

"I hope, by the way," Viktoria added with a little smile, "that nobody's been upset by the strange underwater noises we've been making. . . . No fishermen or anything?"

"No," replied Meg, "there've been no reports of aliens or mysterious booms in the night that I've heard of. What about those microvents you mentioned at the news conference?"

"I keep hoping, but so far we haven't found any true ones, none of the sort I'm really looking for. I thought I had a few days ago, in fact, but it turned out to be nothing more than another pseudovent."

When they reached the geophysics lab, Viktoria had Meg sit down in front of one computer monitor while she sat before another. Typing madly on the keyboard, the tall blond scientist called up a seemingly endless stream of colored maps and diagrams illustrating the structure, deep and shallow, of the Puerto Rico Trench and the surrounding seabed. As she typed, she talked of features both long-known and newly discovered.

Standing off to one side, Madeira found it hard to decide just how much of it Meg understood. All the same, he found the spectacle fascinating. Not even NASA could have done it better. He was also certain that a lot of it, especially some of the newly discovered features, had burst, fully formed, from Viktoria's very fertile imagination. Give her a computer, he thought, and she can create a universe where none ever existed.

"This is all just great!" Meg exploded during one of Viktoria's infrequent pauses, "but isn't this ship awfully big for the work you and Riki are doing? I mean, why do you need such a big ship?"

An expression of surprise, then anger flashed across Novikoff's face, only to be brought rapidly under control before Meg, who was still looking at Viktoria, had time to notice. "It's all a matter of seakeeping ability, Meg," he replied. "It's very important that we be able to continue operations even in bad weather, especially when we have divers down in the habitat. And the computers need stability, too. Economics is also involved; we can't afford to spend time sitting in port during storms."

"Yes, I can see that," replied Meg, not missing a beat. "You're all doing great work here. But to tell you the truth, one of the main reasons I came was to get some insights on your sense of what's happening in Russia, and Europe, today. I think that's something our readers really want to know more about."

"Of course, Meg," Novikoff said while Viktoria deflated slightly. "We'll do our best, but you've got to understand that this is a time of great change and that none of us here is what you would call an insider. None of us is really close to the center."

"That'll be just fine. What do you, Mike, make of all the conflict, the violence, that seems to us outsiders to be occurring almost continuously in Moscow? Will the radical nationalists, the reactionaries who want to restore the Soviet system, overthrow President Yeltsin? Can he win the next presidential election? Will there be a presidential election?"

"At the moment, Meg, my sense is that we're experimenting, trying out new forms and testing our wings. No, I don't personally believe the ultranationalists will succeed in overthrowing the forces of rationalism and progress, although I do think the next few years will be very interesting. What worries me, and it worries me very much, is that the rest of the world may still not understand what we are doing, may not understand our need to feel our own way into tomorrow."

"And what role does your operation here play in all this? How does it contribute to Russia's struggle to feel its way into the twenty-first century? Back in San Juan, as I remember, you mentioned that President Yeltsin himself is very interested in what you're doing."

"Of course the President is interested!" replied Novikoff, again failing to totally mask his surprise and suspicion. "As Viktoria attempted to demonstrate to you, the scientific work being done on this expedition is of a very sophisticated nature. Notice, for example, that she's doing most of the geophysical work by herself, thanks to some of our newer computer systems. The work she is doing is of great interest to the entire scientific world. It is just this sort of project which illustrates the new directions that Russia is now taking."

Madeira gasped mentally at the sight of Novikoff's attempts to twist and dance his way out of the position he'd talked himself into.

"And much of the work done by Riki and his assistants," continued the Russian, "concerns environmental factors. Comparing the levels of certain pollutants in the sea life here with that in Russian waters, for example. These are things that we must understand if we are to save Russia's environment, not to mention that of the rest of the world."

"Fair enough," Meg said, apparently not ready to dig further at the moment. "Now, about Yeltsin himself? Will he continue to push for reforms or is he just interested in doing whatever he has to, to stay in power?"

"It is my belief that the President is totally committed to

241

reform,'' replied Novikoff, a slight flash showing in his eyes.

"If so, then why are so many of his most progressive advisers quitting or being forced out?''

"All governments experience personnel changes from time to time. There are minor internal disagreements. Changes in viewpoints. Look at your own government.''

"You personally don't expect to be laid off soon, then?''

"Laid off? Oh yes, discharged. No, I very much fear that Russia will need naval officers for a while, yet, although I must tell you that I find my personal interests are more and more going in the direction of this project and others like it. I can't tell you, for example, how satisfying it is to work with Al here. Not only are his skill and judgment proving of great value, but I also feel our collaboration is a big step forward in mutual understanding between our two nations.''

Meg glanced briefly at Madeira and bestowed on him a smile of minimal tolerance.

Here it comes, he thought, his stomach tightening. Now tell me, Al, how's the recovery going? You know, the submarine. And why the hell are you working so hard to hide it from me and everybody else? Why are you all lying to me!

Without saying a word to him, Meg turned to Viktoria.

"Mike's a naval officer, but you're a scientist plain and simple. Where do you think your country is headed?''

Madeira exhaled the breath he'd been holding.

Viktoria sat in silence for several seconds, then answered. "Russia will move forward,'' she said slowly. "In time, Russia will be a totally modern nation. It will still have its own . . . flavor . . . but it will no longer be odd or backward. Except when it wants to be.''

As she spoke, Madeira sensed a faint rushing, or pounding, in the air. Glancing out the open porthole, he was shocked to see the jet-black afternoon sky and to realize the ship was being assaulted by a powerful squall. Then he became aware of the big cat's occasional shudders as furious gusts slammed into her.

God! he thought. How did I miss this thing?

Was he losing his weather sense? Had he been underwater too long? Out of it? He hoped not. A sailor with no weather sense was soon a dead sailor.

"What about Zhirinovsky and his ultranationalists?" demanded Meg.

"He's a politician," Viktoria replied. "He and the others will do what they will do, but progress will come anyway."

Was it an act, wondered Madeira, or did the statement reflect Viktoria's true feelings?

"On to another question," Meg said.

"Of course," Novikoff said with a smile.

"It appears to many of us that Russia is rebuilding the Soviet Empire. Would you care to comment? Especially about Russian troops reoccupying every one of the so-called Confederation of Independent States?"

"Meg," answered Novikoff, waving his hand gently in the air as if he were brushing away cobwebs, "that is exactly what I meant about being misunderstood. Non-Russians seem to forget that most of those areas have been part of Russia for centuries, for longer than the United States has existed. And don't you please forget that Chairman Khrushchev was Ukrainian. He was born in Kiev. And Stalin himself was Georgian. Not, of course, that any of us now take any pride in him."

"What about Serbia?"

"They were all behaving like wildmen. And it was NATO and the UN who asked us to go in and restore order and justice, which we are in the process of doing."

And then Meg attacked, demanding an explanation for the continued huge concentrations of Russian Federation troops in Belorussia, Ukraine, and Georgia, all of which had been part of the Soviet Union and had recently declared their independence.

Novikoff sighed. "A strong central government, a strong source of guidance and discipline, is essential in the modern world, Meg. Succession is a very tricky thing. You Americans know the importance of a strong government as well as anybody. Look at the last forty or fifty years of *your* history."

He paused a moment, then continued, "Russia right now is going through what America did during the years following your Revolution. This, what you are watching right now, is our true revolution! The events of the Soviet era, the past seventy-five years, have been just the prelude."

Madeira watched and listened and at times felt like laughing at Novikoff's sincere, and totally canned, replies. And at Meg too, for that matter. She was trying so hard to get her scoop by tripping Novikoff up on geopolitics, asking the same questions every other reporter in the world was asking, when the exposé of the decade was dangling right beneath her.

A phone buzzed. It was the helo pilot calling to insist that they leave before another squall hit. Meg argued and threatened but finally agreed.

"Okay, Chet," she ordered, "I want a few shots: one of Viktoria at her computer, one of Riki studying one of these specimens, and then one of Viktoria, Riki, and Mike sitting around a table talking like they're having a conference."

"You've got it, Meg," said Uribe, jumping into action.

After ten minutes of posing, the event was photographically recorded and Novikoff led the way out of the lab and onto the deck.

When they arrived on the helo pad, Meg shook hands with Viktoria and Novikoff and thanked them. "You go ahead and get in, Chet," she said to Uribe.

She then turned to Madeira, who was standing several feet from his employers. "Al," she said in a low voice with a big, phony smile, "they're really quite good. Viktoria and Mike have put together a real good act, but Mike can't hold his rum for shit! Back when you were in San Juan he came up to my condo, had a few too many, and ended up prancing around bragging how important this operation is and how they'll make him an admiral if it all works out."

Oh God! thought Madeira as his mouth threatened to drop

open. She'd pulled the Mata Hari move on the mercurial Russian.

"There isn't a politician on earth who gives a fart about an oceanographic survey except as an opportunity to be photographed on the cutting edge or to show how much he cares about the environment. And they don't make people admirals for running them either, so I decided there has to be more to it. Real scientific expeditions, even Russian ones, don't send armed thugs like your friend Chief Officer Chernov to greet the press. So I dug a little more. You, for example. Your reputation isn't just for deep-diving operations but for deep salvage and recovery, especially under circumstances that aren't clearly kosher. And the CIA's involved. Somehow. So what is it? An airplane? A nose cone? A submarine? What are we doing here?"

"Viktoria and Riki gave you an excellent account of the expedition's objectives." Madeira squirmed inwardly as he spoke. He hated telling outright lies, and he also hated not being sure he was on the right side.

"Bullshit! But I'll find out. My editor's behind me on this. I had to beat up on him, but now the little wimp can almost taste the Pulitzer I'm going to get him. See ya later...."

She winked at Madeira, waved at the Russians, and stepped into the helo.

Chapter Twenty-four

Goddamn Novikoff and his big mouth! thought Madeira as
he relived Meg Jefferson's wink. Novikoff was fooling himself if he thought he could play that carelessly with the media pros, among whom Madeira now unhesitatingly included
the red-haired reporter. Now, thanks to Novikoff's folly,
Madeira was certain that the press would end up eating
Mike, and the whole operation, alive.

What the hell. What did he care if the hotheaded, and
very naive, Russian blew his own security wide open?
Maybe it was better that way. The recovery wasn't secret
because Madeira wanted it that way. Madeira's job was to
recover the wreck. Let Mike and Viktoria, Jen and Charlie
worry about the political ramifications, about who would
pitch whom out of office if the rest of the world found out
the Soviet navy had left a sunken nukie moldering fifty
miles from Puerto Rico, vomiting radiation.

But, damnit, he had gone to a lot of trouble to help maintain the cover, and he resented the possibility that it was all
in vain.

He returned his attention to the video screen in front of him and stared for a moment at the sharp-edged gash in the wreck's side. And at the shadows that seemed to dance within it. What would they find after they cut through the pressure hull? A horde of mutant sea monsters? The errant and unhappy souls of the crew? A blazing atomic inferno?

Of course not. After they cut through the pressure hull they'd find themselves in a galley and messing space. Fold-up tables and benches. Electric ovens. Refrigerators. Pots, pans, stoves, china, and silverware. No monsters. No lost souls. No mushroom clouds.

Then he realized that somebody was standing silently behind him, staring intently over his shoulder at the wreck's flickering image. He turned and found himself facing Vasily Chernov.

"Mr. Chernov. What brings you in here?"

"Curiosity, Captain. What do you think we will find in there?"

"A ratty old reactor leaking radiation."

"And what else?"

"All the usual garbage, as far as I know. What is it that you expect will be found there?"

"There are rumors all over the ship, Captain. Gold? Who knows?"

And the same rumors had probably been all over the St. Petersburg waterfront, thought Madeira, beginning to wish he'd never made up the story about gold to throw Cornie off the track. "You should never believe rumors, Mr. Chernov."

"It has been my experience that many rumors are based on some true fact."

"The only true fact I know is that there's an old reactor there."

Chernov mumbled something sharp in Russian and marched out of the operations center.

Good riddance, thought Madeira as he heard the door slam behind him.

Why was Chernov so interested in what might be in the

247

William S. Schaill

submarine? Could that be what he was doing when Madeira caught him going through his papers? Hadn't Novikoff suggested that he was untrustworthy? And hadn't both Bukinin and Timon indicated that he was in with the Mob? Was this little encounter significant enough to mention to Novikoff? Was Novikoff even the right person to go to?

Was there something in the storeroom?

He'd have to think about it.

"Okay, Alexi, hit it!" he finally said, returning his attention to recovering the wreck.

"Captain?"

"Sorry. Position the cutter, and when you're ready, light off the laser and start cutting."

"Yes, sir."

He continued watching the moniter as the technician maneuvered the cutter down the track about halfway to the mud, then into the cutaway portion of the wreck. With a silent bang the glowing bubble suddenly burst to life at the tip of the cutter as the high-amperage electrical current excited an artificial crystal that, in turn, emitted the thin, burning beam of intense light.

Madeira was faintly amused to note that for Alexi the novelty still hadn't warn off. Excitement showed in his eyes and his jaws attacked the chewing gum with renewed vigor as he guided the almost magical burning light through the distant, deep waters.

There really was something wrong with Novikoff, thought Madeira as he continued to stare at the monitor. Nothing about him rang true anymore. He was becoming increasingly erratic. More than erratic, in fact. Unpredictable. Was he insane or was it something else? Something more calculated?

And he was getting worse with every passing hour.

Madeira forced his full attention back to the video monitors and the straight, black line that was already appearing on the pressure hull's surface. "Alexi, you're an ace at that now."

"Yes, sir. I have the power!"

"Where did you come up with that?"

"What, sir?"

"I have the power!"

"Television, sir. American television."

"Oh!"

Madeira leaned back in the chair and closed his eyes, telling himself he wanted to think some more about Novikoff. About the whole operation, for that matter.

God, was he tired! The lifting straps were all in place, but the last half-dozen tunnels, starting with number twelve, had been complete bastards.

Right after Meg had sprinted off into the stormy skies Madeira, Timon, and Grivski had returned to the wreck and tackled tunnel number twelve again with the newly repaired cutter.

And again, the cutter had gone crazy. This time it refused to tunnel up after passing under the wreck. Finally, when the last few feet of tube were slipping down the hole on one side of the sub and nothing had reappeared on the other, Madeira had told Timon to cut the power. He then let Grivski crawl down the tube to recover the damn thing.

While the cutter was being hauled up to the surface again for further repairs, they'd had to recover the tube, which didn't wish to be recovered.

Tunnel number twelve had set the tone for the rest. Each of the last six had involved some sort of breakdown or failure. Of the cutter. Of the communications system between the divers and the Beluga.

And, in one case, of one of the tubes itself. Number fifteen had torn in half, pulled itself apart into two pieces when it was about halfway under the wreck, and then filled with silt. They'd had to let the cutter dig itself out to the far side of the wreck and disconnect its power cable so they could drag the cable back out. Then, more hours had been wasted reconnecting the power cable, which had to be done in the Beluga's access trunk, with the lower hatch open, after the water had been driven out by high-pressure air, and waiting for a replacement tube to be sent down.

William S. Schaill

But it was all done now, he thought with an audible sigh of relief. And, as far as he could tell, none of the problems were the result of sabotage. They were just the almost inevitable screwups that always occur on salvage jobs. In this case they'd just all happened at once.

His thoughts drifted to Viktoria. He wondered what she was doing right now. Was she dreaming? Were her dreams happy ones? He liked the idea of Viktoria lying, asleep, with a smile on her face. Whether or not she was a spy.

"Captain! Captain Madeira!"

He was instantly awake, although groggy. "Yes, Alexi? What's up?"

"The radiation level, sir. The radiation detectors on the cutter show that the water coming out the cut in the pressure hull is at least one thousand times more radioactive than the outside water."

"Shit!" mumbled Madeira as he scanned the monitors and tried furiously to think clearly. "Stop cutting!"

"I already have, sir."

"Then inform Captain Novikoff."

"He said he will be right here, sir."

The radiation was supposed to be isolated in the engineering spaces. What was it doing on the mess decks? Was it really a messing space? What about the space just aft of it? Between it and the reactor room? Was that really a storeroom? What was stored in it? Was there something else they weren't telling him?

"What do you think, Al?"

God! Madeira thought as he turned to Novikoff. The man's ability to move with the speed of light was amazing.

"Is this compartment really a messing space? Or is there something I haven't been told?"

"You know as much as I do. You've seen the plans." Madeira noticed a strained edge to Novikoff's voice as the Russian spoke.

"All right, then, what about this storeroom? What's in it?"

"As far as we know, it only has repair parts."

250

"What about the sub's weapons? Any of them nuclear?"

"No. The submarine was experimental. She wasn't carrying any weapons at all."

"Then the explosion, or whatever made that hole in the deck, must've also blown out two bulkheads, both the one between the reactor room and the storeroom and the one between the storeroom and the mess decks."

"That would have to be a very powerful explosion," observed Novikoff, his strain still very evident. "One would expect to find more external evidence of such a blast."

"Unless it was directed," Madeira said, thinking immediately of sabotage. "Or, unless there's additional damage on the bottom, under the mudline where we can't yet see it." The sort of damage, for example, that might be caused by an American antisubmarine torpedo.

"We have two choices that I can see," continued Madeira after a long, uncomfortable silence. "Either we try to patch up what we've done and go home, or we cut a hole and send in a SeaFairy to take a look."

"I don't see that we really do have any choice, Al."

"Neither do I."

The two SeaFairies hovered a few feet above the round hole Alexi had cut in the pressure hull. The ROVs' thin, black tethers, now wrapped in extra chaffing gear, looped down slightly, then trailed up behind them.

Madeira studied the edges of the hole a few minutes, then shrugged. They looked smooth enough, but he knew they were bound to be slightly serrated. "Okay, that'll have to do. Send one in."

While one of the ROVs continued to hover, supplying a view of the hole, the other slowly descended into the dark opening, its floodlight providing the wreck's first internal illumination in more than three decades.

As advertised, the compartment was filled with what appeared to be messing gear. On shelves. In bins. Stacked on deck. All partially obscured by thick layers of silt, corrosion, and biogrowth.

William S. Schaill

"Turn it about a hundred and eighty degrees, Alexi. We should only be about two meters from the bulkhead."

Sweating heavily, Alexi slowly spun the ROV. As the bulkhead swung into view, Madeira hoped the tether didn't foul on any of the cut pipes or decaying shelving.

"Down, Alexi. Drop it about a meter . . . goddamnit! That's the problem. The watertight door's wide open. They didn't have time to close it."

"Or maybe there was nobody left alive to close it," Novikoff said darkly.

Madeira shuddered slightly. At what had happened. At what now had to be done.

"This door still doesn't explain the radiation, Mike. How's it getting into the storeroom? Could they have left that door open, too?"

"Maybe that bulkhead was also damaged by the explosion. But that's not our concern at the moment," he added quickly. "For now we'll just secure that door and complete the recovery. As long as the radioactive material is isolated, we can proceed."

"Down some more, Alexi," said Madeira. "I want to get a close look at the hatch."

The hatch looked fine, he decided. Both the door and the frame looked functional, once over thirty years of marine growth was cleared away.

But he knew that no matter how well preserved or functional it looked, it wouldn't function. That was the First Law of Salvage. Or maybe it was the Second. Just like the cutter and tube.

"Okay, Alexi. Bring the SeaFairy out."

"Yes, Captain."

"Mike," he said, shifting his glance to the monitor hooked to the ROV still hovering outside the wreck, "I'm going to have to go down and install a patch over that hatch if we want to contain the radiation."

"Let Timon or Grivski do it."

"I'm afraid I'd better do this one. Otherwise, they're not going to think I've earned my million bucks." As he spoke,

Madeira noticed that the SeaFairy seemed stalled just inside the hole.

"Who cares what they think!"

"Unless you order me not to, I'd like to handle this."

"As you wish."

"What's the problem, Alexi?" Madeira asked as he turned slightly away from Novikoff.

"I think the tether is fouled," replied the technician, his voice a mixture of irritation and unease. "It won't come out."

"Move the other SeaFairy in. See if we can see what it's fouled on," Madeira said to the other ROV's operator, who was sitting beside Alexi.

"Yes, sir."

I remember now, he thought as the monitor showed the tether disappearing into the shadows of the mess decks. It's the Second Law of Salvage. The First Law says that any line or tether that can foul, will foul.

"Get it down deeper!" Novikoff snapped.

"I am afraid to, sir," said the operator.

"I agree with him," Madeira said quickly, determined to head off even worse trouble. "Get that second unit up and out, Alexi! Try to take your unit down, then move it to the right, then try up again. . . . But gently!"

Novikoff lapsed back into silence.

Letting me hang myself, Madeira thought.

The ROV rose again to the opening and stopped, clouds of silt now swirling all around it and billowing up, out of the wound. Madeira looked over at Alexi, whose face was now glistening with sweat. "Let's try it one more time."

The next, and last, try was as much of a failure as the first.

"All right!" said Madeira finally. "We're going to have to clear it by hand when we get down there. Can you get it to settle down to the deck?"

Alexi tried everything he or anybody else in the room could think of and failed. The SeaFairy couldn't settle lower than about a foot above the messing space's deck. So the tiny ROV spent the next four hours hovering, trapped among the wreckage, waiting to be rescued.

It really is the fast lane to hell, thought Madeira as he stood in the ooze alongside the wreck and guided his eyes along the trapped ROV's tether up into the hole. All the usual risks of entering a wreck, plus the hot water. A soup a hundred—no, a thousand—times hotter than the already hot stuff surrounding the wreck. Death was just pouring out of the thing.

There was nothing to do now but do it. He'd just have to work faster and better than ever before.

"Let's go, Grivski. Follow me."

"Yes, Captain."

Madeira grabbed the cutter's framework and pulled himself up the cold, black side of the wreck. Grivski, dragging a big strongback patch, followed a few feet behind him.

When he reached the hole, Madeira planted his feet on the lower edge and looked down into the submarine.

Thanks to the SeaFairy's wavering lights, he could see both the deck and the bulkhead and a hundred additional, shadowy forms. In the middle of the little open space available hung the ROV itself, edging back and forth in angry impatience like a wasp trying to get out through a closed window.

"Alexi, can you edge it over to starboard to make some room for me to get down?"

"Yes. I'll try."

The ROV retreated slightly, grazing the bulkhead as it did. "That is the best I can do, I think."

"Roger," Madeira replied, as he lowered a weighted descending line. After tying the line off to the frame, he turned to Grivski. "Tie that patch off and get comfortable just as fast as you can. This water isn't doing either of us any good."

Grivski emitted what sounded like a snort as he tied the patch off to the framework, allowing it to hang down along the sub's side. He then placed his feet beside Madeira's and hooked one arm around the framework. "I'm ready."

"Okay, I'm going down." He lowered himself over the edge of the hole and into the galley. Above him, Grivski tended Madeira's tether.

"How does it look? Can you find the hangup?"

"So far, so good, Mike. I'm on the deck now . . . about ten feet from the SeaFairy. . . . Okay, I can see the problem. The tether's caught on a section of shelving. . . . It's wrapped around something."

"Can you get at it?" demanded Novikoff.

"I think so. I've got my hand on it now." As he reached up, the SeaFairy sheered suddenly toward his outstretched fingers, its sharp little propellers spinning furiously. "Damn!" he mumbled.

"What?" Novikoff asked.

"The ROV almost bit my hand off!"

"Oh."

"There!" he said after several moments of grunting. "I think I've got it! Alexi, try to take her up slowly."

With Madeira holding the tether clear of all visible obstructions, the SeaFairy rose slowly, drifting from side to side as it went.

"Bravo!" said Alexi, congratulating primarily himself. "It's out and the tether is all clear."

"Take it on up, then," Madeira said, now fumbling in a silty darkness that was relieved only partially by the light mounted on his helmet. "Take 'em both up."

"Al," Novikoff interjected, "I think it might be a good idea for the ROV to go back in, with you guiding it, so we can see what you're doing."

"I sure as hell don't. It'd be in the way, and I don't have any time to waste keeping it from fouling again." He could feel a gentle flow of water past him. It had to be coming from the next compartment, the storeroom, and from the reactor room beyond.

"I'd still like to see what you are doing."

Madeira thought he detected a note of irritation in the Russian's voice.

"I'm standing in what's left of a well-maintained galley, damnit! In fact, this sub's cooks were good men. Despite whatever hell the ship went through, most of the stuff looks like it's right where it should be. . . . I'm leaving the galley and working my way through the mess decks. They're in pretty good shape, too, although some of the tables and benches are loose. . . . Okay, I'm at the hatch now. . . . Knife edge looks pretty good. I'm going to clean it off a little, then I think we'll be able to pop the patch right on."

Madeira intentionally neglected to mention that he'd also glanced carefully around to see if any of the cooks were still there, ready to do what they could to give him a hand.

If they were, they were keeping well hidden.

He stared a moment at the door, his light beginning to penetrate into the storeroom beyond. Then he bent down and thrust his head through the opening.

"Hurry!" It was Grivski. "You have no time to explore."

What the hell? thought Madeira. The Russians were determined to keep him out of that storeroom! Novikoff had insisted he not cut through it, and now Grivski was hopping from foot to foot to keep him from even looking in. Was there something in there he wasn't supposed to see?

And then a second, equally chilling thought hit him. Yes, hurry, you stupid bastard, he thought. Your diving dress provides only so much protection against the radiation. He grabbed the pinch bar and chipping hammer hanging from his belt and started to clean the knife edge against which the watertight door sealed.

After cleaning along the top and sides he knelt down to work on the bottom. With his hammer chipping mechanically on the knife edge, his mind and eyes concentrated on what might be in the forbidden, dimly lit murk before him.

He squinted into the darkness and began to see. The storeroom was filled with shadows. The shadows of shelving, lockers, and storage bins, all undoubtedly filled with engineering spares. The shadows of a small, built-in desk. The shadows of cables and piping running fore and aft. The ephemeral shadows of motion, of what might be living things of some rare family and order.

And arrayed along each side of the passageway running down the center of the compartment were still more shadows. Four in all, maybe six; it was hard to see. Big shadows. Lumpy shadows. Shadows that had nothing to do with the ship's engineering systems. Shadows, he felt certain, that didn't belong there at all.

They were stacks of what looked like artillery projectiles, he decided. Although they didn't seem to be pointed. Containers of some sort. Canisters of something. Bundled together and piled on what looked like pallets.

What sort of cargo would the Russians have been shipping, via experimental nuclear submarine, to Cuba? Right in the middle of the Missile Crisis? What came in smallish canisters and wasn't terribly heavy?

The answer seemed obvious, unless the sub was headed back to Russia, in which case the canisters undoubtedly contained rum. But then, the Russians don't drink that much rum, do they?

Only two questions remained to be answered. Were they biological or chemical? And were they still potent?

"Captain Madeira!"

"Yes, Grivski?"

"Our time is short!"

Yes it is, thought Madeira. And I've had enough of this shit. He opened his mouth, about to tell Novikoff that he was coming out of the wreck and up and wanted to talk to him in private. Then he thought about Grivski. Grivski breaking arms and ribs. Grivski pounding faces into pulp. Grivski standing between him and the surface. Tending his tether. What was it Novikoff had said? Grivski and Mendalov would see him . . . us . . . through?

He was a prisoner, he now realized. A fat little mouse caught in a trap baited with a million dollars, a jar of ego balm, and the vision of redemption, of making up for a lifetime of screwups.

As long as he did his job he was valuable alive to Novikoff. But would he remain so once the Russian learned that Madeira knew about the cargo they'd tried so hard to conceal?

He very much doubted Mike would ever want him to set foot ashore again. He would, without doubt, turn to his strong right arm, Grivski, to make sure that knowledge of the canisters remained buried forever.

A ray of hope suddenly burst out of the gloom.

Meg Jefferson.

Novikoff wouldn't dare harm her. Next time she appeared, and Madeira felt confident that she would return, he'd change sides. Tell her the truth and hitch a ride with her to San Juan. To hell with the million dollars and to hell with Jen and Charlie.

Somehow, he suspected Grivski and Novikoff wouldn't let it happen that way. Still, it might be worth a try. In the meantime, his only hope lay in finishing the job quickly and seeing no evil along the way.

Mike, he thought, I won't mention them if you won't. And the same for you, Grivski.

"Okay," he finally said, "it looks pretty clean. I'm returning to the galley."

"Yes, Captain," replied the Russian as he dropped a short guyline down to the galley. He then manhandled the heavy patch itself into the hole and prepared to lower it.

Madeira grabbed the guy. "Okay, lower away!"

"Lowering away," Grivski replied. "Do you want me to come down after it to help you?"

"No. There's not enough room. I can handle it."

Madeira looked up to watch the patch descend, a growing black blob. Then, just a foot or two out of his reach, it seemed to stall.

"It's stuck," mumbled Madeira as he yanked impatiently on the guyline. Every extra second he spent screwing around with this patch, he thought, was undoubtedly shortening his life by hours. Or days.

The patch shuddered, then resumed its slow fall, bringing down with it an entire section of thoroughly rusted shelving along with an oven and a sink. A thousand pounds of tangled metal and wiring toppled over onto him, crushing him onto the deck and burying him just as thoroughly as any fossilized dinosaur ever was.

Chapter Twenty-Five

Ninety-seven.

The number glowed in high relief, cutting through the thick fog that seemed to fill his head.

Or maybe it was only ninety-three.

He took a shallow, painful breath while he continued to root through the haze. Novikoff had said ninety-seven, he decided, his thoughts now starting to flow faster. Viktoria had mentioned ninety-three. However many it was, they'd all died. Right here. More or less where he was lying.

It'd probably started as something small and easily corrected, he thought. That's how most of them seem to start.

But it hadn't been corrected. Or it'd been corrected wrong, or too late. Then indecision, impatience, confusion, and fear. One thing had led to another, and finally . . . BOOM!

It had to have been a high-pressure steam line. The line had burst with the force of a hundred pounds of TNT, blasting the fatal hole through the pressure hull and filling the reactor compartment with its equally deadly, acidlike vapors. Anybody in the compartment at the time was probably killed almost instantly, his flesh and lungs parboiled.

Madeira tried to open his eyes and discovered they already were open. The absolute dark wasn't in his head after all. It was all around him.

Was his helmet light working? He tried to feel it with his right hand and found the arm pinned to the deck. He tested his left, only to discover it too was totally immobilized. Shaking, he tried to take a deep breath and felt only more pain.

My air supply! he thought as tendrils of panic creeped across his still-muddled mind. The supply valve must be damaged. Or the controller. He reached for the valve, having already forgotten that neither of his arms could move.

"What happened? Are you okay?" He was alert enough by now to realize the voice must be Grivski's.

"A bulkhead . . . something . . . fell on me." As he spoke he realized that something big and heavy was sitting on his chest, making breathing nearly impossible.

"Must've pulled it down on myself," he continued with painful slowness. "I'm pinned to the deck."

"Are you injured, Al?" It was Novikoff this time.

Madeira tried to move his arms again, then his legs. Nothing would budge, although none of them hurt, either. He tried to wiggle his fingers and toes and found he could.

"I'm okay . . . chest hurts a little. Something heavy's pinning me down. Grivski, can you see anything down here?" As he grunted out each breathless phrase he nudged the chin switch inside his helmet, slightly increasing the dress's internal pressure and relieving some of the weight on his chest.

"No. The whole space is filled with shit in the water."

"Don't worry about that, Grivski," snapped Novikoff, "go in and get him!"

"No, Grivski, stay where you are!" Madeira shouted feebly, thinking of every disaster he'd ever seen or heard of and determined to prevent this from becoming yet another.

He could see the usual pattern developing. Some stupid

bastard yanks too hard on a guyline and manages to topple a hundred tons of shit onto his own head. A second, equally stupid bastard jumps blindly into the same black hole. Now there are two stupid bastards, both injured, trapped in the wreck. Soon the wreck's score will be ninety-nine, or ninety-five, depending on whether you believed Viktoria or Novikoff, to nothing.

And the game was far from over.

"I want Timon or Mendalov, it doesn't matter which, to suit up and come tend our tethers before Grivski even thinks of coming in here."

"But that will take time" insisted Novikoff in what sounded suspiciously like a whine.

"Grivski can't get in right now anyway," Madeira replied in what he hoped was a calm and convincing tone. "Not until the crap in the water clears up. If he tries he'll just end up killing both of us."

"I am not afraid to go in right now!"

"I'm the one who's afraid, Grivski!"

"Okay, Al. You're the salvage master," relented Novikoff after a long pause.

And it's also *my* ass, Madeira thought as he tried to relax. And *my* chromosomes, for that matter.

Unfortunately, he'd already done everything he could think of to save himself. There was nothing he could hammer or twist or pull; nothing he could do to relieve the agony of lying on the very edge of life and death.

Mike Novikoff stood in the operations center, looking over Alexi's shoulder, and fumed.

It didn't matter what Madeira knew or didn't know, just as long as he got the wreck up to the surface. Once the wreck was up he would readdress the whole question, but in the meantime the American had to be kept alive. Not even an American could salvage the sub if he was already dead and buried in it.

His fists clenched, the Russian naval officer glanced around the room. "Mr. Chernov, I'm pleased to see that you

continue to take such a strong interest in this project," he
snapped upon spotting the chief officer.

"Yes, Captain, we have all put so much time and effort
into it; it is natural that one would be interested."

Indeed it is, thought Novikoff, and I'm sure your friends
on the St. Petersburg docks would also like to know. Unfortunately for you, you picked the wrong gang of thugs to
join up with.

Madeira heard, or felt, the wreck groan, as if it were shifting or collapsing. Then, to take his mind off the totally unacceptable, he considered the particles churning madly
around him. Mud, sand, rust, and God knows what else. All
hot, hot, hot. Settling on him. Covering him. Working its
way into every crevice and joint in his dress.

He was being embalmed in radioshit! And it didn't even
have to work its way through the dress to hurt him. A half-
inch was almost as good as a hit.

His thoughts returned to the God-knows-what-else in
which he was lying. Under which he was lying. Fifty years
of death and decay. Food. The bodies of countless mutants.
The remains of the crew. It was a graveyard, and he'd already been buried in it.

"Beluga!"

"Yes, Captain?"

"Who's coming to tend?"

"Timon, sir."

"Make sure he brings a chain hoist with him. And a big
pinch bar and a good collection of wire straps."

"Yes, Captain."

Madeira lay there, unable to move, and found himself
looking for Carlos. There he was, all right, standing in a
corner of Madeira's mind. He was there, just as Madeira
knew he'd be, but he looked very unhappy. And didn't seem
to have anything to say.

This time he *is* embarrassed, Madeira decided, because
he can't think of anything to suggest. Or because he knows
something he's afraid to tell me.

Madeira realized he was growing light-headed and wondered vaguely if maybe something was wrong with the air he was getting so little of.

Not wishing to think further of that possibility, he studied the thin trail of silt that was drifting across his faceplate. At least the water was alive, he thought. Flowing oh so slowly out of the storeroom. Circulating, almost, like the blood in a living creature.

He could almost feel the hot silt settling on and around him. He wiggled, hoping to dislodge some of it.

Circulating! How the hell could it be circulating? This was the only opening that hadn't been closed off.

Thermal circulation?

"Mike, goddamnit! Could the reactor still be operating?"

"What makes you think so?"

"The water. . . . Water's still flowing out the storeroom door, but we've closed off all the other entrances. The only explanation I can think of is that the reactor's still heating the water."

"That's very possible, Al." It was Viktoria's voice. "Especially with a unit as badly designed as this one. Even in well-designed systems there are always some reactions going on and some heat being generated. No matter how far in the control rods are pushed."

"Can it go critical?"

"No. If it were going to do that it would have done it by now. This is not totally unexpected. Is the water noticeably warm?"

Not totally unexpected! he thought. Why the hell didn't anybody mention it to me?

"No," he replied to Viktoria's question, having decided it didn't matter at this point why nobody had told him. "The water doesn't feel at all warmer. There must be a very small temperature difference. Just enough to get it moving." But if it's still running, added Madeira to himself, then it's still making more plutonium.

"I doubt it will prove a problem, but we'll keep an eye on it."

Madeira sighed. At the moment, the reactor's heat production was probably the least of his worries.

By the time Timon had managed to suit up and drag the rescue equipment over to the wreck, the slowly circulating water in the storeroom had cleared to the point where Madeira could see one edge of the large, black mass sitting on his chest.

"Timon's here, Captain," Grivski reported. "We are ready."

"What can you see? Can you see . . . me?"

Christ! he thought. He'd almost asked if Grivski could see *them*! Him and Carlos.

"I can see your light, sir, and some of the shelves."

"Very well, come on down whenever you're ready." Carlos and I will be right here, waiting for you, he added to himself.

Within seconds, or so it seemed, Grivski's hulking mass was bent over him, digging him out from under the remains of the galley. First one arm, then the other became free. Madeira quickly discovered, however, that he was still pinned just as firmly as before.

"Stand by. I'm going to lift this oven off you."

Madeira watched his shadowy rescuer and held his breath, hoping that his dress, which appeared to be intact now, wasn't torn by the oven's removal. He could feel the pressure on his chest lessen. And then it was totally gone.

But still, he was unable to move. Something was holding his thighs.

"It's good you told Boris to bring that hoist. I will need it to get this shelf up," grunted Grivski.

While Grivski and Timon rigged the hoist, Madeira lay quietly, waiting. He was still covered by a thickening layer of radioactive silt and fanned by a slight current of radioactive water issuing from the storeroom.

Then, to his great joy, he felt a deep, protracted groan echo through the thick, dark waters. It was the agony of corroded steel fighting and losing to the force of leverage.

"You should be free now. See if you can stand."

William S. Schaill

Madeira pulled his legs slowly toward him, overjoyed that they still worked. He then rolled over and rose first to his knees and then carefully to his feet.

"Okay . . . I'm okay," he announced a few minutes later. His chest hurt like hell, but he assured himself that no ribs were broken. If something really were broken, he reasoned, he wouldn't feel like going on.

"What about your controls, Al?" It was Novikoff.

"They seem fine. Otherwise, I doubt I'd still be talking."

"Okay."

"Let's get this patch installed, Grivski, and get the hell out of here!"

"I can do that. You return to the Beluga."

"Now that we're both already here, it'll go faster if we do it together. We've both been here way too long anyway."

"As you wish."

"What do you want me to do?"

"You just keep tending those tethers, Timon."

Between them, it took Madeira and Grivski less than ten minutes to install the patch and tighten it down, hopefully trapping the most radioactive particles in the reactor, turbine, and storerooms. Along with the gently warming water.

It took another half hour to collect their gear and slog their way back to the Beluga.

"Lock out those brushes," said Madeira as the divers halted under the access trunk.

"Roger," Mendalov replied just before the lower hatch popped open and three long-handled scrub brushes dropped down.

They scrubbed each other down repeatedly and hoped the slowly moving ocean waters would contribute to the decontamination of their dresses. Then Madeira, followed by Grivski and Mendalov, crawled into the trunk. After the air pressure had been reduced to only a few atmospheres, the two Russians pushed Madeira into the hyperbaric suite, then joined him.

"Mendalov," grunted Madeira into the phone after re-

266

moving his helmet, "is this hooked up so I can talk directly to *Asimov*?"

"Yes, Al," Novikoff replied. "I can hear you fine."

"I want Alexi to start cutting right now. While he's finishing off the pressure hull the Beluga's going to surface to reprovision. You're going to have to help Mendalov dock and load, because the rest of us are still going to be in the pot."

Madeira paused. Was he letting paranoia get the better of him? His fear of Grivski? His distrust of Novikoff? Was he panicking? Taking that first hasty and ill-considered step toward the edge of the cliff?

"Okay."

"Then we're going to finish cutting through the bottom, rig the lift, and be done."

"Alexi's already started."

"Roger."

"These are all still radioactive, sir," Timon said as he ran a Geiger counter over Madeira's dress. "What do you want done with them?"

"How radioactive?"

"Not enough to kill us right away."

"Throw 'em into the trunk, then. Since we don't have any others, we're going to have to try cleaning them again."

"Yes, Captain."

Madeira turned to the other Russian. "Thanks, Grivski. You saved my life."

"It was my duty."

Madeira studied the man's cold eyes. Grivski was telling the absolute truth. There was no joy there. No pleasure at having saved a shipmate. Not even any satisfaction at having cheated death for at least a short time.

For Grivski, neither life nor death seemed to exist, except as a technical consideration. If he felt any thrill at all, it was as the result of having carried out his orders promptly and efficiently. He would feel exactly the same, Madeira suspected, if he'd just finished polishing some brasswork. Or garroting a small baby.

Then Madeira glanced at the InstaRad radiation badge taped to his stomach. Damn! It was pink bordering on an angry red. He didn't need Grivski to kill him. The radiation would do a good enough job on its own.

His thoughts returned to the canisters in the storeroom. Maybe he should ask Novikoff about them. He played with the idea. It was very tempting; it would surely relieve the horrible anxiety that continued to fester within him.

But it would be a very serious mistake to do so, he decided with a slight shudder. He might well pay more for those few seconds of nervous relief than they were worth. Monkeys who see nothing tend to live longer than overaged salvage divers who ask too many questions.

He'd like to be able to discuss it with Carlos. Or even better, with his father. Carlos was the expert at getting out of trouble. Carlos's brother, Al's father, was the only member of the family bright enough to avoid unnecessary trouble in the first place.

Maybe he should've paid a little more attention to his father's approach six months ago. Or twenty-five years ago, he added ruefully.

Chapter Twenty-six

"How do you feel, Captain?" Timon asked as he and Madeira knelt in the soft, radioactive muck that filled the submarine's cramped bilges. "Dr. Galin told me you received a dose of almost fifty REM yesterday."

"I seem to be okay. Olga says the most likely symptom will be nausea or diarrhea, but I feel fine so far. Check back with me in ten years."

"But you shouldn't be here now," persisted the Russian diver. "Your exposure builds up over your lifetime and this shit around us is hot. The three of us can finish up without you taking more risks."

"I'm being paid for the risks, Boris, and it's not as hot here as in the reactor compartment. Anyway, I'm not even in the same league as some of your people at Chernobyl."

"They're all dead men!" spat Timon, ending the conversation for the time being. "Fools led by fools led by fanatics."

Unable, thanks to the silt-filled water, to see any further than his own imagination, Madeira slowly forced the hand

William S. Schaill

laser's pulsing, faintly glowing ball across what felt like, and should be, a steel I beam.

Suddenly he jerked his left hand back toward him, cursing as he did.

"What?" demanded Timon.

"I almost ran the laser over my fingers," Madeira said. "I once knew a guy who did that with an arc welder. Sliced off all four of them and never felt a thing until it was too late."

Someone else on the circuit, not Timon, chuckled.

The last four days, Madeira thought, had been sheer hell. And he'd brought in all on himself. Ever since he'd decided to pick up the pace.

Once Alexi had finished cutting the hull above the mudline, Grivski and Timon had cleared a path across the galley and mess decks and repositioned the cutter's frame on the internal deck. The two Russians had beat a hasty retreat to the Beluga and Alexi had made very quick work of the deck.

Then the really nasty part had begun.

Working in pairs, round the clock, the four of them had removed the deck section by section. With the bilges now open they were free to grab hand lasers and attack the sub's bottom and the thick, longitudinal beams that made up its complex backbone. Each had spent hour after miserable hour bent over, kneeling, lying, wallowing in the radioactive muck. All the while, their full mental powers had to be centered on the dimly flickering balls.

"You must be more careful!" scolded Timon. "Especially now. This job is becoming more and more dangerous as time passes. It looks to me like you have put yourself right in the middle of the biggest dangers. I personally would like to see you go home in one piece."

Madeira listened, convinced the Russian wasn't just talking about diving accidents. Did Timon know about the canisters? Was he really a friend? What about Viktoria?

"They're all sicker than dogs!" snapped the major as he grabbed a stanchion. Despite, or perhaps because of, its

270

great mass, the dry dock shuddered and yawed outrageously as it lumbered before the growing following seas.

"Yes, sir," the sergeant replied, "but our people will all perform their duties as required."

"I'm sure they will, Sergeant. We have no choice now. I doubt the crew will give us any trouble. Nobody's paying them to get killed."

"Will they be able to load the submarine into the dock in this weather?"

"We'll anchor somewhere calm. *Asimov* will notify us where in another day or two."

"And later? After we have removed the cargo from the submarine?"

"Yes. We'll be back at sea then. That may be tricky, transferring it to the yacht. But it will be done and we'll be gone long before anybody can be notified."

"Beluga, this is *Asimov*. We are waiting to start."

"Captain?" Timon asked.

"I want to run over it all one more time in my head, Boris. Just to make sure we haven't missed anything."

"What's the holdup down there?" Novikoff demanded before Madeira had finished speaking.

"Sorry for the delay," said Madeira into the microphone, trying not to show his irritation, "but I want to take another five minutes to check a few things and make sure we're totally ready."

"Five minutes. That's all we can spend on it. The weather's deteriorating rapidly."

The weather's definitely not improving, Madeira thought as he glanced at one of the two monitors showing the view in the tunnel between *Asimov*'s hulls, but another five minutes won't make much of a difference. What *would* make a difference would be if he'd managed to overlook something important.

"Roger."

"It's almost over for her now."

"Yes, it is," Madeira answered, looking at the wreck on

the monitor. Once they'd finished it was highly unlikely anybody'd ever visit her again. "You think the ghosts will be happy to be left alone?"

"Some of them may still be in the part we're taking with us."

Fortunately, thought Madeira, I'm not among them.

"I want to check the other side one more time," he said, not wishing to further consider his near entombment at the moment. He then glanced up at the monitor displaying the wreck as seen by the SeaFairy hovering on its other side. "Start at the stern and move slowly up to the cut."

Timon nodded as he moved the little ROV's controls.

"I will say, and I don't care who hears me, that I'm glad this will soon be over," Timon said, echoing Madeira's own thoughts. "This hasn't been an enjoyable job!"

"No, it hasn't," replied Madeira, hoping to hell that no more diving would prove necessary.

The SeaFairy had reached the cut and was hovering there. It was as clean and sharp as could be, and all the straps were in place and secured to the double lifting wires. Just to make sure they hadn't missed anything, he'd had Timon and Mendalov stretch a wire across the wreck, then draw it down through the cut, much as a magician might pass his wand through the saw space where he'd just cut his assistant in half.

The wire had gone straight down to the bottom. Unhindered. There might still be something they'd missed under the ooze, but he didn't believe it.

He looked up at the scene between *Asimov*'s hulls. At the massive, greased-smeared lift wires rising up out of the water. At the seamen, visible here and there, standing, waiting for orders, or for something to happen. At the growing seas now starting to crest as they rumbled down between the bows and into the tunnel.

It certainly wasn't what he'd call prime lift weather.

"*Asimov*, commence lifting when ready. Keep an equal strain on all wires."

"We are starting to lift, Beluga." It sounded like Bukinin, but Madeira couldn't be sure.

"Okay," said Timon, excitement building in his voice. "I can see the straps getting tight."

Madeira found himself holding his breath as he watched the straps stiffen, then felt a grinding rumble shudder through the intervening water. He could imagine the lift wire, miles of it, running slowly through the pairs of huge blocks that multiplied each pound of force applied at the surface by almost sixteen.

Thousands of foot-tons of brute force.

The wreck's old, he thought, its steel tired. It's always possible the straps will just cut through it. Like slicing through a hard-boiled egg. He could almost see the plates buckling and the whole mess being neatly chopped into a dozen red hot parts, each spewing countless radioactive particles into the Atlantic. The reactor collapsing, then going critical.

He was letting his imagination run wild again. "Boris. Take a look at number seven."

"Don't worry so much, Captain. It looks okay to me."

Madeira looked up at the little fan, which rattled and clacked away, doing nothing more than stirring the damp, hot air.

"Beluga, is the payload moving? We have as much tension on these wires as they can take."

Madeira returned his attention to the two surface monitors. The lift wires were now bar-tight and vibrating like violin strings. Every now and then, one performed a strange sort of hop as the ship moved underneath it.

Then he studied the ROV's transmission.

"Roger, *Asimov*, we have a suction problem," Madeira said after watching absolutely nothing happen for several minutes. The sub had settled comfortably into the bottom over all those years. Snuggled into the ooze. Almost put down roots. And the deep mud wasn't about to give up its treasure without a real fight.

"Slack off all your wires," continued Madeira. He

William S. Schaill

wished the expedition had a second ship, one that could pull on a wire rigged at right angles to the wreck, thereby rolling it and breaking the suction. Not that he could guarantee that approach would work any better than any other.

"We're slacking off. Do you want to try to parbuckle it?"

Fortunately, thought Madeira, he'd warned Novikoff that something like this might happen. Otherwise the Russian would undoubtedly be hopping up and down and shouting by now. With success seeming to be so close, no more than a thousand-foot lift away, the son of a bitch had gone almost critical himself.

He continued to study the stubbornly unmoving mass of steel. And the ooze. And the great wires rising up into the overlying murk. "Not yet. Before we spend a lot of time rerigging to parbuckle, I want to try to lift just the stern. To tip it forward slightly."

"What happens if the stern breaks off?"

"Then we're in deep shit, but I don't think it will. The wreck's holding up very well. I want to heave around gently on one, two, and three."

During the pause that followed, Madeira could faintly hear Novikoff and Bukinin shouting at each other.

"Okay," Novikoff said finally, "we'll try it."

"Roger," replied Madeira. "Boris," he continued, turning to his companion, "I want to get closer to the stern so we can see what's happening."

"Closer?"

"Closer. But not so close the damn thing can bite us."

Timon lifted the worksub clear of the ooze and crept forward, keeping a careful watch on the wreck all the time. Madeira, meanwhile, kept the SeaFairy, still on the other side of the wreck, out of trouble.

"We're ready to heave on them now," Novikoff said as Timon was settling the Beluga back down on the bottom.

"Roger. Heave around."

Again Madeira held his breath, staring intently at the video monitors. He could see the three straps rise ever so slowly from the ooze. He could feel the rasping moan as they embraced the wreck's cold steel.

And again, nothing happened.

"What now, Al?" Novikoff's exasperation was all too obvious. The Russian has no future in the salvage business, thought Madeira. His frustration level's simply too low.

Then again, he thought, why the hell am I laughing? What sort of a future do I have?

"Maintain the lift on one, two, and three and have Bukinin give the ship a little kick forward. Dead slow for about a minute. No more!"

A thousand feet over Madeira's head, *Asimov*'s thirty-plus-thousand-ton mass surged forward slightly as Bukinin moved the engine controls. The lift wires stretched even tighter and the straps rasped again against the wreck as the ship strained off at an angle.

A trickle of bubbles appeared here and there along the wreck's bottom. The trickle suddenly expanded into a chain, then exploded into an almost solid white curtain, which shot up toward the surface.

At the base of the curtain, puffs of ooze rolled out and away. Could that be what Viktoria's mythic microvents look like? wondered Madeira briefly.

"She's going, Boris. She's twisting," he shouted. "We're breaking her free! *Asimov,* stop engines!"

"Look!" shouted Timon as he pointed at one of the monitors.

By the time Madeira looked it was already too late. Wire number one was tearing off the last ten feet of the wreck and there was absolutely nothing he could do to stop it.

"Goddamnit to hell! *Asimov*, stop engines and heave around on all lift wires!"

"If that whoreson tears the wreck apart I'll have Grivski kill him right now," Novikoff snarled in Russian as he stared in horror at the monitor in the operations center. "He'll never live to see the surface again."

275

William S. Schaill

"You selected him yourself, Captain," said Viktoria carefully, pondering Novikoff's statement.

"I also selected *you* myself."

Viktoria clamped her mouth firmly shut and edged away from him as Novikoff returned his full attention to the monitor.

Who was it, she asked herself again, who *really* chose you? Yeltsin? Primakov? The General Staff? The Mafia even?

Why were you selected? And what are you really supposed to be doing?

"Okay, *Asimov*," said Madeira, regaining control over himself. "It is essential that you keep heaving around on all wires."

"Heave around! What the hell do you mean heave around? You've just torn the stern off the wreck!"

"Keep heaving around!" Madeira repeated as calmly as he was able. His worst suspicions were now absolutely confirmed. Novikoff had been a staff officer for most of his career. A political fixer of some sort. "It's broken free of the suction and is bouncing along the bottom. Once we get it well clear of the bottom we can stop and investigate."

"We can investigate better on the bottom."

"If we try to bottom it now we'll tear it into twenty pieces. . . . Now, keep heaving!" He watched the dark mass of steel scrape and bang its way across the ocean floor, its plates bending and twisting as it went. What, he wondered, was happening to the reactor?

Then he glanced at the monitor showing the tunnel between *Asimov*'s hulls. The orderly tangle of massive lift wires were all twitching and hopping now. It was as if they were giant fishing lines, each with a sea monster securely hooked and fighting back for its life.

"Al." Novikoff suddenly sounded as if he were struggling to reason with a child, or a madman. "Millions of lives may be at risk if we've fouled this up."

Why the sudden change in tone? wondered Madeira as

the sweat poured off him. He must be scared. Scared the wreck's going to pop open and spew canisters all over the bottom. Where everybody can see them. Where it'll take a year to find and recover them all.

"Just keep heaving, Mike. This is what you're paying me a million dollars for."

"I'm glad you haven't forgotten who's paying you."

So much for Mr. Nice Guy! thought Madeira.

"I'm ready to take the SeaFairy in to investigate the damage on your order," Timon reported.

"Roger. I'll tell you when," replied Madeira.

"Very well!" Novikoff said. "We're continuing to heave around, but I want you to get in there and investigate the damage as soon as possible!"

"Roger, *Asimov*. Keep heaving until I tell you to stop."

Madeira and Timon scanned the monitors intently, both underwater and topside, hoping to spot any new trouble before it had time to develop into something bigger.

"*Asimov*, how're you doing with number one?" Madeira asked, more than merely eager to have the now-useless stern lift wire removed totally from the water so it couldn't possibly get in the way.

"We're working on it."

Madeira and Timon watched in silence as the thousand-ton treasure, cradled in the net of lift wires, rose inch by painful inch clear of the bottom. Forgetting, for the moment, the damage to the stern, he couldn't help but believe that victory was beginning to take shape.

God! he thought, savoring the strange euphoria reserved for salvors. Is it really out of the mud and headed up? Over two million pounds of steel and muck.

And ghosts. No salvor could ever afford to forget about the ghosts.

"It looks good, Captain. Very good," beamed Timon.

"Sure as hell does. This's one of the smoothest lifts I've ever seen." Despite the rough start, he added to himself. "We'll be under way in another twenty-four hours."

"What about the goddamn stern!"

277

Shit, thought Madeira. He'd forgotten Novikoff could hear every word they said.

"Roger. We'll send the SeaFairy in now to check on that."

"We'll stop heaving," Novikoff said as Madeira nodded to Timon.

"No. Keep heaving. Everything's going too smoothly to stop. We'll check it out on the way up."

With Madeira guiding it, the SeaFairy flitted in, under and around the wreck's mangled stern, transmitting both video images and radiation readings as it did.

"You getting our transmissions, Mike?"

"Yes, it looks like you tore off some plates and cut a gash in it. But the radiation doesn't seem elevated."

"No," Madeira agreed with a sense of relief. "It looks like they managed to keep that door closed."

According to the plans, the little compartment all the way aft was a narrow storage space. If the wreck had been a fully operational combat sub it would undoubtedly have been the aft torpedo room. Whatever it was, or could have been, it wasn't leaking radiation.

By now the ocean bottom had disappeared into the great monochrome darkness below. The only visual reference remaining was the ghostlike wreck itself, which seemed to Madeira to be holding up very well after over thirty years on the bottom.

"We've got another day or so of watching the grass grow," said Madeira as he tried to stretch. "Make yourself comfortable. I'm going to check on Mendalov and Grivski, then I'll relieve you in a couple hours."

"Watching the grass grow?"

Madeira studied the scene on the monitor. The swell, nasty and from the east, was running a good fifteen feet with white, tussled tops as it rolled down between *Asimov*'s twin hulls. The mass of lift wires was tending aft while forward, between the bows, the sky glowered in grim shades of gray.

"Okay. Let's surface, but keep away from the wires. Stay well forward."

Fifty feet below the worksub, the wreck tugged and jerked at the greatly reinforced wire net they'd just completed installing around it. If it weren't for the catamaran's great size and stability, the whole maneuver would have been impossible. Even as it was, the wires were as lively as any Madeira'd ever seen.

"As soon as I reach the landing stage, you go down again."

Timon nodded his understanding and moved the worksub's joystick forward.

Madeira, wearing a wet suit and life vest, climbed into the upper access trunk and closed the lower hatch.

"We're on the surface now."

"Roger," Madeira replied into the waterproof comm unit. "I'm opening the upper hatch now."

"Don't get wet."

The hatch popped open just as a swell swept over the worksub's deck and cascaded down onto Madeira. Goddamnit! he thought as he fought his way up out of the flooded trunk and into the gloom that dominated the space between *Asimov*'s two hulls. He closed and dogged the hatch, then grabbed a handrail just as another swell thundered over him. Wiping his face, he looked around quickly and spotted the small landing stage they'd rigged for him right at the research ship's waterline. Novikoff was standing on a gallery just above the stage.

"Here, Al. Take this," the Russian shouted. Madeira watched as Novikoff's arm snapped around and a light line arced through the gloom.

Neatly done, for a staff officer, thought Madeira as the line snaked past him and landed across the Beluga's deck, about four feet away. Moving as fast as he could, he grabbed the line. After wrapping it around his waist he threw a bowline in it, then caught his breath as the next swell rolled down and lifted him off the worksub's deck.

"We're almost there," he panted jubilantly as Novikoff

pulled him up on the landing stage. For a moment he almost forgot that the canisters might yet prove to be the death of him, not that Novikoff had shown any indication that he knew Madeira knew. "Another fifty feet, then we stop everything off and get on our way."

Novikoff smiled. "I will admit I had my doubts, but it all seems to be working out."

Madeira looked aft at the straining wires and then up at the gallery, which would serve as his control station.

Was that a flash of red he saw? A head of burning red hair?

"Is Meg Jefferson here?" A wave of hope, almost relief, swept over him as he asked, totally drowning any amazement he might have otherwise felt at his newfound fondness for the fiery reporter.

"No. . . . What makes you think that?"

"I thought I saw her standing up there in the gallery."

"I don't think she'll be back until after we've transferred the wreck to the dock and returned to San Juan."

"Oh!" Madeira replied. Where, he wondered, was the media when he needed it?

"Al," said Novikoff, beaming, "your part of this operation is almost over; it will be in a few hours. Despite my many worries it has all gone very well, and I've decided to have a little party tonight to celebrate. After supper."

"Damnit, Uribe!" Meg Jefferson shouted as the press photographer jumped aboard the big sportfisherman Meg had browbeaten her editor into chartering for her, "I've got them this time!"

"Oh!" Uribe said. "I thought you had them last time, only then you backed off."

"I wasn't sure then. I didn't have anything solid enough to be sure, but now I do."

Both had to shout to be heard above the rumble of the boat's two big diesels.

"What changed your mind?"

"A few days ago I called a guy I know in New York and asked him to do a little more research on Madeira. He called back this morning. It seems the engineer on that Cape Cod whaleboat Madeira drives has been going around telling everybody that Madeira's been hired by the Russians to help them salvage a Russian sub filled with gold."

"Gold! That's shit. The guy must be drinking."

"I'm sure he has been, and I agree that the gold bit is shit, but I'm certain it's really gold for us."

"What?"

"It's a cover of some sort. The engineer, who my friend says isn't too bright, must have overheard something, so Madeira made up the gold bit to get him off the track. But I'll bet both my boobies that what he overheard had something to do with salvage. . . . That *is* what Madeira does. They really are picking up something out there, and they're willing to tell such big lies about it that it's got to be interesting."

"You're a spiteful woman, Meg," said Uribe, laughing. "You can't stand their trying to con you."

"It's not spite. It's business. The Statehood Plebiscite's old news now, especially since they chose the safe, boring Commonwealth route again, and The Big Oil Spill's getting a little tired, too. Whatever they're up to on that 'research ship' is big. You don't send big ships to do little jobs. And big jobs make big news."

"So we're going to go out and visit them again?"

"Not right away. We're going to go watch them, from a distance. And then, when I think the time's right, we're going to ambush them."

"You're going to grab them by the balls and make them sing, right, Meg?"

"Right, good buddy."

Meg waved at the boat's skipper, who was already on the flying bridge with his piratical gold earring glinting in the pale sunlight. Having caught his attention, she pointed out the marina entrance, out toward the gray, stormy ocean. The skipper nodded at the mate, who cast the dock lines off, then revved the engines still further and backed quickly away from the dock.

The ambush was on.

Chapter Twenty-seven

Asimov steamed slowly northeast at slightly less than three knots through the dark, utterly starless night. With each sea, the big catamaran rose sluggishly, only to have its ascent immediately checked with a shudder as a thousand tons of radioactive junk jerked up short on the lift wires.

"Boris, do you know what's in the storeroom?" Viktoria asked as the two of them stood on deck, sheltered, in the lee of the ship's huge deckhouse.

"No, Commander. Don't you?" replied Timon, puffing on a cigarette.

"No. But you're certain there's something there?"

"Yes. Captain Madeira saw something, and ever since he's been very edgy, frightened, I would say. Sometimes, when he doesn't think Grivski's looking, he looks at Grivski with a very strange look."

"And what about Grivski?"

"Yes. I think he knows what it is; I think he's known all along."

"Does he . . . ?"

"Yes. He knows Captain Madeira knows."

"Then everybody seems to know but you and I?"

"I don't think that animal Chernov knows what's there, although he does seem to suspect that something is, and I doubt Captain Bukinin knows either."

"Do they matter?"

"Chernov may, if he's as in with the Mafia as he seems to be."

"Has he done something you haven't told me about?"

"It's what he doesn't seem to be doing. I don't think he's smuggling anything back with him from Puerto Rico."

"He's concentrating on something else, then. Like whatever's in that storeroom . . . or the plutonium. Grivski and the commandos should be able to protect that."

"That may not keep the Chechens from trying."

"Chechens? Chernov's not Chechen. What makes you think it's a Chechen gang he works with?"

"Rumors, mainly. You're right, we can't be sure it's Chechens, but I'd bet it is."

"Whoever it is, they may try. But what I really want to know about is that storeroom!" As she spoke, Viktoria wondered if Boris Yeltsin knew what was in there.

Madeira paused at the rail to savor the strong, wet wind blowing in from starboard. The natural seasonings, salt and ozone, tasted good, almost as good as life itself. He swayed slightly, keeping time with the ship's shallow, jerky pitching as rumbling, gray-white waves rolled out of the surrounding dark and shattered on *Asimov*'s high sides. Thin clouds of spray, thrown up and over the ship, drifted rapidly across the deck before disappearing again into the night.

There was an electricity in the air, he thought. A sensation of crackling energy and limitless relief. Of well-being and clarity.

He, Al Madeira, had recovered the nastiest wreck to come along in some time. And he'd done it with a tiny crew in what would be record time if records of such things were kept.

He took another deep breath, and his spirits sagged. The job *was* done and the customer, Novikoff, did seem happy, but it was becoming increasingly hard to tell what the Russian really felt. And the contents of the storeroom continued to nag. They were probably just ancient history, something Moscow wanted to sweep under the rug to avoid embarrassment, but he'd just keep his mouth shut about them.

And hope that Grivski wasn't instructed to make sure it stayed shut.

They'd all been very lucky, he decided. No diving accidents. No deck seaman injured or killed by snapping wires or falling weights. And his own total radiation exposure for the operation, while high, was not so high as to guarantee him a glow-in-the-dark future.

Yes, everybody had been lucky. Everybody but Rustoff. And the guy who was supposedly killed in New York.

He glanced up at the TV camera mounted under the boat-deck overhang and the camera stared intently back at him. He'd soon be free of them, too. And he'd be a million dollars richer, although the money somehow still seemed unreal, a joke.

Habit, however, was not dead. The voyage wasn't over, he reminded himself. Just to make sure their luck continued to hold, he wandered down and aft along the inboard side of the starboard hull. As he went he inspected each of the lift wires, its chaffing gear, the huge steel stoppers bolted around each lift wire, and the wire straps leading from the stoppers to the huge bollards.

With every wave the ship shuddered and the wires hopped and thumped slightly out of time with the ship's movements. The weather was going to get worse, he thought, and this really was a half-assed way to move the wreck, but the Russians had given him no choice. All he could do was cross his fingers.

When he reached the stern he crossed over to the other hull and started forward, continuing his inspection.

"Hello, Captain!"

The voice, coming out of the darkness, startled him. He

William S. Schaill

turned and saw the seaman assigned to keep an eye on the lift wires standing next to a bollard, smoking a cigarette.

"Hello . . . Arnoff," replied Madeira, hoping he had the man's name right and suspecting that the greeting had pretty much exhausted the sailor's knowledge of English.

Arnoff smiled broadly and waved slightly but said no more. Madeira smiled hard and nodded, and then, after an awkward moment, continued his inspection.

Everything appeared to be in order, although the wires' liveliness did cause his heart to miss a few beats.

After examining the last, most forward wire on the port side he climbed the ladder to the boat deck and paused, looking again out into the Atlantic's perpetual storm.

It's still there, he thought as he glanced out over the port quarter. A faint white light that seemed to flash every now and then as if being obscured by the churning, heaving seas. No green running light, though. It must be too far away for the running lights to be visible.

And now there was another, he realized. Another faint white light more or less abeam to port. But it was the one astern that was most interesting, because it had been there for several hours.

It could, of course, be anybody. A fisherman. An inter-island freighter. A yacht. Maybe even a guardian angel with red hair.

He found the thought that he was looking to a smart-ass reporter for salvation slightly nauseating. Especially since any threat to him might be no more than the product of his own paranoia.

"Attention! Attention!" Bukinin shouted, waving a glass of vodka, as Madeira walked into the main salon. "It is *Asimov*'s first millionaire! Tell us, sir. What do you intend to do with all this money? It is enough for a thousand honest Russians to live on for a lifetime."

Good question, thought Madeira. The drunken captain's question both irritated and discomforted him, since he had neither a plan nor a pressing need for the money. Not unless some slimy bastard in Washington decided to take his pension away.

Maybe he should give it back. Make it possible for a thousand Russians to live a lifetime. He'd had his fun, after all. No amount of money could provide the high he felt after snatching the wreck from the ocean. But even if he did give it back he doubted any starving Russians would see so much as a kopek. The Russian government would certainly find other uses for it.

"Don't quite know yet, Captain. Maybe I'll give it all to the church . . . or to the Republican Party."

Bukinin glowered at him, then returned to his conversation with Vasily Chernov. Clearly, whatever rapport Madeira thought he'd developed with the captain was nothing more than a figment.

Madeira stood for a moment in the middle of the room as the ship listed slightly, then sideslipped hesitantly down the face of a wave. The second mate was telling a joke of some sort, in Russian, to the chief engineer and one of his assistants. Riki and Novikoff were earnestly discussing something about which Riki looked far from pleased. It could be a happy hour almost anyplace in the world.

Almost.

They were all there to celebrate *his* victory over the ooze, the cold, deep waters, and a thousand tons of radioactive scrap, and yet he felt totally out of place. It was as if he were a party crasher. Somehow, once again, he was the outsider. And had been all along.

This is insane, he thought as he stepped over to the sideboard, then grabbed and popped open a beer bottle. Why did he feel as if God was about to lean down from above and squish him with His thumb?

Must be getting another cold, he decided. He always experienced the sensation of light-headed edginess just before the viruses struck with their full force. Either that or Carlos was trying to whisper something to him that he wasn't quite hearing.

"Congratulations!"

He felt Viktoria's arm slip through his. Without thinking, he pressed it against his side.

"Thanks, but it was a team effort."

God! she looked good, he thought. Cool. Hot. Sparkling and totally desirable.

Could it be the gold earrings? Of course not. They were just a highlight.

"No reason for you to be modest," she said slowly and quietly, her lips very close to his ear. "You led the operation. You made all the difficult decisions and did the most dangerous work. You deserve the credit . . . and every penny of your pay. That fool Bukinin is just jealous."

Her arm was cool under his and her hip pressed against his leg. He could feel himself tensing, feel a glowing, gnawing anticipation growing within him as caution and prudence shrugged their shoulders, covered their eyes, and sidled away.

Tonight, he was the victor and he wanted her. To hell with Grivski and Novikoff and the canisters. And so what if she worked for Russian naval intelligence?

"For a spy, you're very beautiful."

"We all are. . . ."

Novikoff glanced at them and smiled thinly, then returned to his conversation with Riki.

"Shouldn't you visit Woods Hole this summer? Discuss microvents with the people there?" He found himself leaning slightly toward her.

"You still don't believe they exist, do you? Anyway, I thought you were going to visit Russia."

"I'm still thinking about it. Has there been any identification of that vessel following us?"

"Following us? Why would anybody want to follow us?"

"I can't imagine."

"Mike thinks it's either your government or Meg Jefferson."

"He's probably right. Whoever it is can't be enjoying the ride at the moment. They have to be beating their brains out."

"What are you going to do after you go home?"

"Count my money, then go back to whale-watching. See what comes up."

The crowded, poorly ventilated room was hot and stuffy, thick with the smell of heavy food, alcohol, cigarette smoke, and human bodies. Madeira turned to the only relief he could imagine, the cool challenge sparkling in Viktoria's sapphire-blue eyes. Tonight he was the victor, he reminded himself. Tomorrow, his job done, he might very well be dead, victim of some totally believable accident.

He leaned forward and kissed her. Briefly but firmly. She responded with a deep, hard hunger that matched his own.

Mike Novikoff pressed himself against the starboard rail as *Asimov* continued to lurch and stagger through the growing seas and cursed his own stupidity and lack of self-control. He'd gotten drunk again, just like in San Juan. Not *as* drunk, but drunk enough. Too drunk for the most important night of the operation. The *only* night of the operation.

He listened to the groaning of the ship, the thudding of the waves on her sides, and the working of the lift wires as he willed his head to clear. There was 30,000 feet of water beneath the keel, the deepest part of the Puerto Rico Trench. Should the wreckage break loose tonight, nobody who didn't already know about its cargo would ever learn of it. And even those few who did know of its existence would assume it had gone down with the rest.

Blow, wind, blow! he thought. The worse the weather, the more believable the wreck's loss would be. Just as long as Grivski and Mendalov got the stuff out beforehand.

Novikoff lit a cigarette and inhaled deeply. Then he headed for one of the hatches that led down to the galleries built into the inner hulls of the ship. A moment later he heard a noise. He stopped in the shadow of one of the big deck winches and turned in time to watch Vasily Chernov stagger out a door in the superstructure, across the deck, and then disappear slowly down the very hatch for which he himself was headed.

Novikoff remained in the shadow of the winch, his fists beginning to clench. The chief mate was still sniffing around, trying to learn more about the cargo, just as he had been doing for most of the voyage.

He started to shout at Chernov, to engage him in conversation, to keep him from going down the hatch, but then decided it was better to let him go. Chernov was an irritant, and had been all along. He was also still a threat, perfectly capable of blowing the whole operation wide open.

The chief mate had been drinking heavily at the party, thought Novikoff, and now his luck had run out.

Moving quickly, his head beginning to clear, Novikoff sprinted to his quarters and then returned to the hatch. He paused a moment to listen, then stepped quietly into the hatch and started slowly down the ladder into the ship's starboard hull. As he descended, the roaring, pounding boom of the seas slamming into the ship's hull and echoing up and down the tunnel became stronger and stronger. He stopped when he reached the first landing and waited. The ship shuddered and the vibration continued, amplified by the singing lift wires. When he heard bumbling, uneven footsteps punctuated by mumbled curses echo up from a deck or two below, he started slowly down the next ladder. And then the next, with equal care.

Four decks down, Novikoff paused again to listen. Then he stepped into the short passageway leading to gallery number four. Ahead he could see the chief mate, standing in the gallery looking out into the tunnel.

The sound of his approach covered by the tunnel's roar, Novikoff slipped up behind Chernov.

"Vasily," he said in a loud voice.

Chernov turned, his eyes dull and only half focused from the vodka. "Captain Novikoff. Just the man I wanted to see. What is that man doing down there?"

Novikoff looked out into the center of the tunnel where Mendalov, wearing a wet suit, was securing a rubber boat to one of the lift wires. "There's some material in the wreck which is still classified. They're going to recover it before the wreck goes into the dock. . . . You were told about this some time ago."

"I don't remember being told such a thing," Chernov replied. "Tell me, what's really in that submarine? What are you taking from it?"

"There's nothing in the wreck that's of any concern to you and your Chechen friends, Chernov!"

"Everything is of interest to me and my friends," said Chernov, reaching for a fire ax mounted on the bulkhead.

"You're a faithless pig, Chernov," Novikoff shouted, his anger overcoming him. "You've sold out, betrayed your Motherland to the Chechens for a few rubles!" he continued as he drew the pistol he'd returned to his stateroom for.

Chernov burst into a slobbering laugh. "The Motherland, Novikoff? The Motherland means no more to you than to anybody else. The dollar now rules the world. Ask your Georgian friend, Avalaridze!"

"What!"

"You were followed in San Juan, Captain. You were seen talking with Niko Avalaridze."

Novikoff's fury exploded, as did his pistol, right into Chernov's face. "I have no interest in money," he shouted, each word punctuated by another explosion in the pistol's chamber. "We're not in with him, although he may think we are. We're using him for the good of Russia, to save Russia from American overlordship."

Panting slightly, Novikoff watched Chernov collapse to the deck, his lower jaw burst, his nose gone, and the back of his head now missing.

"You should have paid more attention to the warning I gave you in New York," he concluded.

Chernov was long past paying attention to anything.

Continuing to pant, more from emotion than exertion, Novikoff dragged the bloody body to the rail and, with a heave, lifted it partway over. Just one more drunk lost overboard on a dark night, he thought. Then, hearing a noise behind him, he let the body slump back on the deck and turned to find Grivski standing there with his huge arm wrapped tightly around Timon's neck.

"He followed you down here, Captain," said the Russian robot.

"Another irritant!" Novikoff said, beginning to calm himself as he thought through the possibilities. "A reformer . . . A reformer who was widely known to hate Chernov . . . And who was shot while in the act of murdering this ship's chief mate. Do you understand me, Grivski?"

"Yes, Captain."

"The murderer and the victim will be found together. Both dead."

The ship shuddered as she rose to a particularly large sea. A second later a loud thump echoed through the tunnel, a thump much louder than the wreck's normal banging and slapping.

Novikoff turned and looked just in time to see one of the huge, greasy lift wires heave itself up into the air, arching briefly like a whip being drawn back for the blow. It then slumped back into the water again and started to trail slightly aft, just missing Mendalov, who was swimming like hell for the small stage just aft of the gallery.

"Shit!" Novikoff shouted. "The wreck is breaking away. Grivski, you see to Timon and make sure it's convincing!"

"Yes, Captain."

The Russian naval officer than ran out of the gallery and up the ladders to the main deck.

"Stop playing with that!" snapped Avalaridze as he caught Ari tinkering again with the radio direction finder in *Velociraptor*'s darkened pilothouse. The Maxi yacht, now about five miles east of *Asimov*, was dealing very gracefully with the growing seas. Niko's stomach clearly wasn't.

"Okay," Ari replied, "but how can we be sure it'll work?"

"It'll work," said Arnold, the skipper, out of the darkness, "just as long as you don't fuck up the frequency setting. We'll pick up the signal five minutes after they set the rubber boat adrift. Then we just home in on it."

Chapter Twenty-eight

Something rock hard slammed into the door.

Once.

Then the door flew open.

"Out of bed, Al! We've got real trouble!"

Madeira awoke instantly, and wished he hadn't. His mouth felt like the Gobi Desert at high noon, and his head was pounding with a furious intensity.

He rolled over, squinting into the dim light from the passageway and expecting to see Viktoria next to him, curled slightly in sleep, a slight, relaxed smile on her face.

"She's not here anymore. Now, get the fuck up!" Novikoff shouted as he flicked on the overhead light.

Madeira stared at Novikoff a second, then at the pistol the Russian was waving around. He wanted desperately to doze off, to drift back to the very recent past, the hours he and Viktoria had spent in another world. He knew to do so now would be fatal. "What the hell's going on?"

"The wreck's breaking loose!" replied Novikoff, shouting. "One of the lift wires has already snapped, and others are bound to go at any time now."

Madeira felt deathly ill and knew it wasn't just the beer.
"Where'd she go?"

"Back to her room to get dressed."

Only then did the message really get through the alcohol-induced blockade of his mind. "The wreck's breaking loose?"

"Yes!"

"Shit!" groaned Madeira as he got to his feet and started to dress. Damnit! he thought as he tried to get his foot into his trousers, why the hell's the ship rolling so damn much? Then he recognized, with dismay, that the exaggerated rolling sensation was only partly the work of wind and sea.

How'd Novikoff gotten Viktoria out of the bunk without waking him? Madeira wondered illogically. His throbbing head, he decided, might provide a possible answer. Then he realized that she'd obviously left long before Novikoff had burst through the door.

He noticed a faint, rapid popping sound.

"Who's that firing?" he asked. "If the wreck's breaking loose, why is somebody firing an automatic weapon?"

"Grivski. He's trying to stop Timon before he kills anybody else."

"What? Who do you think he killed?"

"Chernov. He shot him to death."

For the first time, Madeira looked closely at the Russian. "What's that all over your clothes?"

"Blood. Chernov's blood. I tried to help him, but it was much too late. Everybody knows that Timon hated him."

Sharks! he thought bitterly. Lane Williams said he'd be swimming with the biggest, meanest sharks ever born, and the admiral'd been right. While simple Al Madeira had ambled along, laughing and scratching like an orangutan and worrying about all the obvious things, like Grivski's fists, Novikoff and the others had been . . . what?

He still didn't understand what the hell was going on around him.

The deck beneath his feet tilted, then slid and shuddered in a new way. "Stop the ship, Mike!" he almost shouted, his alcohol-addled brain now focusing entirely on the treasure he'd so painfully wrested from the ocean deeps. Jesus! To lose it now!

"What?"

"How many cables did you say have parted?"

"One when I left the tunnel."

"It's at least two now; I just felt one go. We've got to slow way down before the wreck slips out of the net." He paused briefly, feeling the deck's jerky ups, downs, and occasional sideslips. "Don't come to a complete stop, that'll just make it worse. Turn into the seas and slow to bare steerageway!"

Novikoff grabbed the telephone and called the bridge.

"Okay," Madeira said, tying his last shoe. "Let's go! You have a weapon for me?"

"No. I want you to concentrate on saving the wreck. Leave Timon to Grivski and me."

With Novikoff leading, they raced along the dimly lit passageway and down the ladder to *Asimov*'s main deck. The sporadic bursts of gunfire became louder and more distinct as they went.

There was a distant shout of triumph. Then silence.

The instant their feet hit the main deck they pounded aft, slaloming around barely visible bollards, cleats, winches; hurtling over lift wires running across the deck and over the side; and ducking to avoid guy wires and a hundred suspended obstacles of one sort or another.

"Mendalov!" panted Novikoff as he skidded to a halt.

"Yes, Captain," replied the wet-suited shadow that separated itself from the huge deck winch directly ahead of them.

"Where's Timon now?"

"Dead, Captain. Grivski shot him a couple minutes ago."

"Bullshit!" exploded Madeira, still choking on disbelief.

"What!" Novikoff said.

"Timon didn't kill Chernov! He hated his guts and he would have liked to kill him, but he didn't! You're feeding me another line of shit."

"Enough!" Novikoff snapped. "Mendalov, you go find Grivski and tell him to meet us in gallery four. Then you inspect and secure all the remaining wires."

"Yes, Captain."

"Al, you come with me. You're going to do what we're paying you to do," ordered Novikoff as he holstered his pistol.

Was there no way out of this garden of delights, Madeira wondered as he followed Novikoff back along the dimly lit, gear-cluttered deck and down the ladder to gallery number four.

The first thing Madeira saw when they reached the gallery was the wet, lumpy red clump that had been Vasily Chernov's head. Next to it lay Timon, dressed in work pants and a dive jersey and riddled with small-caliber holes. Despite the gruesome evidence, Madeira was more convinced than ever that Boris had *not* killed Chernov.

Grivski appeared, glanced briefly at the bodies, and stepped over to Novikoff. That makes four sons of bitches, he thought. One dead, three to go.

A blast of Russian erupted from the speaker mounted on the bulkhead. Novikoff spun and stared at it a moment, his fury appearing to grow. Then he shouted back at the speaker.

"What was that?" Madeira asked, wondering if Novikoff would even bother to answer him.

"Bukinin. . . . Meg Jefferson *has* been in that boat that's been shadowing us. She's demanding to come aboard."

Meg Jefferson! The press, like the cavalry, riding to the rescue! Hope flared briefly, then died. There was no way she could save him now.

"What did you tell him?"

"To keep her off, to do whatever's necessary." Then he turned to Grivski and spat out a long stream of angry Russian. Grivski nodded, then trotted off.

Do whatever's necessary! thought Madeira, reminding himself that condemned men still have one big advantage over those already executed. And, under the circumstances,

what choice did he have? Maybe if he played it straight he'd
live.

Somehow.

He leaned over the rail and looked down. Although *Asimov* had slowed, the tunnel was still filled with the booming echoes of flowing water, straining, twisting, chafing steel, and pounding machinery. It was the cries of the innocent dead, thought Madeira. Of all the millions who've died at sea due to betrayal or deceit, not to mention their own limitless stupidity.

Six wires were gone now, the aftmost six. They descended from the opposite side of the tunnel and didn't reappear on this side. Despite their great weight they seemed to trail slightly aft. The ship must be moving more than he'd realized.

"What do you suggest, Salvage Master?" Novikoff asked.

Madeira looked down again at the meat that had been Boris Timon. *That* had been Novikoff's one conclusive error. All the rest was believable. Chernov was a scumbag and deserved to die. But Boris hadn't been the executioner. Not that it made any difference at this point.

Madeira knew he had no choice but to play out his role to whatever end awaited. They owned the ship and they had the guns.

Suddenly there was motion. Out of the corner of his eye, Madeira noticed a movement way off to the left, astern. He turned and looked just in time to see the ghostlike white shape of a big sportfisherman surge across *Asimov*'s stern, rolling and pounding in the nasty seas.

The boat appeared to have stopped and turned, and its high, flaring bow was now inserting itself between the catamaran's two hulls as the growls of its twin diesels became audible. In the next second Madeira could see the mass of red hair, glowing in *Asimov*'s working lights, on the sportfisherman's flying bridge.

Meg raised a power megaphone and said something. It sounded like "I've got you clowns now!"

Madeira continued to watch as a string of large raindrops—or were they black snowballs?—tumbled from above onto the boat.

One after another, so rapidly as to seem like one continuous detonation, the grenades exploded, each a vapor-hot ball of orange flame and invisible shrapnel. On the third or fourth detonation, the boat itself burst into a solid, rectangular mass of flame that completely filled the end of the tunnel.

The flaming mass fell back behind *Asimov* where it started to roll violently in the ship's wake. It burned for another minute or two and then disintegrated in one final explosion.

As usual, thought Madeira, Grivski has executed his orders with total thoroughness. Nobody could have survived the explosions.

"Okay," said Novikoff after the roaring echoes of the final explosion had been carried away, "let's find you some scuba gear. We've got work to do."

As the Russian spoke he was looking over Madeira's shoulder.

Following Novikoff's glance, Madeira turned and found himself staring into two blue eyes that snapped with an icy, high-voltage fury.

"Viktoria!" Novikoff said. "I warned you about these people!"

"Yes, Captain, you did," she replied, glancing quickly at Timon's body, then back at Novikoff.

"The Mafia, the Fascists are everywhere these days."

"Yes, they are."

Novikoff and Mendalov then stepped off to one side and started talking quietly, while Viktoria glanced out into the tunnel, at the rubber boat that remained tied to one of the lift wires.

"He was mine, Captain!" she said, turning back toward Novikoff and the diver. "Timon was mine. He was neither Fascist nor mafioso, and he didn't kill Chernov, because Arnoff saw you do it."

"What?" Novikoff demanded, his thoughts caught be-

William S. Schaill

tween two conversations. As the Russian captain spoke, Mendalov spun, reaching down for the diving knife strapped to his right leg.

A pistol appeared in Viktoria's right hand and three shots slammed into Mendalov's left side, an inch or two below the armpit.

Even as those first three booms were still echoing up and down the tunnel, Novikoff reached for his own side arm. Viktoria fired three more times, pulping the Russian naval officer's chest and driving his body backward against the rail.

"Oh, goddamnit!" she shouted as the sickly yellow-white clouds of muzzle gasses billowed in the tunnel's normally cool air. She glanced up at the TV camera, which was aimed at the wreck, then reached for the telephone and punched the button for the bridge. "This is Commander Galin," she said, "put Captain Bukinin on.... Then wake him up!"

She waited a minute or two in silence, studying the pistol in her hand, while Bukinin was called from his sea cabin.

"What's going on down there?" demanded *Asimov*'s master.

"I've just shot and killed Captain Novikoff. He appears to have lost his mind or he may be engaged in some conspiracy.... Either way, he disobeyed his orders. He killed Timon, who worked for me, and Chernov."

"Oh?"

"I am now in command of this operation, Captain.... Do you understand? Our orders neither required not justified the execution of Boris Timon, or of your toadie Chernov, either. Novikoff was always unstable. We are here to solve a problem, not to make still more."

"Are you sure he had no reason to do these things, Commander?" boomed Bukinin's voice in her ear after a long pause. "What makes you so sure you know what Captain Novikoff's orders really were? And whose orders are you following?"

Viktoria shuddered slightly, her light coveralls failing to keep out either the Atlantic's cool dampness or the gnawing unease, the near certainty that there was still so much more to know than she knew. "I am following the orders issued to me by the commander in chief of the Russian Federation Navy, Captain, and so shall you. And it doesn't matter what Novikoff thought his orders were. I ask you again, do you understand where your true duty lies?"

The deck rose and fell, the remaining lift wires hopped and groaned, and the waters continued to snap and pound against the ship's steel plates.

"Yes, Commander," Bukinin replied finally. "My orders are the same as yours, to solve a problem for Russia. And I will, of course, respect your naval commission."

Madeira glanced down at the four blood-soaked bodies and then astern, where he assumed Meg and her crew now also slumbered beneath the cold, rolling seas. Was there any chance that this was maybe the end of it?

"Very well," Viktoria said, staring out into the darkness astern. "You are to arm your men and find Grivski. He may be able to tell us what, if anything, was on Novikoff's mind. I want him alive."

"Yes, Commander. Where is the other? Mendalov?"

"He's also dead."

"Ah!"

Continuing to hold the phone to her ear, she took a deep breath and wondered how much longer she could count on her naval commission to intimidate the merchant master. Then she turned to Madeira. "Okay, Al. Before you go into that storeroom you have to save the wreck. How do you intend to do it?"

He looked at her a moment. She's as mad as all the rest, he thought. Doesn't she realize it's hopeless?

Then again, nothing is really hopeless. That's the Third Law of Salvage.

"I don't know yet. I'm going to have to start by taking a look at it. Then I'll probably have to try to reconnect the damaged lift wires."

"What do you want done with the ship?"

"Keep her exactly as she is."

William S. Schaill

"Captain Bukinin!" she said into the phone.

"Yes, Commander?"

"Keep the ship exactly as she is now. Do not change speed or heading."

"Yes, Commander."

He stood on the edge of the stage and looked down into the water that surged past a foot or so below his feet. Past the nightmarish tangle of wires he himself had created and through the oil slick–like surface. His full attention was directed deeper, at the fearful shadow that hung, unseen, below. He could feel the darkness it pulsed, the call to eternity.

Why am I doing this? he wondered. For that mad bitch with the blue eyes? For the whales? For myself?

The five-pound chunks of lead tugged at his waist and the steel Scuba tank pressed against his back.

He jammed the mouthpiece between his teeth and inhaled. The air tasted okay. He counted the pairs of lift wires . . . two, four, six, eight, ten, eleven. That's where the blast hole in the deck was. Near number eleven. He'd use it as a descending line.

Madeira leaned over and grabbed the waterproof dive light. Then, holding his mask in place with one hand and the light, his weight belt, and tank harness with the other, he stepped into the dark, endlessly deep Atlantic.

Bobbing slightly, struggling to get his raggedy breathing under control, he waited for the wreck to come to him.

Even before the first wires reached him, he could feel the sub's dark presence; feel its pressure wave elbowing him aside. Then the first pair of wires were on either side of him, singing quietly with stress as they cut through the water.

He felt as if he could reach down with his toe and touch the monster below. But would it bite? Would it take his foot off at the ankle? At the knee? Or at the hip?

Then the second pair of wires slipped past.

During the few seconds it took wire number eleven to reach him, Madeira concentrated on getting both his breathing and thinking under control. After all these years, he thought, he still hadn't mastered these most basic of diving skills.

He grabbed the thick, grease-covered bundle of steel strands and dragged himself down. When he reached what was left of the deck he paused and hung on, staring at the blast hole. It was wide open again, just the way he and Timon had cleared around it. The strongback patch was nowhere to be seen. The damn thing was wide open and trailing an invisible plume of radiation.

Timon was a good man, he thought, wondering if he'd meet him again. And how soon. Maybe he hadn't told Madeira everything he might have. Maybe he'd even been reporting every word Madeira'd uttered to Viktoria. But that was all to be expected.

Novikoff had murdered the son of a bitch, Novikoff and Grivski, and they'd done it with the coldest of calculation. It had nothing to do with Timon's loyalty to Mother Russia. Novikoff had needed somebody to accuse of murdering Chernov, and Timon had somehow been convenient.

The wreck shuddered and rolled, reminding Madeira that he was there to try to save the reeking mass of rust. He would mourn Timon later.

Then he noticed the two cargo nets, their corners pulled up to shape them like baskets, hanging down below the rubber boat. Novikoff had been preparing to remove whatever was in the storeroom. And Chernov must have gotten in the way.

Madeira grabbed one of the lift wires and pulled himself carefully down along the wreck's side, shining his light on the other lift wires as he went. The sensation of menace was overpowering, of being a gnat on the hide of a huge, dark monster. A living monster that groaned and twisted and shifted madly in its efforts to escape the web the gnat had created to imprison it. And all the while it seemed to radiate the flavor of evil.

Even before he reached the bottom he knew the wreck was lost, that it was only a matter of time before the monster would succeed in freeing itself. Six lift wires had failed by now, and more would soon follow. In the process, large portions of the harness he'd built around the wires were being torn away. The wreck was hopping and slipping from side to side, lunging forward and falling aft. And starting to tear itself apart.

There was nothing he could do now. Indeed, the effort had probably been doomed from the beginning, from that very first meeting in New York. Long-distance tows of large submerged wrecks had been done before. Many times. In fact, he'd even done one or two himself. But they were always very, very risky. They failed as often as they succeeded; more often probably. And even when they did succeed they were usually nightmares along the way. If it hadn't been for the political factor, the need for secrecy, he would have insisted on loading the wreck into the dry dock right at the site.

But that was all ancient history. As would be the wreck in a few minutes. It was the canisters he wanted to know about now. They weren't ancient history; they were very, very current. During the past couple of months at least half a dozen people had died because of them, and he wanted to know why.

He started up one of the lift wires, careful to keep his hands and feet from slipping between the wire and the wreck. When he reached the deck he dragged himself over to the hole, taking care to avoid becoming entangled in the cargo nets. This, he decided, would be the quickest way in. Far faster than trying to remove the patch he'd placed over the door between the storeroom and the messing space in which he'd been trapped earlier.

He shined the light into the darkness. All around, squat, silt-robed shapes hovered in the shadows. They all should be glowing, he thought as he stared down into the machinery spaces. They're all red hot, yet they look as quiet, and dead, as the contents of an unopened pharaoh's tomb.

Madeira continued to hang on to the edge of the hole, looking into it, feeling the tortured metal skin vibrate slightly as his dark treasure was dragged ever so slowly to the northeast.

And the water flowing out was now noticeably warmer than that of the surrounding Atlantic.

"Okay!" he snapped to himself. "Do it! The longer you wait, the more likely it is that the wreckage will slip."

He jackknifed and pulled himself down into the hole, through the turbulence at the boundary, and into the relative calm of the reactor room.

Calm, perhaps, but filled with terror. On all sides, above and below, wires, pipes, and who knows what else reached out of the thick darkness and grabbed at him. And all the while, the entire mass hummed and vibrated with psychopathic glee as it spewed silent, invisible radiation in all directions.

And yet he couldn't get over the sensation of peacefulness that seemed to dominate the space. He stared a moment at the reactor itself, the cause of the ship's death.

A defective design, everybody seemed to agree. Too bad for the crew. Most of them were probably good guys, but that's the way it is. Sooner or later we all get the same. In his own case, he thought, it'd probably be very much sooner.

He felt the wreck shudder and slip slightly.

By force of will alone he returned his attention to the door between the reactor room and the storeroom. It looked open, just as they'd suspected.

The wreck shuddered again.

He sculled carefully down, hoping to keep from further agitating the silt, and edged toward the door. Shining his light ahead of him, he pulled himself through, into the storeroom.

As before, a row of skids piled high with canisters ran along each side of the path down the middle of the space. The skids had clearly been well secured, since they were all still in two neat lines and none had toppled over.

He felt the grinding shriek of steel. Then the wreck shuddered and plunged like an out-of-control elevator. There was a dull clang as the overhead hit his tanks and a dense cloud of silt billowed up from the deck.

Shit! Shit! Shit! he screamed silently, torn between the urge to run and the now-absolute conviction that it was essential that he save one of the canisters.

After a second of indecision he forced himself forward and down and grabbed one of the cans. All the while the wreck continued to drop away from him.

Surprisingly, the canister came free after the briefest of tugs, the steel banding securing it to the pallet having long since been reduced to little more than an illusion by rust.

Turning, with one arm wrapped around the canister, Madeira felt his way back toward the door through the water now totally opaque from the resurrected silt. Panic bubbled within him, on the verge of exploding, while the wreck continued to shudder and drop as it slipped out of the net.

Carlos? Are you with me, Carlos?

Jesus Christ! He couldn't find the door. The whole damn wreck seemed to be spinning and rolling. He didn't even know which way was up anymore.

"I'm sorry, Al," said Carlos finally, "but this time you've really done it. You know I'd do anything for you. Anything! But for once I've got to agree with your dad. You shouldn't have gone back for the canister. That was incredibly stupid. Now not even I could get myself out of the trouble you're in."

Would he continue to obey her? Would he obey her at all, for that matter? And what was he up to right this minute?

Viktoria was so preoccupied with Bukinin that she didn't notice the first twitches of the lift wires. Only when the screeching and groaning skyrocketed in intensity was she forced to take notice. Leaning far over the rail, she watched in surprise, then fear, and finally a growing horror as the lift wires launched into a mad dance in tune with the cacophony that thundered up and down the tunnel.

She continued to observe with morbid fascination as a large swirl took shape in the dark water below her. There was, she noticed, a large hollow in the middle. A giant, swirling dimple.

And then, with what sounded like a sigh, the wires relaxed suddenly, as if exhausted by their brief frenzy.

The phone buzzed. "What happened?" Bukinin bellowed as soon as Viktoria answered. "Have we lost the wreck?"

"Yes, Captain. The wreck is gone." And the mystery in the storeroom will remain hidden forever, she added to herself with more than a touch of bitterness.

"I await your orders, Commander!"

She looked out again at the swirling waters and smiled bleakly. That, at least, answered one of her questions. Now that the operation had become a hopeless fiasco, Bukinin was more than willing to let her lead the retreat.

"Recover all these wires, Captain," she ordered, "and then head home to St. Petersburg."

"Very well, Commander."

"And tell the dry dock to turn around and go home also. We have no wish to draw any more attention to ourselves at this point."

While Bukinin bellowed a string of orders over the PA system directing the recovery of the net and wires before they fouled the propellers, Viktoria continued to lean on the gallery rail, staring down into the water. Not only was the wreck gone, but so was Al Madeira. Gone, just like that! She snapped her fingers unconsciously. Just like Leo.

Things weren't going any better for her at the moment than they seemed to be for Russia.

She permitted herself to wallow a few minutes in a totally unprofessional despair.

Grivski! she thought with a start. He's still loose. She still had to ensure that he was both neutralized and preserved for interrogation. She also had to maintain control over the ship until they got back to Kronshtadt. Biting her lip, she chewed on those two related problems.

Then the ocean belched.

She felt the thump as the shock wave, generated over a thousand feet below, slammed into *Asimov*'s plates and lifted the ship's stern. Quickly looking aft, she saw a dome of boiling white water rise out of the dark sea, a portion of it driving into the tunnel.

It's all glowing! she thought in mild amazement as countless billions of bioluminescent plankton violently protested the trashing of their environment.

A fitting tribute, she decided. What better memorial to Al Madeira than for the sea to burst into green flames upon his death?

Chapter Twenty-nine

"Cornie!" shouted Frank Urban, owner of the whale-watcher *Evie G*, across the crowded barroom. "You heard anything from your boss recently? How's he doing with that Russian sub filled with gold?"

Cornie placed his almost-empty beer mug down on the bar. After wiping his mouth with the back of his forearm, he turned on the stool and faced Urban. "Ain't heard nothing from him, Frank. . . . Makes me think, though, that he's doing just fine. If they hadn't been able to find it he'd be back by now, and it he was having some other problem he'd have called me."

"How about Carlos? He heard anything?"

"Not that he's told me."

"You sure he's not just chasing women someplace down south?"

"He's working on that sub, Frank. Trust me."

Urban turned back to his companions and said something that caused them all to burst into gales of laughter. Cornie made a point of not noticing.

William S. Schaill

*   *   *

It was like being in a clothes washer. Water, dense silt, and bigger, harder objects of all description surged and churned around Madeira as the wreck spun, skidded, and rocked violently. All the while the rasping, grinding groans of steel on steel filled his ears and mind.

Kicking madly, he drove himself down toward where the door should be. He had to get out! There was no time to think, no time to worry about radiation or eternity or anything in between. There was only time to act. And pray.

He found the door and pulled himself through into the reactor room just as the wreck slipped free. Blunt end down and liberated from the wire supports Madeira had so carefully crafted, it plunged toward the bottom. As it fell it started to slowly turn end over end, pivoting as the blunt end rose and the pointed stern descended.

Totally blinded by the tarlike water, bruised and disoriented, Madeira lost all sense of direction and even concious purpose.

Which way to go now? What to do next?

He hadn't the slightest idea. He understood what was happening and no longer believed he had any choice about what would happen.

Something grabbed at his hand. He yanked it back to him, then curled up into a frightened, defensive ball. "It had to happen someday," reflected that part of his brain that was still rational, "and it seems to be happening right now."

Everything was spinning and churning around him. All was darkness. His world had come to an end, he thought bitterly. He bit down hard on the mouthpiece and clutched his arms even more tightly around the canister and across his chest.

Something solid was pressing against his back, forcing him down. Every breath was a struggle. The wreck was headed home, and it seemed to be taking him with it. Along with the rest of its crew, the unfortunates it had nabbed the first time.

But appearances proved to be deceiving. Driven by its

310

own momentum, the dense, silt-filled water was sloshing and spinning to a beat different from that of the wreck itself. Slopping out any opening it could find, the soupy mass chose to carry Madeira along with it in its escape.

His head and chest snapped back, up into the blast hole he had used to enter. His back arched and his feet were forced down. In the next instant the wreck, like Jonah's whale, vomited. Still clutching the canister, Madeira was rocketed out the blast hole and back into the dark and disturbed ocean.

Even as he emerged from the hole he could feel the wreck still grabbing at him, determined to take him down with it. He kicked furiously. Up. Up where his unseen bubbles were going. Up to life.

In. Out. In. Out. He wanted to gulp the air and cherish it, hold it forever, but his training forced him to breathe as steadily as possible and to exhale thoroughly.

It's behind you now, below you, he told himself. The worst is over. There's no reason to panic. You've still got plenty of air.

But air wasn't the problem. The problem was still the wreck! The hungry, goddamn monster that had almost added him to its lost crew. The mass of rust and steel might be gone now, far below and still sinking, but he would always be a prisoner of its memory.

It would always be waiting just below the surface of his thoughts.

His head burst through the surface, only to be overrun by a cresting wave. He kicked frantically, determined to keep above the next wave.

The canister! Yes, he still had it, clutched under one arm. But he'd lost the light somewhere.

There she was! *Asimov.* Twenty-five yards away, fifty at most, although it's always hard to tell at night. Towering over him, her dim working lights making it appear that the waves had been cast from an oily black pewter.

Twenty or thirty yards, if that. But in these seas? Holding

the canister? A nightmare! And if the ship was still going forward, an utter impossibility.

But she didn't seem to be moving much, if at all. Holding her own, at worst.

Had Bukinin stopped to look for him?

Fat chance!

Maybe Viktoria'd ordered him to.

That seemed faintly possible, although most likely they'd stopped to recover the lift wires.

He dove back down under the inky water. Deep enough to avoid the waves' full power but shallow enough to still feel their rythmic rising and falling. He kicked, sixty of the most powerful thrusts he could muster. As he forced his way through the thick, living dark he could feel the fluid flow of the next approaching wave. It started as a slight, uplifting pressure against his face mask. It flowed along his body, down his chest and stomach, causing his spine to flex slightly, continued past his groin, then finally down his legs.

It felt right. It felt as if he was holding his course directly into the seas.

Then he surfaced again, to regain his bearings.

Not bad! A little off to port, but *Asimov* was clearly closer. How long had it been, he wondered, since the wreck broke loose? How far below him was it at this very moment?

He dove again and repeated the process. He wasn't *that* good a swimmer, he knew. The ship must be blowing down on him.

Panting, tearing through his air supply like a drunk through a bottle of bourbon, he surfaced from the third dive to find himself nose-to-butt with one of *Asimov*'s towering sterns, which was dimly, though adequately, defined by the tunnel's working lights.

There's a ladder here somewhere, he thought as the ship's bow pitched down into the trough, throwing the stern high into the invisible night. A row of steps, formed of one-inch steel bars bent into U's and welded to the transom.

The stern hung suspended, almost directly above him.

Then, with a whoosh and a hiss, it started down like a thirty-thousand-ton flyswatter. And he was the bug.

Christ! he thought. Where the hell's that ladder!

Far below Madeira the wreck continued to twist and shudder as it fell slowly through the heavy waters, headed for its final resting place in the depths of the Puerto Rico Trench.

When it reached eleven hundred feet, less than a hundred deeper than Madeira had found it, the coiled spring of a pressure detonator pressed against its stops, causing a very simple electrical circuit to snap closed.

But nothing happened! The detonator was electrical, and the batteries by which it was powered had long since died. It was, therefore, unable to trigger the surge of power that would detonate the blasting caps set into the huge scuttling charges placed in the sub's bilges, right under the machinery. Almost a ton in all, the charges were designed to totally destroy the reactor. They had been placed by a paranoid nation determined to ensure that, no matter what, the Americans would never learn the details about their marvelous new technology.

And then, maybe fifty feet farther down, a second spring reached its limit and a backup detonator snapped. This time the system was based on percussion, physical contact, instead of electricity. The hammer snapped, driving the pin into a cap of fulminate of mercury. In less than an instant the entire charge detonated. The sides of the wreck bulged, forced apart by the mass of rapidly expanding gasses, and then burst, freeing the great, surging bubble to begin its frothing trip to the surface, expanding almost geometrically as it went.

The wreck must be halfway to the bottom by now, thought Madeira as he rose on a wave and the stern fell past him.

There it was! The ladder. With one or two kicks he could reach out and grab it.

But somehow he had to ditch his fins in the process. He couldn't climb the ladder with them on. He couldn't remove them once he was on the ladder, because he only had two hands, one to hold on and one to hold the canister, and he couldn't ditch them now, because he'd never be able to reach the ladder without them.

Time! There was no time to ponder the fine points! If he didn't get out of the water soon he'd either be drowned or pounded to death by *Asimov*'s barnacle-covered rump.

He kicked hard, once, twice, then lunged out, reaching for one of the passing rungs. He managed to snag it just as it plunged underwater, dragging him with it.

With his free hand he forced the canister down between his legs and squeezed his knees together hard while the hand continued on to his right fin, which he cast off.

He was then free to concentrate on hanging on as he was dragged deeper and deeper into waters that seemed determined to tear him loose from his handhold.

Eventually, he could feel the stern's plunge slowing, then coming to an end. In a matter of seconds, he thought, it would rise as the ship's twin bows dove into the next trough. He grabbed the canister with his free hand while he used his finless foot to locate another rung. The ladder shot skyward, dragging him up through the water with increasing fury, just as he located a rung and jammed his foot into it.

With the canister wedged between him and the ship, and both hands maintaining a death grip on the upper rung, he was dragged clear of the water just as the ocean belched violently.

He could feel the ship's steel skin resonate to the rumble of the detonation long before the great dome of water heaved itself out of the depths and chased him halfway to the sky.

Another three seconds, he thought, and I'd be dead, my guts jellied by the shock wave.

He looked down, back over his shoulder. The boiling mass now stretched as far as he could see and continued to swell up at him. And it was alive—glowing, pulsing a bright greenish-white light.

There must, he realized, have been a scuttling charge. Could it possibly have been a nuclear one?

He doubted it. But whatever kind of charge it was, it was big, big enough to generate vast amounts of highly radioactive silt. Silt that would remain suspended for months as it moved north with the Gulf Stream. Silt that would become part not only of the food chain but of the medium itself, the ocean.

He was still staring stupidly at the green-burning sea when the stern reached its zenith and started down again.

He had to get up on deck, he realized, snapping back to his more immediate problems. He couldn't hang on forever, or even for much longer. He pushed himself back from the hull and looked up. Thirty feet, at least. He'd never make it unless he ditched the heavy, bulky scuba gear, burning that one last bridge behind him.

The elevator continued down, burying him in the seething, glowing maelstrom. This, he decided, was what it must have felt like when one of Cornie's pious ancestors set out to prove you were a witch.

He forced his body tighter against the ship and used one hand to trip the quick-release fastenings on his tanks, which slammed him hard on the head and then disappeared into the watery dark.

Then he ditched the remaining fin.

As the ship paused, preparing to rise yet again, he forced the canister behind his weight belt. The instant he burst through the heaving surface he started to climb, pulling himself up one painful rung after another. With each step his middle-aged shoulder muscles screamed. With each step the canister jabbed painfully into his gut and hipbone.

Almost thirty feet to go. Roughly thirty slippery rungs, each a brutal torment to his bruised arches, which benefited not at all from his dive booties' unpadded soles.

Up the ship went, and up Madeira went. Down the ship went while Madeira continued to struggle up. Finally he pulled himself over the toe rail and under the lifeline. Then he collapsed, exhausted, in the scuppers.

"Captain!"

A shadow stood in the darkness, shining a flashlight on him. From the shadow's voice and outline he guessed it was one of the Russian seamen, one who'd never seemed to know much English. One, as he remembered, who seemed to have been interrogated with special vigor by Grivski.

"Yes. Has the ship been damaged? Are they recovering the wires? What is Captain Bukinin doing now?"

The seaman stared at him, his eyes reflecting the dim light. He shrugged, as if to say "I don't understand a word you're saying and haven't the slightest interest in doing so."

A wave of rapid Russian boomed out over the PA system. The sailor turned slightly to listen, then turned back toward Madeira, who could have sworn the man now had a slight, grim smile on his face.

The seaman shined the flashlight on Madeira again, nodded, then ambled slowly away, leaving Madeira lying, panting, on the heaving deck.

What the hell's the next step? he wondered, checking to see that he still had the canister. He doubted Bukinin would be very happy to see his new little treasure. Of greater practical importance, he wasn't sure how Viktoria would feel about it either.

The sound of many voices shouting in Mach 2 Russian suddenly hit him, carried aft by the wind. Then the rapid cracking of automatic-weapons fire.

He sat up, convinced at first that a full-fledged mutiny had broken out. Then he felt the deck rumble and heard a faint splash. Then another.

He crawled over to the inboard side of the deck and looked down into the tunnel just in time to see another lift wire splash into the Atlantic. Bukinin, or whoever was in charge, was obviously not wasting the time to recover them. At least part of the crew was busy jettisoning the lift gear, which seemed to suggest that there was no mutiny in progress. The rest, he decided, must still be hunting Grivski down. Hunting him down like the carefully trained and hopelessly vicious pit bull he was.

He wondered how many Grivski would take with him.

Then he wondered where *he* stood. And why so many people had been killed. And what Novikoff had been planning to do.

The canister, he decided. The answers had to be in the canister.

He asked himself how the Russian authorities were going to react when *Asimov* arrived back at St. Petersburg empty-handed.

What had Lane Williams said about outside experts making the best scapegoats? And they're probably just as useful dead as alive.

Asimov's decks, he decided, were no safer tonight for him than they were for Grivski. Accidents do happen, especially when you're aboard a Russian ship and don't even speak Russian.

It had to be done, Viktoria told herself as she climbed ladder after ladder to get from the gallery, overlooking where once the wreck had been, up to the bridge. She couldn't spend the rest of the return voyage hiding in the gallery shouting orders to Bukinin over the intercom. If she was to maintain any authority that her naval commission might still provide, she would have to do it in person.

The slightly oily stainless steel of the ladders felt deathly cold to her touch. The painted steel bulkheads on all sides and the cold, dank-tasting air reminded her of the cell that she now believed almost certainly was waiting for her when they got back to St. Petersburg.

That dismal thought, and the memories of her mother and father, made her shudder.

Shooting Novikoff had been a terrible mistake, at least in terms of her own future. The more she thought about it, the more convinced she was that it wasn't entirely a matter of Novikoff's losing control. Her former superior, for some reason, must have viewed Chernov as a threat. Arnoff, unfortunately, while in position to see the two executions, had been unable to hear so much as a word.

Even worse, she was now equally convinced that Novikoff was, indeed, operating under orders different from her own. All along, he'd been doing exactly what he claimed to be: carrying out his orders.

But whose orders? She hated to believe that Yeltsin would order the murder of innocent, loyal Russian sailors. She was more prepared to believe that certain reactionaries in the government might very well do so—assuming the objective was of sufficient importance. But what was the objective? Now, with the wreck and its cargo gone, she would never know.

When she emerged from the hatch onto the boat deck she paused to catch her breath. The fresh air, and the storm itself, calmed her anxieties slightly by expanding her perceptions, by reminding her that there were powers even greater than the Russian government. Then she charged up the next ladder.

"Have you contacted St. Petersburg?" she demanded of Bukinin the moment she entered the pilothouse.

"Yes, Commander," replied Bukinin, his face a blank. "They have just replied, and they are not happy. They are demanding more information on how Captain Novikoff died. What are we to tell them?"

"The truth, Captain."

"I'm still not sure I know or understand the truth."

"Incomplete though it is, we will tell them the truth as I have explained it to you." Viktoria found herself almost envying *Asimov*'s master. All along he'd been following the orders of the senior naval officer aboard his ship. He would probably come out of the whole affair in one piece.

The expression on Bukinin's face changed briefly to one of almost concern, or even sympathy. "Are you sure you know what you're doing, Commander?" he asked quietly.

"No, Captain," she replied with a sigh, "I'm not at all sure."

Bukinin then turned back to his own multitude of problems—those of getting his damaged ship home.

Madeira lay on *Asimov*'s high, wet fantail and listened to the night wind moan and howl. For the moment he seemed safe enough, hidden among the shadows, just one more dark, sodden lump, but he knew that could all change in an instant. He had to get himself completely out of the way of the hunt. True safety, of course, would require him to get completely off that godforsaken ship—and that became his primary goal—but in the meantime he had to get out of the line of fire.

The chattering of distant automatic-weapons fire galvanized him. It sounded like it was far forward, so maybe the hunting party's attention was concentrated there for the moment. He grabbed the canister and started forward, slowly, at a crouch, keeping to the shadows, trying to reach out around him with his ears and eyes.

So far, so good, he thought when he came to a stop at the watertight door that Bukinin had stormed out of the day Rustoff was shot. But now he had a crucial decision to make. Should he stay on deck, where it was dark and where he might not be seen? And where, if he was seen, he would almost certainly be shot.

Or should he open the watertight door and walk to his stateroom along well-lit passageways, where he could easily be seen if there was anybody around to do so?

The answer was obvious. They weren't hunting him. Not yet, anyway, based on the sailor's reaction a few minutes before. At the moment nobody probably cared about him. If anybody saw Al Madeira in a passageway, he or she might be a little surprised that the American had survived, but nobody would shoot him. Not right away. But if he stayed on deck he wouldn't be Al Madeira, guilty only of returning from the dead. If he stayed on deck he'd be a dark shadow. An obvious target for a crew out hunting shadows of both present and past.

Chapter Thirty

"Hello," Madeira said with as much of a smile as he could muster when Viktoria threw open the door and stormed into her stateroom. "Get him yet?"

She stopped short and stared at him as he sat on her bunk, now dressed in chinos and a polo shirt. Her distracted expression changed quickly to one of surprise and then of amusement.

"I'm impressed, Al! You're more than just solidly competent, as Mike Novikoff used to enjoy describing you. You're a magician."

"Not a very good one. That Customs officer, Perez, was much better. I seem to have lost the wreck and poisoned half the Atlantic in the process."

"Don't give yourself so much credit. You were hired to recover part of a wrecked submarine, not to protect it from a pack of lunatic Russians."

"Then you think I'll still get my million dollars?"

"Ummm . . ."

"Did you get Grivski yet?"

"No, not yet, although Bukinin thinks he has him trapped on deck somewhere."

"There's been so much shooting that I assumed they must already have him."

"No. Most of the shooting has been sailors shooting at shadows, except for a few. They've been shooting at each other. It's just like back home; there're a lot of old grudges being settled tonight."

"Casualties?"

"Three deaths that I know of, and two wounded. And I'm sure there'll be more, either now or when we get back home." Viktoria slumped into the chair in front of her desk, her fatigue and unhappiness now clear.

"Do you have any idea why Novikoff killed Chernov?" asked Madeira.

"No. Maybe he just threw another tantrum, maybe he completely lost his mind. I suspect, though, it had something to do with what was in that storeroom."

She paused a moment, then turned and skewered him with her electric eyes. "Nobody, Al, will tell me what was in there."

He looked at her a moment, torn by the indecision that had been plaguing him for some time, still unsure of her objectives and loyalties, squirming mentally under her glance.

"Do you know what this is?" he finally asked as he pulled the canister out from under the blanket and handed it to her.

Viktoria glanced at the dingy cylinder, then turned her full attention to it, reading the barely legible Cyrillic stencils running along its sides. Her eyes widened slightly. "Do *you* know what it is?"

"It's a biological or chemical warfare agent of some sort." He waited, wondering when the pistol hanging at her side would appear, pointed at him.

"It's chemical. It's one component of a binary nerve agent called Compound 2734. Were there many of these?"

"Fifty or so . . . along with a similar number of slightly larger ones."

"Dammit! That would be the other component. Neither is particularly toxic by itself. You have to mix them to achieve the full horror."

"Then Khrushchev was giving Castro chemical weapons during the Missile Crisis?"

"So it would appear."

Viktoria paused a moment, an expression of shocked understanding crossing her face. "Al, Compound 2734 is an especially foul weapon. It's unstable and unpredictable. Some people vomit their guts out, and I mean that literally, when exposed to it. For others death results from inflamed nerve cells. The cells in the brain and spine, nerve cells everywhere in the body, just explode! Sometimes it acts immediately and sometimes it takes up to a week for the symptoms to appear. It was useless on the battlefield. We never did come up with a good use for it except out-and-out terror."

"Is there an antidote?"

"Supposedly, but I understand that it only worked part of the time. I told you, this stuff is so dangerously unpredictable that it scared even our people. That's why we stopped making it in the sixties. Only a lunatic would try to use it. It was only good as a Doomsday Weapon."

"How was it supposed to be . . . applied?"

"Either as a liquid or an aerosol, as I remember." She lifted the canister up to her ear and shook it. "This sounds like it's filled with liquid. The other canisters would have a gas in them. The canister with the gas fits into the end of the one with the liquid. When the bomb, or missile, is armed the ends puncture and the gas bubbles into and mixes with the liquid. Then the device is detonated at a low altitude and the stuff is blown all over. It's introduced through the nose and mouth as people breathe and eat, and it doesn't take much."

"Novikoff must have known it was there."

"Of course he did! That's why he didn't want the store-room cut through or entered."

"Then his real mission could have been to get this shit back to Russia before anybody could learn about it. To destroy the evidence. But that's all ancient history now."

"Don't underestimate the power of ancient history, Al," said Viktoria, a look of pain slowly taking over her face. "Look around you! Look at what once was the Soviet Union! People everywhere are killing each other over feuds that go back hundreds and thousands of years. The ghosts can still kill."

"You're starting to lose me, Viktoria."

"Al," she replied, her exasperation showing, "don't you ever listen to the news? Yeltsin's in trouble! The economy's a mess and the citizens are confused. They're hungry and frightened, and it won't take much to make them do something really stupid. The only way he can survive the winter is with Clinton's support plus a lot of luck. Both moral support and money. Yeltsin needs America to love and trust both him and Russia. Think what the media could do with a Russian submarine full of the most awful chemical weapon I can think of. What would the American public say? Talk about ghosts from the past! Even if it was over thirty years ago. Once the media got hold of this we could forget about love and trust and foreign aid!"

"Let's look at it from another angle for a moment. Could Novikoff have been planning on stealing this stuff?"

"What for? I told you, it's almost impossible to use. Only a madman would want it. Chernov was the gangster, anyway."

"I can think of several madmen who might buy it."

"No. Novikoff was a reactionary, maybe, but he would never have worked with gangsters. He was third-generation Soviet navy!"

"So many dead!" Madeira said, thinking of all the mangled bodies, living and dead, and especially of Timon.

"That's the world we live in!" snapped Viktoria, feeling more than a tinge of guilt at her own institutional involvement. "There aren't any innocent parties involved in this! Not you. Certainly not me. Not even Meg Jefferson. She was as much of a . . . a gunslinger . . . as anybody. Even her crew was undoubtedly paid well for the risk."

What about the whales? thought Madeira. Do even I really believe that they count?

Oh, goddamnit! "Viktoria, does this compound work only on humans?"

"I doubt it works just on humans, Al. It probably has some effect on most or all mammalian nervous systems."

There was a scraping sound in the passageway.

Shit! thought Madeira, eyeing the weapon at Viktoria's side. Then he relaxed. If it'd been Grivski they'd both be dead by now. It must just be a rat out looking for a late-night snack.

"You know what this means?" Viktoria finally asked after a minute or two of deep thought.

"I thought you just told me."

"It means that I really have just made the biggest mistake of my life. I'd originally planned to demand that Novikoff explain what he was doing, but when I saw Boris lying there I lost it. Then Mendalov went for his knife. . . .

"Now I understand that he was ordered to get rid of this stuff at all costs. Now I'm the one guilty of insubordination and murder."

"Then you think Yeltsin knew about the cargo?"

"I'd like to think somebody else ordered the cover-up," replied Viktoria, her face now as bleak as the Siberian night to which her father had been consigned so many years before, "but I can't be sure."

She's terrified, he suddenly realized with surprise. Almost in shock. She doesn't know what to believe.

"Who's in command of *Asimov* at the moment?" he asked.

"I am," she replied, "but I don't think that'll last for long. I'm sure Bukinin's in communication with Kronshtadt right now. . . ."

"And?"

"And as soon as they understand that Novikoff was shot, and that I did it, they will make Bukinin understand that I just killed the man chosen by the highest of the high to carry out their orders."

"Viktoria, I don't think he was covering up anything. He was planning to take the stuff. There were two cargo nets rigged under that rubber boat, just waiting for Mendalov to fill them with canisters."

"I'm sure that had something to do with his plan for getting rid of them."

"I doubt it. What did you learn about Niko Avalaridze?"

"Who? I never heard of him."

"He's a Georgian import-export type who sat next to me on the flight from London to St. Petersburg and didn't bother going through either Customs or Immigration. Then I saw him again in San Juan. It was just too much of a coincidence, so I told Novikoff about him. Novikoff said he'd check into him, which means, I should think, that he'd tell you to check into him."

"Yes, he always gave me things like that to do, but he never mentioned Avalaridze. This proves nothing! He may have been one of our own intelligence people."

"Novikoff suggested that, but I don't think so, somehow," said Madeira.

"How badly was the ship damaged by the blast?" he continued, returning to what seemed to him the next most immediate concern. "It feels as if the port engine was damaged. Or the shaft was thrown out of alignment."

"Yes. The port shaft is damaged, we're only running on one engine, and we're also taking on water."

Madeira tensed again as the scraping sound returned.

"That's a rat, Al," Viktoria said. "If you're going to be a Russian sailor, you have to get used to rats."

"That's all done now. I'm turning in my leg irons and going back where I came from."

Just as Madeira finished, the night erupted into a hurricane of sound as deep, thick Russian erupted from loudspeakers from one end of the ship to the other.

"What's that?"

"It's Bukinin calling off the hunt and asking Grivski to report to the bridge."

"Did you tell him to do that?"

"No. Maybe I'm not in command anymore."

"Good-bye, Viktoria," Madeira said as he reached for the canister. "This ship isn't a healthy place for me. Bukinin thinks I'm already dead, so he won't even miss me, but if he were to stumble on me . . ."

He paused a moment, looking at her. "It's not a very healthy place for you, either."

"No," she answered, "it's not. Would you mind if I came with you?"

Madeira studied her a moment. She certainly wasn't begging; she was only asking a favor.

Did he owe her anything?

Not really.

What about last night . . . tonight?

Maybe he did owe her something, even though she *had* been using him all along and probably would do it again if she felt it would help her new Russia.

"Okay. Let's go, then." A pair of extra hands might prove very useful, he told himself. He could never trust her, but loving her would be no problem. "What about the camera in the passageway?"

"That's not hooked up, or it wasn't an hour ago."

He stood a moment with his hand on the doorknob. What was outside? Had the scraping sound been somebody repairing the camera? Or had it been Grivski?

"Do you have a spare pistol?"

"No. Just this one. Do you want it?"

Hell! he thought. She uses it better than I do. But I'm the one about to walk out this door. "Yes," he replied, holding his hand behind his back. "Have you reloaded?"

"Yes."

This is ridiculous, he thought. Grivski wouldn't be hanging around in the passageway waiting for them. If he was after them he'd have already broken the door in and shot them while they talked.

Swallowing hard, Madeira opened the door and looked out into the seemingly empty passageway, first to the left and then to the right, then up at the TV camera.

"It looks okay. . . ."

"By the way," asked Viktoria as they hustled aft along the brightly lit passageway, "where are we going?"

"South or southwest, depending on what the seas are doing."

"Do you think they're looking for you yet?" Madeira asked as he peeked around the corner and along the port boat deck, his eyes focused on the dimly lit workboat hanging in its gravity davits.

"They must be by now. Does anybody besides me know that you've returned from the grave?"

"One of the seamen, I'm not sure I ever knew his name, saw me, but he seemed more interested in finding Grivski." Had the man reported Madeira's all-too-unlikely return to Bukinin? Had he even considered it worth reporting?

Probably not, at least not until the hunt for Grivski was called off.

"The boats all have alarms on them, right?"

"Right. Whenever a boat is lowered it's indicated on the bridge, but the system is a very basic one. I can wire a shunt so it doesn't go off."

Madeira stared hard out into the darkness, sensing as much as seeing the huge seas thundering out of the east, pounding the ship's side and then boiling past. Once in the boat would he run before the dark, bearded monsters and head for Santo Domingo? Or take them on the quarter and aim for Puerto Rico?

Either way, their chances of survival were only slightly better than if they stayed aboard *Asimov*. He found himself wallowing in the prospect of pending disaster, carefully examining, almost savoring, every gruesome possibility.

He forced himself to return to the present. They had to

keep moving! Bukinin would, by now, be looking for Viktoria, but he might still be ignorant of Madeira's survival. They had to get the hell away before he had time to put it all together.

"What will you need?"

"Pliers," she replied, "and a screwdriver."

"There's a small toolbox in the boat, or at least there's one in the starboard workboat, so there should be one in this one."

"Good."

As Viktoria spoke, Madeira was listening intently. To the wind. To the boom of the seas hitting the ship. To the hull's sullen creaks and groans. To at least one or two somethings that were rolling loose around the deck.

And there was something else there too, he thought. Something that wasn't keeping time with nature's beat.

"Al?"

"I thought I heard something."

They crouched and listened for several minutes, unable to pinpoint anything. The clock's still running, thought Madeira.

"I'll go get the tools," he finally whispered. "You take this and make sure nobody sneaks up on me."

After handing Viktoria the pistol he edged from shadow to shadow across the deck to the boat's forward davit, its arching arm faintly visible in the night. Clutching the canister, he paused again, listening. Then he climbed the slick rungs welded to the davit and pulled himself up into the use-battered boat.

The toolbox was precisely where he expected it to be, in a small cabinet next to the engine controls.

"Viktoria, here!" he whispered as he dangled the oily box over the side of the boat.

"Okay," she replied. "I've got it."

"Then start on the alarm."

"Okay."

After carefully stowing the canister in the cabinet Madeira

felt around for the dipstick and checked the fuel tank. It was full.

Then he took a moment to stand and look out on the heaving madness all around. It made little difference for a ship the size of *Asimov,* although Bukinin clearly had his hands full with only one engine, but it was going to be hell in the workboat. Especially headed more or less downwind.

The ship rolled and he caught a flicker in the darkness, the briefest of flashes, out of the corner of his eye. Something had moved over near the life-jacket locker. Or so he thought. It might have just been something blowing past the working light. A piece of paper tumbling across the deck. A puff of spray.

His breath caught as he waited, wishing to God he had bionic vision capable of cutting through the thick night.

The ship rolled again, and he started to slip. He caught the boat's gunnel and waited.

Practically everything moved: The ship, the seas, even the boat shifted slightly in its gripes. Everything moved but the shadows around the life-jacket locker. They remained rock-solid and totally unmoving.

A loudspeaker someplace nearby exploded to life, Bukinin's voice thundering into the wet night.

"What the hell's he shouting about now?" hissed Madeira over the side of the boat.

"They still don't seem to have found Grivski. Bukinin's telling him I'm the traitor and begging him to come help find me."

"How're you doing with the alarm?"

"I'm almost done."

"Good." Madeira clambered out of the boat and down the davit. "Have you ever launched one of these?"

"No," she said, putting the pliers and screwdriver back into the metal box. "My expertise is tectonic shields and intruding on other people's privacy."

"Stand back, then." Madeira's last word came out as a grunt as he tripped the manual release on one of the davits. He hustled to the other and tripped its release, then stood back and watched. The boat and the two hooklike arms from which it was suspended all rumbled down an inclined track toward the ship's side. As they went, the arms slowly tilted out so that when they reached the end of their tracks the boat would hang suspended out over the water.

"That alarm system was completely unnecessary," remarked Viktoria, almost shouting to be heard over the davit's groaning rumble.

"We're totally committed now," Madeira shouted, turning to look at her. "We can only hope they're not sure exactly which boat it is. . . . And we have to be gone by the time they do figure it out."

Then he saw the knife glint in the dark air a few feet behind Viktoria. And the face above it!

Huge, hard, and somehow misshapen, an outward and physical reflection of the monstrosity of his soul, but all too recognizable. Even in the dim light.

It was Grivski.

Chapter Thirty-one

"Arnold!" Ari shouted, "why haven't we picked up anything yet? They dumped the submarine over half an hour ago so they must have launched the boat before that—"

"I don't know, damnit! Maybe the beacon's not working. Or they forgot to turn it on. Maybe that explosion, whatever it was, sank it."

As he spoke, the skipper realized that suggesting the last possibility had been a serious mistake. Hoping for reassurance, he turned to Niko, only to encounter an expression even colder than Ari's. "I'm not the one who fucked up here . . . It was whoever you have aboard that ship!"

"We'll continue looking," Niko said after a long pause. "We may be able to find it after the sun comes up."

I sure-as-shit hope so, Arnold thought, concluding that he should never have taken this particular smuggling job.

The davits rumbled to the ends of their tracks and slammed into the stops with a loud clang. The boat's gunnel was now at deck level, already beginning to pound against

Asimov's side. And Grivski was reaching, stumbling forward through the shadows, seemingly intent upon grabbing Viktoria's neck with one arm while his other hand waved the large, glinting knife in wild circles.

The boat shuddered as the ship pitched into the next wave. A moment later a cloud of spray drifted aft through the working lights. Madeira stood a moment, almost frozen. He then realized that Grivski was bellowing nonstop at the top of his lungs. In Russian.

"Grivski's right behind you, Viktoria," he shouted, coming out of his daze. "Dive forward!"

It was all he could think of to do at first. Then he noticed the four-foot steel bar used to crank the davits back up in the event of power failure. He grabbed the bar and charged Grivski, attempting to insert himself between the enraged Russian and Viktoria, who was already sprawled on the deck, fumbling with her holster.

He swung the bar, aiming at the arm holding the knife, and continued on, hoping to ram his shoulder into Grivski's chest. All the while, Grivski continued to bellow.

The bar slammed into Grivski's arm and the knife flew into the air and overboard. The Russian stumbled backward, then grabbed his injured arm and finally collapsed against the life-jacket locker.

Madeira, stunned at first at the success of his initial charge, recovered. Grivski was an animal. Madeira thought of the men aboard *Asimov* whom he had seen the Russian brutalize. Then he thought of the many more to whom Grivski had undoubtedly done even worse in the past. Finally he thought of his own fear. Grivski was a brutal killing machine with no soul and no reason to live.

He lunged forward to finish the job before the Russian could revive. To beat and kick him to death. To pound his skull into jelly. To make Grivski feel a little of what he'd made so many others feel.

Then he stopped. Grivski had been beyond feeling, and maybe even beyond moral responsibility, for years. A mad dog. A robot. No more.

Up to that moment Madeira had been absolutely terrified of Grivski. But now he found it impossible to fear the cringing mass of protoplasm he saw before him. And with the fear had gone the hatred.

Feeling neither fear nor hatred, Madeira was unable to kill.

He studied the fallen man carefully. The son of a bitch was *already* finished. And had been from the start. Something was wrong with his left leg, and the whole side of his head and face were covered with blood. He was just sitting there now, his empty eyes staring into eternity with neither interest nor understanding as he continued to mouth his now-silent tirade.

They, Bukinin and his crew, had succeeded in hunting him down and didn't even know it. One of them must've hit him with automatic fire. Or maybe he'd fallen somewhere. Or both. He'd probably been wandering the ship like that for hours.

Madeira shuddered. He found it all too easy to imagine Grivski's odyssey: maddened by pain and the blow to his head and aware only that he was being hunted for some reason that was probably incomprehensible to him; one step removed from death and totally unaware of his return to grace.

He looked within himself and once again saw shadows of Grivski. Under different circumstances, if he had been born in Russia . . . He tried to cast the thought aside, to tell himself Grivski was no more than a rabid dog and his own empathy just a sign of weakness, but was unable to do so.

"Get in the boat, Viktoria," he shouted over his shoulder. "Grivski's done. Keep an eye on him, but I'm sure he can't hurt us now."

Viktoria replied with three rapid shots.

Madeira watched, fascinated, as Grivski's body hopped, hopped again and then again, seeming to nod and shrug in fatalistic acceptance of each additional blow to its collapsing chest.

"In our position, Al, only a fool would take any chances at all."

He started to tell her that she was getting entirely too damned fond of firing that pistol but restrained himself. She was undoubtedly right. You shoot mad dogs not because they have sinned but because they are dangerous.

In fact, Viktoria was probably doing Grivski a favor.

Madeira paused again. To catch his breath. To clear his head. To push aside the distracting moral questions. To tell himself that Grivski really hadn't been human. To look at the seas and gauge the wind. To feel the ship's motion. To wish he felt more at home inside churches.

In seas like these, he thought, and with only one shaft, *Asimov* must be a whore to handle. He could feel her trying to pivot, to force her way to port. Bukinin had a great deal to keep him busy.

"Do you know how to trip the release hooks on the falls?"

"No."

"Get in here, then, and I'll show you."

After providing a brief demonstration and explanation of how to disconnect the boat from the ship once the boat was in the water, Madeira returned to the steering position and cranked the engine over.

The diesel groaned and whined.

How much longer could it possibly take Bukinin to catch on to what they were doing? Even with his other problems he was bound to realize something was happening.

Sweating despite the cold, wet wind, he jammed the starter down again. Goddamn the Russians and their sloppy maintenance!

The engine groaned again, caughed, then caught. Stifling a shout of relieved triumph, he apologized mentally to the Russians, to those like Timon, anyway, for slighting their maintenance habits. Then he leapt back onto *Asimov*'s deck, released the brake on the davit, and jumped back into the boat as it dropped into the churning Atlantic.

The end of the whole miserable affair was in sight, he

assured himself. They'd return to Puerto Rico and he'd give Nash the canister and the story. Then it'd be over for him, anyway. Let the sharks decide whether the canisters are ancient history or a warning of things to come. Let them decide what to do about the toxic blob that was now headed north with the Gulf Stream.

The instant the workboat's bottom hit the water, Madeira cast off the aft fall and put the engine into gear. "Cast off forward," he shouted as he turned slightly to port, trying to ride the crest of the ship's secondary bow wave.

Unable to see what Viktoria was doing, he concentrated on steering . . . and on wondering just how radioactive, and toxic, was the water that was splashing over the side of the boat.

There was a short, violent ejaculation in Russian. Then: "Okay. It's off."

"Okay, now the painter."

"The what?"

"The bowline."

"Okay, it's off now too."

Madeira gunned the engine and started a slow turn to port, away from *Asimov*'s dark mass.

Now what course? he asked himself. South to Puerto Rico or slightly east of south? The Dominican Republic was probably closer, but he wanted to go to Puerto Rico. And if he missed the Dominican Republic he might end up in Haiti, which didn't seem the place to be at the moment.

A little east of south, then. Say one seven zero. One seven zero, if the seas would let him steer that once they emerged from *Asimov*'s lee.

The dirty gray light of dawn found them cold and wet as the open workboat surfed before quartering seas.

Madeira glanced forward at Viktoria, crouched down on the deck, sheltering in the lee of the steering console. Then he glanced aft at the great curling mountain thundering down on them. He tensed, as he already had a thousand times since leaving *Asimov*, and tested his grip on the wheel.

It was an absolute miracle that they hadn't broached, swamped, and sunk during the night, when the huge black waves had roared out of nowhere, curling and foaming, and tossed the boat forward and to the side, just like the plaything of the gods that it was. He had been able to see little or nothing. It had all been a matter of feel, and very good luck.

But they *had* survived, and now he could see the waves coming.

A sense of elation, almost ecstasy, threatened to overcome him. Life was no longer about brutality, escape, and survival. The past had already been driven from his consciousness by the challenge of the present. It was once again as it had been in his youth, an all-consuming, heroic quest and contest: the search for the mythic perfect wave and the struggle to use and master it; the determination to shout into the wind and subdue it. He was one with the boat and the wind and the water, and knew he always had been.

Some might say Madeira was hovering at the very edge. Others might say he'd gone over it.

"We're making very good time," he shouted to Viktoria. "Ten, maybe fifteen knots, and most of them in the direction of Puerto Rico."

"Good!" she replied.

"We've probably already made a good twenty or twenty-five miles. . . . I figure at most we've only got another hundred to go."

"Excellent!"

Asimov was nowhere to be seen, although Bukinin must have finally detected them on radar even if nobody saw them leave. But then, Bukinin knew nothing of the canister and undoubtedly had his hands full saving his crippled ship.

If all went well, if he didn't lose his nerve, if Viktoria didn't suddenly draw her pistol and shoot *him* three times in the chest, they'd be ashore in Puerto Rico by mid- or late afternoon. Where in Puerto Rico they'd end up he wasn't quite sure. It's a big island, he reassured himself, over a hundred miles long. He couldn't possibly miss it entirely.

Unless he'd totally miscalculated, of course. Or the compass was screwed up. Or the engine died.

But somebody'd find them. The area was thick with shipping. Interisland freighters. Airplanes. Cruise ships. Fishermen. The Coasties, for that matter, were supposed to be everywhere. Saving Haitians. Chasing druggies. Arresting Haitians.

Taking his eyes off the cresting seas a moment, he scanned the gray horizon.

Nothing!

They were all alone. He hadn't seen another vessel, or even a light, since they'd left *Asimov*.

It was just him and the Atlantic, he thought with manic pleasure. The air was definitely sweeter. The blood, the betrayal, the brutality; all the filth of the past few months had been stripped away and carried off by the cleansing wind.

The stern lifted and started to slide to starboard, driven by the now-arrived wave. Madeira spun the wheel to starboard and waited, ready to shift the rudder rapidly the other way. The boat caught the wave and galloped forward, racing down its infinitely long face, charging at the back of the next wave ahead.

All around, the foaming crest hissed and snapped and occasionally slopped aboard.

The wind blew, the engine roared, the waves hissed and cracked, and the low gray-black clouds tumbled westward, wrestling with each other every inch of the way.

Fear and uncertainty were forgotten. Time, life, death all became nothing. Madeira was now totally enthralled by the process, by the magnificent drama in which God was so graciously permitting him to participate.

"Al, are you hungry? You must be hungry!"

The trance was broken for the time being.

"What do we have?" shouted Madeira, shifting a part of his attention away from wind and waves for the first time in hours and turning to face Viktoria.

"Not a great deal," she replied, standing next to him now

and holding on to the steering console. "Survival biscuits, water, something in a can."

Madeira felt the stern lift and, without thinking, spun the wheel. His shoulders were tired and his legs painfully stiff, he realized, but he was winning at a game in which he knew defeat equaled death.

"The biscuits probably aren't bad," he thought aloud, "everybody in the world seems to use the same recipe. But that stuff in cans . . ."

"You want biscuits, then?"

"Biscuits and some water, please."

"Do you know what you're getting into?" he asked a few moments later, after munching on a biscuit and downing a dozen small cups of water. "Do you plan to ask for political asylum? What about your family, or has all that changed?"

"Don't worry," she shouted with a slight smile. "You just get us to Puerto Rico. I know exactly what I'm doing."

Madeira wanted to continue the conversation but found it just too difficult to make himself heard above the engine. Anyway, Viktoria seemed to have drifted off into a world of her own again and the Atlantic, he decided, required his full concentration.

"Al! You see that ship?"

Madeira tore his mind off his duel with the elements and looked off to starboard, where Viktoria was pointing. My God! he thought as the boat rose on a wave and he was able to see the approaching vessel clearly. She was no more than half a mile away and headed right for them. How had she gotten so close without his noticing her? He felt a jolt of disappointment. He didn't really want to be rescued, he realized. He wanted to finish the job himself, to drive the boat through the storm and into San Juan. Then the boat topped the wave it had been climbing and started to plunge madly down the other side. Madeira had to return his full attention to the struggle.

"What is that?" asked Viktoria as he schussed the mountain wave. "It looks like some sort of a cruise ship, but it's too small, isn't it?"

By now the boat had started to climb the next wave and Madeira could look off to the side again. The other boat had turned to parallel their course. "It's a yacht, I think. Some sort of a Maxi yacht. It must be some big celebrity, or a drug dealer. Who else would ride around in a Gucci boat like that?"

As he spoke he realized that there were several people aboard the Maxi yacht looking at them through binoculars. Again the boat topped a wave, and Madeira had to look away from the Maxi to concentrate on saving his own modest yacht.

"Al!" Viktoria shouted suddenly. "They're turning away, they're going away just as fast as they can, the bastards!"

"We'll make it, Viktoria," he replied with almost a sense of relief. "Don't worry."

"I know we will. Strangely enough, that's not one of the things that's worrying me at the moment."

Then she laughed. "I can see that boat's name now."

"What is it?"

"*Velociraptor*—it's perfect. The boat looks just like those lizards in that movie."

"Isn't that land up ahead?"

Madeira looked first at Viktoria, then in the direction she was pointing. So great had been his absorption in his renewed duel with death that he'd failed to lift his eyes, to see the solid gray mass of land rising up ahead out of the waves and stretching much of the way across the indistinct horizon.

"Yes. Let's assume it's Puerto Rico."

He had no way of being sure, but it looked as if they were headed for about the middle of the island.

"I'm going to hold this course for a while until I get a better idea of where we are, but I think we might be able to make it to San Juan by dark."

"Okay."

An hour or so later, thinking he might have spotted the glint of Condado Beach's resort high-rises, Madeira changed course slightly to the east. It was only after he'd settled on the new course that he realized Viktoria had taken the canister from the locker and was standing in the stern, examining it. He continued to watch as she set the can on the gunnel, stepped back, and drew her pistol.

"What the hell're you doing?" he shouted, stepping toward her, then realizing that he couldn't leave the wheel for even an instant.

"Watch!" she said as she fired into the canister, punching two large holes in it and blowing it over the side.

"Shit!" he snarled as she fired again, before the canister had time to sink. A towering, acrid rage flared up within him. It rose from his gut, tore through his chest, and billowed into his head, causing his eyes to throb as if scorched from behind by a blowtorch. He didn't care whether Boris Yeltsin lived or died—unless, of course, he really was ultimately responsible for Timon's murder, in which case he hoped to see him in Hell—but he'd risked so much, and suffered so much, to preserve the canister that he damn well wanted to deliver it to somebody.

"It's better this way, Al," she said, turning to him and reholstering the pistol. "Our people—my people, that is—will be able to control the story rather than having to watch the CIA use it however they wish. There's no physical evidence now; it's all just a tale told by a slightly eccentric retired American naval officer."

"You still hope you can go home someday," he mumbled, his rage already subsiding, "and you've decided Novikoff really was in with gangsters. . . ." He glanced astern. There was no sign of the canister amidst the monstrous, tumbling seas.

"Something like that. I want to see Russia reborn. I want to be part of it. I'm not as sure of Yeltsin as I once was, but I still have to keep my bet on him."

She unbuckled the holster belt and tossed it and the pistol

over the side. "That might prove difficult to explain after you get us back safely ashore."

By the time Madeira got them around El Morro and into the only slightly choppy waters of San Juan Bay, the sun had long since disappeared and the fuel tank was close to dry.

"Have you ever steered a boat?" he asked as he throttled back.

"Once or twice."

"Good. Take this wheel a few minutes. I've got to get my joints working again."

"Yes, Captain!"

Madeira stepped back to allow her to take the helm and collapsed on the first step, intense flames of pain shooting up his legs.

"Al!"

"I'll be okay," he grunted. "My legs've locked up. You keep your eyes out for any traffic. It'd be very embarrassing to be run down at this point in the operation."

It must be almost nine, thought Madeira as he pulled alongside the largely darkened ferry terminal and spotted the security guard standing, hands on hips, waiting for them. It was the same fellow who'd almost had him arrested the night he was beat up.

"Keep off!" shouted the guard. "No landing permitted!"

"*Buenas noches,*" Madeira replied with a smile. "We're from the Russian research ship that's been in and out a few times the past month or two. If you check your records you'll see we have blanket authority to use the terminal as our landing." Madeira suddenly realized that he was still shouting, even though they had left the cold, loud sea wind behind them and were now surrounded by an almost quiet, tropical night.

The guard looked skeptical but unsure of himself. He did seem to remember Madeira.

"My name's Madeira," he continued in a quieter tone, offering his ID card as he spoke. "I'm that retired naval officer who's acting as liaison with the Russians.''

The guard studied the card, then Viktoria.

"The ship's completing some experiments a few miles offshore. She'll be in in the morning. We have to make some arrangements ahead of time. The State Department has been notified. . . .''

Maybe, thought Madeira as the guard continued to study the card, the friendly approach was a mistake. Maybe he should have screamed and shouted even more. Pounded his fist on something. Taken the imperial approach.

"Very well,'' the guard said at last. "How long will you be here?''

"An hour,'' lied Madeira. "Two hours absolute maximum.''

The guard nodded, then sauntered away into the warm darkness.

Madeira secured the boat, then headed for the pay phone, digging into his pocket for change as he went.

"Will this help?'' Viktoria asked, offering him her calling card.

"No, thanks. I'm making a local call.''

"To your CIA contact?''

"I think I'd better.''

"I would if I were you.''

The phone rang three times, then was answered. By Jen.

The CIA agent's harsh voice and demanding tone triggered a sudden, overpowering wave of intense dislike, almost hatred, which swept over Madeira, causing him to rethink the whole situation.

If he took Viktoria, and the story, directly to Jen and Nash they'd want to immediately take control of the data. Manage it. And if the data were to be managed, then Al Madeira would also have to be placed under management.

But his successful battle with the sea had brought out the most basic, undomesticated elements of his character. If he wanted to be managed he'd have tried harder to stay in the navy!

He hung up without saying a word. Let them think some deep-breather was onto them.

The trick to this fugitive business, he decided, is speed. Make the right moves and make them fast.

"I'll need your calling card after all," he said, turning to Viktoria.

"Did your control tell you to turn me in directly to Moscow?"

"No," Madeira laughed. "I hung up on her without identifying myself. I want to call a friend of mine, Lane Williams."

"Admiral Williams? We know about him; we've never been sure just what to make of him."

"If things work out you'll be meeting him within the next twelve hours."

"That sounds good to me."

"I wonder if I can direct-dial from here."

"Of course you can! You can direct-dial from almost anyplace in the world these days. In fact, as soon as you are done I'd like to call a friend of mine."

"In St. Petersburg? I thought you didn't have any friends anymore."

"In Moscow. There are hundreds of millions of people in Russia. Even I still have a few friends left. "I hope.""

Chapter Thirty-two

"What flights to Miami do you have tonight?" Madeira asked, gasping slightly as he spoke into the telephone. He was hot and sticky, his face burned fiercely from the sun and wind, and the phone booth stank. Probably, he suspected, because of him.

"We have one leaving in about forty-five minutes," replied the voice on the phone, "but that's completely sold out. Then there's one at ten thirty-five."

"Any seats open on that?"

During the ensuing pause he looked carefully around for thugs with baseball bats and saw none. It was still too early for them, he decided.

"Yes," the reservations clerk finally said, "first class only."

"We'd like to reserve two, please."

"And the names on the reservations?"

"Just a minute," he said into the telephone. He stuck his head out the door. "Are you still coming?"

"I wouldn't miss it!" Viktoria said.

"Galin and Madeira," Madeira said into the phone.

"Will you need a car in Miami, Mr. Galin?"

"No. . . . I'm Madeira. . . . Yes!" He felt a creepy, crinkly sensation run up and down his spine. It's just the salt drying, he reassured himself. Then, to make sure, he glanced out of the telephone booth, hoping *not* to see Nash, Jen, or Grivski.

"Would you like me to arrange one for you?"

"Yes."

"What size please?"

"Midsize."

"Thank you. I'm reserving two seats, one in the name of Galin and one in the name of Madeira, on our flight seven-twenty-five to Miami leaving from Munoz International Airport at ten thirty-five tonight. Please go to the counter just as soon as you get to the airport to purchase your tickets. I'm also reserving a midsize car for you in Miami. Will you require accommodations in Miami, Mr. Madeira?"

"No. No, thank you."

"Very well. And thank you for flying with us."

Madeira hung up and stepped out into the fresher, if not fresh, air along the front of the terminal. "We've got a little more than an hour to get to the airport."

"Okay," Viktoria replied as she stepped into the booth. "This shouldn't take more than a few minutes."

"Please make it as quick as you can."

"I will. What did you say that Georgian's name was?"

"Avalaridze. Niko Avalaridze."

While Viktoria called Moscow, where it was five in the morning, Madeira stepped out onto La Marina in search of a cab.

He waved at the first one he saw passing. Miraculously, the cab slowed, then swerved out of traffic and slammed to a stop right in front of him. "Yeah!" said the cabbie.

"Yeah!" Madeira replied, without thinking or knowing why he did. "Can you wait a second?"

"Yeah!"

Madeira turned and stepped right into Viktoria, who was standing directly behind him. "That was quick!" he said.

345

"You said we're in a hurry."

Madeira opened the door and waved Viktoria in. "To the airport," he said as he followed her in and slammed the door behind him.

"Which one?" asked the driver.

"The international one," Madeira replied, wondering if the driver was really in any doubt at all.

The cabbie turned and floored the accelerator, thereby managing to slam Madeira back onto the seat.

He started to say something to the driver, then thought better of it. Then he started to say something to Viktoria . . . and thought better of that, too. He settled back into the seat, took a deep breath, and immediately realized his body had turned into jelly.

During those long, painful, and glorious hours in the workboat it'd been almost possible for him to believe he was still twenty-five and free to shout into the storm. But the ride was over now. He was an out-of-shape retired naval officer again. A middle-aged guy who was stuck in the middle and felt compelled, for some reason, to see the mess through to the end.

After a moment's thought he rephrased his self-evaluation: He was an old guy who had no choice but to see the damn thing through to its bitter end.

When the cab slammed to a stop at the airport terminal, Madeira reached for his wallet and looked in.

"Damnit! All I've got is three dollars."

The driver spun around, murder in his eyes.

"Don't worry," Viktoria said quickly. "I've got enough."

They rushed through the door and across the concourse, filled with bored, sad-looking people sitting and waiting, to the counter.

Yes, their reservations were all in order. Madeira handed the girl his charge card.

"No luggage?" she asked.

"No," said Madeira.

"I'm terribly sorry," she reported a minute or two later, "but they've declined your card."

Goddamnit! thought Madeira, painfully aware of the mass of people standing behind him in line, all but a few trying to look off into space as if they were somehow totally unaware of his disgrace. Could he possibly have forgotten to mail the payment in the confusion just before he left for St. Petersburg? Would there be a pile of dunning notes waiting for him when he got home? Assuming, of course, they didn't send him directly to Leavenworth. Without passing Go.

"Here, Al. Use this one."

Madeira turned and looked at Viktoria, then stepped aside so she could present the card, which proved to be good as gold.

"I'm surprised your cards still work," Madeira said quietly after they'd settled into their seats on the plane.

"It'll take them a while to cut me off."

Madeira looked tiredly around the cabin. At least they didn't stand out too much. In fact, their misshaped and abused clothing fit right in with the outfits worn by the other tourists.

Back in the normal world, he thought as the engines' roar rose to a scream and the plane accelerated down the runway.

Determined to keep moving just as fast as he could, Madeira practically sprinted through the jetway and out into the boarding area at Miami International. He paused a minute to allow Viktoria to catch up. While he waited, he examined the small crowd.

Good! There wasn't a soul there he knew. And none seemed to have any interest in him, although quite a few clearly found Viktoria fascinating, the men staring boldly at her, the women studying her out of the side of their eyes.

After glancing at the overhead signs Madeira led the way to the left, down the corridor, down an escalator, and out into the baggage-claim area.

"Al, I've got to go to the bathroom!" Viktoria said as

they stopped just inside the door to allow Madeira to look for any obvious signs of trouble.

"Okay," Madeira said. "I'll meet you at the Easy Rental Car desk. . . . It's right there along the wall with all the others."

"Roger," she replied with a grin.

Only after she'd disappeared into the ladies' room did Madeira remember they needed her credit card to rent the car.

Unable to do anything positive until Viktoria reappeared, Madeira walked over to the fence surrounding the baggage carousels and leaned on it. Then he continued to study the crowd as it fought over the luggage.

Several minutes later he saw Viktoria walk out of the ladies' room and head directly for the pay phones. Then, when she reappeared, he headed for the Easy desk.

"How's Moscow?" he asked as he intercepted her about twenty feet from the car-rental desk.

She smiled at him. "Confused . . . Unhappy . . . Certain that nobody's telling them what really happened . . . Worried about what it might mean."

"What about you?"

"I seem to be very much on their minds," she replied, taking his arm as she did.

"We need your credit card to get this car."

"It's really not fair that they're not going to give you the million dollars you earned."

Forty minutes later they were turning right out of the Easy lot, located in a very intimidating area of worn warehouses and dark streets at the edge of the airport, onto LeJeune Road. Three minutes later they took the off-ramp up and onto the Dolphin Expressway. In another twelve minutes, after passing the darkened building in which The Trans-Caspian Trading Corporation maintained its Miami offices, they turned onto Route 821 South, toward the Keys.

"We didn't appreciate that little shuffle of yours in San Juan, Al!" Jen hissed as Madeira sat down next to her in a conference room at Boca Chica Naval Air Station, just north of Key West. "It made us look like morons."

Madeira turned, about to tell her she *was* a moron, then reminded himself that he was supposed to be a grown man. "Where's Nash?"

"You have no need to know."

"He's in Washington, isn't he? Doing damage control."

Jen looked as if she wanted to spit at him.

"Very well," said Admiral Williams, who, despite not having been on active duty in years, took it upon himself to get the meeting rolling. "I think it's best to start at the top. Ms. Armbruster here has just flown down from Washington to give us our marching orders."

As he spoke he nodded to the petite young assistant secretary of defense seated at the head of the conference table. She couldn't be over thirty, thought Madeira. Not that it mattered a whit to him.

"Basically," started Armbruster without preamble, "we're pissed. The heads-ups you've been providing have sucked! Nobody told us this was going to happen, and now, all of a sudden, SOSUS reports a humongous, unexplained explosion off Puerto Rico and the President's about to be zapped for your fuckup!"

As she spoke Armbruster stared directly at Jen, who opened her mouth to interrupt and then slammed it shut.

"So what's the plan, Ms. Armbruster?" Williams asked after everybody had stared at his or her hands a few seconds.

"The plan is . . . First, this bullshit about chemical weapons never happened."

"What!" Madeira said, almost rising in his chair.

"NOAA has already sampled the water, and while they did find some odd chemicals there, the only toxins are radioactive. It doesn't matter now anyway, the whole situation in Russia's just too damn unstable." As he listened to Armbruster, Madeira glanced at Viktoria. The Russian appeared deep in throught, her brows heavily furrowed.

"Normally we'd be on a case of environmental genocide like this with both feet," continued the assistant secretary of defense, "but we've got too much invested in Yeltsin to let the details get out, at least not until we've had a chance to restructure it. Understood? If anything appears in the media, you're all dead!"

Madeira looked out the window as a crew of weekend warriors pedaled their P-3B Orion antisubmarine patrol plane down the runway, the concrete almost blindingly white in the not-quite-tropical sun. In the distance the shallow, blue-green waters of the placid, near-shore Atlantic sparkled invitingly.

He wasn't particularly fond of airplanes but wished he were with the Airedales today. Then he thought about Meg Jefferson. Would she and Ms. Armbruster be soul sisters? Or bitter archenemies?

He suspected they would have been at each other's throats the instant they met.

"What about the glowing blob?" asked one of the uniformed naval officers. Like the majority of those present, he was a legal specialist.

"He's real pissed about that, too! Why should *we* lose points over that when *you* screwed it up?" This time she looked at Madeira.

"We might consider initiating an enforcement action against the polluters," suggested a Coast Guard officer.

"You mean sue the Russians? I already told you we don't want to make any trouble for them now."

"If *we* were handling it we'd also include the Agency, and Madeira here, as defendants. He's the contractor, isn't he? Charge him with willful negligence . . . fraud, even. Might not be necessary to mention the Russians at all."

Jesus! Madeira thought. The first Coastie I've ever met with a sense of humor.

Unless the bastard was serious.

"Other than that," continued the Coast Guard officer, "I have little to suggest. This falls well outside our standard pollution-control protocols."

"Something real has to be done!" Madeira said, thinking

350

of the whales. "There must be some colloidal agent we can use."

"What?" Armbruster snapped, looking at him as if he were making fun of her.

"We need a gelatin or something like it we can spread over the surface which will sink, taking the radioactive particles with it. If we can get most of it to settle on the bottom of the Puerto Rico Deep, it'll be out of the food chain. Let it rot there for a few thousand years."

He noticed the Coast Guard officer was about to say something, undoubtedly something clever, and decided to head him off at the pass. "Bury it in the Deep, just like the Coast Guard did with that oil barge that was leaking off San Juan a month or two ago."

"How about aluminum sulfate?" offered one of the naval officers. "The stuff they use in swimming pools."

"That won't work very well in salt water."

All eyes turned to Viktoria, who, up till now, had remained totally silent, listening in fascination to the workings of the United States government.

"Dr. Galin's right," said Lane Williams, "but there's been some real progress in the sewerage-treatment business the past few years. I was reading not long ago about some new flocculents and an ion-buffered additive that sounds like just what we need. I'm sure we can come up with something."

"We're not going to let you dump more chemical poisons into the ocean!" Armbruster snapped. "I've already recommended the formation of a joint Defense Department–EPA Task Force to come up with some solid, defensible answers, and I've got backing all the way up. We're going to touch all the bases and get the right names to sign off on this. In the meantime we're going to do whatever's necessary to defuse this, to ensure it doesn't develop into an issue."

"We'll come up with something safe, Ms. Armbruster."

"Are you a qualified ocean scientist, Admiral? What have you published recently?"

"As I'm sure you're aware, Ms. Armbruster," growled Williams, "there's considerable evidence that shock waves aid the flocculation process; they tend to jam the particles together, and if some of them are sticky they stay stuck."

"What?"

"We might consider dropping depth charges periodically around the blob while we treat it with the flocculents. I shouldn't think we'd want to do it any closer than five or ten miles, though. All we want to do is massage the thing. We don't want to burst it."

"Depth charges!" Armbruster shouted. "You're out of your mind. How's that going to look? I'm not going to just stand by and let you rape the ocean again. I haven't agreed to anything. What documentation can you provide that any of this works?"

"Nothing's been passed on by the FDA, but I think it's worth a try. Why don't you see what your certified experts think?"

Armbruster stared at him, her expression one of contempt and irritation. "You're a dangerous man, Admiral. A danger to yourself and to everybody else on Planet Earth."

"If we're going to do anything, we'd better do it quickly," said Madeira while Lane Williams glowered back at the assistant secretary of defense. "Once this thing disperses, once it's moved north of the Deep, it's going to be too late!"

"All right!" Armbruster erupted. "This meeting's over for now. But I don't want any of you leaving the base until I tell you to."

"I'm sorry, Al," Viktoria said as they walked out of the Boca Chica Admin Building.

"You mean about Compound whatsis?"

"Yes."

"What the hell's the story on that?"

"My friend in Moscow thinks the liquid component almost undoubtedly deteriorated somewhat over the past thirty years. And salt water is not a good medium for controlled chemical reactions. There are too many other things floating around for the components to react with.''

It was close to midnight when the plane bearing the Vice President's media adviser, as well as a science adviser of some sort, landed at Boca Chica. Twenty minutes later the meeting, with an expanded quorum, had been reconvened.

''I'm sure you'll all be pleased to learn,'' began the media adviser, ''that so far we've managed to keep a lid on this thing. Nobody, except SOSUS and the Russians, seems to have noticed the explosion. Indeed, the only problem so far has been the reporter and her boat, and everybody seems willing to believe they were storm victims. The Coast Guard, of course, is out looking for them right now.''

''Yes,'' Lane Williams replied, ''that's all very good news.''

''So now all we have to do is decide how to handle this long term, which is why Dr. Clark and I are here. We would have called you all to Washington, but we don't want this affair to appear in anybody's appointment book until we're totally sure we understand it.''

''Very reasonable!'' Williams rumbled. ''Would you like a recap?''

''Yes. Ms. Armbruster has given us a summary, and I've gotten the CIA's version, but I'd also like to have Captain Madeira run over it again as he saw it. . . .''

''We've got a very dangerous situation on our hands here,'' said the media adviser an hour later, after Madeira had told his tale and been cross-examined on it. ''The safest path, I think, is to flood the area with observers and establish a high-powered study group. At the same time we'll have to act to ensure that everybody understands we didn't create the problem . . . without actually accusing the Russians of anything, of course.''

''We could also do what we can to contain the damage,'' interrupted Madeira after brooding awhile on sharks and whales.

"You mean your idea for dumping chemicals on it? Dr. Clark here feels that's a very long shot. There's a good chance we'll end up taking more flak for trying it than if we do nothing."

"But if it works," Madeira insisted, "it'll be historic! The first even partially successful treatment of a problem of this sort."

Chapter Thirty-three

"What the hell do you mean 'she's gone'?" shouted the phone in his ear.

"The admiral was up at five-thirty, making coffee. There was no sign of her. No note. Nothing at all. It was is if she'd never been aboard," Madeira replied. "And nobody else in the marina saw anything."

"I knew we should've taken her into custody. I should never have trusted you and that Alzheimer Admiral to baby-sit," Jen said bitterly.

"For what? What could you have arrested her for?"

"Murder. Violation of civil rights. Have you forgotten that smart-ass reporter? Your Russian chick was involved. Somehow."

"She was there, but she certainly didn't do it. Anyway, that happened on a Russian ship in international waters, and she's a commissioned Russian naval officer. You can't arrest her for that. All you can do is protest to the Russian government."

"Where've you been the past hundred years, Madeira!

None of that matters anymore. If there's a violation of the United States Code anywhere, by anybody, the Justice Department can authorize a closure action ... just as long as we have de facto control over the subject person. Anyway, she's also a party to a major act of pollution—that's international law—and she entered the United States illegally!"

Standing on the fantail of Williams's ancient yacht, watching the sun rise over blue water and white sand, Madeira shrugged his shoulders. It must be jealousy, he thought spitefully. Jen was jealous of Viktoria because Viktoria was prettier than she. "You're absolutely right, Jen. Your failure to take her into custody when you could was more than just negligent. It was criminally negligent! If I were still a federal officer I'd order your immediate arrest. . . . You are still at Boca Chica, aren't you?"

"Go to hell, Madeira!"

"What name did you tell them was on her calling card?" asked Lane Williams as the Orion patrol plane droned south. Below, the shallow waters of the Silver Bank sparkled in the noon sun, while off to starboard loomed the gray-green outline of Santo Domingo's mountainous profile.

And somewhere, way off to port and miles over the horizon, a Russian tug plodded slowly northeast, towing an empty seagoing dry dock filled with bored, edgy naval commandos.

"Hashimoto Electronics . . . or something like that."

"And the Visa card?"

"The same," Madeira replied with a chuckle tinged by a note of irritation. He really couldn't decide if he was totally enchanted by Viktoria or if she made his skin crawl. Either way, she had the getaway act down to a science.

"She's a fascinating woman, Al," remarked Admiral Williams as he looked out the window. "You do seem to come up with the best damn dates!"

Madeira looked down at the two American destroyers maneuvering on the flat ocean far below. As he watched, a large whitish-blue circle formed far astern of one. A smaller, and almost benign, version of the blast that created the now-invisible blob. The other ship, he knew, was there to ensure that no whales got too close. In fact, none had been detected so far.

"I was surprised they finally went for it. They seemed to have their hearts completely set on smoke and mirrors."

"It was the 'historical' bit you threw in, Al. They're all obsessed with making the history books, as you damn well know. After all these years you're finally beginning to think like a shark yourself, and I'm not sure if I like it or not."

"Do you believe Jen?" Madeira asked, changing the subject as he continued to look out the window. "Do you think they really can't pick up any trail?"

"They'll eventually find something, but by then it'll be too late."

"Then they didn't take her themselves?"

"No. Jen's not that good a liar, although you and I are going to have to watch our backs from now on. We're both right at the top of their little list." Williams chuckled.

"What about her own people?" wondered Madeira. "They could easily trace all calls made on that card."

"No. I'd swear she left under her own power. She'll pop up again when she's ready."

"There they are," Williams said, pointing out the window. Below and off to the south, three huge Air Force C-5As were clearly visible as they thundered low over the flat, deep-blue sea, pouring dense clouds of thick, gray-green powder on it.

"It seems to be working," remarked the retired admiral. "The samples they took after Tuesday's application indicate an eighteen-percent reduction to a depth of one hundred feet. Those are the figures I saw, anyway. I have no idea what they'll tell the public. With four or five more we should get maybe fifty or sixty percent, hopefully down all the way to the bottom. After that it'll be too dilute for us to be able to do much.

"It's not perfect, but then this *is* real life."

Yes it is, thought Madeira. Real life. All you can do is make the best of what you've been given.

"What're they telling the media we're doing?"

"At the moment they're saying we're testing a new wave-suppression system the Coast Guard hopes to use."

"Then they're still not sticking their necks out about the explosion?"

"No. Not yet. Not until they've convinced themselves what we're doing is salable to the electorate."

"What about the depth charges?"

"Testing the system's susceptibility to shock."

"Who came up with that one? You?"

"No. Ms. Armbruster. She's very much a team player once the White House tells her what the plan is."

"It's dead calm down there! They'll see through it in no time."

"Then she'll restructure it if necessary."

What the hell did he care? thought Madeira as he looked out at the splotchy, almost-flat sea.

Things were looking up for his pals the whales, he decided, and he could certainly hope Viktoria was okay. But an overpowering sense of dissatisfaction lingered. He'd lost the sub, lost the canister, and now, worst of all, he'd probably never get the chance to find out if he loved or loathed Viktoria.

"You stupid bastard!" he mumbled, causing Admiral Williams to turn toward him with an expression of amused interest.

"Me, Admiral. I'm the stupid bastard. I'm too damn old to be walking around demanding perfection. I've got to learn to go with the flow."

"I hope not, Al. If you do you won't be nearly as much fun to know."

Part Three
May 1994

Langley, VA (United States of America)—On May 25 a CIA informant in the Russian Ministry of Defense reports that a Russian citizen of Georgian extraction named Niko Avalaridze, along with his cousin Ari Kostaveli, has been arrested for treason. It is the informant's understanding that the pair's offense is in some way related to the effort to recover a Russian nuclear submarine. The informant also indicates that Russian security forces expect neither traitor to live long enough to stand trial.

The Agency elects to take no action with respect to the report. This decision is based, in part, on the horrifying revelations concerning Russian double agents being made in connection with the arrest and interrogation of Aldrich Ames, a high-level CIA officer found to be in the employ of Russian intelligence, and the resulting lack of confidence in many American informants in Russia. Furthermore, as noted by the evaluating officer, this data is not in conformance with official U.S. policy concerning the submarine's recovery and loss.

Truro, MA (United States of America)—Al Madeira receives a postcard from St. Petersburg, Russia, which reads: Al, We were both right! There are so many different kinds of rats in Russia. I will be visiting Woods Hole in June. Signed: V. Madeira responds immediately to the return address, requesting further details so he can meet her at the airport.